STEALING
MONA LISA

STEALING MONA LISA

A Mystery

Carson Morton

Minotaur Books

New York

This is a work of fiction. All of the characters, organizations, and events portrayed in this novel are either products of the author's imagination or are used fictitiously.

STEALING MONA LISA. Copyright © 2011 by Carson Morton. All rights reserved. Printed in the United States of America. For information, address St. Martin's Press, 175 Fifth Avenue, New York, N.Y. 10010.

www.minotaurbooks.com

Library of Congress Cataloging-in-Publication Data

Morton, Carson.
  Stealing Mona Lisa : a mystery / Carson Morton. — 1st ed.
      p. cm.
    ISBN 978-0-312-62171-1
  1. Swindlers and swindling—Argentina—Fiction.   2. Art—Forgeries—
Fiction.   3. Leonardo, da Vinci, 1452–1519. Mona Lisa—Fiction.   4. Art
thefts—France—Paris—Fiction.   I. Title.

  PS3613.O77863S74 2011
  813'.6—dc22

                                                        2011009099

First Edition: August 2011

10 9 8 7 6 5 4 3 2 1

For my parents,
Connie and Carson

Based on a true story . . .

It has been said that nothing ever happened that couldn't be improved in the retelling. In this spirit the chronology of certain events has been altered for the purposes of the narrative.

STEALING
MONA LISA

Prologue

PARIS—1925

The sight of the horse-drawn hearse and its macabre attendants, rising like a specter out of a vaporous late-morning mist, stopped Roger Hargreaves dead in his tracks.

Tethered to a black leather carriage, four black horses stood unnaturally still, the polls of their heads adorned with towering red plumes. Three monks—hands clasped and faces obscured by the cowls of their coarse robes—contemplated the cobblestones beneath their feet. An undertaker in a long black coat sat on the carriage bench, his gaunt face emerging from beneath a shiny stovepipe hat. The morbid tableau took up fully half of the first of three small courtyards known collectively as the cour de Rohan, a leafy oasis at the edge of Saint-Germain-des-Prés.

The ghostly scene filled Hargreaves with the eerie feeling that somehow they had all been waiting there just for him.

Resisting the urge to turn on his heels and go back to the lively bustle of nearby boulevard Saint-Germain, Hargreaves took a step forward. The lead horse and the undertaker slowly turned their heads, almost in unison. Momentarily transfixed by the driver's blank expression and penetrating stare, Hargreaves acknowledged him with a slight nod, a gesture that was returned almost imperceptibly. He averted his eyes and rechecked the address written in his small reporter's notebook: 23 cour de Rohan, presumably one of the narrow, clustered three-story, pink-hued stone residences hiding behind the twisted trees and wild ivy vines snaking around their windows. He thought for a moment of asking the undertaker which house it might be but quickly discarded the notion. He had no desire to communicate with this man. Besides, he was a reporter; he could locate a simple address.

Hargreaves looked at the name in his notebook. Eduardo de Valfierno, some kind of marquis or something. Of course, half the society of Paris laid claim to one title or another these days. Whoever he was, he claimed to have information regarding the theft of the *Mona Lisa*—or what was it the French called it? *La Joconde*—from the Louvre Museum back in 1911. Old news, of course. It had been recovered not too long after the incident, but there might be a story there. The marquis had contacted his newspaper, the *London Daily Express*, by telephone and arrangements had been made. To save expenses, the paper's editor had wired Hargreaves—already on assignment in Paris—with instructions. At least it would be a change of pace from covering the *Exposition Internationale* at the place des Invalides. If he had to write another article about the wonders of Art Deco furniture, he'd drown himself in the Seine.

Trying to ignore the undertaker and his assistants, Hargreaves stepped past them through a partially opened gate into a tiny courtyard. Luck was with him. Attached to the wall next to a large green door, partially obscured by a sprig of ivy leaves, was a wooden plaque with the number 23 etched into it. He lifted a brass knocker in the shape of a cat's head and tapped it three times onto a well-worn plate. As he waited for a response, he couldn't resist one more look back through the wrought-iron gate at the hearse.

"Can I help you, monsieur?"

Hargreaves turned, startled. A short, heavyset woman in her

late sixties stood in the open doorway, her hands placed defiantly on her hips.

"Bonjour, madame," he said, removing his bowler hat. "Robert Hargreaves. I've come to interview the marquis de Valfierno."

The woman regarded him with the icy stare of a stern school-mistress. Then, with a dismissive snort, she turned sideways and pressed her back against the door panel, not quite inviting but per-haps challenging him to enter.

Hargreaves stepped past her into a small, darkly lit foyer. "Those men in the courtyard," he said in an attempt to make conversation, "they make quite a spectacle."

The woman said nothing. She closed the door and led him into a sitting room cluttered with unmatched furniture, its windows adorned with fussy draperies. He tried to place the aroma in the air. Jasmine, perhaps. Something strangely exotic, anyway, mixed with an unpleasant musty odor.

Lowering herself onto a high-backed wooden chair, the woman indicated a plush sofa. Hargreaves sank into the worn-out springs. Forced to look up at her, he felt like a schoolboy about to receive a scolding for some infraction or other. A silence followed, broken only by the snorting of one of the horses in the courtyard.

"Madame," Hargreaves began, "I believe you have the advan-tage of me."

"I am Madame Charneau," she said sharply. "This is my boarding-house."

Hargreaves nodded. More silence.

"The marquis," he asked after a moment, "is he here?"

"The marquis is one of my lodgers," Madame Charneau replied.

"May I . . . see him?"

"You are a writer, are you not?" It sounded more like an accusa-tion than a question.

"A correspondent, yes. For the *London Daily Express*."

"And you're compensating the marquis for this . . . interview." She said the word as if it were something unsavory.

"An arrangement has been agreed upon, yes." Hargreaves shifted uncomfortably on the sofa.

"The marquis is a great man, I'm sure," she said, as if she did not believe it for a moment. "He is also three months arrears in his rent. And he is very ill. You noticed the hearse outside."

"Well, yes. Of course."

"My brother is an undertaker. As a favor to me he has diverted his men from a local job."

"The marquis is that bad?"

"I'll be blunt, monsieur. If you wish to see him, you will give me the money now. I will apply it to his rent and to the doctor's fees."

Hargreaves's throat tightened. "Madame, I'm . . . not sure I can do that . . ."

She began to rise to her feet. "Then I bid you good day."

He was beaten. Not wanting to go back to London empty-handed, he held up his hand in a gesture of surrender. Madame Charneau stopped in midrise and lowered herself back down, a smug half smile on her face. Hargreaves removed the wad of franc notes he had prepared and, after giving it a brief, regretful appraisal, offered it to her. The moment she took it from him, her disposition underwent a complete sea change.

She sprang to her feet and chirped, "You see, monsieur, the mist has lifted. It will be a lovely day after all."

With a lighter step than Hargreaves had noticed earlier, she led him out into the foyer and up a staircase to the first floor. On the way up, he surreptitiously checked his pocket watch. A French colleague had tickets to see the American sensation Josephine Baker and her Revue Nègre tonight at the Moulin Rouge. He was not sure he entirely approved of such spectacles, but this was, after all, Paris. At any rate, he hoped that this interview would not take up too much time.

On the first-floor landing, five doors and another narrow staircase leading upward lined the hallway. Madame Charneau opened the first door to her right and led Hargreaves into a dark, airless room. In the gloom, he could just about make out a figure lying beneath a thick blanket on a brass bed. Madame Charneau went to the window and snapped back a heavy drape, bathing the room in harsh light. The man in the bed shielded his eyes and turned his face to the wall.

Madame Charneau was all bright, cheery efficiency as she smoothed out his bedsheet and straightened his blanket.

"You have a visitor, Marquis," she said eagerly.

The man in the bed made no movement as Madame Charneau pulled up a wooden chair and motioned for Hargreaves to sit.

"This is Monsieur Hargreaves. He's come to hear your stories."

With some reluctance, Hargreaves slowly lowered himself onto the chair.

"Well, I'll leave you two alone, then, shall I?" Madame Charneau moved to the doorway.

"I'll be close by if you need me," she added before leaving the room and closing the door behind her.

Hargreaves stared at the back of the man's head. His thick hair was an almost luminescent white, matted from lying on the pillow.

"Marquis," Hargreaves began, but Valfierno, his face still turned to the wall, raised his hand to stop him. Then he slowly turned his head back toward the light, his eyes squinting against the glare. Without looking at Hargreaves, he pointed to a side table littered with various pitchers and bottles.

"Of course," Hargreaves said. "You're thirsty."

Grateful to have something to occupy himself with, Hargreaves lifted a pitcher of water and filled a tumbler. He handed it to Valfierno, who impatiently brushed it aside, spilling some of its contents onto the bedcover. He pointed to the table again. Next to the water pitcher sat a half-full bottle of what appeared to be gin or vodka.

"The bottle?" asked Hargreaves.

Valfierno nodded.

Hargreaves picked up the bottle and found a sticky shot glass in the clutter of the tabletop. He filled it and held it out to the man. Valfierno propped himself up on an elbow, took the glass, and thirstily poured the clear liquid down his throat. Savoring the experience, he handed the empty shot glass to Hargreaves and lay back with an expression that approached contentment, or perhaps it was simply temporary relief from pain.

Then he began to cough explosively.

"Are you all right?" Hargreaves asked, thinking that he had just hastened the older man's demise.

The coughing slowly subsided, like a rumble of thunder fading into the distance.

"I have felt better," he allowed. His voice was hollow, as dry as parchment. Then, for the first time, he looked directly at the Englishman through rheumy, bloodshot eyes. His lips curled into a faintly sardonic smile and he added, "but thank you for asking."

Though Hargreaves estimated that the man was perhaps not yet sixty years old, he was aged beyond his years, his unshaven face sallow and drawn.

"You brought the money?" Valfierno asked, his voice clearing and gaining resonance.

Hargreaves hesitated. "Ah, yes . . . the money. Truth be told, I gave it for safekeeping to Madame Charneau."

"That witch!" Valfierno spat out, bringing on another series of racking coughs. "I only wish to live in order to torment that *putain* longer." He coughed again and shook his head in resignation. "Never mind. There's not much time left. Are you ready?"

Hargreaves nodded and dug his small notebook and pencil from his jacket pocket.

"Quite ready. Our readers, I'm sure, will wish to hear the story of the theft of the world's greatest painting in great detail. I've prepared some questions—"

Valfierno cut him off with a sharp gesture of his hand.

"No questions! No answers!"

Hargreaves drew back at the outburst.

"Don't worry," Valfierno said, his voice softening. "You won't leave empty-handed. I'll tell you a story. Do you like stories?"

"If they are true," Hargreaves replied tightly.

Valfierno nodded. "Then I'll tell you a true story."

Valfierno's head sank back deeply into the pillow and he stared up at the ceiling as if looking for something hidden deep in the cracks of the plaster. "Have you ever been to Buenos Aires, Mister . . . ?"

"Hargreaves, and no, I haven't had the pleasure."

"Pleasure indeed," Valfierno said, ignoring the impatient sarcasm in Hargreaves's voice. "The fragrance of the jacaranda trees fills the air; *parilla* cafés lure you in with their enticing aromas; and the tangos played by the *orquestas típicas* torment the soul with their elusive promise of love."

Making a fist and holding it to his heart, he turned to look directly into the reporter's eyes. "Have you ever experienced *le coup de foudre*, Mr. Hargreaves? Have you ever fallen in love at first sight?"

Hargreaves bristled. "I shouldn't think so."

"Did you know that a man can fall under the spell of a woman and not even realize it?"

Hargreaves was getting nowhere. He had to get this man back on track. "You mentioned Buenos Aires."

Valfierno turned his face back to the ceiling. His eyes drifted shut and for a moment Hargreaves thought he was falling asleep, or worse. But then they shot open, a sparkling intensity shining through the milky haze.

"Yes," he said, "Buenos Aires. That is where my story begins."

Part I

Bait the hook well, this fish will bite
—Shakespeare, *Much Ado About Nothing*

Chapter 1

BUENOS AIRES—1910

The marquis de Valfierno stood tapping the knob handle of his gentleman's cane into the palm of his hand at the foot of the steps of the Museo Nacional de Bellas Artes. His Panama hat shaded his face, and his spotless white suit helped to reflect the sharp South American sun, but he was still uncomfortably warm. He could have chosen to stand at the top of the steps in the shadow of the museum portico, but he always preferred greeting his clients at street level and then walking up with them to the entrance. There was something about ascending the steps together that fostered easy and excited conversation, as if he and his client were embarking on a momentous journey, a journey that would enrich both of them.

He checked his pocket watch: 4:28. Joshua Hart would be punctual. He had amassed his fortune by making sure his trains ran on time. He became one of the richest men in the world by filling those trains with passengers reading his newspapers, and loading them with mountains of coal and iron bound for his own factories to forge the steel for a new America.

4:30. Valfierno looked across the plaza. Joshua Hart—titan of industry—came on like the engine of one of his trains, a stout barrel of a man, robust at the age of sixty, clad in a black suit despite the heat. Valfierno could almost see the thick smoke curling upward from the stack of his stovepipe hat.

"Señor Hart," Valfierno said as the shorter man planted himself in front of him. "As always, it is an honor, a pleasure, and a privilege to see you."

"Save the horseshit, Valfierno," Hart said with only a slight hint of ironic camaraderie. "If this godforsaken country were any hotter, I would not be surprised to find out it was Hades itself."

"I would think," said Valfierno, "that the devil would find himself at home in any climate."

Hart allowed a grudging snicker of appreciation for this remark as he mopped his face with a white silk handkerchief. Only then did Valfierno take notice of the two slender women, both dressed in white, lacy dresses and both taller than Hart, collecting behind him like the cars of a loosely linked train. One was in her fifties, the other in her thirties perhaps. Valfierno had dealt with Hart on a number of occasions through the years, knew he was married, but had never met his wife. He could only assume that the younger woman was his daughter.

Valfierno doffed his hat in acknowledgment and looked to Hart for an introduction.

"Ah, yes, of course," Hart began with a hint of impatience. "May I introduce my wife, Mrs. Hart . . ."

Hart indicated the younger woman, who smiled demurely and only briefly made eye contact with Valfierno.

". . . and this," Hart said, a hint of disapproval in his voice, "is her mother."

The older woman did not respond in any way.

Valfierno bowed. "Eduardo de Valfierno," he said, introducing himself. "It is a pleasure to meet you both."

Mrs. Hart's face was partly obscured by the wide brim of her hat, and Valfierno's first impression was of white, smooth skin and a delicately pointed chin.

Mrs. Hart's mother was a handsome—if somewhat worn—woman whose placid smile was fixed, as was her gaze, a blank stare concentrated on a point behind Valfierno's shoulder. He felt the urge to turn to see what she was looking at but thought better of it. Was she blind? No, not blind. Something else.

"I trust that you ladies are enjoying your visit," he said.

"We haven't as yet been able to see much," Mrs. Hart began, "but we're hoping that we—"

"Dear," Hart cut her off with forced politeness, "the marquis and I have business to conduct."

"Of course," Mrs. Hart said.

Hart turned back to Valfierno. "Let's get on with this, shall we?"

"By all means, señor," Valfierno replied with a brief look to Mrs. Hart as she gently brushed a fly away from her mother's shoulder. "After you," he added, gesturing with a flourish of his hand.

He had expected the ladies to go first, but Hart immediately started to pound up the steps. Mrs. Hart seemed to hesitate for a moment so he decided to follow her husband without waiting.

Valfierno made a point of keeping one step behind and below Hart in a deliberate attempt to keep their heads at the same level. "You will not be disappointed, señor, I can assure you."

"I'd better not be."

Valfierno glanced back down. Mrs. Hart was gently leading her mother up the steps.

As they reached the top, Valfierno pulled out his pocket watch.

"The museum closes in fifteen minutes," he said. "Perfect timing."

They walked into the lobby, stopping and turning as Mrs. Hart and her mother entered behind them.

"I think it best if you remain here in the lobby," said Hart. "You understand, don't you, dear?" His tone was solicitous but firm.

"I just thought that Mother and I would like to see some of the—"

"We'll come back tomorrow . . . when you'll have more time to appreciate the art. I did say that I thought it best that you stay in the hotel. Now please, do as I say."

Valfierno sensed that Mrs. Hart was about to protest, but, after a brief pause, she averted her eyes and simply said, "As you wish."

The look Hart gave Valfierno was unmistakable: enough talk. With a brief nod to Mrs. Hart, Valfierno led him off through the museum.

The two men made their way through a large atrium, moving through the hazy dust suspended in the shafts of late afternoon sun. The few patrons who remained were already moving in the opposite direction on their way out.

"If I may say so," Valfierno began, "your wife is quite lovely."

"Yes," Hart said, clearly distracted.

"And her mother—"

Hart cut him off. "Her mother is an imbecile."

Valfierno could think of no response to this.

"She has no mind left," Hart continued. "Useless to bring her along in the first place, but my wife insisted."

A moment later, Valfierno and Hart stood before Edward Manet's *La Ninfa Sorprendida* mounted on a freestanding wall that ran down the center of the long gallery known as Sala 17. A zaftig nymph is clutching a white silky robe to her bosom to hide her nakedness. She is turned toward an intruder who has caught her sitting alone in a sylvan forest, perhaps preparing to swim in the pool behind her. Her eyes are wide with surprise, but her full lips, parted only slightly, suggest that, although she is startled, she is not ashamed.

Valfierno had stood here many times before and he always wondered, who was the intruder? A complete stranger? Someone she knew whom she expected to follow her? Or was Valfierno himself—or anyone else who stood in awe of her—the intruder?

"Exquisite, is it not?" Valfierno said, less a question than a statement.

Hart ignored him. He stood staring at the painting, sizing it up with the suspicious gaze of a man trying to find fault with a racehorse he's thinking of buying.

"It's darker than I thought it would be," Hart finally said.

"Yet the soft light of her skin draws one's eye out of the darkness, wouldn't you say?" Valfierno prompted.

"Yes, yes," Hart said, the impatience in his voice betraying his growing agitation. "And you tell me that it's one of his most celebrated works?"

"One among many," Valfierno allowed. "But certainly highly regarded."

Never oversell. Let the painting and the client's avarice do all the work.

Valfierno let the ensuing silence hang in the air. Timing was everything in such matters. Let Mr. Joshua Hart of Newport, Rhode Island, drink it all in. Let him absorb it until the thought of leaving Argentina without the object of his obsession was unimaginable.

"Señor Hart," he finally said, glancing at his pocket watch, "only five minutes to closing."

Joshua Hart leaned his head toward Valfierno, his eyes darting back to the painting. "But how will you get it? All of Buenos Aires will be up in arms. They're bound to catch us."

"Señor, every museum worth its salt has copies of its most important works ready to put up at a moment's notice. The public at large will never even know it's missing."

"But it's not the public I'm worried about. What about the police? What about the authorities?"

Valfierno had expected this, the moment when the client has second thoughts and tries to convince himself he has traveled thousands of miles to admire the object of his lust but now fears that the risks involved are too great.

"You overestimate the capabilities of the local authorities, señor. By the time they manage to organize their investigation, you'll be smoking a cigar on the deck of your ship staring out across the water at the Florida coast."

Hart floundered for a moment, searching for objections. Finally he said, "How do I even know that you won't deliver a copy instead of the real thing?"

This was the question Valfierno had been waiting for. He

glanced up and down the narrow gallery. They were alone, and not by chance. Valfierno stepped toward the painting, motioning Hart to join him. Hart's face tightened with anxiety, but Valfierno encouraged him with a reassuring smile. Hart looked up and down the gallery before he took a step forward. Valfierno removed an ornate fountain pen from his pocket. Taking his time, he unscrewed the cap, placed it on the rear of the barrel, and offered it to Hart, who reacted as if it were a lethal weapon.

"Go on, take it," Valfierno encouraged.

Hart gingerly accepted the pen. Valfierno took hold of one side of the bottom of the frame and carefully tilted it away from the wall.

"Put a mark on the back of the canvas. Your initials if you like. Something you'll recognize."

Hart hesitated.

"Time is running short, señor." It was said without haste or concern. A simple statement of fact.

Hart's breathing became short and labored as, leaning into the wall, he gripped the lower corner of the frame with his left hand and scribbled something on the back of the heavy canvas. Valfierno let the bottom of the frame fall gently back into position, checking to make sure the painting was level.

"I hope you know what you're doing," Hart said, handing the pen back.

Valfierno replaced the cap over the nib of the pen. "Leave the rest to me."

On their way out of the gallery, Valfierno and Hart passed a lanky young maintenance man in a long white blouse, his cap pulled low over his face as he leisurely pushed a mop across the wet floor. A temporary sign, GALERÍA CERRADA, had been hung on the side of the archway. Hart gave the man a look of contempt as he was forced to step over a small puddle. He didn't register that Valfierno and the maintenance man exchanged a fleeting glance, Valfierno giving him a slight, knowing nod as he passed.

Valfierno, Joshua Hart, and the two ladies were the last patrons to leave the museum. Hart hurried down the steps first, clearly in an agitated state. Valfierno descended with Mrs. Hart and her mother.

"Tomorrow," he began, "you will have much more time to enjoy the pleasures of the museum."

"Yes," said Mrs. Hart. "I hope so."

Joshua Hart was waiting at the bottom of the steps, his back toward them. As soon as they had stepped onto the plaza behind him, he turned and shot a challenging question at Valfierno. "So, what happens now?"

Valfierno looked around to make sure they were out of earshot of anyone. "I will bring the item in question to your hotel in the morning."

"I have to tell you," Hart said, "I'm starting to feel uncomfortable about this whole thing."

A certain degree of last-minute resistance from a client was not unusual, of course, but Valfierno had not expected this much from Hart.

"There is nothing to be concerned about, I can assure you."

"I will need some time to think. Perhaps this was not such a good idea after all." Hart was talking more to himself than to anyone else.

Valfierno had to change the subject quickly. The last thing he wanted was for his client to dwell too much on the possible risks involved.

"I think you need to get your mind off it for a while," he said in his most soothing voice. "Evening is falling. The coolness in the air invites exploration of the city."

"You call this cool?" Hart said. "I can hardly breathe."

"Indeed," began Mrs. Hart in response to Valfierno, "we had spoken of perhaps a visit to the zoo." Her voice sounded hopeful but tentative.

"A magnificent idea," Valfierno said, grateful for the young woman's inadvertent help. "It remains open until at least seven, and the jaguar exhibit is not to be missed."

"My mother is quite looking forward to it, aren't you, Mother?"

The older woman gave only the slightest reaction, more to the touch of her daughter's hand than to her words.

Hart took notice of the women for the first time since exiting the museum. "Don't be absurd," he said, masking his irritation in a cloak of concern. "It's far too hot for that, and the streets are too dangerous at night. It's best that we go back to the hotel."

Mrs. Hart's lips parted slightly as if she was about to respond, but she said nothing.

Valfierno felt the sudden urge to support the young woman's wish.

"I can assure you," he said, "the streets are perfectly safe in this area."

"And who are you now?" Hart asked pointedly. "The mayor?"

Valfierno smiled, cocking his head slightly. "Not officially, no."

Valfierno was pleased to notice a brief smile flicker across Mrs. Hart's face.

"It's time to go," said Hart curtly, turning to his wife. "Come, dear." And without waiting for the women, he began striding across the plaza.

"Until the morning, Señor Hart," Valfierno called after him.

"I must think," Hart shot back with a dismissive wave of his hand. "I have to think."

Mrs. Hart acknowledged Valfierno with a slight nod before collecting her mother and following her husband.

Valfierno removed his hat. "Ladies," he said in farewell.

Hart and the two women were swallowed up by the crowds drawn out by the cooling evening. Taking a deep breath, Valfierno brought a white handkerchief up to his brow and allowed himself to sweat for the first time all afternoon.

———

Inside the gallery, the young maintenance man in the white blouse stood before Manet's *La Ninfa Sorprendida*. Checking one more time to make sure he was alone, he stepped forward and, with his left hand, tilted the bottom of the frame away from the wall. Reaching behind with his right hand, he applied pressure to the back of the canvas and pushed it up until he had exposed its bottom edge. Gripping it, he slowly pulled downward as if he were drawing a window blind closed. Bit by bit, he revealed a second painting, an identical copy, the one he had secured behind the original the evening before. He tugged steadily until he had removed the second painting without disturbing the masterpiece still occupying its frame.

He let the frame swing back gently to the wall and started to roll up the copy, noting the initials "J.H." written on the back in stylized letters.

"Who closed this gallery?"

The sound of the authoritative voice startled him. It came from the direction of the gallery entrance hidden from this angle by the freestanding center wall. One of the museum guards, no doubt.

The echo of footsteps told the young man that he had only seconds left before discovery. With rapid wrist motions, he finished rolling up the copy. Slipping the cylinder beneath his long blouse, he walked briskly to the end of the gallery farthest from the entrance. He turned the corner at the end of the center wall at the same time the guard turned the corner at the opposite end, so neither one saw the other. Walking rapidly toward the gallery entrance, he matched his stride to the sound of the guard's footsteps coming from the opposite side of the wall.

"Is anyone here?" he heard the guard say as the young man slipped through the gallery entrance past the sign he had posted. Crossing the main atrium, he entered a corridor used only by museum staff. He hurried to a side entrance, produced a key, and unlocked the door. Letting himself out, he closed the door behind him and walked off into the gathering evening.

Chapter 2

Shadows lengthened and early evening breezes cooled the humid air as Valfierno leisurely made his way back to his house in the Recoleta district. Tipping his hat to a pair of well-dressed *señoras*, he thought of Émile back in the museum. There had been no point waiting for the young man. He might have had to sequester himself in the building until everyone went home as he had to the night before when he placed the copy behind the real painting.

One way or another, Émile would return with the canvas sometime this evening, Valfierno was sure of it. In any event, he had done his part and it was out of his hands for now. It was always possible, however unlikely, that Émile would be discovered in the act, but he could not afford to worry about such a possibility before it happened. He needed all his energy to consider the issue at hand: the growing likelihood that Joshua Hart would renege on his agreement to exchange fifty thousand American dollars for what he believed to be Manet's original *La Ninfa Sorprendida*.

Valfierno considered Hart's state of mind. The man had traveled to South America for one purpose: to purchase a stolen painting for his collection, the same collection that Valfierno had played no small part in assembling. Valfierno had always supplied him with perfect forgeries, but Hart was absolutely convinced they were all original. Hart had traveled to Paris, and to Madrid, but this was the farthest he had ventured. Perhaps that had something to do with his trepidation. And why had he brought along his young wife and her apparently feeble-minded mother? For all his civility, he hadn't seemed particularly concerned with their comfort or enjoyment.

Mrs. Hart was at least thirty years Hart's junior and, from what Valfierno had observed from their limited interaction, quite an attractive woman. Perhaps Hart had brought her along to keep an eye on her, to keep her within sight at all times, to shield her from temptation. And perhaps giving in to his wife's desire to have her mother accompany her was his one concession. Valfierno wondered how Hart could have ensnared such a lovely young woman. *I suppose*, he thought, *that's why God invented money.*

He turned his thoughts back to the problem at hand. What would he do if Joshua Hart decided to go back on his agreement? Too much was at stake to allow that to happen. Valfierno would have to come up with something, some kind of insurance, but at the moment he had no idea what it would be.

Valfierno's attention was distracted by a commotion in a side alley. A gang of street urchins—pathetic creatures that poverty and injustice had set as a plague upon the streets of Buenos Aires—had surrounded a genteel young woman, pestering her for money. The woman's clean white dress contrasted starkly with the boys' dirty rags. At the sight of Valfierno, she rushed toward him and threw herself into his arms like a drowning victim grasping for a life belt.

"Señor," she pleaded in English, "please, they're like a pack of animals!"

The youthful beggars swarmed around, importuning both of them with well-practiced vigor.

"*¡Señor! ¡Señorita!*" they cried out, "*¡Por favor! ¡Unos pocos pesos! ¡Tenemos hambre! ¡Tenga la compasión, por favor! ¡Señor! ¡Señorita!*"

Valfierno put one arm protectively around the young woman's shoulder.

"I see you've met our little ambassadors," he said, and then, holding his cane aloft for emphasis, called out, "*¡Vete, bestias pequeñas!*"

But his gesture had no effect on the diminutive rabble, their grubby soiled hands reaching up like the tendrils of some multi-headed creature. In one swift move, Valfierno passed his cane to his left hand and dug into the pocket of his jacket. He withdrew a fistful of coins and cast them into the alley as far as he could. Like a flock of pigeons scrambling for crumbs, the boys chased after the glittering treasure, jabbering incoherently.

As the street urchins fought for their share of the silver and copper coins, Valfierno quickly led the young woman away.

"Thank you, señor," she said. "You're very brave."

"It was nothing. The streets are full of these unfortunate wretches. One can hardly blame them for their misfortune. Are you all right?"

"Only thanks to you, señor."

She looked up, and Valfierno got a good look at her for the first time. She was perhaps twenty, with large green eyes set like emeralds beneath a pair of perfectly arched eyebrows. Somehow, she had managed to shape her wide, sensuous mouth and full lips into an innocent, humble smile worthy of Botticelli's Venus.

"You're an American," he said.

"Yes. I'm a student. At the *universidad*. Although I'm afraid my Castilian is very poor."

"It's fortunate, then, that my English is very good."

She nodded and glanced down coyly.

"I'm not sure the streets are safe for a young woman alone," he continued. "Where are you going? Perhaps I should accompany you to your destination."

"No, señor. I'm fine, really. I'll stick to the main street until I get back to my room. You've been more than kind. I really should go."

And, with one more innocent smile, she deftly spun away and floated off down the street. He watched her for a moment before noticing that the yapping voices of the street urchins had stopped. He took a few steps back to look down the alley. The little beggars were gone, but something curious caught his eye. A few coppers, even a silver coin, still lay on the ground where he had tossed them.

Valfierno looked back in the direction the young woman had taken, but she was nowhere to be seen. He hesitated for only an instant before patting his coat over his inside pocket, the pocket where he kept his billfold.

The pocket was empty. The billfold was gone.

He patted his watch pocket. Also empty.

Valfierno smiled.

"Good job, boys. You earned your money today."

The young woman stood once again surrounded by the street beggars, their arms outstretched and their grubby little fingers clutching at the bills she distributed to them from Valfierno's wallet.

"Plenty for everyone," she said in Castilian. "We caught a big fat fish this time."

She stood in a litter-strewn alleyway sheltered from the view of anyone on the main street. The boys yammered with exhilaration as they collected their rewards. But in the midst of the excitement, the tallest boy noticed something over Julia's shoulder and froze. The other boys followed suit, their eyes growing wide with fear and surprise.

Julia turned. Blocking the alleyway stood the gentleman in the fine white suit. A uniformed *policia* stood next to him, a look of smug satisfaction on his face. Strangely, the gentleman's expression seemed to suggest that he was more amused than angry.

The frozen tableau shattered as the boys scurried away like insects caught in a beam of light. With youthful agility they scampered over walls and fences, leaving the young woman alone with all avenues of escape cut off.

"Señor," she said, reverting to English with all the sincerity she could muster, "once again you have saved me from those terrible boys . . ."

Valfierno chuckled. "You know, if it had just been the money in the wallet, well, you would have earned it. But I'm afraid that the watch you took holds some sentimental value for me."

Still smiling, he held out his hand. Her innocent expression turned quickly to one of resignation. She shrugged and stepped forward, placing the wallet and the pocket watch into his palm.

"I'm afraid the wallet is not quite as heavy as it was," she said, trying to soften her guilt with a coquettish smile.

"I didn't expect it to be," Valfierno said. "And may I say that your Spanish has improved greatly since I saw you last."

"I know this girl, señor," said the *policía*, stepping forward and grabbing her arm. *"Una carterista gringa.* This time she will spend a long time enjoying our hospitality."

"Please, señor," she appealed to Valfierno, "you helped me once. The prisons here are terrible places for men, let alone a defenseless female."

"Oh, I don't know," Valfierno said. "I have the feeling that you'll be able to take care of yourself. What is your name?"

"Why should I tell you?" She bristled.

"No reason at all."

She looked to the *policía* and then back to Valfierno.

"Julia . . . Julia Conway."

"The marquis de Valfierno. At your service."

As the *policía* held her in place, Valfierno walked in a circle around them, sizing her up.

"I beg you, señor," she pleaded. "I won't last a day in that hellhole."

"Actually," Valfierno considered, "there may be an alternative, a way for you to repay me and get out of this predicament."

"Now wait just a minute," Julia said, turning her head from side to side to keep him in view. "I don't know what kind of girl you think I am, but—"

"Don't flatter yourself," Valfierno interrupted as he removed the bills still remaining in his wallet and handed them to the *policía.* "Thank you, Manuel. I'll take over from here."

"De nada, señor." The *policía* released Julia's arm and gave her a dirty look before walking off.

"No, I had something else in mind entirely," said Valfierno, offering his arm to her. "A little job to take advantage of your skills."

Julia hesitated. His expression was hard to read. She had just robbed him and yet he seemed more amused than anything else. Whatever he was up to, he was enjoying it. And, if it involved the use of her own particular talents, then perhaps she would enjoy it too.

"Well?" he persisted. "What do you say?"

She shrugged. And took his arm.

Chapter 3

Mrs. Ellen Hart sat at a small burnished mahogany table in the living room of her husband's luxury suite in La Gran Hotel de la Paix. Her mother sat across from her, staring out a bay window at the flickering gaslights lining Avenue Rivadavia. The older woman wore the same expression she always did. Her face revealed only a vague contentment, as if she were looking through the world around her to some distant, happy place and time. Ellen wished she could talk to her mother about even the most mundane day-to-day things; she thought of how wonderful it would be just to hear her voice again, to look into her eyes, to tell her—to tell anyone—what lay in the deepest recesses of her heart.

She thought of the last words her mother had ever spoken: "I'm tired, dear. I think I should go and lie down for a while." It was the last time that she could be sure her mother had actually looked at and recognized her. She had helped her onto the daybed in their New York apartment, the one next to the large window overlooking Central Park. Her mother looked into her eyes and smiled a silent thank-you. Then her lids closed and she drifted off into what started as sleep but ended as a coma, the result of a stroke that took her silently in her dreams. It had been more than a week before she regained consciousness. Their family doctor pronounced her physically healthy, with no impairments to limb or body, but her mind was a different story. Perhaps in time, he said.

But it had been fully ten years now, and Ellen knew in her heart that her mother would never return to her, that she would have to be content with the living photograph she had become. With a lot of help, her mother had learned to take care of many of her own needs almost to the degree she could before the stroke. But what she never regained was the power of communication. Ellen had no idea if any of the words she spoke to her mother were understood. But Ellen could still see her, could still feel her hand, could still put her arms around her, and could still smell her hair. And with these things she had to be content.

The door to the master bedroom opened and Joshua Hart appeared, collarless, his shirt hanging over his trousers.

"Dear," Ellen said pleasantly but a bit surprised, "you're not dressed for dinner yet."

"What did you say?" he asked distractedly.

"Dinner. It's past eight o'clock."

"Oh, we're not going to dinner," he said as if she should have already known that. "Just arrange to have something brought up."

"But Mother and I have just finished dressing, as you can see . . ."

"Well, perhaps you should have asked me first," he said curtly.

"But I did, dear. We talked about it this afternoon."

"I've simply too much on my mind," he said, irritation showing in his voice. Then he took a deep breath and added in a forced, soothing tone, "You understand, don't you, dear? And it certainly doesn't make any difference to her."

Ellen turned to her mother, but the older woman's eyes were fixed on some distant point beyond the window.

"I just thought," she began, "that it would be nice to go out for a while."

"I'll make it up you when we get back to New York," he said in a patronizing tone. "If you want something to eat, please arrange for it to be brought up."

He sat down on a chair at a small desk and picked up a newspaper, bringing the conversation to a close.

"I did suggest," she said tentatively, "that we not come with you on this trip, that we stay at home."

Hart looked up from his paper, clearly annoyed that she would not drop the subject.

"You are my wife," he began, as if explaining something to a child. "Wherever I go, you go. That is the way it will always be. Try to remember that."

She lowered her eyes and calmly responded, "Of course, dear."

He sighed impatiently, gave up on his newspaper, and stood up. He held out his hand.

"Ellen," he said, conciliatory now, "please try to understand. I have much to consider. This is a very serious business. I'll make it up to you when we return. I promise I will."

She nodded with a resigned smile as she took his hand.

He lifted hers and kissed it. "Now," he said briskly, "I have work to do." And with that he turned and disappeared back into his bedroom.

Ellen took hold of her mother's hand, gently squeezed it, and said quietly, "You must be hungry. I'll arrange for some dinner, shall I?"

Walking through the gaslit streets of the Recoleta district, on the way to Valfierno's house and an uncertain future, Julia Conway began having second thoughts and considered bolting. But she quickly discarded the notion. Where would she go? Back to join forces with those horrible boys and their leering, suggestive remarks? Back to trolling the streets for easy targets? No, there was something about this elegant, self-possessed man that intrigued her. She'd give him a chance and find out what he had in mind, assuming of course he didn't try anything funny. If he did . . . well, he wasn't bad-looking—for an older man—but even pickpockets have their principles. And it wouldn't be the first time someone tried to take advantage of her. She had handled herself before and she was confident that she could handle herself again.

She tried to draw him out concerning his plans for her, but he revealed little, only reassuring her that she would come to no harm. By the time they reached Valfierno's house on the Avenida Alvear, she had discovered only that he seemed to possess a limitless talent for charming evasiveness.

"This is your house?" she asked as they passed through a decorative wrought-iron gate onto a cobbled path shaded by a line of blossoming magnolia trees.

"The house has been in my family for generations."

Julia followed Valfierno toward a three-story mansion that was actually relatively small and modest compared to the other grand houses in the area.

"What do you do, anyway?"

"Let's just say that I dabble in fine arts."

Valfierno pushed open one of the carved double doors and gestured for her to enter. Julia stepped into a large circular foyer dominated by a grand staircase leading upward before splitting off to the left and right into the upper reaches of the house.

"Wait here." Valfierno threw his gloves onto a small table. "And try not to steal anything," he added before disappearing behind the staircase.

"Don't worry about me," she responded, her eyes scanning every corner of the room.

In the rear courtyard, inside a converted carriage house lit by both candle and gaslight, Yves Chaudron applied delicate brushstrokes to a faithful copy of *La Ninfa Sorprendida*. As he worked, he referenced a master copy sitting on an easel that stood off to the side. In truth, he could almost have painted the masterpiece from memory. This copy would be number five, or was it six? Of course, he had more time to paint now that his legs had become worse. He probably should force himself to move about more, he often thought, but what use was it? At seventy-six, painting was all he had left; it filled his time practically to the exclusion of everything else. Indeed, he hadn't left the large house for almost a year now. He had little reason to, anyway. He had seen enough of the world outside. Recreating the brushstrokes of the masters was the only thing that gave him pleasure these days.

"Ah, Yves," Valfierno said, striding in, "you are farther along than I had hoped. Excellent. If all goes well, we'll need a replacement before long."

The old man placed the pad of the mahlstick he held in his left hand onto the painting's surface to provide support for his brush hand.

"So," he said, applying paint to the delicate features of the woman's face, "you have reeled in our fish?" The old man's words came out like a long, tired sigh.

"Not quite, but soon. It may require a little more persuasion. You look tired, Yves. It's late. You've done enough for one day." Valfierno considered the painting. "By the looks of things, you're almost finished."

"One is never finished," Yves said. "One can only hope for the wisdom to know the proper time to walk away."

"Then this is that time," said Valfierno. "Besides, I want you to come into the house and meet someone."

In the foyer, Julia stood admiring a particularly exquisite figurine, part of a set that graced the mantelpiece of a large fireplace. She picked it up and examined it briefly before slipping it into a pocket of her dress with deft, practiced efficiency.

"And what do you suppose you're doing?"

Startled, she turned toward the main entrance. A tall young man stood in the doorway. In one hand, he held a crumpled-up white blouse; in the other, a rolled-up canvas.

"I was just noticing how dusty it was up here," Julia replied, running her finger along the mantelpiece for effect.

The young man tossed the blouse and canvas onto a table before striding up to her, suspicion etched on his face.

"Who are you, anyway?" he demanded.

"I could ask you the same thing," she said in her most indignant voice.

"Émile," Valfierno broke in as he walked out from behind the staircase. "You're back. And I see you've met Miss Conway."

"Julia, please," she said with a theatrical curtsy. "Delighted to meet you."

"I just caught her stealing," Émile blurted out.

"How dare you accuse me of stealing. I was just admiring the figurines, that's all."

"Then what's that in your pocket?"

"Why don't you try to find out?"

"Émile," said Valfierno, ignoring their exchange, "you'll have to move your things right away. Julia will be sleeping in your room."

"What?"

"You can sleep over the carriage house."

"But she's a common thief!"

"Who are you calling common?" she protested.

Émile was about to say something when Yves, supporting himself with a cane, appeared from behind the staircase.

"I can't remember the last time I heard such commotion," he said with amusement.

"Let me introduce our master painter," said Valfierno. "Monsieur Yves Chaudron, Miss Julia Conway."

Yves managed a slight bow. "*Enchanté*, mademoiselle."

"Now that's more like it," said Julia with a pointed look at Émile.

Émile responded by swiftly sticking his hand into her pocket.

"Get your hands off me!" she screamed as she tried to push him away.

Émile held up the figurine in triumph. "*Voilà!* She lifted this right off the mantelpiece."

"It's just a copy," said Yves with a shrug. "She's welcome to it."

Émile and Julia glared at each other like a pair of belligerent cats until Valfierno broke the standoff. "Well, now that we've all become better acquainted, I'll show you to your room."

Turning a defiant shoulder to Émile, Julia walked up to Valfierno who, instead of turning to lead the way, stood his ground in front of her and held out the palm of his hand. She gave him a quick look of innocent incomprehension before finally reaching into her pocket and producing a wallet.

Émile's mouth dropped open as he patted his empty pocket. Valfierno took the wallet from her but continued to hold out his hand. Julia shrugged and, with an impish smile directed at Émile, produced a pocket watch.

"She's very good," said Valfierno, taking the watch and returning both articles to Émile, "but you do have to keep an eye on her." He put one hand on Julia's shoulder and gestured toward the back of the house. "This way. And I think it's time that we had a little chat about how you can be of help to us."

Chapter 4

Late the following morning, Valfierno and Julia strolled into the lobby of La Gran Hotel de la Paix. Valfierno, dressed as usual in a spotless white suit, carried a long leather valise. Julia wore the new outfit he had bought her that morning on Avenida Corrientes, and looked for all the world like a proper and genteel young woman.

"Tell me who I am again," she asked playfully as she adjusted her high shirt collar. Valfierno shot her a warning look. "Oh, yes," she said, "your niece. Not very exciting."

"That remains to be seen," he said under his breath as they stepped up to the reception desk.

"May I help you, señor?" asked a tall clerk, his appraising eyes taking aim at them down his long, thin nose.

"Señor Hart's room, please," replied Valfierno. "He's expecting us."

Valfierno knocked on the door to Joshua Hart's suite.

"Remember to be charming," he warned Julia.

"Just watch me."

The door swung open, revealing Mrs. Hart. Valfierno could have sworn that when their eyes met, her face flushed slightly.

"Mrs. Hart," he said, holding his hat to his chest, *"buenos dias."*

"Good morning, Marquis," she responded, quickly composing herself.

This was the first time Valfierno had seen her without her large-brimmed hat. Untill this moment, he hadn't realized how curious he had been to see her face in full. She was really quite striking, though not perhaps what one would call an obvious beauty at first glance. In fact, he had never seen a face quite like hers before. Her irises were a pleasing coffee brown and her eyes turned down slightly on the outside corners suggesting just a hint of sadness. Her nose was straight but a little too wide for her face, though this was more than compensated for by a perfect, naturally pink rosebud of a mouth.

"Eduardo, please," he corrected her. "And this is my niece, Miss Julia Conway. She's visiting from New York."

"Please, do come in."

The suite consisted of a large sitting room with furnishings that would have been considered passé in a Parisian hotel but passed for the height of elegance in Buenos Aires. Doors to the left and right led, Valfierno assumed, to the bedrooms. Mrs. Hart's mother sat at the small table by the bay window. She stared out without acknowledging the visitors.

"I'll let my husband know that you're here," Mrs. Hart began, but before she could take a step, Joshua Hart barreled out of the master bedroom, towel in hand, his suspenders draping loosely down his trousers.

"Valfierno, I was wondering when you'd show up—"

He stopped in midsentence when he noticed Julia, his demeanor visibly changing. He wiped the residue of shaving cream from his face, tossed the towel onto a table, and tucked in his shirt.

"Good morning, Señor Hart," Valfierno said. "May I introduce my niece, Miss Julia Conway. As I mentioned to Mrs. Hart, she is visiting from New York, and her discretion in this matter goes without saying."

"Very pleased to make your acquaintance," Hart effused, hoisting his suspenders up to his shoulders. "Please excuse my appearance."

"That's quite all right," Julia said with a slight curtsy. "It's a pleasure to meet you, sir."

"Valfierno," said Hart as he picked up his jacket from the back of a chair and slipped it on, "you never told me you had such a beautiful niece."

"An embarrassment of riches," said Valfierno with a glance to Mrs. Hart, who quickly looked away.

As an afterthought, Hart said, "You've met my wife already."

Julia nodded gracefully.

When Hart finished adjusting his jacket he stepped forward, took Julia's hand, and kissed it with a flourish.

"Charmed, I'm sure," he said.

Julia let out a perfectly modulated giggle of embarrassment. *She really is very good*, Valfierno thought.

Hart motioned her to a padded chair. "Please, make yourself comfortable."

Julia sat down, making an elaborate show of rearranging her dress.

"Well," Valfierno began, "shall we get down to business?"

Hart's demeanor became suddenly serious. He turned away, smoothing the front of his jacket as he mumbled, "I suppose if we must."

Valfierno opened the valise and removed the rolled-up painting. "We had to cut it from its frame, of course, so there is some minor loss around the edges but nothing significant." He partially unscrolled the canvas and pointed to the inked initials in a lower corner on the back. "Your mark, is it not?"

Hart examined the mark closely. After a moment, he looked up. He seemed almost annoyed that he could find no fault with it.

"There's been no news of a theft," he said, an accusation more than a comment.

"A copy already sits in its place on the wall of the gallery. They waste no time in such matters. It would be bad for business."

Hart turned away. "I don't know. I'm still not sure if it's wise to go through with this."

"But señor," said Valfierno in a reassuring tone, "it *is* your mark."

"Yes, yes, it's my mark," Hart said impatiently. "But what I'm telling you is that I'm not sure it's such a good idea anymore."

Valfierno acted as if this were of no consequence at all.

"That's a pity. You've traveled such a long way."

"This country makes me apprehensive. What if they should stop me at the docks?"

"A few American dollars will smooth over any difficulties, I can assure you."

"I must have more time to consider," Hart said. "Come back in the morning."

"I understood that you were leaving tomorrow," Valfierno began. "Don't you think that would be—"

Hart stopped him with a sudden outburst. "I said I need more time!"

Everyone froze for a moment. Then Hart turned to Julia and forced a smile. "Such things are not decided lightly, you understand."

Julia nodded graciously.

"Of course not," said Valfierno in complete agreement. "You shall have all the time you require. What time is your boat scheduled to leave tomorrow?"

"Half past eleven," said Mrs. Hart, trying to be helpful but eliciting only a disapproving look from her husband.

"Then I shall meet you at the docks in the morning," said Valfierno as he rolled up the painting. "Shall we say at ten?"

Hart hesitated. The only sound in the room was the rustling of the canvas as Valfierno finished rolling it up.

Valfierno broke the silence. "And perhaps we can convince Miss Julia to join us once again."

"Oh, I'd love to," said Julia, adding, "that is, if Mr. Hart doesn't object."

Julia looked at Hart, an angelic, hopeful expression on her face.

My God, Valfierno thought, *next she'll be telling him how much she loves all the big boats!*

"Of course not, my dear," Hart said. "It would be a pleasure."

"Then it's all settled." Valfierno slid the painting back into the valise. "Come, Julia."

As Julia rose from the chair, her purse slipped from her lap to the floor.

"Allow me," Hart said, bending down to retrieve it.

"Oh, that's quite all right," said Julia, reaching for it herself. Her sudden movement resulted in a collision with Hart, forcing her to momentarily clutch at his jacket for support.

"I'm so sorry, my dear," Hart said as he picked up the purse and held it out to her.

She straightened up and took it from him. "No, it was my fault entirely."

"No, it was very clumsy of me," Hart insisted.

"Well, señor," Valfierno broke in, "no permanent harm seems to have been done. We shall take our leave." He pulled the door open and said, "Julia . . ."

With a final smile and curtsy into the room, Julia walked past him into the corridor. "Until tomorrow then," Valfierno said with a deferential nod before following her out.

Hart closed the door behind them. He turned to see his wife standing motionless, looking at him.

"Lovely girl, is she not?" he said, a little uncomfortably.

"Very lovely," she replied before sitting at the table and covering her mother's hand with her own.

"Well," was all Joshua Hart said before disappearing into his bedroom.

In an alleyway near the hotel, Julia handed Hart's wallet and passport to Valfierno.

"Charming," said Valfierno.

"All in a day's work," she said, trying to be dismissive but not able to completely suppress a delighted smile.

"Here." Valfierno handed her back the wallet. "This is yours to keep."

"I'd rather have a cut of the take."

"Don't be greedy," Valfierno admonished as he pressed the wallet into her hand. "And besides, there is no take yet, and might never be if things don't go according to plan. Now go back to the house. I have more work to do."

"The old guy's wife is pretty," Julia said, looking to him for a reaction.

"Is she?" Valfierno said lightly.

"Not that you would notice," she said with a sarcastic flair before turning away with a flourish and strolling off.

Of course Mrs. Hart was pretty, Valfierno thought, turning his attention to the passport. But what concern was that of his?

Chapter 5

Valfierno spent the remainder of the morning seated in a small café with a view of the entrance to La Gran Hotel. His plan depended on Joshua Hart's reaction to the discovery that his passport was missing. The goal was to exploit Hart's vulnerable position by offering a simple quid pro quo: Hart would buy the painting in exchange for a supposedly forged passport provided by Valfierno. The trick would be to accomplish this without creating suspicion. It would also require another meeting with Hart today, and that meeting would have to be by chance.

Valfierno hoped that, after discovering the loss, Hart would leave the hotel for the U.S. consulate on Avenida Sarmiento in the Palermo district. He knew that it could take as much as six weeks to obtain a new passport. Hart would use his influence to expedite the process, but it would still take at least a week. Hart would return to the hotel frustrated and in a foul mood. Valfierno would then contrive to bump into him on the street. He wasn't sure exactly what he would say to the man, but he always thought best on his feet.

The noon hour went by with no sign of Hart. Then, in the early afternoon, Valfierno's vigil was rewarded by the sight of Mrs. Hart escorting her mother out of the hotel's entrance. He had to make a quick decision: Wait for Hart, or take advantage of this potential opportunity?

Placing some coins on the tabletop, he rose and followed the two women at a discreet distance as they turned down a busy street dotted with bistros. Within minutes, Mrs. Hart had seated herself and her mother at an outdoor table shaded by a jacaranda tree on the patio of a small café.

Valfierno paused for a moment before crossing the street. As he drew closer, a splash of color caught his eye. The blue, almost purple panicles of flowers adorning the tree perfectly matched the colors on Mrs. Hart's wide-brimmed hat.

"Mrs. Hart," Valfierno said, stopping at their table and feigning surprise, "what an unexpected pleasure."

She looked up, a little startled. "Marquis . . ."

"Oh, no," Valfierno said, removing his hat as he stepped closer to the table. "Eduardo, or Edward if you prefer. I really must insist."

Mrs. Hart gave him a polite smile.

"I see that you have discovered one of Buenos Aires's best-kept secrets." Valfierno took in the bistro with a sweeping gesture of his arm. "The *asador* here prepares the finest *chinchulines* in the entire city."

"I thought a stroll and perhaps some tea would do my mother good," Mrs. Hart said, "though we are expected back soon. Would you care to . . . join us?"

"Oh, I wouldn't dream of intruding."

With a quick look to her mother, she turned back and said, "I wish you would. We wish you would."

"Just for a moment, perhaps." He pulled out the remaining chair and seated himself.

"The dish you mentioned," Mrs. Hart said, "the chef's specialty . . ."

"Ah, yes. *Chinchulines.* I believe in the American South they are referred to as chitlins."

"I see," she said with an amused grimace. "Pig's . . ." She gently motioned toward her stomach.

"Indeed," said Valfierno. "You mentioned tea. I recommend *yerba mate.* A local specialty and quite delicious."

Valfierno summoned the *camarero* and ordered for the three of them. Tea and cakes. When the man had left, Valfierno made some comments concerning the weather and the quality of the various bistros located on this particular street, and then lightly inquired about their opinion of Buenos Aires.

"In truth," Mrs. Hart replied, "we have not had much opportunity for sightseeing. My husband prefers to stay in the hotel much of the time."

"That is unfortunate. Buenos Aires is known as the Paris of South America, a reputation well deserved."

The tea arrived with sweet cocoa cakes. Valfierno, cautious about seeming too inquisitive, confined his remarks to those concerning the food and drink. He insisted that they drink their tea through the *bombillas*—the traditional metal straws the *camarero* had provided—which Mrs. Hart did with some amusement. As they ate and drank, a rather long and slightly awkward pause developed. Valfierno hoped that it would be Mrs. Hart who broke the silence. He was not disappointed.

"I have to . . . apologize for my husband," she began with some hesitation. "This trip has been very stressful and, though I can't say that I fully approve of his intentions in the matter of the painting, you must understand that his concerns greatly contribute to his mood in general and his indecisiveness in particular."

"Of course," Valfierno said, waving it off. "I fully appreciate his misgivings. He must be comfortable with the transaction before proceeding, that is a given."

They exchanged solicitous smiles.

Another silence followed. Valfierno had hoped she would have mentioned the loss of her husband's passport by now. He sensed that she wanted to open up to him but was holding herself back for some reason. He had to raise the stakes; it sometimes required a bold stroke to penetrate even the most outer boundaries of intimacy.

"I am curious about one thing, however," he began tentatively.

"Yes?"

"Well, forgive my frankness but . . ."

He paused, making a point of displaying his reluctance to continue. As he had hoped, Mrs. Hart's expression took on an inquisitive air, which he took as tacit permission to proceed.

"Mrs. Hart," he continued, "if I may be permitted to say so, you are a beautiful woman . . ."

"Marquis . . ." she said, seeming to take umbrage at the remark but revealing with a slight blush that she was also flattered.

"I am only stating the obvious. My point is . . . it seems to me that you could have had your pick of any eligible man. To what does Mr. Joshua Hart owe his good fortune?"

"Marquis," she said in an obvious attempt to project more indignation than she apparently felt, "I'm afraid that does not concern you."

"Of course not," Valfierno conceded. "My impudence is exceeded only by my curiosity. Well, I feel I've taken up too much of your time already."

He placed some coins on the tabletop.

"Oh, that's not necessary," Mrs. Hart protested.

"Indeed not," Valfierno said as he lifted his hat and rose from the table, "but it is my pleasure. I believe I will see you again in the morning."

"Oh, but something has happened," she said. "A crisis has arisen."

Valfierno breathed an inner sigh of relief. He thought for a moment that he had played his hand too aggressively. He slowly lowered himself back into the chair, concern etched on his face.

"A crisis? What sort of crisis?"

"Well, you see," she began, hesitating for a moment before continuing, "it would seem that my husband has lost both his wallet and his passport. In fact, he suspects that one of the housemaids may have stolen them."

"Surely he can just go to the bank, and to the American consulate for a new passport," suggested Valfierno.

"Money is not the issue. But his passport . . . He telephoned the consulate immediately only to be informed that, at best, it would take a week or more to produce a replacement. The return trip takes almost two weeks. Two days following our scheduled arrival in New York, he is chairing a meeting to discuss the consolidation of the East Coast railroads."

"You know a great deal about your husband's business," Valfierno said.

"Is that so odd? He thinks I have no interest whatsoever in his affairs, but I know more about them than perhaps he would even wish. And I know that if he is not at this meeting, it could cost him a great deal of money."

"That *is* a crisis," Valfierno agreed.

"So you see," Mrs. Hart concluded, "if my husband is forced to stay in Buenos Aires one day longer than he has to, I fear that he will become quite unbearable."

Valfierno leaned back, tapping his lips with his fingertips. He took his time; he didn't want her to think that he had known all along what he would say next. Then, as if a sudden light had been switched on in his head, his eyes snapped back to hers, and he leaned forward eagerly.

"I believe, Mrs. Hart, that our meeting today was fated to occur. I'm a man of many connections. I am sure that, with any luck, I can find the necessary papers for your husband by tomorrow morning."

"You could do that? You *would* do that?"

"Certainly." He paused before adding quietly, "For you especially."

At this, she drew back, her expression, which an instant before had registered enthusiasm, suddenly guarded.

"And of course," Valfierno amended, "for your dear mother as well."

"We would be most grateful. You're very kind."

He nodded a slight acknowledgment, but then a shadow of concern flickered across his face, accompanied by a weary sigh.

"Is something wrong?" Mrs. Hart asked.

"Well," Valfierno began, emphasizing his apparent reluctance to

continue, "there is still the small matter of my business arrangement with your husband."

"The painting."

"I know you don't approve," Valfierno continued, "but there
was significant risk involved in obtaining the item, not to mention
expense."

"I can well imagine," she said guardedly.

"Your husband seems to be unsure whether he wants to see our
agreement through to a mutually beneficial conclusion. If he were
forced to stay in Buenos Aires for a week or more, I would have
more time to convince him that his fears are unfounded."

She sat back in her chair, unable to hide the disappointment in
her face. "I fully understand. You have your own considerations in
this matter."

"And I'm not just thinking of myself, you understand. There are
others involved who have also put much at risk."

"Of course, you must do what you think is right," she said as
evenly as possible. "Now, I think we should be getting back to the
hotel." She placed her hand on her mother's arm.

"Please," said Valfierno, briefly touching her forearm. "Mrs.
Hart. I mention these things only because they bear mentioning.
I have no intention of going back on my previous offer. Naturally,
there will be some small expense involved, but your husband shall
have the necessary papers by the morning."

She was about to speak when he held up his hand.

"No, it's settled. I am delighted to be of assistance. The agreement between your husband and myself should not be your concern." He had accomplished all he could. In Hart's eyes, Valfierno
would have legitimately learned of the loss of his passport from his
wife. He could now contact Hart and offer his services. Naturally,
it would only be fair to expect the consummation of their original
deal concerning the painting before a "forged" passport could be
produced on such short notice. It smacked a little too strongly of
blackmail for Valfierno's taste, but he saw no alternative. He felt

strangely guilty about his manipulation of Mrs. Hart, but it had been unavoidable.

"Now, if you will excuse me, I will make the necessary arrangements."

As he picked up his hat and pushed back his chair, he noticed Mrs. Hart glance nervously at her mother as if seeking guidance.

Before he could rise, she spoke hesitantly. "Perhaps . . ."

"Yes?"

"Perhaps . . . there is a way that both you and my husband can benefit from this situation."

Valfierno's heart began racing. Was it possible that she was about to make this even easier?

"And how would that be?" He settled back into his chair.

She turned again to her mother, and Valfierno could sense the longing she felt to share this with her. Finally, she turned back to him, a thin mask of resolve on her face.

"You could tell my husband . . ." She hesitated.

Valfierno encouraged her with an inquisitive look.

She drew in her breath for an instant before letting the words rush out. "You could tell him that you will produce the passport only if he buys the painting."

"Mrs. Hart," Valfierno said with genuine astonishment, "you surprise me."

She leaned forward. "It would only be fair considering the amount of trouble you've gone to." She said this with unexpected fervor, but she quickly caught herself, straightening up as she added, "And, besides, I know that my husband, despite his misgivings, would still like to have the painting in his possession."

This was more than Valfierno could have hoped for. Directly proposing the exchange ran the risk of making Hart suspicious. Or Hart might feel cornered and simply refuse out of hand. But if his wife presented the idea and told him that she had thought it best to agree—at least in principle—Hart would be more inclined to go along with it. Of course, he might reproach his wife for agreeing on his behalf, but Valfierno justified this by telling himself that it was also to her and her mother's benefit to leave Buenos Aires as soon as possible.

"As you said," Valfierno mused, "for our mutual benefit."

"I'll tell him." She was fully committed now and warming to her idea. "I'll tell him that I met you on the street, that we talked, and that you outlined this proposal. Time was of the utmost importance, so I took the liberty of agreeing in his name to the arrangement. Don't you see? It solves everyone's problems. You will be paid for your efforts, and we will be able to return to New York tomorrow."

Valfierno pretended to weigh this in his mind as he marveled at her enthusiasm for the idea.

"He may be less than pleased that he was not consulted in the matter," he finally said.

"The money is not important to him," Mrs. Hart said, trying to sell the idea now. "He has some concern about the authorities, yes, but it's nothing compared to his desire to leave your beautiful city as soon as possible."

Valfierno looked away, tilting his head and forming his face into an expression of amused uncertainty.

"Well," she challenged him, "what do you say?"

Valfierno looked at her, letting the moment stretch a bit longer before an appreciative smile formed on his face.

"I say, Mrs. Hart, that you are a most remarkable woman."

Mrs. Hart was clearly pleased that he had accepted her proposal. But her smile lasted only a few seconds.

"Well, then," she said, composing herself. "Mother, we should be going."

Valfierno rose as Mrs. Hart gently guided her mother to her feet.

"We will see you at the dock tomorrow morning at ten o'clock," she said, gathering up her hat and long white gloves, "an hour before the boat leaves."

"And you are sure you want to do this?"

"Yes, I'm quite sure. Good day to you, Marquis. Come, Mother."

As Mrs. Hart guided her mother back in the direction of the

hotel, Valfierno experienced a strange combination of feelings: exhilaration in the knowledge that his plan had succeeded beyond all expectations, and a measure of guilt for having involved her.

Turning to go, he noticed a single white glove lying on the ground beneath the table. He picked it up and was about to call after her when he stopped himself. He felt the silky fabric of the glove between his fingers, hesitated a moment, then slipped it into his pocket.

Chapter 6

At dinner that evening, Julia proved to be an entertaining guest, at least to Valfierno and Yves. Émile said little as the meal progressed. Valfierno's housekeeper, Maria, served *carbonada criolla*, a thick beef stew spiced with sliced pears. Despite the uncertainty of what tomorrow was to bring, the group ate heartily and made short work of a number of bottles of dark red Tempranillo wine. After finishing a dessert of sweet honey cakes, Valfierno and Yves peppered the newcomer in their midst with questions.

"So how exactly did you pick up your particular talent," Valfierno asked, rubbing the tip of his thumb and forefinger together to illustrate her unique aptitude.

"Yes," added Yves. "Tell us, how old were you when you got started?"

She took another sip of wine and smiled proudly. "Eleven."

"Eleven?" Valfierno was impressed. "Why such a late start?"

Valfierno and Yves shared a friendly chuckle, but Émile simply stared into his half-empty glass of wine.

"Go ahead and laugh," she said good-naturedly, "but eleven actually is a bit late."

"And have you ever been caught?" Valfierno asked. "I mean, before yesterday?"

"As a matter of fact, I was caught red-handed the very first time I tried to pick someone's pocket."

"Oh, dear," Yves said, amused at how casually, even proudly, she said it. "That was unfortunate."

"Actually, it was just the opposite," she corrected him, "because I was caught by my uncle Nathan."

"You tried to pick your own uncle's pocket?" Valfierno asked in amazement.

"No, Uncle Nathan was teaching me *how* to pick pockets."

"Then I think we need to hear a little something about this Uncle Nathan of yours," Valfierno said before signaling Maria to refill Julia's glass.

"Well," she began, "let's just say he was the black sheep of the family . . ."

Her father was a midlevel banker in Manhattan, and she had lived a very prosaic middle-class life in Fort Lee, New Jersey, just across the Hudson River from the city. Her family had always considered Uncle Nathan something of a pariah, someone to be scorned or at best ignored. But to Julia, he was her most intriguing relative by far. Not that his reputation was ill deserved: He had spent three long years at Sing Sing Correctional Facility in upstate New York for check forgery. He had apparently learned his lesson and bid farewell to the world of crime. Though, in the eyes of most of the family, he traded that world for one even more reprehensible: show business.

He made his living touring the frayed edges of the vaudeville circuit in an act that consisted of picking the pockets of audience members to the amusement of their working-class brethren.

He was assisted in this venture by one Lola Montez, his comely—at least in the flattering glow of the dim stage lights—assistant, another sore spot with his family.

But not to Julia. On the rare occasions when Uncle Nathan

came in from the road, she would spend as much time as possible with him, soaking up his sordid tales of the squalid yet exciting world of show business. And he delighted in passing down the one talent that he had mastered above all others: the art of pickpocketing. He traveled extensively and regaled her with stories of his foreign adventures, particularly in London, Paris, and Barcelona. He even taught her some French and Spanish, the latter of which had proved particularly useful lately. As he would always say, the larger the audience, the greater the number of suckers.

She was a quick study, and Uncle Nathan insisted that he could have made a killing with those small hands and long slender fingers of hers. He even hinted that one day Julia could join him onstage and, between the two of them, they would elevate the act to a level that would draw the attention of the higher-class promoters in New York and Chicago. The notion stoked her dreams, populating them with visions of a thrilling and romantic future.

And then one day her mother announced that Uncle Nathan was dead, shot by his assistant Lola's cuckolded husband. Her family was not a bit surprised. Julia's world became suddenly very dull indeed.

The day after her sixteenth birthday, she ran away from home, her head full of the promise of far-off adventures and her pockets full of the dollar bills that her mother kept in her sewing basket "for a rainy day." It had even been raining that day.

The money took her from New Jersey to Charleston, South Carolina, where she found Uncle Nathan's skills invaluable. She fell in with a group of young prostitutes and came up with a foolproof scheme. Acting the part of a lady of the street—though never in fact playing that role, she assured her listeners—she would fawn over and cajole an eager john only to fabricate some perceived insult and stalk off in disgust. By the time the man realized that he had been relieved of his wallet, it was too late.

In most cases, the poor fool would drag himself meekly back to his home and family. But she knew that sooner or later, someone would be sufficiently motivated to go in search of her. So she never stayed in one place for too long and kept moving south, following the Florida East Coast Railway all the way to the burgeoning city of Miami. After she wore out her welcome there, she boarded a steamer for São Paulo, Brazil, eventually making her way to Buenos Aires.

"And now," she concluded, "it looks like I've come about as far south as I can go."

"Indeed," Valfierno said. "Tierra del Fuego holds very little promise for someone in your line of work."

"Besides," she added casually, "the local police relieved me of my American passport months ago."

"Well," said Yves, "that's quite a tale. Don't you think, Émile?"

Émile looked at Yves and shrugged. "If it's true."

Julia gave him a look.

"True or not," Valfierno said, "it makes for a hell of a story."

"I'll drink to that." Yves raised his glass.

"You've been very quiet," Julia said to Émile, a hint of challenge in her voice. "Don't *you* have any amusing anecdotes?"

"Even if I did," Émile answered, "I wouldn't have been able to get a word in edgewise."

"No fighting at the table, *enfants*," Yves said in his most avuncular manner.

"I'm going to bed," announced Émile, rising from the table. "*Bonne nuit.*"

"*Buenas noches*, Émile," said Valfierno.

"Don't forget this." Julia held out Émile's pocket watch.

Émile swiped the watch and stalked off.

"You shouldn't tease him so hard," said Valfierno after Émile had left the room.

"He's a big boy," she said, draining what was left of the wine in her glass. "He can look after himself."

Later in the evening, Valfierno and Yves sat in the warm glow of candlelight in the carriage house, Valfierno puffing on a cigar and each holding a glass of Tempranillo.

"I don't know what Émile's problem is," Yves said. "She's a very engaging young lady."

"She's always picking his pocket," Valfierno said with a shrug. "He hates that."

The carriage house was an art gallery in itself. A number of easels supported copies of various masterpieces in different states of completion. Scores of other canvases lay stacked against the walls, mostly Yves's original work. It had always been Valfierno's considered opinion that, even though Yves's paintings seemed to lack the precision of the copies he created, they possessed a distinctive, compelling style of their own.

Yves's original work fit into two categories. In the first, buildings with inward-leaning walls loomed over narrow streets as if they were about to pounce on the small unsuspecting pedestrians below; muted washed-out hues added to the sense of oppression. In the second, people, their clothing rendered in unnaturally bright and piercing colors, sat at outdoor cafés and leaned into each other much the same as the walls of the buildings had, but the mood was intimate, sensual even. Bright sunlight cast long, vivid shadows that contrasted with the luminous colors threatening to burn through the canvas itself.

"You know, my friend," Valfierno said, taking a sip of wine, "they are really quite good. Your own pieces, I mean. You should spend more time on them."

Yves shrugged off the compliment. "How can I? You work me like a mule." But he smiled as he said it.

"After we have successfully concluded our current business, we'll all take a break. No more copies for a while. You can concentrate on your own paintings. How does that sound?"

"Like hard work," said the old man.

"And copying the masters is not?" challenged Valfierno.

"The most difficult part has already been done. The choice of subject. The composition. The lighting. The technique. Still, as you know, I always manage to find a way to leave my own mark."

Valfierno smiled. Master forgers usually couldn't resist making a small, virtually undetectable alteration in the compositions they were duplicating. Anyone taking the time to count the number of pearls in the nymph's necklace in the painting in the museum would, after taking delivery of his new purchase, find himself the beneficiary of one extra pearl for his money.

"My point is," Yves continued, "that technique can be learned. But the inspiration comes from another place altogether, a mysterious place, a hidden place." He tapped his chest with his fist. "It is possessed only by the true artist."

"You underestimate yourself," said Valfierno. "Inspiration is just another word for heart, and you always find a way to put your heart into all your work."

The old man decided to accept this. "True enough. Without the heart, it's only paint and canvas."

"Then it's settled," Valfierno declared. "You'll create an original work just for me. A commission, if you will. Who knows, I might even pay you."

Yves smiled in response, took a long drink from his glass, and asked, "So, will we catch our fish tomorrow?"

Valfierno pondered this for a moment.

"I believe that Mr. Joshua Hart of Newport, Rhode Island, will complete the transaction." Valfierno took a sip of his wine before amending, "That is, with the kind assistance of *Mrs.* Joshua Hart."

Chapter 7

Joshua Hart impatiently checked his pocket watch again. Behind him on the dock, his wife stood with her mother. Mrs. Hart clutched the handle of a bulging carpetbag, anxiously tilting her head upward to scan the sea of faces.

The hull of the 11,000-ton Allan Line steamship *Victorian* loomed above them, an overhanging cliff of gray steel. The blare of horns punctuated the babble of the uniformed crew members and burly stevedores as they struggled to board a throng of people.

"Where in blazes is he?" Hart demanded of his wife, who could only shake her head and shrug in response.

At that same moment, Valfierno stood with Julia just out of sight behind the wall of the nearby customshouse. He held the long leather valise containing the painting. Émile stood out from the wall observing the American and his party milling about on the dock.

"The boat is set to leave in fifteen minutes," Émile said, nervously checking his pocket watch.

"Patience," said Valfierno. "Timing is everything."

Émile looked at his watch again before turning to Julia for support. But all Julia did was to annoy him with a teasing glance at his timepiece, which prompted Émile to thrust it into his pocket.

On the dock, a man in a dark blue uniform bellowed out a last call for boarding.

"Confound it!" Hart snapped. "Where the devil is he?"

"There!" Mrs. Hart called out, unable to restrain her excitement. She pointed at Valfierno pushing his way through the mass onto the dock. Farther back, Émile and Julia hurried after him, but when Julia stepped onto the dock itself, Émile came to a halt. Julia stopped and looked back at him.

"What's the matter?" she asked.

Émile stared down at the wooden dock and the water glinting below, visible through the cracks between the planks.

"You're not afraid of water, are you?" She said it more as a childish taunt than a real question.

Émile gave her a stony look.

"That's ridiculous," he said, right before stepping purposefully onto the dock and striding past her into the crowd.

Farther on, Valfierno walked up to Joshua Hart.

"Where the devil have you been?" Hart asked angrily. "You've almost made me miss the boat."

"Forgive me," Valfierno said breathlessly. "Our carriage lost a wheel."

Émile and Julia emerged from the crowd and stopped behind Valfierno.

"Who is this?" Hart demanded, indicating Émile.

"My assistant, Émile. He helped me to procure the papers."

"How good to see you again, Mr. Hart," Julia said.

She stepped forward, extending a hand toward him in greeting. But she tripped over her own feet and fell forward, forcing her to grab onto Hart's coat lapels for support.

"Oh, forgive me," she said. "I'm all left feet."

He briefly acknowledged her but was too distracted to take much notice.

"Well, have you got them?" Hart demanded, turning away from Julia.

"Of course." Valfierno nodded to Émile. The young man produced a passport with various papers sticking out of it. Hart reached for it, but Valfierno put his hand out to hold Émile back.

"First things first, señor," he said with mild reproach.

Hart hesitated.

Don't tell me he still has misgivings, thought Valfierno. *He couldn't still be thinking of waiting it out here in Buenos Aires for the consulate to come up with a new passport.*

Careful to keep an expression of complete indifference on his face, Valfierno turned to Mrs. Hart. To the casual observer he was simply acknowledging her with a polite smile, but he held her eyes longer than necessary.

Mrs. Hart hesitated for just an instant before saying, "Dear, the ship is about to leave."

Hart turned to his wife with a sharp look before giving her a grudging nod. She stepped forward and held out the carpetbag. Valfierno motioned to Émile, who handed the passport to Mrs. Hart with one hand as he took the carpetbag with the other. Joshua Hart snatched the passport from his wife and opened it, taking out the papers as Émile checked the contents of the bag.

"I trust you'll find them satisfactory," Valfierno said.

"Yes," Hart replied a little warily. "They almost look like the originals . . ."

"And this, I believe, is also yours." Valfierno handed the valise containing the painting to Mrs. Hart.

"Please, señor," called out a uniformed officer, "you must board now."

With a look to Valfierno, Hart allowed himself to be guided by the officer to the gangplank. Mrs. Hart followed close behind with her mother. She had just started up the walkway when Valfierno stepped forward.

"Mrs. Hart," he said, "I believe you may have dropped this."

He held out the white glove he had retrieved from the café. She stopped and looked at him, barely glancing at the glove.

"I believe you are mistaken, señor," she said smoothly. "The glove is not mine."

She smiled politely, her eyes holding his for another moment.

Then she turned her attention back to her mother and continued up toward the deck, leaving Valfierno holding her glove.

Fifteen minutes later, the *Victorian*'s horn sounded a blaring farewell to Buenos Aires as tugboats nudged its massive hull from the dock. Ellen Hart stood with her mother at the railing. Nearby, Joshua Hart commiserated with another well-dressed man about the good fortune they shared in finally leaving such a godforsaken place.

On shore, Valfierno and Julia watched from the edge of the dock as the ship began its journey up the estuary of the Rio de la Plata to the vast South Atlantic. Émile stood a few steps behind them. Julia pulled out a pocket watch with a flourish and consulted it.

"Right on time," she said, holding up the timepiece for Émile's benefit.

Immediately, he checked his pocket but, to both his relief and embarrassment, found his own watch exactly where it should be.

On the deck of the steamship, still in conversation with the other gentleman, Joshua Hart absentmindedly patted his watch pocket. He stopped midsentence, thrust his hand into it, and fished about frantically with his fingers as if somehow he would find his watch hiding in there.

Nearby, Ellen Hart looked across at Valfierno standing on the receding dock. She resisted the urge to wave good-bye. She watched the man in the white suit until he blended in with the crowd and wondered if he had also been watching her.

On the return trip from the harbor, Valfierno announced to the group that they would celebrate the successful conclusion of their business with a dinner that evening at La Cabaña Las Lilas. Yves rarely went out these days, but Valfierno would do his best to persuade him.

"Julia," Valfierno said as they approached the house, "your skills proved invaluable to us. I suspect our fish might just have managed to wriggle off the hook without them."

"All in a day's work," she said, shrugging it off. "Maybe I've even earned a full cut now." She made a point of looking directly at the carpetbag that Émile held in the hand closest to her. Then she looked up at him and smiled demurely, making him frown and shift the bag to his other hand.

"Don't worry," Valfierno assured her. "I always reward those with useful talents."

"Did I mention," Émile began, a little too loudly, "how close I came to being caught the other night when I retrieved the copy from the museum? A few seconds more and they would have had me."

"You must be very brave," Julia said, playing the ardent admirer to the hilt.

"I would be out of business without your resourcefulness, Émile," Valfierno said with appreciative sincerity.

"Come," he added as they reached the gate in front of the house. "Let's deliver the good news to the master painter."

Inside, Valfierno went straight through to the courtyard. Émile began to follow but Julia put a hand on his arm, gently restraining him.

"Would you like this?" she asked, producing Hart's pocket watch.

Émile looked at the watch. "No, thank you," he said tightly. "I have my own."

"Are you sure?"

Face flushing, Émile forced himself to resist the temptation to check his pocket. He was about to say something, but thinking better of it, walked away.

"But this one is solid gold," she called after him teasingly.

Crossing the courtyard, Valfierno considered the type of painting he would commission from Yves. A portrait was the most obvious choice, of course, but perhaps it would be best to leave the subject entirely up to the artist. Yes, he would have the freedom to paint whatever he wished.

Valfierno entered the carriage house studio and saw Yves sitting with his back toward him, contemplating the new, almost-completed copy of *La Ninfa Sorprendida*.

"The fruits of our labors, old friend," said Valfierno, placing the carpetbag on a table. "No more work today. The celebration begins immediately."

The old man didn't respond. He often fell asleep at his easel. Valfierno stepped forward and placed his hand on Yves's shoulder.

"I think you'll want to wake up for this—"

Yves slumped forward. Before Valfierno could prevent it, the old man rolled from the chair to the floor onto his back.

Valfierno knelt down. Yves's face was ashen. His open eyes, their pupils dilated, stared blankly at the ceiling.

Valfierno put his hand on Yves's cheek. His skin felt icy cold. He was quite dead.

Chapter 8

The ornate mausoleums and marble crypts of the Cementerio de la Recoleta dwarfed the simple headstone that marked the final resting place of Yves Chaudron.

Valfierno stood alone by the grave site staring at the simple inscription: "Yves Chaudron. June 14, 1834–April 25, 1910. Eternal Rest His Final Reward."

Valfierno had just buried the main reason that he had left Paris almost ten years before.

Yves Chaudron had made a foolish mistake. He tried to pass off a copy of an El Greco as the real thing to an English businessman in Paris. Yves was an excellent forger but a very bad con man. The Englishman became suspicious and reported him to the Prefecture of Police.

Yves came to Valfierno, for whom he occasionally did some work, and asked for help. As it turned out, he arrived at precisely the right time. Valfierno had grown disillusioned with the scene in Paris; the market for creatively obtained works of art had cooled and he had been thinking of making a change for some time. He made a deal with Yves immediately: They would leave France together for the fresh territory of Buenos Aires in Valfierno's home country of Argentina.

There would be less scrutiny from the authorities there, and he could dip into the pool of newly minted American millionaires trying to establish their influence in the expanding South American markets. It promised to be an exciting, not to mention lucrative, change of scene. In return for Valfierno's help, Yves Chaudron agreed to provide his services exclusively.

Buenos Aires felt like a bit of a backwater after Paris, but he never regretted his decision. Valfierno took frequent trips to the United States to drum up business with the nouveau riche from Boston to Philadelphia. He eventually amassed an impressive clientele, but since the Wall Street Panic of 1907, customers had been harder to come by. Joshua Hart had weathered the storm better than most, but even he had required months of persuasion before agreeing to come to Buenos Aires.

Now, everything had changed.

"Good-bye, old friend," Valfierno said, looking down at the headstone. "If there is a God you can do his portrait, and if there is a heaven you'll have endless vistas for your paints and brushes."

Émile and Julia stood some distance away, observing Valfierno.

"Didn't the old man have any family?" she asked.

"No one," Émile answered without looking at her.

"Friends?"

"The marquis was his only friend."

"Sad to die alone," she said. After a moment, she added, "I wonder who'll come to my grave when I die."

Émile ignored her.

"Perhaps *you* will," she added with a flirtatious smile.

"Oh, I'll come, all right," he said, walking away. "I might even do a little dance."

"Wonderful," she called after him. "In that case, I'll leave instructions to be buried at sea!"

That night, Valfierno sat in the carriage house studio, a glass of Malbec in his hand, an almost empty bottle on the floor next to him. Two candles cast circles of light in the darkness, illuminating the haphazard gallery of canvases, Yves's life's work. Valfierno had placed one of Yves's original canvases—an outdoor café scene, frantic with life—on the easel. The copy of *La Ninfa Sorprendida* lay faceup on the floor. It looked finished, but Valfierno knew that it probably wasn't. Not that it mattered now.

Despite the clutter, there was a palpable emptiness to the space. The magnificent art was still here, but the artist was gone; the heart of the room had grown silent.

"I just thought I'd check up on you," Émile said from the doorway. Valfierno said nothing. "Are you going to stay up all night?"

Valfierno kept his eyes on the canvas. "What will you leave behind, Émile?" he asked quietly.

"I'm not going anywhere," the young man replied.

"At the end of your life," Valfierno clarified, "what will you leave behind?"

Silence hung in the air for a moment before Émile finally spoke. "Does it matter?"

"I don't know," Valfierno mused. "To the one leaving this world, perhaps nothing, but to the ones left behind . . ." Valfierno shrugged.

"The trick then," Émile began, almost talking to himself, "is not to have anyone to leave behind."

"My young friend," Valfierno said with a sigh, "of all the things you can learn from me, that shouldn't be one of them."

"You should go to bed," Émile urged. "The sun will be up soon."

And with that, Émile withdrew and clattered up the stairs to his room above the carriage house.

Valfierno lifted the glass to his lips and emptied it. He considered refilling it but changed his mind. Slipping his hand into his pocket, he pulled out Ellen Hart's white glove. He felt the silky texture between his fingers before lifting it to his nose. The faintest hint of fragrance evoked the whisper of a memory that lay tantalizingly beyond his reach, or perhaps it was only the scent of the flowering trumpet trees drifting in on the warm night air.

He lowered his hand and looked around the empty room. "You were right, old friend," he said to the darkness. "Without the heart, it's only paint and canvas."

By the time the candles melted down to petals of wax dripping onto the tabletop, and the promise of dawn washed the room in pale gray light, Valfierno had made his decision.

Chapter 9

Émile stood on the dock, well back from the edge, restlessly shuffling his feet.

"Relax," Valfierno said. "This won't be your first sea voyage. Look at it as a grand adventure."

"I'm fine," Émile insisted a little too strongly. "I just don't know why we have to leave on such short notice, that's all."

"Once a decision is made," Valfierno said, "there is no point in delay. We need a new collaborator; it's as simple as that. And Paris is where we shall find him."

Émile apprehensively scanned the crowd.

"What do you keep looking for?" Valfierno asked.

"Nothing," Émile replied. "I'd better go and see what those porters are doing with our luggage."

The young man threaded his way back through the crowd. Yes, Valfierno thought, their master forger was dead. Now they had to return to Paris to find another one. That was reason enough, of course, but there was something else. The seed of a plan had begun to take root in his mind, a scheme that, if it succeeded, could change everything.

"She's here," Émile called out, suddenly reemerging from the crowd and pointing back up the dock. His words came as a dire warning. "I told you she'd follow us."

His thoughts interrupted, Valfierno turned to see Julia break through the crowd behind Émile. He was not surprised.

When he had first announced his plan to move the operation back to Paris, she had been thrilled. He had pointed out to her, however, that she could not possibly come with them. She had pleaded, first to Valfierno, then to Émile, to be included in their plans. Valfierno listened to her arguments but remained firm, reminding her that she had enough money now to do what she wanted, even return to the United States. He had arranged for her to get a new passport, though she wouldn't have it for another month. The house was to be let to the family of a local businessman, but Julia would be able to live there until they moved in. The housekeeper, Maria, was staying on and could keep an eye on her.

Finally, Julia had given up and retreated to her room. She hadn't emerged even when Valfierno and Émile left this morning. Valfierno was a little surprised that she had capitulated so easily. Apparently, she hadn't.

"I'm coming with you," she announced as she drew to a halt in front of him. "Nothing you can say will stop me." Valfierno thought he detected genuine fear behind her eyes despite her show of bravado.

"There's nothing I need to say or do to stop you," he said. "For one thing, you have no ticket and the ship is completely booked. For another thing, you don't have a passport. And by the time you finally get one, you will see the wisdom in all of this."

In truth, there had been no available berths on the steamship for some time, but Valfierno had been so eager to implement his plan immediately that he had used his considerable influence and paid a huge premium to obtain passage for himself and Émile.

"But why don't you want me to come with you?" she asked, unable to keep the petulance out of her voice.

"My dear, it's simply not possible. Émile and I are returning to France. It is his native home and my chosen one. We're not coming back."

"But you told me yourself how useful I am."

"Yes, and you have been paid very well for your skills."

"Émile," she said, appealing to the young man, "don't you want me to come with you?"

Though he tried not to look at her, his eyes met hers for a brief instant before he quickly turned to Valfierno.

"We have to get on board." He started for the gangplank.

"Don't worry, *mi querida*," Valfierno said, leaning forward and gently kissing Julia's forehead. "If anyone can take care of herself, it's you. *Buena suerte.*"

Julia watched the two men walk up the gangplank. She wanted to call out but knew there was nothing more she could say. Frantically, she looked around the crowded dock as if somehow it held the answer to her problem. Returning her gaze to the ship, she caught Émile staring down at her from the railing before he looked away and drew back, disappearing onto the deck.

A sudden commotion drew her attention. A well-dressed young woman hurried along the dock waving frantically and screaming, "Wait! Wait!"

Two local men dripping with sweat kept pace on either side, both loaded down with suitcases and hatboxes. Clearly this woman had cut her departure time too close and had almost missed the sailing.

Julia didn't hesitate. As the hysterical woman dashed by her, she stepped out into her path.

Chapter 10

The steamship slid effortlessly across the mirrorlike surface of the ocean, the sun blazing like a beacon ahead. Émile had spent most of the trip in his cabin, but on the morning of the final day, only hours before they were to dock in Le Havre, Valfierno convinced him to come up on deck to enjoy the perfect weather.

"I don't suppose you remember much of Paris," Valfierno said. "You were only a boy when we left."

"I remember the smell mostly," Émile said, grimacing at the thought. "And the streets. And how cold it could get at night. And how hungry I was all the time."

Valfierno looked at Émile standing back from the railing, marveling at how much he had changed since those days. He was tall now, though still a bit gangly with the awkwardness of youth. His facial features, taken separately, were unimpressive: his eyebrows too thick, his eyes a little too deeply set, his nose and ears too pronounced, his mouth too wide to fit comfortably between his cheeks, all ending in an elongated chin that made his face too long. But somehow the combination of all these elements made for an appealing, even handsome face. If he would only smile once in a while, Valfierno thought, that would make all the difference. And he was clean, of course, and well groomed, unlike the street urchin he used to be, as black with dirt as a chimney sweep.

Like Buenos Aires, the streets of Paris were pitifully full of such boys, begging, stealing, marauding in packs, eternally harassing, and in turn harassed by the local authorities. One did one's best to avoid them, to ignore them whenever possible, but they remained an omnipresent feature of the city. The worst thing you could do was to look them in the eye, especially if you felt any sympathy toward the creatures. Once they got a whiff of pity, they would swarm around you like a flock of hungry seagulls, their little hands reaching up for coins or, worse, burrowing into your pockets for anything they could find. But Émile had been different. Émile had saved his life.

It began, as these things often do, with a woman. Her name was Chloe, and she was the wife of Jean Laroche, an art dealer on rue Saint-Honoré. On the surface, Laroche was an honest dealer in fine art, but his real money came from selling fake masters, and in that side of his business he worked closely with Valfierno. Chloe was the kind of woman whose presence alone constantly reminded men of their sexuality and, to make matters worse, she was extremely flirtatious. Valfierno enjoyed her playful advances but never took them seriously. After all, she flirted with everyone. Everyone, that is, except her husband. And her husband was a jealous man.

At first, when the four young ruffians had cornered him in the alleyway off rue Saint-Martin, he thought it was a simple robbery. Thugs—dubbed *apaches* by the newspapers for their vicious brand of lawless violence—often roamed the streets at night. Valfierno was not worried initially. He had enough francs in his pocket—or so he thought—to appease them. But when the largest youth, apparently the leader of the pack, informed him they had a message from Monsieur Laroche, he knew he was in trouble. As they proceeded to beat him to the ground, he had allowed himself an ironic thought: *If I'm to be killed by these ruffians, it's a pity I'm not guilty of the crime they're punishing me for.*

And killed he knew he would have been, if it hadn't been for Émile.

As Valfierno lay on the rough cobblestones trying to protect himself from the flying boots and clubs, he had all but given up any hope of survival when the punishment suddenly stopped. He heard the *apaches* murmuring to each other and risked opening his eyes. Their attention was riveted on the slight figure of a young boy standing on the other side of Valfierno's prostrate figure.

"And what do you think you're doing?" the leader demanded, appraising the boy. *"Allez, gamin!* Off with you before you get a boot up your ass!"

But the boy didn't move. He just stood there observing the scene with an expression of almost innocent curiosity. One of the young *apaches* stepped over Valfierno and raised his club as if to hit the boy. The boy flinched instinctively but held his ground.

The *apache* with the club turned to the leader and shrugged.

"Go on," said the leader. "Clobber the little bastard if he won't move."

The *apache* turned back to the boy, brandishing his club once again. The boy just looked at him.

"Ah, to hell with it." The *apache* lowered his weapon and returned to the group. "There's no fun in this. It's too easy. You clobber him if you want to."

"Merde," the leader said. "We've done enough for one night, anyway. We've given this dandy a lesson he'll not soon forget." The others agreed and, with a few parting kicks for good measure, the *apaches* melted away into the shadows.

Valfierno looked up at the boy through swollen eyelids. "What's your name?" he asked.

The boy hesitated for a moment. "Émile."

"Well, thank you, Émile. I was beginning to get the distinct impression that they didn't like me. Are you hungry, Émile?"

It was weeks later, after the boy had been cleaned up and moved into the attic bedroom of the house Valfierno rented on rue Edouard

VII, that Valfierno casually asked him why he hadn't run away that night.

Émile gave Valfierno a puzzled look. Hadn't it been obvious?

"You were lying in my spot."

Valfierno looked back out over the sea.

"Yes, Paris is a hard city for many, but a city full of opportunity for those with the right talents."

Émile made no response, simply nodded his head in a desultory manner. In fact, he had said very little since they left Buenos Aires. Valfierno knew all too well of Émile's aversion to water, but he also imagined that he was apprehensive about returning home. He had tried to draw him out on a number of occasions, but each time he had been unsuccessful. Something else was bothering the young man.

"Let's take a walk," Valfierno suggested.

As they began to stroll around the promenade deck, Valfierno thought he would try a different tack.

"I'm sorry that we couldn't include Julia in our plans," he said casually.

"Why be sorry?" Émile said. "She was more trouble than she was worth."

"She had her talents. Without her, I'm afraid we would have lost Mr. Joshua Hart and all our work would have come to nothing."

"We would have thought of something. We managed without her for years before and we will again."

"I suppose you're right," said Valfierno without much conviction.

"Nothing was safe around her," Émile continued, warming to the subject. "She was little more than a common thief."

"And what are we, Émile?" Valfierno asked. "Uncommon thieves?"

"It's entirely different. For one thing, she could never keep her hands off anyone's watch, especially mine."

"Yet you still have it," said Valfierno.

"No thanks to her," Émile said, turning a corner beneath the captain's bridge. "If I never see her again, it will be too soon."

Émile glanced at Valfierno as he said this and didn't see the woman coming from the opposite direction in time to avoid an awkward collision. "I beg your pardon, madame . . ."

"Perhaps, monsieur, you should pay more attention to where you are going," said Julia Conway.

"How did you . . . ?" Émile sputtered in shock. "What are you doing here?"

"Same as you, of course, going to France." She casually handed him back his pocket watch. "Here. I've got to keep in practice."

Completely flustered, Émile took it from her.

Valfierno appraised her. "So," he said evenly, "from pickpocket to stowaway."

"Who are you calling a stowaway? I stole my ticket fair and square."

"Little good it will do you when we dock," said Émile. "They'll never let you into France without a passport."

"Why don't you let me worry about that," she said as she sauntered away from them along the deck. "I can take care of myself, remember?"

Émile stared at her receding figure. Valfierno put a hand on the young man's shoulder.

"I thought she wouldn't give up so easily," Valfierno said with admiration before starting off again.

Émile stood for a moment longer before turning on his heel and following him.

Valfierno and Émile passed through the line at the Le Havre customshouse with no difficulty. The necessity of a quick departure from Buenos Aires had always been a possibility so Valfierno made sure that Émile always had a current French passport. After retrieving his stamped passport from one of the customs officials, Valfierno pulled Émile aside. Julia was standing in line a little way behind them, and he wanted to see how exactly she planned to pass inspection.

When Julia's turn came, a middle-aged customs official opened her passport and perused it. Looking up from his desk, he gave her an appraising stare. She returned his gaze with the prettiest, most innocent smile she could muster.

"Is anything wrong, monsieur?" she asked demurely.

"If you don't mind me saying, mademoiselle," the man replied, "you look much younger than your birth date would indicate."

"I don't mind in the least," she said with a coy sideways glance. "In fact, under different circumstances, I'd want to hear much more of what you have to say."

Taking notice of the looks he was beginning to get from some of the other officials, the man stamped the passport, held it up to her, and mumbled, "Welcome to France, mademoiselle . . ."

Julia smiled sweetly and took the passport. As she paraded past Valfierno and Émile, she turned to them with a smile on her face.

"What are you waiting for?" she said before moving off into the crowd.

"*Bienvenu á France,*" Valfierno said to no one in particular before he and Émile picked up their bags and followed her.

Part II

To have what we would have, we speak not what we mean.
—Shakespeare, *Measure for Measure*

Chapter 11

The locomotive clattered across the verdant French countryside, its billowing plume of smoke and steam staining an otherwise cloudless sky. Inside a private compartment, Valfierno sat with his face buried in a day-old copy of *Le Matin*. He had hardly spoken a word since the train had pulled out of the station at Le Havre.

Émile sat next to him by the window, across from Julia, his gaze fixed on the passing landscape, less from interest than from a desire to avoid making eye contact with her. He could not stop thinking about how easily she had insinuated herself into their small party. And she was oblivious to the fact that she was intruding. In fact, she seemed as enthusiastic as a schoolgirl on a Sunday outing.

"It's exciting, isn't it," Julia said, catching Émile glance at her.

"What is?" Émile said, looking back out the window and trying to sound casual.

"Everything. The boat ride, the train, Paris."

Émile gave a noncommittal grunt. "We're not even there yet."

"I mean the anticipation. It's exciting."

"What do you know about Paris?" he challenged.

"Only what I've read in books. I know it's the City of Light, the city of romance, or so they say."

Émile rolled his eyes. "Then I can imagine the types of books you've been reading."

"Can you?" she asked, a slight challenge in her voice. "There was one book that was very good indeed. What was it again? I think the writer was Hugo something or other. No. Something Hugo. Victor Hugo. That's it. It was a very big book. It had romance, war, escaped prisoners, orphans, sacrifice. It really was very good. What was it called? A funny name. Something about everyone being miserable all the time. Have you read that one?"

Émile turned to her. "*Les Misérables*," he said in a way suggesting that only idiots would not know that name. "And you haven't read it."

"I have too. I just couldn't remember the name. Ask me any question about it. Go on. Ask me."

"Forget it." Émile turned his head back to the window.

"You haven't read it, have you?" she chirped with triumph. "You have no idea what I'm talking about."

Flushed with victory, she looked over at Valfierno, catching a brief, amused look from him as he peered above his newspaper. Looking out the window, she allowed herself to become mesmerized by the lines of trees receding toward the hills, all moving at different speeds according to their distance from the train. As she allowed the gentle rocking of the carriage to lull her into a half sleep, she remembered fondly the time that Uncle Nathan had told her the entire story of *Les Misérables*. Perhaps one day she would actually read it.

Valfierno, Émile, and Julia stepped onto a crowded platform lit by rays of sunlight filtering through the vast arched skylights in the coffered ceiling of the Gare d'Orsay. Julia stood transfixed, turning this way and that to take in the merry-go-round of color and noise all around her. Émile, on the other hand, put a great deal of effort into appearing blasé as he found a porter to collect their luggage on a hand cart.

"Come," said Valfierno to Julia. "But behave yourself. We're here for much bigger game than silk handkerchiefs and pocket watches."

Valfierno led them up the steps to the main level where, after negotiating the throngs of travelers, they passed beneath a massive gold clock through the main entrance. They emerged into a wide, tiled courtyard bathed in sharp sunlight. Julia stood for a moment, looking around. To her left, the mansard-roofed baroque buildings lining the narrow rue de Lille provided a tantalizing preview of the city that lay behind them; to her right, the Pont Solférino leapfrogged across the river on its cast-iron arches. A soft breeze drifting off the water tempered the pungent yet vibrant fragrance of the sprawling city.

Valfierno wasted no time in engaging the services of a motor taxi driver. They were not fifteen minutes from their destination, but he chose a much longer route to take them on a tour of the central city.

Following Valfierno's instructions, the driver took them along the river to the Pont au Double, where they crossed to the Île de la Cité and drove past the great cathedral.

"Notre-Dame," Julia said enthusiastically as she peered through the side window. "I'm right, aren't I."

"The spiritual center of all France," said Valfierno.

"Looks like the begging center too," she said, taking note of the line of ragged supplicants—legless, blind, twisted, and hunched over—who lay in wait for the tourists exiting the cathedral.

"Where are the gargoyles?" she asked, looking upward out of the open taxi window.

"On the roof, of course," said Émile. "Where else would they be?"

They continued across the Pont d'Arcole to the Right Bank, where they turned west and motored past the Louvre and the Jardin des Tuileries. Entering the place de la Concorde, they curved around the obelisk of Luxor rising from the center of the expansive public square.

"Looks like a copy of the Washington Monument," commented Julia.

"If anything, my dear," Valfierno said mildly, "it would be the other way around."

"Anyway," she said, shrugging, "ours is a lot bigger."

Passing between the Horses of Marly, they turned onto the Champs-Élysées leading straight as an arrow up toward the Arc de Triomphe.

"It's so wide," said Julia, marveling at the rows of elm trees interspersed with kiosks and columns plastered with newspaper pages and advertisements.

"Napoleon wanted his streets wide enough to parade his army on, and too wide for people to build barricades across," Valfierno explained.

"He could do whatever he wanted," added Émile. "After all, he had already conquered most of Europe."

"I refer, of course, to Napoleon the Third," Valfierno corrected him as gently as possible, "Napoleon Bonaparte's nephew."

Julia gave Émile a teasing smile. "I suppose it can get confusing with so many of them," she said.

Émile fell silent as the taxi joined the circle of motorcars and horse-drawn carriages circling the Arc de Triomphe. After two circuits, Valfierno directed the driver to turn south to the Pont d'Iéna.

Passing the Trocadéro Palace with its towers like architectural donkey ears, they drove onto the bridge. Before them, the great iron structure named for its architect and builder Gustave Eiffel loomed ahead, dwarfing every other building within sight.

"I've never seen anything so tall," Julia said, peering up at the intricately framed iron structure. "Or so beautiful."

"They say," Valfierno began, "that the writer Guy de Maupassant hated it so much that he used to eat his dinner every day in its restaurant just so he wouldn't have to look at it."

"Émile," Julia said in a teasing lilt, "perhaps you should take me there for dinner sometime."

Émile made no response.

"Indeed," Valfierno added, "there are many who still consider it nothing more than an eyesore, a standing heap of scrap metal."

Émile tried to act as if he had seen it all before, but he couldn't resist craning his neck for a better view of the intricate latticework growing like iron vines climbing to the sky.

"Napoleon's final resting place," Valfierno said with a flourish as they drove past the golden dome of Les Invalides.

"The nephew or the uncle?" asked Julia eagerly.

"The uncle," said an amused Valfierno.

Their tour almost over, Valfierno directed the driver onto boulevard Saint-Germain.

"*Voilà, le Quartier Latin!*" Valfierno announced with a sweep of his hand.

They were immediately immersed in a bustling hive of activity where every possible stratum of Parisian society was on display: ladies dressed in the latest *style moderne,* laden with hatboxes; gentlemen trapped in uniform dark suits showing off their individuality with an endless variety of elaborately sculpted mustaches and beards; young women in *coiffes bretonnes,* their arms full of dresses, food baskets, or bouquets of flowers, hurrying off to deliver their loads to their household employers; old men sitting beneath striped awnings in front of cafés, solving the problems of the day in a haze of pipe smoke; old women in drab gray, loose-fitting clothing, peeling potatoes and selling vegetables from under wide umbrellas.

"We're almost there," said Valfierno a moment before the driver honked his horn to protest an autobus cutting in front of him on the congested street.

Valfierno pointed and the driver turned left onto rue de l'Eperon, then immediately continued his turn onto rue du Jardinet. At the end of this quiet narrow street they pulled into the cour de Rohan. As the motor taxi came to a halt on the bumpy cobblestones, Valfierno whispered in the driver's ear and the man hopped out to remove a bag from the roof of the vehicle. A plump middle-aged woman, her hair sweeping up into a tight bun, emerged from a small gated inner courtyard to greet them.

"But who is this?" asked Valfierno with theatrical flair as he stepped out of the taxi. "I had expected Madame Charneau to greet us, not some beautiful young chambermaid."

"It will take more than flattery to make me forgive you for being gone so long," Madame Charneau said, smiling as she reached up to corral an errant strand of hair. "But then again, not much more."

"You remember Émile," Valfierno said as the young man stepped out of the taxi.

Madame Charneau clapped her hands together like a proud mother. "The boy becomes a man. It is so good to see you again, Émile."

Émile, more than a little embarrassed, quietly endured her embrace. Behind them, Julia stepped out of the taxi and gazed up at the tall, narrow houses rising from the courtyard like perfectly sculptured canyon walls.

"And this is Mademoiselle Julia Conway."

"And where did you find this one?" Madame Charneau asked with obvious approval.

"It would be more accurate to say that she found us," commented Valfierno.

"The marquis was kind enough to let me accompany him," said Julia with a sly look to Valfierno.

"*Bienvenue.* You are most welcome to my humble house."

"Madame Charneau runs the best boardinghouse in all of Paris," Valfierno said.

"The cleanest, anyway," Madame Charneau corrected him.

"The best and the cleanest," Valfierno continued. "She will take good care of you."

"Aren't you going to stay here too?" asked Julia, an edge of concern creeping into her voice.

"Émile and I will be sharing a modest pied-à-terre on the Right Bank," replied Valfierno.

"Well, what bank is this, then?" Julia asked.

Valfierno gave her his best Gallic shrug. "By the process of elimination, the Left."

"As I mentioned in my last cable," Madame Charneau said, handing Valfierno an addressed envelope bulging with a set of keys, "as soon as I received your first telegram, I located this house for you. It should suit your purposes well. It's on rue de Picardie, a very quiet street. It's not bad for such short notice and the rent is quite moderate. I have arranged for a car as you requested. It will be waiting for you in a garage on rue de Bretagne just at the end of your street."

"Thank you, madame," Valfierno said. "Your services, as always, are invaluable."

"Simply my way of welcoming you back where you belong."

"But wait a minute," Julia said to Valfierno. "Why can't I stay with you?"

"Impossible," Valfierno replied. "Our house will be much smaller than the one in Buenos Aires. Madame Charneau will make you extremely comfortable."

"Come with me, child." Madame Charneau gathered up Julia's bag. "You must be tired from your journey."

Julia stepped up to Émile and placed her hands on his chest in a gesture of appeal.

"But you will come back for me," she said, more a question than a statement.

Émile pulled away and climbed back into the taxi, but Valfierno stepped forward and put a reassuring hand on Julia's shoulder.

"Tomorrow," he said before turning and joining Émile in the backseat. "We begin our work tomorrow."

The taxi swung around in the small courtyard and drove off, leaving a black cloud of smoke spreading out on the cobblestones. Julia wondered if they intended to abandon her here. To reassure herself, she opened her hand and looked at Émile's pocket watch.

She smiled. Now they would have to come back.

Chapter 12

Thirteen acres of manicured flower gardens and expansive lawns graced what once had been a scrubby promontory of land nudging out into Rhode Island Sound. Maintaining the grounds—dotted with scores of statues that had been copied from the French palace at Versailles—was a job that consumed the services of five full-time and twelve part-time gardeners. Windcrest, the great house itself, with its stunted towers, mullioned windows, marble columns and pilasters, was an impressive if uneasy marriage of French Renaissance and Elizabethan styles. To keep it running, it required the services of no fewer than fifteen live-in house staff.

Joshua Hart had spared no expense in creating the most imposing edifice in all of Newport. He had commissioned the great Boston architect Robert Peabody to design and build the Beaux Arts mansion ten years before in 1900; it had cost him almost two million dollars, twice as much as any of the other "cottages" that graced the shoreline.

Inside the house, Hart's middle-aged butler, Carter, and Tamo, a young Filipino houseboy, carried a wrapped frame down a set of narrow steps leading to a vast cellar. Hart had paid a small fortune to an expert craftsman to mount *La Ninfa Sorprendida* in an appropriately carved antique, gilded frame. The bulk of the man's fee had secured his absolute discretion in the matter.

"Careful there!" Hart bellowed from the foot of the stairs.

Ellen Hart stood next to him. She was usually not invited into her husband's domain, but he always insisted on her help whenever a new painting was added to his secret gallery. Indeed, these occasions were the only time she was permitted to share in the pleasures of his collection.

As the two men reached the cellar, Hart took the frame from Tamo.

"That's all. Off you go," he said, sending the young boy bounding back up the stairs. Of all his servants, only Carter was allowed to venture beyond this point.

Ellen led the way through the vast basement—sealed at great cost against ground moisture—to a large door just beyond the entrance to a well-stocked wine cellar. From her pocket she took the key he had given her a few minutes earlier, placed it in the keyhole, and turned it. She pushed open the door and stepped inside, feeling for the electrical switches on the wall.

"Just the top switch," Hart said.

She flicked the top switch and one bulb came on just inside the door, revealing a high-ceilinged room about thirty feet square. Rows of paintings, barely visible in the dim light, hung from the walls like spectral images.

Within fifteen minutes, working in the semidarkness, Hart and Carter had unwrapped and mounted Manet's *La Ninfa Sorprendida*. As soon as the job was finished, Carter withdrew without a word. Hart wiped his forehead with a handkerchief and became aware of his wife still standing by the door.

"Thank you," Hart said in a tone that was as dismissive as it was polite.

Ellen nodded and left the room, pulling the door closed behind her.

As soon as she was gone, Hart flicked on the remaining three switches in quick succession. A battery of strategically placed floodlights flared to life, illuminating his subterranean gallery. He stood as he always did, in trembling awe and silence as his eyes drank in his collection of masters. In truth, he would have been hard-pressed to name each of the paintings and their artists, with the exception, perhaps, of his most recent acquisitions. The important thing was possessing these works of art. They were his and his alone. Unsuspecting fools viewed reproductions, hastily mounted to cover empty spaces on walls in countless museums, but there was only one person in the world who could look at the genuine masterpiece, and that one person was Joshua Hart.

After a moment, he turned away from the paintings and walked to the rear of the gallery where a small door was set into the wall. Removing a single key from his inside jacket pocket, he unlocked the door, turned the knob, and walked inside.

Ellen Hart slowly ascended the steps to the main level of the house. At the top, she stopped for a moment and looked back down to the dark cellar. Her husband would stay by himself in his cavernous lair for hours surrounded by the things he loved most.

She would not miss him.

Chapter 13

On the morning following their arrival in Paris, Valfierno and Émile drove into the cour de Rohan in an open Panhard-Levassor motorcar to find Julia waiting for them outside Madame Charneau's boardinghouse. Without a word, she climbed into the backseat and returned Émile's pocket watch. He took it from her without comment. An amused Valfierno drove out onto boulevard Saint-Germain and turned right onto rue du Bac. As he crossed the Seine over the Pont Royal, he gave Émile and Julia a sketchy outline of what he wanted them to do. He pulled up to the archways leading to the place du Carrousel—one of a number of entrances to the Louvre Museum— and Émile and Julia climbed out.

"Remember," Valfierno told them, "you are newlyweds. Wander about. Get a feel for the place."

They pressed him for more detailed instructions, but he told them that he just wanted them to stroll around and observe.

"Pay particular attention to the Denon wing," Valfierno added as he shifted gears, "but above all enjoy yourselves. You're young! You're supposed to be in love! It's Paris!"

Émile watched the car pull away and wished he were in it.

"Well," Julia said, taking Émile's arm with evident relish, "shall we?"

Beneath the high, arched ceiling of the long Grande Galerie in the Denon wing, a pair of maintenance workers clad in long white blouses struggled to attach a wooden glass-fronted box to the wall. Nearby, two gentlemen stood in the center of the hall observing. One of them, a distinguished-looking white-haired man dressed in a finely tailored Italian suit, was none other than the museum director, Monsieur Montand. Next to him stood Police Inspector Alphonse Carnot of the Sûreté. Middle-aged and portly, he wore a suit that had not improved in appearance since he purchased it from a charity shop on the place de la Bastille many years ago.

"I tell you, Monsieur Montand," said Inspector Carnot with evident pride, "these new shadow boxes are the latest in security. They'll put an end to these anarchists and their defacements."

Inspector Carnot was getting to the point in his career where he would have to distinguish himself soon if he hoped for further advancement. He had always suspected that his height—more precisely his lack thereof—had held him back. His bulk and his low center of gravity gave him the appearance of a child's spinning top, but the inspector took himself very seriously indeed. Following an incident in which one of these new self-styled anarchists had spit on a Raphael, he had been called in to suggest improvements in museum security. He had persuaded the director to place the more prominent paintings in wooden shadow boxes where they would be protected behind a sheet of glass. He was convinced that his part in this innovation would be an important step toward his much sought after promotion.

"Patrons are already complaining that the glass is much too reflective," said Montand, peering at the inspector through his thin-framed spectacles. "They come to see great art, not their own faces."

"Better to be reflecting their faces than dripping with anarchist spittle, eh, Monsieur Director?"

Farther down the Grande Galerie, Julia and Émile strolled arm in arm through a typical weekday crowd of bourgeois couples.

Most of the gentlemen seemed vaguely bored, while the ladies appeared more interested in each other's fashions than the artwork on display. A few copyists had set up their easels along the gallery, and sprinkled here and there, a military officer bedecked in medals shared a laugh with the newly acquired demimondaine on his arm.

"This place is much larger than I thought it would be," Julia commented.

"It's the greatest museum in the world," said Émile. "What else would you expect?"

"I don't know," she replied with a shrug. "I've been to some museums in New York, which are also pretty big."

"There's no comparison," said Émile. "Look at all these masterpieces."

Julia stopped to consider a Botticelli Madonna hanging on the wall next to a Fra Diamante Madonna.

"Half of them seem to be of the same thing, a mother and her baby. Where are the flowers?"

Émile's response to this question was an attempt to shrug her off, but she wouldn't let go of his arm.

"So," she continued, "do you have family in Paris?"

"Oh, yes," replied Émile. "I have a huge family: uncles, aunts, grandparents, nieces, nephews. Too many to count. They're all filthy rich and keep inviting me to live with them on their country estates."

"An orphan, huh?" Julia said, glancing at yet another Madonna and Child. "So how did the marquis get stuck with you?"

"Look." Émile stopped and finally untangled himself from her arm. "We're supposed to be observing. Getting ideas. Not carrying on useless conversation."

"But we still have to look the part, don't we?" She rethreaded her arm through his and rested her head against his shoulder.

The piercing crash of breaking glass shattered the serenity of the gallery. Everyone's attention turned to the two maintenance men who had just dropped the shadow box they had been attempting to install.

One of the men, tall and thin, with a sharp, hawklike face, glared at the other, a barrel of a man with eyes far too small for his broad face.

"*Idiota!*" the tall man snarled in Italian before reverting to French. "Look what you've done."

"It's not my fault if my hands sweat," replied the heavyset man holding out his small pudgy hands as evidence.

The museum director and Inspector Carnot approached the workers.

"What on earth do you think you're playing at?" Montand demanded.

The men removed their caps and the taller one hunched his shoulders in an attempt to make himself appear smaller.

"I am sorry, Monsieur Director. It was an accident."

"It was incompetence!" bellowed Montand.

"If my gendarmes displayed such incompetence," chimed in Inspector Carnot, "I would fire them immediately."

"The box is heavy, monsieur," said the tall man. "Next time we'll be more careful."

"Too heavy for you, is it?" said Montand, glancing briefly at the inspector to make sure he was making an impression. "Well, it won't be the only thing that's too heavy, because time will be hanging heavy on your hands from now on. You're both fired."

The stout maintenance man looked shocked. His tall companion took on an indignant expression. "But it was an accident," he said.

"Where are you from?" Inspector Carnot asked, his nose twitching as if he were sniffing the man out. "Are you even French?"

"No, signore. I am Italian."

"Italian," Carnot said with a dismissive snort. "That would explain it."

The Italian straightened himself up to his full height.

"You French are all the same," he began deliberately. "You steal the greatest art in the world then display it as if it were your own."

"Careful what you say to an officer of the law!" warned Carnot, his face turning red.

"The two of you have five minutes to get out of my museum,"

Montand declared. "I'll find someone competent to clean up this mess. Your final week's pay will cover the damages."

As Inspector Carnot and Montand stalked away, the stockier worker screwed up his cap in his hand and quietly said to the retreating figures, "But I'm French . . ."

Nearby, Émile pulled Julia away from the scene.

"Come on," he said. "We've got work to do."

The finely tipped paintbrush applied highlights to the bosom of the gently smiling woman. Another brush added texture to the surface of a lake in the distance behind her; another added lines to a winding road snaking back to an outcrop of jagged rocks. One brushed a thick swirl of greenish-brown paint to the crown of hair plastered tightly against the top of the woman's head. Yet another stroke gently washed a translucent quality onto the skin of her hands, one resting on top of the other. Another shadowed the side of her long, thin nose, and yet another rendered shading to the lips in an attempt to convey just the right smile.

A group of art students sat with their brushes, paints, and easels in the Salon Carré in front of *La Joconde, The Portrait of Mona Lisa* by Leonardo da Vinci. The painting sat within the confines of a shadow box, its glass window reflecting the forms of the students and the milling crowds behind them. The students' canvases—in varying degrees of completion—were of different sizes, none exactly the same dimensions as the modest panel on the wall. At seventy-seven by fifty-three centimeters, the original looked quite small placed, as it was, between Correggio's *Mystical Marriage* and Titian's *Allegory of Alfonso d'Avalos*. The shadow box it sat in made it appear even smaller.

Copying was permitted—even encouraged—as long as the dimensions differed from the original Leonardo masterpiece. The art instructor, his face almost completely obscured by a thick, graying, tobacco-stained beard, floated behind his students in a billowing smock, making various sighs of approval or grunts of displeasure.

Behind the amateurs stood a thickly massed group of museum patrons intently focused on the woman in the painting, their hushed comments revealing an almost religious awe. Émile and Julia slipped in behind the crowd, Julia craning her neck over people's heads for a better view.

"What are they looking at?" asked Julia.

A few of the patrons glanced back at her, disapproval on their faces.

"*La Joconde*, of course," Émile replied. "What else would it be?"

"And how do you know all this?" Julia challenged him.

"The marquis would bring me here as a child," he replied, "and I paid attention."

"So what's so special about this one?" she demanded.

Émile gave her a look halfway between pity and disgust. "It's only one of the greatest paintings in history," he said.

"Is there anything in this museum that isn't great?" she asked sarcastically.

Émile shushed her.

"And if it's so popular," Julia continued, lowering her voice to a whisper, "why doesn't the marquis copy it and sell it to someone?"

Émile grabbed her roughly by her arm and pulled her back away from the crowd.

"Keep your voice down!" he said sternly.

"Well, why doesn't he?"

"Are you insane? *La Joconde* is the most famous painting in the world. No one would ever be insane enough to buy it."

Julia shrugged as Émile walked away. She looked back to the painting. "I don't even see what all the fuss is about," she said to no one in particular. "She's not even all that pretty."

A little while later, Julia and Émile emerged from the museum and walked along the quai du Louvre.

"It's such a lovely day," enthused Julia. "Let's go down the steps and walk beside the river."

A stone stairway led down near the Pont des Arts to a wide cobblestone embankment almost at water level.

Émile held back. "We should go," he said. "We don't have time to waste."

"Who's wasting time? We might need to go down there during our getaway. We should reconnoiter."

"Why would we go down there when we can just cross the bridge?"

"I don't know," she said impatiently. "Come on, the exercise will do us good. Besides, what am I going to do by myself all afternoon at Madame Charneau's house?"

Émile said nothing, so Julia took hold of his arm and dragged him down the steps.

In one direction the embankment was almost blocked by a group of barbers shaving men seated in the shade of the bridge, so they turned in the direction of Notre-Dame. A light, fresh breeze wafted off the river, gently ruffling the water's surface.

"Funny place for a barbershop," said Julia, "don't you think?"

But Émile didn't seem to hear a word she had said. Instead, he detached himself from her arm and moved away from the water's edge closer to the hewn stones of the high retaining wall.

"Why are you all the way over there?" Julia asked.

"It's less windy," Émile replied, seemingly more interested in the wall than the river.

"Suit yourself," she said with a shrug. "Oh, look!"

A long riverboat, half full of sightseers sitting on deck chairs on its wide-open deck, pulled into a small dock ahead of them on the embankment.

"What kind of boat is that?" Julia asked eagerly.

"It's a *bateau-mouche*," said Émile after a brief glance.

"Let's go for a ride. It'll be fun."

"Absolutely not."

"Oh, please," Julia pleaded in an exaggerated childlike whine.

"Go on if you want," he said irritably. "I've had enough of this." He hurried along the embankment a short distance before climbing another set of steps back up to the street-level quay.

"Afraid you'll get seasick?" she shouted. Then she gave up and followed him, muttering to herself, "Spoilsport."

Chapter 14

Valfierno sat at an outside table in front of the Café de Cluny at the corner of boulevards Saint-Michel and Saint-Germain. His chair faced the street, as did all the others on the small terrace. After all, one spent time at a café not to escape the world but to observe it. Since he had arrived ten minutes ago, he had derived great enjoyment from witnessing the ebb and flow of the colorful stream of people coursing along the boulevard as if it were a human tributary of the Seine. A pair of young women, daringly hatless to show off their bobbed hair, sashayed arm in arm along the narrow pavement in front of him. As they passed, they turned their heads to give him an appraising glance. His acknowledging nod elicited smiles from the women, which quickly turned into shared giggles as they disappeared around the corner. He suddenly realized how much he had missed Paris.

"Eduardo!"

Valfierno turned in the direction of the jovial voice. The stocky man standing before him held out his arms in a wide gesture that said: *Well, here I am. Isn't it wonderful?*

"Guillaume," Valfierno exclaimed, rising to his feet and extending his hand.

"None of that," the man said as he stepped forward, his arms enclosing Valfierno in a tight embrace. "*Mon Dieu.* I see you still use that same cologne. I never forget a face or a smell."

Apart from the fact that he had gained quite a bit of weight, Guillaume Apollinaire had changed little since Valfierno last saw him. He still embraced life with such fervor that he radiated energy and vigor. Valfierno could always recharge himself just by being around the man; on the other hand, he was also taken best in small doses.

"It's good to see you," Valfierno said after extricating himself from the bear hug and gesturing to a chair.

Guillaume Apollinaire removed a short-brimmed hat and mopped small beads of sweat from his brow.

"You never even said good-bye, you know," Apollinaire said with an admonishing waggle of his finger.

"Please accept my apologies," said Valfierno with a slight canting nod of his head. "Everything happened so quickly at the time."

"I always suspected it had something to do with the wife of that art dealer, Laroche. What was her name?"

"Chloe."

"Ah yes, the beautiful Chloe, beautiful as a rose with thorns to match."

"Actually," Valfierno explained, "I didn't leave Paris until sometime after that incident."

"Incident indeed," Apollinaire said. "Those despicable street *apaches*." He leaned forward, his eyes narrowing. "You know, I always suspected that when that little minx couldn't entice you into her bed, she told her husband that you had tried to seduce her. She knew what his reaction would be."

"I wouldn't think that even she would be capable of such a thing," Valfierno said.

"You never know what a woman is capable of until you disappoint her, mark my word."

"And you," Valfierno began, trying to change the subject. "I understand that you have not been idle, that you have published a book."

"An epic, no less," said Apollinaire expansively. "*L'Enchanteur pourrissant*, a poetic discourse upon the hazards of love." He leaned forward theatrically. "Merlin the Enchanter becomes captivated by none other than Viviane, the Lady of the Lake herself. He reveals all his secrets, which, naturally, leads to his undoing. He has even foreseen it all yet is helpless to resist her charms. You see? In the end, all men would willingly go to their doom simply for the vague promise of a woman's pleasure."

"It sounds . . . fascinating," Valfierno said, distracted, "although surely not every man is so lacking in willpower."

Apollinaire shrugged. "Perhaps not, but life is worth living only when you give in to temptation at least once in a while."

A waiter wearing a long black apron appeared. "Ah," Apollinaire said eagerly, "there's our man!" Valfierno ordered another Petit Noir, Apollinaire, brandy. The larger man dominated the conversation, reminding Valfierno of all the wonders and pleasures of Paris he had missed. Valfierno mentioned only that he had done quite well with his importing and exporting business in Buenos Aires but had decided that the time had come to return to Paris.

"Importing and exporting," Apollinaire commented, weighing the words. "I don't suppose that would include certain works of art of dubious provenance."

"Let's just say that the customer's desires must always be catered to."

"Speaking of which," Apollinaire said, "how is my old friend Monsieur Chaudron?"

Valfierno sighed. "I'm afraid he is no longer with us. His health was never good, though I like to think the agreeable climate of South America extended his days."

"What a pity. A man of such prodigious talents. I am afraid they were wasted on those little copies he poured his heart and soul into."

"A man must make a living," Valfierno said.

"There you are wrong." Apollinaire fixed Valfierno with his stare. "A man must create a life. There's a big difference."

There was a long pause as the waiter brought fresh drinks.

"Guillaume," Valfierno finally began, "there is a reason I asked you to meet me today."

"Of course," Apollinaire said. "For my amusing and stimulating company."

Valfierno smiled. "Certainly for that, but also for something else. It's the reason I returned in the first place. I know you were always involved with new artists trying to establish themselves in Paris. I assume you still are."

"But of course. It's the most fascinating thing about this city. You wouldn't believe what's been going on. As soon as the Impressionists were allowed into bed with the Classicists, along came the next group of renegades. They don't even have a name yet, though I've proposed one that I'm hoping will catch on. At first I thought perhaps the term Art-Anarchists, but I discarded it. I'm playing with another one now, Surrealists. What do you think? Too obscure?"

"But surely that's the point, isn't it?" Valfierno added, "But tell me, do these . . ."

"Surrealists."

"Do they make any money?"

"Of course not. That would ruin everything."

"Then I was wondering if perhaps you knew one who is well trained, well versed in the classical style of painting, who might be interested in making some money, and whose scruples are . . . let's just say flexible."

"A forger, you mean," Apollinaire clarified.

Valfierno allowed this with a flourish of his hand.

"As it turns out," Apollinaire said, "I may have just the man for you. He has achieved some success in his own circle but little beyond that. He's grown tired of the work he's been doing and the people he knows, and even went so far as to move away from Montmarte, if you can believe that. Looking for inspiration or some such. I mean, I can understand the need for fresh ideas, but moving from Montmartre . . ."

He let the thought hang as if it were the most absurd notion in the world.

"What is his name?"

Apollinaire hesitated for a moment before answering. "His name is . . . Diego. In fact, he has a small studio not far from here."

"Where exactly?"

"Oh, around the corner on rue Serpente, but you won't find him there. He has been dabbling in high-quality museum copies to sell to tourists. How is that for inspiration? As it turns out, I just saw him not an hour ago, set up on the other side of the river on the quai de la Mégisserie. You'll know him when you see him. He'll have the highest prices and the worst sales technique."

"Thank you," Valfierno said, putting down some francs on the tabletop.

"But I warn you," Apollinaire said with a sly smile, "he can be a little difficult at times."

Eduardo de Valfierno sauntered by the line of dark green stalls sprawling along the parapets of the river walls along the quai de la Mégisserie. Enjoying the early afternoon sunshine, he politely waved off the numerous invitations to buy collections of supposedly rare stamps or to inspect antiques guaranteed to be genuine. He strolled past stalls filled with old books and colorful postcards with the casual but confident gait of a man without a care in the world. Occasionally he stopped to pick up a faux antique Chinese vase or examine the thread of a Persian rug, but he always declined when presented with prices that would start astronomically high before tumbling with astonishing speed.

He was particularly interested in the stalls that displayed copies of the great masterpieces. Some were not bad, though most were hopelessly amateurish. Even so, Valfierno never insulted the artists, only begged off respectfully, commenting that it wasn't exactly what he was looking for. None of these artists could possibly have been the man Apollinaire had described.

Finally he stopped at a stall prominently displaying various-sized copies of *La Joconde* painted on wooden panels. They were, by a large margin, the highest quality work Valfierno had seen so far. The artist, a solidly built young man with a shock of dark hair that constantly threatened to fall over his eyes, sat at his easel working on another one. Holding an unlit briar pipe in his mouth, he paid no attention to his potential customer. Or so it seemed.

"No charge for looking," muttered the artist without taking his eyes from his work.

"These are not bad," said Valfierno, "not bad at all."

The artist put down his brush and relit his pipe.

"Perhaps you'd even like to buy one," he said in a tone that suggested he was already bored with their exchange.

Valfierno wondered about the man's accent. Italian? Spanish perhaps? And still the artist had not made eye contact with him.

Valfierno checked a price tag. "The prices seem a bit steep."

The artist resumed his painting. "You need to see the Tuscan in the next booth but one down that way," he said. "He churns them out by the hour."

"No," Valfierno said. "I'll take this one."

The artist looked up at Valfierno for the first time, giving him an appraising stare, almost as if he was suspicious of a customer who was willing to pay his price. Then he turned back to his work as if a sale was of no consequence to him.

"Can you deliver it?"

The man turned back to Valfierno. "Do I look like a postman to you?" His tone was even, but it held a hint of a challenge.

Valfierno smiled as he retrieved a wad of francs from his pocket. This had to be Apollinaire's artist.

"I wonder, my friend," he asked, peeling off the notes, "if you might be interested in doing a little work for me."

"And why would I want to do that?" asked the man, resuming his painting.

"What would you say if I told you that I could get you a thousand times more for one copy?"

"I would say that you are either a raving lunatic . . . or a brilliant judge of talent."

Valfierno held out the money. "My name is Eduardo de Valfierno."

The intense young man peered at the offering for a moment before looking up. Slowly and deliberately, he put down his brush and rose to his feet. He was quite a bit shorter than Valfierno, yet with his stocky build and wide-legged stance he gave the impression of an implacable bull. He took the money and slipped the wad into his pocket without counting it.

Valfierno extended his hand in greeting. The artist considered it for a moment.

"I am José Diego Santiago de la Santísima," he said, grasping it with a firm, almost aggressive grip.

"A pleasure to make your acquaintance, Señor—"

"Diego will do."

"Señor Diego."

Diego bowed his head slightly before sitting back down at his easel to take up his brush and resume his work.

"I notice," said Valfierno, "that you're painting with your left hand. Leonardo was left-handed, was he not?"

"It is essential in making a good copy."

"Then perhaps that's the reason you're so good."

Diego stopped his brushwork and looked up at Valfierno. For the first time his lips formed into a hint of a smile.

"No," he said. "The reason I'm so good," he switched the brush to his other hand, "is that I'm right-handed."

Chapter 15

The great white battleship, bristling with guns, pennants flapping wildly in the wind, steamed toward its prey, a sleek three-masted wooden schooner. The warship's sharp prow sliced through the water like a blade. In a desperate move, the schooner tacked hard to starboard to avoid a collision, but it was too late. The metal ship's underwater snout struck the sailboat's hull with sickening force. The sailing vessel flipped over onto its side, only its broad linen sails saving it from completely capsizing.

A young boy dressed in a sailor suit stood hooting in triumph at the edge of *le petit bassin* in the Tuileries Garden. On the other side of the large circular pool, another boy, wearing a dirty yellow *tablier* and sabots, whimpered to his mother about the injustice perpetrated by the wind-up tin warship against his defenseless sailboat. Oblivious to the drama, scores of men reclined on rented chairs around the periphery of the circle, reading their newspapers beneath the straw boaters jauntily perched on their heads. In the center of the pool, coruscating with the orange flashes of Chinese goldfish, a fountain shot water into the air, forming a misty plume in the light breeze.

In the shade of a nearby chestnut tree, a group of men and women squatted in various poses around a checkered tablecloth spread out on the grass. Bread crumbs littered the cloth; in its center, a wicker basket held the remnants of various wedges of cheese and denuded stalks of grapes. Half-empty bottles of red wine stood guard over the leftovers. Madame Charneau, her back leaning up against the tree trunk, seemed determined to finish off the sole remaining baguette. Émile and Julia sat across from each other on the ground, Julia's attention constantly distracted by the parade of Parisian society couples strolling arm in arm along the central path, the Axe Historique.

Diego squatted with his knees sticking out at a wide angle, steadying a bottle of wine as he drained its contents into his glass. Valfierno, one arm resting on a raised knee, considered a red grape he held between his thumb and forefinger. In the background, the various wings of the Louvre surrounded the large open courtyard that led into the gardens.

"There is a problem," said Émile with an air of forced authority.

"There are no problems," Valfierno corrected him, "only challenges."

"A challenge, then," said Émile, a little exasperated. "With the installation of these new shadow boxes, it will be impossible to place a copy behind any of the protected paintings. It just can't be done."

"Good point," said Valfierno, "but, in this case, a moot one."

"After all," Julia said, "not every painting is in one of those boxes."

"But the painting we want will most surely be part of that exclusive group," Valfierno pointed out.

"And which painting would that be?" she asked.

"That's a stupid question," said Émile. "We won't know which painting until we've found our customer. It's what he wants that counts."

"Émile would be right," Valfierno began, "under normal circumstances."

"You see," said Julia, savoring a small triumph, "not so stupid after all."

"This time," Valfierno continued, "the painting will come first.

We'll concentrate all our efforts on one piece, something that any-one and everyone will want."

"Such as?" asked Émile.

Valfierno turned to the new member of their party. "Señor Diego . . ."

The artist was in the process of pouring the glass of red wine down his throat. He took a final gulp before laying the glass on its side on the lawn. Wiping his mouth with the back of his hand, he reached behind him to produce a panel draped in cloth. With a flourish, he removed the cover like a matador pulling back his cape, revealing a remarkably accurate reproduction of *La Joconde*.

Madame Charneau covered her mouth, stifling a sharp intake of air. Julia's face lit up with excitement.

"Hey, wait a minute," she blurted out, turning to Émile. "That's the one you said no one would ever buy."

"They wouldn't dare," Émile insisted. "Besides, it's a solid wooden panel, not to mention the fact that it's in a shadow box. How will we be able to authenticate the copy if the potential buyer can't make his mark on the back?"

"You're right," said Valfierno. "We can't very well sell an un-marked copy when the original is still hanging on the wall of the gallery. So we will have to make sure the original is *not* hanging on the wall of the gallery."

"And how do you expect us to do that?" asked Émile.

"Steal it, of course!" exclaimed Julia.

"Steal *La Joconde* from the Louvre?" Émile was no longer able to remain calm. "It's impossible!"

"Difficult, certainly," Valfierno allowed, "but impossible? Well, we won't know until we try."

Madame Charneau spoke for the first time. "But Marquis, even if we were able to steal it, all France would be up in arms. We'd never get it out of Paris."

"We won't have to. It will stay here in the city."

"It would be like trying to handle a red-hot coal!" she said. "No Frenchman would even dare to touch it!"

"I was actually thinking more along the lines of finding a rich American client."

"They'll search every bag, every case, every box leaving the country," said Émile.

A small girl ran by crying out with delight as she tugged on the box-shaped kite trailing above her. Valfierno watched her for a moment before responding.

"Of course they'll search everything," he said. "But only after the theft."

"Oh, of course," Émile began with a facetious flair. "Why didn't I think of that? We'll ship *La Joconde* to America before we actually steal it!"

"That is exactly what I am suggesting."

Before Émile could say another word, a sudden wind whipped up from the river, billowing the tablecloth and stinging their faces with sand from the pathways. "I also suggest," said Valfierno, "that we repair to Señor Diego's studio across the river."

Diego rented a cluttered basement studio in the Latin Quarter on rue Serpente, a narrow street just off boulevard Saint-Michel. The location, though far removed from the artist enclave of Montmartre, suited him. Though he was only steps away from a bustling café scene, he could work in relative peace and solitude. He also found that being an artist in an area not known for artists not only shielded him from unwanted influences but made him more interesting to the local café girls. As a bonus, the proximity to the vendors' stalls along the riverbank provided him with at least the possibility of earning enough money to pay the higher rent.

Piles of books, stacks of canvases, assortments of brushes, paints, and rags littered the floor. An open door revealed a large closet also littered with supplies. A sleeping cot piled with rumpled blankets was jammed into one corner, a zinc tub in another. Next to the tub, a pot of artificial flowers sat on a wooden stool.

Madame Charneau, Émile, and Julia sat together on a pair of

rustic benches like students in a class. Valfierno stood before them playing instructor; Diego, smoking a Gauloise, perched on a stool off to one side. Between Valfierno and Diego stood an easel supporting a blank wooden panel. The panel was the exact dimensions of *La Joconde*, seventy-seven by fifty-three centimeters.

"Señor Diego will create a perfect copy," Valfierno began. "The copy will be shipped to America before the theft has occurred. No one will think twice about it. It will simply be one copy among hundreds that are exported every day. Following the theft, it will be delivered to its new owner."

"What about the real one?" asked Julia.

"After an appropriate amount of time, it will be returned to the museum. As Madame Charneau pointed out, the authorities will leave no stone unturned while it is missing."

"And the American?" asked Madame Charneau.

"I will tell him that it is only a matter of time before the museum replaces it with the copy they have been saving for just such an eventuality, announcing to a world hungry for news that the masterpiece has been miraculously recovered. Besides, who would our American tell even if he had his suspicions? The police?"

"Are we sure," Émile asked, "that Señor Diego is capable of making a copy that will pass for the original?"

Everyone turned to Diego, who glared at Émile as he slowly removed the Gauloise from between his lips and snorted a stream of blue smoke through his nostrils.

"I am the only man in France capable of doing that job," he said in a low, threatening tone. "The important question is: Are you capable of stealing the genuine article from the museum in the first place?"

"I'm the only man in France capable of doing *that* job," Émile retorted.

The men glared at each other like two tomcats claiming the same alleyway.

"Well," said Valfierno in his most conciliatory tone, "then we are fortunate indeed to have two such capable individuals at our disposal: Señor Diego and Émile, who, by the way, will have to do the job without any assistance from me."

"Where will you be?" asked Julia.

"Unfortunately, my name would rank high on a list of possible suspects of such a crime. It is essential that my alibi be unassailable, and being three thousand miles away at the time of the deed should fit the bill very nicely. And remember, stealing *La Joconde* is only half the job. Finding a customer who is willing to pay the price commensurate with the object in question will be just as difficult."

"I'll do my part," said Émile.

"I know you will," said Valfierno, "but for something like this you will need help."

"He has it," Julia said. "Me."

"Oh, we'll need your help all right," Valfierno said, "on the outside. You'll be working with Madame Charneau. For this job, we'll have to find someone on the inside, someone with intimate knowledge of the museum's inner workings."

"My brother Jacques has done some work in the Louvre," said Madame Charneau eagerly. "He worked on their boilers. He would be ideal."

"He would be ideal," Valfierno agreed, "if he weren't currently residing in prison."

"This is true," allowed Madame Charneau. For the others' benefit she added, "He rigged a bank boiler to explode and tried to make off with the safe in the confusion. Unfortunately, it was heavier than he bargained for, and he made it only as far as the front door before dropping it on his foot."

"Émile," said Valfierno, "spend some time in the workingmen's cafés in the Saint-Martin district. Keep your ears open and see what you can pick up."

"You know," began Julia, staring at the panel on the easel, "it's a funny thing."

"Yes?" asked Valfierno, turning to her.

"Well, if you think about it, if the original has been stolen, and you're only selling a copy, why settle for just one? Why not sell a dozen copies while you're at it?"

Émile snorted derisively.

Julia frowned at him.

"Interesting idea," said Valfierno, considering, "but not very practical. For one thing, creating that many forgeries would take too long. For another, finding that many customers would be all but impossible; the logistics required would be far too complex."

Émile returned Julia's look with a satisfied smirk.

"On the other hand," Valfierno continued, carefully measuring out his words, "*six* copies might be just about right."

Chapter 16

Rue du Faubourg Saint-Martin resounded with the tinkling bells of bicycles. Few workingmen could afford one of these relatively new modes of transportation, but they were increasingly popular among the bourgeoisie who sought out local color in the area's smoke-filled cafés. Tables of rough-hewn men in worn caps and berets crowded the pavements. *Filles de joie*, heavily made up and smoking cigarettes, sat drinking, flirting, and commiserating with the men. Hordes of feral cats rubbed against a forest of legs, begging for a few tossed scraps.

Émile wished that Valfierno had not insisted that Julia accompany him. He knew this area well. As a child of the streets, he had spent much time here relying on the kindness of men with little money of their own to spare. In a way, he thought, there had been little difference between him and the four-legged creatures snaking around their legs. Valfierno had asked him to keep his eyes and ears open and that was what he was doing. Julia was a complication. She fit right in with her easy manner and friendly smile, but he flinched every time she bumped into someone. He imagined her collecting souvenirs from these men and feared their wrath should they catch her in the act.

"What are we supposed to be looking for?" she asked as they pushed their way into a crowded café. "Why did you pick this place?"

"Don't ask so many questions," he said right before a drunken, burly man collided with them both.

"Hey! Look where you're going," Julia protested, but the man just grunted and stumbled by them.

"Watch what you say," Émile warned. "The last thing we want is trouble."

"Here," said Julia, producing some franc notes from the man's wallet. "At least buy me a drink."

Émile was about to scold her when he saw them.

The two men sat at a corner table, both of them slumped over glasses of absinthe, as if they were searching in the emerald-green liquid for some part of their souls that had been irretrievably lost.

"Let me do the talking," Émile said.

"What? Who is it?" Julia asked, but he was already threading his way through the crowd and ignored her.

"*Bon soir, monsieurs,*" Émile said when he reached the table. "Mind if we sit here?" Julia recognized the men as soon as they looked up. They were the two maintenance workers from the Louvre, the ones who had been fired for dropping the shadow box.

"As a matter of fact," said the one with the hawklike face, "we do."

His companion immediately lost interest and returned his attention to his glass of absinthe.

"I know who you are," said Émile.

The man drew back and eyed him suspiciously. "Is that so?"

"You're the two men who were fired from the museum the other day. We saw everything."

"And what if we are?"

"Well," Julia said, "it was a disgrace the way they treated you."

Seeing her opportunity, she sat down in a chair opposite the men. Émile gave her a sharp look before she pulled him into another chair beside her.

"And who are you?" the man asked, his tone suspicious but softening slightly.

Julia opened her mouth to speak, but Émile took the lead. "My name is Émile." He extended his hand in greeting. "We're pleased to make your acquaintance."

The man made no response. Émile withdrew his hand.

"And this is . . ." He hesitated, drawing a blank.

"I'm his sister."

Émile gave her a puzzled grimace before turning back to the man. "My sister," he said, without much conviction.

The other man looked up from his glass. His eyes were unfocused and watery, and his head bobbed around like a harbor buoy as he tried to focus on Julia. "Your sister?" he said. "She doesn't sound very French."

Émile looked at Julia, challenging her to come up with something.

"Because," Julia said with a smug little smile aimed at Émile, "after our parents divorced, our mother took me to America to live with relatives. It was very sad. I was just a little girl at the time."

This seemed to satisfy the man, and he returned his attention to his absinthe.

"My name is Vincenzo," the hawk-faced man finally said. "Vincenzo Peruggia. But just call me Peruggia. And this is Brique."

"Just call me Brique," the other man said, not even looking up.

"Can I buy you both a drink?" Émile asked.

"Why not," said Peruggia.

"Julia," Émile said, holding his palm out to her, "let me see that money, there's a dear."

Julia gave him a look but did as he requested.

Émile ordered a bottle of red wine. After a few drinks, Brique seemed to fall asleep, his face cradled on his folded arms, but Peruggia became talkative. He told them he had come to Paris in search of employment and worked at a number of menial jobs before hiring on at the museum.

"Imagine," he continued, as much to himself as to Émile and Julia, "a true Italian patriot working in the heart of the country that spawned my homeland's greatest enemy."

"And who would that be?" asked Julia.

"Napoleon, of course," he replied, turning to her with his eyes blazing. "Who else would it be?"

"Of course." Then, after glancing at Émile, she added with all innocence, "Which one?"

"Which one?" Peruggia pounded the table with a fist. "The devil himself, of course. Bonaparte."

"Oh, right," said Julia, trying to recover. "Bonaparte. I thought perhaps you meant the other one."

"She really doesn't know what she's talking about," Émile said as he kicked Julia's leg beneath the table.

"Then I will enlighten her," Peruggia began. "His armies pillaged the land of my birth, raping and burning as they went, and he personally plundered our greatest treasures for his own enrichment, the same treasures that hang on the walls of the museum where I worked for those dogs."

"Even *La Joconde* herself," Émile added, egging him on.

The remark seemed to hit Peruggia particularly hard. He raised his glass and drained it in one long gulp. Brique started snoring loudly.

"Yes, even *La Gioconda*," Peruggia said, making a point of using the Italian name, "the greatest treasure of all, displayed to the world as if a Frenchman had painted it."

"It's outrageous," Julia said, looking to Émile for agreement.

"It's criminal, there's no other word for it," Émile agreed as he refilled Peruggia's glass.

But the steam was already seeping out of Peruggia's rant. "Yes," he said, slowly nodding his head, "criminal."

He raised his glass again and started to drink. This was the moment.

"There's something you should know, my friend," Émile began.

Peruggia lowered his glass and fixed Émile with an intense stare. "And what is that?"

Émile leaned closer and spoke in a hushed voice. "There are people in this world, in this city, who can no more tolerate injustice than you."

Peruggia grunted to show that he didn't believe this for a minute.

"I'm serious," Émile said. "There are people who feel as strongly about this as you do."

"Go on," Peruggia said guardedly.

Émile glanced furtively around the crowded room, quickly catching Julia's eye to share a moment of triumph.

"Not here," he said. "There's someone I want you to meet first."

Chapter 17

Make no mistake, signore," Peruggia said, "I would not do this for money alone."

"Of course not, my friend," said Valfierno. "I perfectly understand your motivations. You are a patriot first and foremost. That is obvious."

The two men strolled on the embankment running alongside the gray-green river beneath the quai du Louvre. The first time Émile had introduced them, Valfierno had been a little wary of the brooding Italian. Usually, he could size up anyone with a glance, but the intensity in the Italian's eyes made him difficult to read at first. Peruggia carried himself hunched over like a hunted man trying to be inconspicuous, an innocent victim from a country that had once been cruelly subjugated by the monster, Napoleon. Once he understood the nature of Peruggia's obsession with events that occurred a century ago, his *idée fixe*, it had been easy for Valfierno to focus the man's anger and frustration on the object of his rage: the Louvre and his former bosses. From there, it had been a direct path to the idea that the only way to restore justice in the world, as Peruggia saw it, was to repatriate *La Joconde* itself.

"To return my country's greatest treasure to its rightful place," Peruggia said as they walked beneath the curved iron latticework of the Pont Solférino, "to deliver it from the bloodstained hands of that tyrant Napoleon—that would be the greatest honor I could ever achieve."

The man would make a perfect revolutionary, thought Valfierno. The single-minded conviction of the righteousness of his cause was a powerful motivator. And Valfierno had discerned very quickly Peruggia's penchant for obsessing over details, especially when he believed that the plan was entirely of his own making.

"Let's go through the whole thing again," Valfierno said, drawing him in. "And don't leave out the smallest detail."

Peruggia animatedly described his plan once more as they continued past a flotilla of flatboats tied to the sloping bank. Busy washerwomen hung up clothes on the laundry barges, their children tethered by leashes to keep them from toppling overboard. One large scow offered an open-air pool ringed by long wooden sheds where one might procure a private *cabinet* and a bath for twenty centimes.

Valfierno listened intently to the Italian, occasionally interrupting him with questions and comments, gently guiding him away from the parts of the scheme that were less than inspired and toward the parts that made more practical sense. Indeed, the first time he had heard the plan, Valfierno thought it was too naïve to work, but then he began to see that its power lay in its simplicity.

"With any luck," Peruggia said as he finished, "the painting won't even be missed until the following day."

"You'll need another accomplice besides Émile," Valfierno said. "Your companion, this Brique fellow, can he be trusted?"

"Yes, but it would be best if we didn't tell him anything until the day comes. He works better when he doesn't have time to think about what he's doing. If he's paid well enough, he'll do as he's told."

"He'll be paid well enough," Valfierno assured him. "You both will. I will arrange lodging at Madame Charneau's house for the two of you. It'll make the planning easier."

The Italian looked out across the river at a passing barge as it slipped beneath the bridge on its way downstream.

"Answer me this," Peruggia began without looking at Valfierno. "Émile and the young woman . . ."

"Julia."

"They told me they were brother and sister, but I know they're not. I've seen the way they act together. Like an old married couple. Why did they lie to me?"

"Signore," Valfierno said, "you must understand, they were only trying to be discreet. They had no idea whether or not you were the right men for the job."

Peruggia considered this, nodding slightly. "So there will be no more lies?"

"You have my word as a gentleman," Valfierno assured him.

Peruggia slowly turned to Valfierno, staring intently into his eyes. "I will help you, signore, for one reason and one reason only, to re-store the honor of my country. But I warn you, if I thought for even a moment that you were trying to trick me . . ." The words hung in the air like a dangling sword.

Valfierno felt a momentary tingle of fear, but he looked the man squarely in the eyes.

"Have no concerns, my friend." He extended his hand. "You will return *La Gioconda* to its rightful owners, the people of Italy. You will be received as a hero."

Peruggia's eyes narrowed with intensity. *"Per Italia,"* he intoned solemnly as he took Valfierno's hand.

"Indeed," Valfierno said, struggling to match the force of the man's grip. *"Per Italia."*

The dull, dirty white blanket of clouds brooding over Paris dimmed the light filtering through the great arched skylights of the Gare d'Orsay. Below, hundreds of travelers bustled to and fro: elegant Pa-risian men in stovepipe hats walked stiffly in their tight black suits; women shuffled along in bell-shaped dresses topped with tight-waisted jackets, their circular hats perched on blossoms of swept-up hair; por-ters followed them, struggling with cases and huge hatboxes. Working-class men in berets, wearing worn, baggy blue jackets, some alone, some leading their doughty wives and gaggles of children, struggled with their cardboard suitcases in search of the correct platform.

While Émile waited at the bottom of the electrically powered luggage ramp to oversee the loading of Valfierno's bags onto the waiting train, Valfierno and Julia sat at a table in a small café on the upper level.

Valfierno took a sip of his *café noir* and said, "You probably wish that you were returning to the United States yourself."

Julia took a bite of a *brioche à tête*.

"I've already seen it." She shrugged. "Besides, I like it here. I feel like I belong."

"It's the way most people feel when they arrive in Paris: as if they are coming home for the first time."

They sat in silence for a moment, Valfierno sipping his drink, Julia taking another bite.

"Émile doesn't seem to like me very much," she finally said in an offhand manner.

"He doesn't make friends easily," said Valfierno. "And, to be candid, I think you work very hard at trying to annoy him."

"But I'm just having a bit of fun. Doesn't he have a sense of humor?"

"He's always been very serious, has been since he was a young boy."

"So, how did you find him in the first place anyway?"

Valfierno eyed her suspiciously.

"I promise I won't make fun of him," she added.

He smiled and related the story of his close brush with death at the hands of the street *apaches*, and Émile's timely rescue—leaving out Madame Laroche and her jealous husband.

"Goodness," she said, "that was a bit of luck. And you never found out anything about his background?"

"I didn't say that."

"So tell me."

Valfierno hesitated again.

"I won't tease him no matter what you tell me. I promise."

"There's nothing to tease about," said Valfierno.

"Well?" Julia prompted.

"I'll tell you what I know," he said, leaning toward her, "but only in hopes that it will perhaps give you a better understanding of the boy."

"Absolutely. I can be very understanding." At Valfierno's skeptical look she added, "When I want to be."

Valfierno glanced up at the ornate golden clock on the arched translucent glass wall at the end of the terminus. Satisfied there still was time, he turned his attention back to Julia.

"When I first found him, or perhaps I should say, when he found *me*, he was a very quiet boy. He hardly spoke at all and indeed didn't seem to remember anything from his life before he started living on the street. I didn't press him. But he was plagued by bad dreams. He would wake me up in the middle of the night screaming. He often called out a name: 'Madeleine, Madeleine!' I would ask him about his dreams the next morning, but he would never respond. I'm not even sure he remembered them.

"I shared my concerns with Madame Charneau, and she remembered a tragic incident from a few years before. A family of four—mother, father, boy of eight or nine, and his sister of seven— were picnicking on the banks of the Seine north of Paris. The river was swollen with recent rain and it was late in the season so there was no one else about. It seems that the parents went for a walk and left the boy to watch over his sister. The two children were apparently climbing on a large tree jutting out over the water when the girl fell in. The boy tried to reach her, but the strong current must have quickly pulled her away. The parents returned to find the boy frantically pacing up and down the bank calling her name, but the girl was nowhere to be seen. Her body was never found, lost forever in the winding downstream channels of the river."

"That's terrible," Julia said.

"The distraught mother drowned herself a week later at the same spot, or perhaps she was trying to find her child—who can ever know? The father vanished soon after, though there was a report that he was seen traveling alone through Marseilles a month later. No one knew what happened to the boy. He simply disappeared."

Valfierno paused. He looked up from his coffee to Julia. "The boy's name was Émile."

"And his sister's name," Julia said slowly, "was Madeleine."

Valfierno took a sip of his coffee.

Julia sat back in her chair. "That would certainly explain why he doesn't like water."

At this moment, Émile appeared through the crowd and hurried up to the table.

"We'd better go down," he said. "The baggage is loaded."

"Well," said Valfierno, placing some coins on the table and rising to his feet, "it would seem the time has come."

Steam escaped from the engine of the polished wood-paneled train as they reached the steps of the carriage.

"The plan is sound," Valfierno said. "Our Italian friend imagines himself part of a crusade. This brings out his talent for focusing on the details of the operation to the point of obsession. Do as he says, but only until you have the painting safely in your possession."

"I still think I would be of more use on the inside," Julia said, "where the action will be."

"Keep your voice down," Émile warned, looking around the platform.

Valfierno gently touched her cheek. "My dear Julia, we've discussed all this before. Think of yourself as a cog in a machine."

"Cogs have no fun at all," she pouted.

Valfierno moved close to her, lowering his voice. "Your part perhaps is the most important of all. It is essential that the object our Italian friend keeps in his possession is a copy, and more important, that he believes with all his heart that it's the real thing."

"That part will be easy," Julia said.

"Your confidence is admirable," Valfierno continued, "but I fear that he is not as predictable as he may seem at times. Take nothing for granted."

"All aboard for Le Havre!" cried out the conductor as jets of white vapor hissed out of the train's steam engine.

"Émile." Valfierno looked the young man squarely in the eyes and placed a hand on his shoulder. "I'm counting on you. And I have no doubt in my mind that you're the best man for the job."

"Don't worry," Émile said confidently. "Everything will go according to plan."

"I hope it will," said Valfierno, "but remember, a plan is only a road map. The important thing is to reach the destination regardless of the obstacles."

Émile nodded, a little less sure of himself now.

Valfierno kissed Julia on one cheek and, as he moved around to kiss the other, he whispered in her ear, "Keep an eye on him for me, will you?"

Julia smiled conspiratorially as Valfierno pulled away and climbed the steps into the car.

The train jerked forward, clattering into life.

"Wish me luck!" Valfierno called out over the increasing racket.

"*Bon voyage!*" Julia shouted as she waved frantically.

"*Bonne chance,*" said Émile.

"So," Julia said to Émile as the train disappeared into its own cloud of steam, "do you really think everything will go smoothly?"

"Of course," said Émile, "as long as you do what you're supposed to do."

"Don't I always?" said Julia with a smile.

And then, before Émile could do anything about it, she stepped forward on her tiptoes and kissed him on the cheek. He drew back, astonished, his hand reflexively going to his face.

"Why did you do that?" he said.

Julia shrugged, a playful smile on her lips.

"I just think we should be friends," she said casually.

She turned on her heels and sashayed toward the platform steps, pausing only for a brief backward glance.

Émile watched her for a moment, a puzzled expression on his face. Then he patted his pocket. Feeling the reassuring bulk of his watch, he allowed himself a relieved smile before following her.

Valfierno settled back into the plush seat of his private compartment. In a little more than a week, he would begin perhaps the most difficult part of the entire operation. He would have to convince not one, but six American captains of industry to each spend a small fortune on a treasure they would never be able to display to anyone else in the world. He had done it many times before, of course, but never on this scale.

He ran through the names in his mind. There were plenty to choose from. He had dealt with them all before and for the most part he would be welcomed. Except perhaps by Mr. Joshua Hart of Newport, Rhode Island. There could be some resistance there.

He ran down the list of the candidates again, thinking about the best way to approach each one. But, as he did, something else kept intruding into his thoughts. He tried to focus but found it difficult. As the train left behind the sprawl of Paris, he reached into his pocket and withdrew a single white silk glove. He wasn't sure why he had bothered to bring it. Ridiculous really.

Shaking himself from his reverie, he replaced it and leaned back into the seat to try to sleep.

Chapter 18

A panel of cottonwood, seventy-seven by fifty-three centimeters, supported by strips of wood on the back."

Diego addressed Émile, Julia, and Peruggia in his cramped basement studio on rue Serpente. He had the air of an impatient professor not particularly eager to share his superior knowledge with his class. He sat on a stool before his easel, which supported the copy of *La Joconde* he had first shown them in the Tuileries. For further illustration, a series of panels in varying degrees of completion lay on a table next to him.

"So it can't be rolled up," Julia commented.

Émile gave a disapproving grunt, but Diego smiled.

"No, *mi querida,* it cannot be rolled up."

Julia turned to Émile. "What?" she challenged him. "I was just thinking out loud."

"Is that what you call it?" Émile said.

"I thought we were going to be friends," said Julia sarcastically.

"It's small enough," Peruggia said. "We'll get it out of there, don't worry."

"If you are all quite finished . . ." Diego said before turning the panel over. "On the back—"

"So what size is this one?" Émile said, interrupting him.

Diego gave him a sharp look. "It is the correct size."

"I thought copies had to be larger or smaller."

"Those are the museum's rules, yes," Diego said, taking a Gauloise from a box on the table and lighting it, "that is, if rules are something that you pay attention to."

Émile bristled at the unspoken challenge. "Rules?" he said, glancing quickly at Julia. "No, I never pay any attention to them myself."

"A real *Cimarrone*, eh," Diego said, referring to the old Spanish name for a wild mustang.

"If you like," said Émile, as if he knew what the word meant.

Diego snorted a slight chuckle as he returned his attention to the panel.

"This particular copy is my master, so to speak. I spent a great deal of time sitting in front of the original—before it was put inside that awful box, of course."

"And no one ever challenged you for having the same-size panel?" asked Peruggia.

"Oh, they challenged me all right," said Diego with a sly smile, "but all I had to do was produce this." He picked up a tailor's cloth measuring tape from the table. "A young lady of my acquaintance was kind enough to cut a segment from another tape and sew it into the start of this one. I would simply place it against the edge of the panel to prove that it was in fact smaller."

"Very clever," said Julia.

Diego shrugged.

"And all the copies you've done so far," began Émile, "are of this quality?"

"Don't be ridiculous," said Diego. "They're good, but not that good."

"But the new ones will be perfect, right?" Émile persisted.

"And what do you think?" Diego snapped, his level of irritation growing with each question. "Now, if I may be permitted to continue, it is vital to remember that the rear of the panel is just as important as the front."

He indicated a light-colored strip of wood vertically attached just left of center at the upper edge of the panel. A bow tie–shaped piece had been added crosswise for reinforcement.

"This dovetail was inserted into the wood to repair a crack caused by some imbecile in the last century when he removed the original frame."

The repair reminded Julia of a small crucifix.

"How did you ever manage to see the back of it?" she asked, clearly impressed.

"It wasn't so difficult," Diego began, playing to Julia's wide-eyed interest. "I was able to briefly visit the photographer's studio when it was being photographed. One of the assistants owed me some money, and so he let me examine it briefly. I thought it would add a nice touch, even though not one in a thousand people would know about it."

"Maybe this assistant could be helpful," Julia suggested to the group.

"We shouldn't change the plan now," said Peruggia.

Émile also bristled at this. "The last thing we need is another—"

"He might have been helpful," Diego interrupted, "but it turned out that he owed money to a lot of people. And not all of them were as forgiving as me. They fished his body out of the river. Apparently he'd forgotten that he couldn't swim."

Diego smiled sardonically at Émile as if he would appreciate this bit of gallows humor. Julia felt a pang of empathy as Émile made a weak attempt at a shared smile.

Diego turned the painting over to the front side and replaced it on the easel, then picked up a blank panel. "Preparation is everything. To keep moisture from the wood, it's first coated on both sides with gesso." Balancing the panel on one knee, he picked up a sticky glass container half full of the dark liquid. "It's made from animal hide. It also acts as a primer for the oil paint."

"How will you make it look like it's hundreds of years old?" asked Julia.

"Five hundred years, in fact," Diego replied. "And don't forget, it's been covered with various layers of varnish over the centuries in attempts to preserve it. But, as in most things, there's a trick to it. I use two layers of lacquer and allow each to dry at a different temperature. This causes crazing on the surface, craquelure, as it's called. Only by comparing each and every hairlike fissure with the original could one tell that they don't exactly match."

"The marquis told me once that forgers always leave a tiny mark somewhere on the painting," said Julia. "Where's yours?"

"I do not indulge in such childish games," Diego said, a smug smile forming on his face. "No one looking at this image would ever find the slightest alteration."

"But how long will all this take?" asked Peruggia brusquely.

"Capturing the genius of a master cannot be rushed. Even by another master."

Diego pointed this last comment directly to Julia. Her attempt to maintain her equanimity was betrayed by a slight flushing of the face.

Soon afterward, Peruggia grew restless and left. His departure put an end to the formal demonstration and Émile drifted off to casually peruse the various canvases strewn about the room. Only Julia still seemed interested, pressing the painter with questions. Diego motioned for her to come closer to the master copy.

"The background is most important," he said, enjoying her attention, "an otherworldly landscape neither real nor imagined. And the lady herself, serenely posed without a care in the world. She sits with her body *contrapposto*, turned slightly away from the observer, but her head turns toward us, as if we have caught her in the middle of some forbidden thought." As he said this, Diego turned to Julia for emphasis, gratified to see that she was hanging on his every word. "Her mouth," he continued. "Is that a smile, the picture of contentment, or are her lips tightly pursed, keeping some profound secret that has endowed her with scandalous or even dangerous knowledge that no one else possesses?"

"That must be difficult to copy," she said.

"One has to do more than just copy. One has to understand. To feel. To inhabit the creator's mind. To re-create the work of a genius, one must be a genius."

From a corner of the room, Émile let out an audible groan.

"Of course," Diego continued, casting a disparaging look at Émile, "when all is said and done, there are certain techniques one must master. For example, there is what the Italians call sfumato, the layering of dark to light, the blending of many colors to blur any sharp lines." To demonstrate, he removed the panel from the easel and replaced it with a large paper pad. Picking up a brush and paint palette, he quickly applied a series of delicate brushstrokes to a blank page. "If it's done correctly, the brushstrokes disappear. It is a way to capture the uncharted depths of a woman's smile, of a woman's heart." Again he gave her a penetrating look that seemed to reach inside her in a way that was both pleasant and unpleasant at the same time.

"Most of these are copies." Émile indicated the various panels strewn about the room. "Don't you have any original work?"

Diego shrugged and lit another Gauloise. "Of course, but not here. I keep them elsewhere so they don't remind me of where I've been. Here I seek something new, something revolutionary. I try my hand at many things. Portraits, for instance. In fact"—he turned back to Julia—"perhaps the young lady would care to sit for me sometime."

"Why on earth would you want to paint me?" Julia asked, pretending not to be flattered.

"There is no greater inspiration than a beautiful woman."

"Oh, I'm sure that would be a masterpiece," Émile said to no one in particular. "Come on," he added, turning to Julia, "it's time to go. We'll leave the *master* to his work."

"I'm staying," Julia said obstinately.

"Suit yourself." Émile snatched up his coat and disappeared up the stairs.

Diego placed the Gauloise between his lips and squinted at Julia through the curling smoke. She allowed herself to enjoy her little triumph for a few seconds but quickly began to wither beneath his gaze.

"He's such a child," Julia said, averting her eyes from Diego back to the painting.

"You find him annoying, don't you?"

"At times."

"And what about me? How do you find me?"

Julia felt a wave of heat flush across her face. She hoped that Diego would not notice.

"Oh, I don't know," she replied, struggling to sound casual. "I don't suppose I've ever thought about it."

Diego let out a laugh. "I don't suppose you have," he said lightly. "But perhaps you should."

"I think perhaps I should be going." She gathered up her things. "Madame Charneau doesn't like me to be late for supper."

"We certainly wouldn't want you to be late for your supper," Diego said as he applied some abstract flourishes to the paper.

"I'll bid you a good evening, then," she said as she hurried up the stairs to the street.

"If you must," Diego said without looking up from his impromptu painting. "*Bon soir, mademoiselle.*"

He raised his brush hand to add something to the pad but changed his mind and instead threw the brush down in disgust. Ripping the sheet from the pad and crumpling it up, he threw it across the studio.

"*Bon soir.*"

Chapter 19

Even though Valfierno had visited the houses of some of the richest men in the United States, he never failed to be awed by Windcrest, Joshua Hart's personal kingdom. Staring out the window of the taxi that had brought him from the train station, he could easily imagine that he was entering the private domain of the royal head of some obscure European principality.

Valfierno had disembarked from RMS *Mauretania* two weeks earlier and checked into the Plaza Hotel across from Central Park. Though he would not be spending much time there, he always used the French Renaissance chateau-style building as his home base in New York.

The morning following his arrival, he had steamed out of Grand Central Station and traveled north along the Hudson River en route to his first destination. From the Van Cortlandt Manor in Croton to Lyndhurst in Tarrytown, the Hudson was studded with the mansions and palaces of America's captains of industry. The opulence of these structures made it easy to forget that they were built upon the backs of thousands of men, women, and children who labored long hours in harsh conditions for little reward.

In a few days of travel, he had visited many of his most valued clients to tempt them with his tantalizing offer. For the most part, his hosts had welcomed him with eager anticipation. As he made his way north, his reception at each stop became an almost predictable routine. First there would be the requisite brandy and cigars served in imposing libraries or on vast verandas overlooking the wide river with its majestic backdrop of the Catskill Mountains rising above the distant haze. Then he would be taken to the secret gallery. This room, off-limits to all but a select few, displayed the artwork the master of the house had obtained by less than honest means. Valfierno always picked out one or two pieces to comment on specifically, often pieces that he himself had provided. And then, finally, it would be down to business as his host inquired about the reason for Valfierno's visit. When Valfierno revealed the name of the painting in question, he was always met first with incredulity until greed and avarice ultimately raised their ugly heads in triumph.

In only a few days along the Hudson, he had been able to successfully conclude agreements for three of the planned six copies. The price he demanded varied depending on the size of his patron's holdings, but it was always extravagant and never less than three hundred and fifty thousand dollars. Yes, the price was ridiculously high, but when would there again be an opportunity to acquire for one's collection the ultimate manifestation of human creativity? It had taken him years to cultivate the confidence of these men, and now the time had come to extract the full value of that trust.

In the weeks following his Hudson River journey, he continued to travel extensively; he found one client on the North Shore of Long Island—the fabled Gold Coast—and one in Chicago. He probably could have found at least two in the great city on the lake, but instead, for his final client, he had made a special trip, traveling by train up the Connecticut coast to the fabled and opulent mansions of Newport. Riding from the station in a cab, Valfierno took note of the many so-called cottages lining the waterfront, each one more ostentatious than the last. *If these were cottages,* he thought, *then the* Mona Lisa *was a* Saturday Evening Post *illustration.*

He handed his taxi driver a ten-dollar bill and told him to wait. A brisk sea breeze animated the great swaths of flowers and reeds in the front gardens. Wide marble steps led up to an arched portico. Before he even reached the massive oak front doors, they swept open as if by magic.

Hart's butler, Carter, greeted Valfierno with practiced deference. "Marquis," he intoned, "welcome to Windcrest. Mr. Hart is expecting you."

Carter led Valfierno into a vast marbled foyer adorned with paintings and sculptures. He recognized a genuine if lesser Klimt, but for the most part the works were not particularly distinguished. Carter walked past the wide central staircase to a small doorway where he gestured for Valfierno to enter.

Valfierno walked into a large library and immediately stopped. Mrs. Hart stood in the center of the room, wearing a light summer frock, her hands clasped in front of her. It was the first time he had ever seen her with her hair down and—though he had certainly not forgotten her—it had been sometimes difficult to conjure up the image of her face. To see it again so suddenly was both a pleasant surprise and a disconcerting jolt.

"Marquis," she said, approaching him, "what a pleasure it is to see you again."

"I assure you, madame," he began, faltering slightly with an unexpected shortness of breath, "that the pleasure is all mine."

Valfierno detected a slight blush when she nodded her head in acknowledgment.

"And it would be greater still," he continued, "if you would call me Edward."

Her only response to this was a slight but genuine smile. "Please," she said, "my husband is expecting you."

As she led him through the library, Valfierno sensed a slight movement out of the corner of his eye. He turned toward the windows and saw her mother seated in a padded chair, focused intently on her hands as she knitted something from a ball of green yarn.

"Madame," Valfierno said in salutation, but she continued her knitting without acknowledging him.

"He's in his study," Mrs. Hart said with a kindly smile.

She entered a narrow hallway at the end of the room. Valfierno followed, captivated by the way she walked. Her feet landed softly, almost directly in front of each other, her hips swaying fluidly and gracefully with each stride. There was not a wasted motion and he imagined that she probably had no idea how pleasing she was to observe.

She led him into a low-ceilinged, oak-paneled study, its windows shuttered against the afternoon sun. Thin shards of penetrating light served only to accentuate the gloom. Joshua Hart was sitting at a massive oak desk. Standing next to Hart was a large man of about forty. His head was shaved bald, and he wore an expensive dark suit tightly tailored to his muscular frame.

"Well, the marquis de Valfierno," Hart said dramatically as he put down a pen and swiveled in his chair. "And how is the mayor of Buenos Aires?"

Amused by his little joke, he looked up at the other man for a reaction. The man obliged with the faintest of requisite smiles.

"I'm well, thank you," Valfierno replied, bowing his head slightly, "but currently I'm residing in Paris."

"I don't imagine you're much more than a councilman there, eh?" Hart quipped.

"No more than an appreciative tourist really," Valfierno said with a sideways glance at Mrs. Hart in an attempt to include her in the conversation.

"I'm forgetting my manners," said Hart, rising from his chair. "This is my new associate, Mr. Taggart. Mr. Taggart is recently retired from the Pinkerton Detective Agency. He now works exclusively for me. There's been labor unrest of late, and I have felt in need of a little protection."

"Mr. Taggart," Valfierno said, acknowledging the man with a slight tilt of his head.

Taggart fixed Valfierno with an icy appraising stare before slowly nodding in response. Valfierno thought that the man's steel-gray eyes and shining naked head gave him the look of a gladiator, transported from a distant time and place and looking quite out of sync in modern clothing.

"And where, pray tell, is your lovely niece?" Hart asked, sitting back down.

"Much as she would have liked to have accompanied me, she is attending school in Paris, studying art."

"Pity." Hart selected a cigar from a silver box. "You must tell her that if she's ever in the States, she should drop by to say hello." Hart looked at his wife for the first time since she had entered the room before adding, "To study my collection, of course."

"Well," Mrs. Hart said, "if you'll excuse me, gentlemen . . ."

Valfierno turned and bowed slightly as she left the room.

"Have a seat," Hart said, indicating a plush leather chair. "You've traveled a long way. I think perhaps some brandy is in order."

Valfierno sat down as Taggart moved to a side table and poured brandy from a decanter into two crystal glasses.

"You know," Hart continued, "it's a funny thing about that forged passport you gave me. As soon as I got back to the States, I got a new one, of course, but try as I might, I couldn't tell the difference between the two. The one you provided even had the correct entry stamp, date and all."

Taggart handed each of the men a glass.

"I use only the most skilled people," Valfierno said, taking the drink. "The work they do is always of the highest order."

Hart made a grudging sound of acknowledgment before raising his glass and downing the dark red liquid in one swig.

As Valfierno took a sip from his glass, he caught the eye of Taggart. The man was staring at him.

"So, Mr. Hart," Valfierno said, eager to change the subject, "how are you enjoying your recent acquisition?"

"Why don't you come see for yourself?"

When Hart flicked on the light switch in his underground gallery, Valfierno's eyes were immediately drawn to the centerpiece of the collection, Manet's *La Ninfa Sorprendida*.

"Magnificent," Valfierno said, spreading his hands wide for emphasis. "This has always been my favorite Manet. Such depth, such emotion. Truly a masterpiece."

"It ought to be for the price I paid," Hart said.

Valfierno turned to see Taggart standing by the door. The big man was staring straight at him, his face a blank mask.

"How about the copy?" Hart continued. "You know, the one that was put up in its place in the museum?"

"It's serving its purpose," Valfierno replied. "I believe they had to lower the lights somewhat to complete the effect."

"Is that so," Hart said, turning his eyes back to the painting. "No need to do that here, of course."

He studied the painting for a moment before turning back to Valfierno, suddenly all business. "Well, let me get to the point, Marquis. I agreed to see you out of courtesy and, I will admit, in hopes of seeing your delightful niece again, but I'm afraid that you've come all the way here for nothing. I have all that I ever desired here within these walls. A man has to know when enough is enough, don't you think?"

Valfierno began to pace slowly around the room. "You have a tidy collection, I'll grant you. The Spanish, the British, the Dutch are all well represented. You have your French masterpiece now, of course, but"—he hesitated as if slowly forming his thoughts—"the Italians are a little underrepresented, wouldn't you say?"

"Don't even try," Hart warned amiably. "Whatever it is you're selling, I'm not buying."

"I had hoped you would say that," Valfierno said with a display of relief. "I have another patron to visit, and in truth, I had promised him first right of refusal concerning the object in question. I came here only as a courtesy. You'll make the man I refer to very happy indeed." As if to drive home the point, Valfierno pulled out his pocket watch to check the time. "Ah, my train. I have a taxi waiting outside. If I leave now, I'll just make it in time."

"Not that it matters," Hart said, trying to sound disinterested, "but who exactly are you going to see?"

"Oh, I never discuss one patron with another."

"Come, come," Hart said, "surely you owe me that much."

Valfierno hesitated, as if considering. Then, after giving Taggart a sideways glance, he walked up to Hart, leaned forward, and whispered the name in his ear.

Hart's eyes widened. "That old pirate! He could buy half the paintings in the British Museum and his collection still wouldn't hold a candle to mine!"

"That's true," Valfierno allowed, "and will remain true. Until, of course, he takes possession of the object in question."

Agitated, Hart stalked around the room, demonstrating with a sweeping arm.

"Nonsense! He couldn't match my collection in a million years. Look at these. Manet, Constable, Murillo, even a Rembrandt! What does he think he's going to get? The *Mona Lisa*?"

The look on Valfierno's face coupled with a slight canting of his head spoke volumes.

Hart's smug expression dissolved instantly.

"Holy Mother of Christ!"

Back in his study, Joshua Hart paced the room, frantically sucking on a cigar.

"And this time," he said, his excitement raising the pitch of his voice, "none of this 'copy in the museum' horseshit. I want to see every goddamn newspaper in the world splashed with news of the robbery. Do we understand each other?"

Valfierno sat in the plush leather chair successfully hiding his own excitement. He regarded an unlit cigar that Hart had forced upon him.

"We understand each other perfectly, Señor Hart."

"How long will it take?"

"It can't be rushed, of course. There is much careful planning involved. Say, six months?"

"And you're positive you can pull this off?"

"I'm staking my life on it. To fail in such an endeavor would be fatal. The best I could hope for would be to spend the rest of my life rotting on Devil's Island."

"Failure is one thing," said Hart. "I can accept that. After all, it costs me nothing; I pay only on delivery. But if I suspected that you were in any way trying to make a fool of me . . ." He paused for effect.

Valfierno smiled casually. "I can assure you, señor—"

"Mr. Taggart," Hart said, cutting him off, then pausing as he walked behind the chair that Valfierno sat in, "please tell us, in the course of your work, how many men have you killed?"

Taggart sat on a wooden chair in a dark corner of the room. At first he didn't answer, but then he leaned forward into a sharp shaft of sunlight. "Depending on how you count," he said, considering, "eleven or twelve."

Hart flicked his cigar ash into a silver ashtray embedded into a small wooden table. "Am I being too subtle for you, Marquis?"

"Too subtle?" Valfierno said, slipping his cigar into his inside jacket pocket and pushing himself to his feet. "Hardly."

"Excellent," said Hart. "Then we have a deal. And, with luck, you may still be able to make your train."

Hart's evident excitement over the deal he had just negotiated made him talkative. Leading Valfierno back through the library to the main foyer, he prattled on about his employees' obsession with such unimportant issues as unsafe work conditions and inadequate housing. It was their constant agitating that had necessitated hiring a man like Taggart in the first place. He was of the opinion that the rabble should be content to be working at all. Valfierno nodded now and again to give the impression of paying attention, but his thoughts were elsewhere. When they reached the entrance, Hart extended his hand and Valfierno took it.

"In six months' time, then," Hart said.

Valfierno turned and saw Mrs. Hart standing halfway up the main staircase. The look they exchanged was brief, but there was something about her expression that suggested she was trying to tell him something, something that could not be spoken. Or perhaps he was imagining it. Either way, it was an image he would conjure up in his mind many times in the months to come.

Chapter 20

But you said you'd marry me! You promised you'd make an honest woman out of me!" Julia stood in the center of the Grande Galerie of the Louvre, her voice loud and petulant.

"I said a lot of things. Why are you making such a scene?" Émile's eyes darted around the gallery; he was all too aware of the attention they were drawing to themselves.

"You men are all alike!"

Museum patrons gave them sidelong glances and whispered to each other in disapproval. Over Émile's shoulders, Julia noticed a guard, a rotund man in his fifties with a large untrimmed mustache, approaching them at the fastest clip he could manage.

"All you're interested in is stealing a girl's virtue," Julia added for emphasis as the guard put his hand on Émile's shoulder and spun him around.

"Please!" the man said, half angry and half pleading, "you must hold down your voices. You're creating a disturbance."

"Monsieur," Julia appealed to him, softening her voice, "you're a man of the world. Would you lead a young innocent girl on with empty promises and then just cast her aside like an old newspaper?"

The guard's flustered reaction was just what Julia had hoped for.

"Mademoiselle," he said, looking around at the patrons watching them, "this is not the place for such talk."

Julia shot Émile a glance. It was his turn to contribute.

"Can't a man have a little fun without having to promise a girl the stars?" he said, warming to the part.

"Oh, you promised the stars all right," Julia said, "but all you've ever done is to drag my reputation through the mud!"

"I beg you, mademoiselle," said the guard, "please keep your voice—" but before he could finish Julia turned on him with even greater fervor.

"Tell him!" Julia appealed to the guard. "Tell him he can't treat a young girl as if she were little more than a woman of the streets!"

"Please," the guard implored her, "you have to be reasonable. You have to keep your voice down."

"Is there not a single man in all France who will defend me?"

Reluctantly, the guard straightened himself and looked up at Émile. "Monsieur," he began in an officious tone, "you should not treat this poor young woman with such disrespect."

Julia glanced down at the small brass ring clipped to the guard's belt. It held a single key.

"Now the whole world's on her side," Émile exclaimed. "If you only knew how difficult she can be! If you only knew what she puts me through!" For emphasis, he threw up his arms dramatically and stalked away.

"Thank you so much, monsieur," Julia said, touching the guard's arm. "You're a true gentleman, so rare these days."

Flashing her sweetest smile, Julia threw her arms around the man and hugged him closely.

"Mademoiselle," he pleaded.

In one swift move, she unclipped the key ring and palmed it. She let go and stepped back, giving him one final smile before bustling away. The guard, his face now almost crimson in color, removed his kepi and mopped his brow.

A moment later, Julia met Émile in a small utility room at the end of the adjacent Salle des États. Checking to make sure they were unobserved, she handed him the brass ring with the single key dangling from it.

"Are you sure he didn't notice?" Émile asked.

"I'm sure, but he will notice soon enough if you don't hurry."

Émile removed a small tin from his pocket and flipped open the lid, revealing a raised bed of wax. He lifted the key to his mouth and warmed the notched tooth with his breath before carefully making an impression of both sides in the soft wax.

"Don't take all day," Julia said, keeping a lookout.

"It has to be done right," he said slowly and deliberately.

"Come on," she hissed as he finally closed the lid and handed her back the key ring.

She wiped away the waxy residue with a handkerchief, slipped it into the pocket of her coat, and hurried back to the Grande Galerie.

"Monsieur! Monsieur!" she cried as she skittered across the floor toward the guard, who instinctively drew back. "Wonderful news. I don't know how to thank you." She planted herself in front of him, breathless, clasping her hands together beneath her chin. "Your stern reprimand has done the trick. He's agreed to marry me. And it's all because of you. You are my hero!"

As she said this last, her hands flew apart to embrace him, knocking off his kepi in the process.

"Oh, I'm so clumsy! Let me get that."

"No, please, mademoiselle," he sputtered, "you mustn't make a fuss."

As he bent over to pick up his hat, she clipped the key ring back onto his belt.

Flustered, he straightened up and replaced the kepi onto his head, adjusting it to make sure it was tight.

"Well," she began, "I really must be going now. I must tell *Maman* the good news right away!" And with that she floated off, leaving the man with a wide-eyed, slightly dazed look on his red face.

Émile waited at the top of the wide staircase leading down to the lobby. Julia ran up and threw her arms around him.

"We did it!" she said.

"Yes, we did," he agreed, giving her a rather reserved pat on the back. "But let's not overdo it."

They separated and she smoothed out her coat.

"Well," she said, "I think we make an excellent couple."

She threaded her arm through his and they started down the steps.

Chapter 21

The shipping clerk at the Hudson River Import and Export Company on the west side of Manhattan had reason to be pleased with Valfierno's arrival. The well-dressed gentleman appeared every month or so like clockwork. He would show up two or three days in a row until the package he was expecting had arrived. And he tipped very generously indeed.

"Ah, and you've all the luck today, sir," the clerk said, his West Cork brogue only slightly smoothed by years of living in New York. "I think I have the very thing you'll be looking for."

Ignoring several other customers, the man retrieved a rectangular crate, three and a half feet by two and a half feet and five inches deep. He placed it on the counter.

"Makes number six, if memory serves," the clerk said brightly.

"Yes, and I believe the last."

"You'll be needing some help out," the clerk suggested eagerly.

"Thank you, I can manage."

Valfierno produced a crisp twenty-dollar bill from his pocket, four times his usual tip.

"Thank *you*, sir," the clerk said, beaming. "Thank you indeed, sir."

Valfierno simply nodded and, with a slight acknowledging bow to the clerk's neglected customers, lifted the crate and left.

———————

As a well-known importer of fine arts copies, there was nothing unusual about Valfierno returning to the hotel with his new deliveries. It was perhaps odd that he preferred taking the crates up to his room without assistance, but his eccentricities were equally well known to the hotel staff. And, after all, he was French, or Italian, or from some such country. In any case, he certainly wasn't an American, and unconventional behavior was to be expected and must, within reason, be tolerated.

Back in his rooms, Valfierno carefully opened the crate. He removed a panel wrapped in cloth and put the wooden crate aside. After the panel was unwrapped, it took only a brief look at the finished result to satisfy him. From the very first copy, Valfierno had been impressed with Diego's work. This one was so accurate that he wished he could compare it to the original hanging in the Louvre. He knew it would stand the scrutiny of anyone but the most astute art expert.

Diego had protested at first that it would be impossible to create seven copies—including the one that was to end up in Peruggia's hands—in the time allotted to him. Therefore, a compromise had been reached. The copies would be of varying quality and would arrive from Paris in order of that quality, beginning with the lowest. Valfierno knew who his customers would be, and it would be easy enough to match the quality of the copy to the perspicuity of its buyer. Indeed, the very first copy he had received—though an excellent reproduction—was earmarked for a particular captain of industry who was more or less blind.

The copy he held in his hand was actually the penultimate version; the final version was to remain in Paris and had to be of sufficient quality to fool Peruggia, who was soon to have an intimate, though hopefully brief, acquaintance with the original.

Valfierno carefully replaced the cloth around the panel and carried it to a large closet off the sitting room. He placed it with the five others, all similarly wrapped, leaning against the rear wall. He touched each one in turn, starting with the one closest to the wall, the first copy he had received. One, two, three, four, five, six. The set was complete.

Walking back into the room, he picked up his copy of the book Apollinaire had written: *L'Enchanteur pourrissant*—The Rotting Enchanter. It was a strange alchemy of modern and classical verse chronicling Merlin's obsession with the Lady of the Lake. This infatuation results in his entombment in a cave, a fate that strangely he doesn't seem to mind at all. A little esoteric for Valfierno's taste.

Valfierno put the book down and stepped to the window. The Manhattan skyline spread before him, the setting sun reflecting in the windows of the tightly packed forest of buildings. An image of Ellen Hart formed in his mind, but he forced it away by turning his thoughts to his cohorts in Paris.

"*Bonne chance, mes amis,*" he said aloud. "*Bonne chance.*"

All he could do now was wait.

Part III

We are not thieves, but men that much do want.
—Shakespeare, *Timon of Athens*

Chapter 22

Vincenzo Peruggia sat fully clothed on the narrow bed in his first-floor room in Madame Charneau's boardinghouse. He had arisen and dressed sometime after midnight, his restless mind and the unusually warm evening having made sleep impossible. As the first light of dawn painted the room in sepia tones, he thought of all he must accomplish over the course of the next few days. If things went according to plan, by tomorrow night he would be in possession of one of the most revered paintings in the world. He would have completed the first step in fulfilling his dream of restoring the dignity of his native country.

He had been living in the boardinghouse for almost six months now, as had his companion, Brique, who was quartered in a room across the hall. It was decided early on that it would be unwise to tell the slow-witted Frenchman anything beyond the day and time he would be needed to help in an endeavor that would earn him enough money to live comfortably for many years to come.

With the exception of Brique, they were all acquainted with each other's role in the plan, but there was one vital part that was known only to Peruggia, and to him it was the most important part of all. He understood that people took him for a fool at times. Valfierno had assured him that ultimately the painting would be his to return to its rightful home. But Peruggia knew that it was up to him alone to guarantee that this would happen.

There was no particular hurry this morning. They would not need to arrive at the museum until the afternoon, about an hour before closing time. But Peruggia grew impatient sitting on his bed, his mind racing, and he could wait no longer. He checked his pocket watch: 7:45. He decided it was time to wake his companion and fill him in on the plan for the next two days.

Peruggia knocked on Brique's door. There was no response. This in itself was not unusual. Brique often returned late into the night, almost too drunk to stand. He would spend much of the following day sleeping it off, snoring with enough force to rattle the nerves of the rest of the house's occupants. But this time the room was silent. Peruggia knocked again, louder. Still no response. He pushed the door open. The room was empty. The bed had not been slept in.

Peruggia roused Julia and Madame Charneau, who hurried to the local *boulangerie* for fresh bread, stopping at the Hôtel de Fleurie to use the telephone in the lobby to call Émile.

Within a half hour they were all gathered together in the kitchen. Madame Charneau stood making coffee in a press pot. Émile sat at a long wooden table across from Julia. Peruggia nervously paced the room.

"That must have been him I heard last night," Madame Charneau said as she sliced a baguette on a wooden cutting board. "It was almost midnight when he went out, but I never heard him come back."

Peruggia thought of the noise that woke him in the middle of the night. He had dismissed it as just the sound of Brique coming home and banging his door shut. But he must have been leaving.

"No one was supposed to go out last night," Émile said to Peruggia. "You were supposed to keep an eye on him."

"A man gets lonely sometimes," Peruggia said.

"Your friend seems to get lonely quite a lot," Julia added lightly.

"So where is he?" Émile asked, his agitation lending his voice a sharp edge.

"Probably out cold in some alley clutching an empty bottle of absinthe," Madame Charneau said, "or lying in a stupor in some whorehouse. It's a good thing he knows nothing of the details of the plan."

"Except that it was to be today," added Julia pointedly.

"This could ruin everything," Émile said.

Peruggia stopped pacing and turned to Émile. "He still has time."

"But what shape will he be in?" Émile asked. "We'll have to put it off."

"We can't do that," said Julia.

"She's right," Peruggia agreed. "The time has come."

"But we can't do it without three people on the inside," Émile insisted.

"We *have* three people," Julia said.

"Not if Brique doesn't get back in time," Émile said, his exasperation growing, "or if he's incapable of—"

"It won't matter," Julia insisted. "We'll still have you, Signore Peruggia"—she paused before adding—"and me."

Émile's fist landed on the table. "Don't be ridiculous!"

Julia held up the palms of her hands to punctuate her reasoning. "What's the difference? Three is three."

"Three *men!*" Émile said, exasperated. "Three capable *men!*"

"Oh, your third man was really capable, let me tell you." Julia rolled her eyes.

"I'm telling you," Émile said, appealing to the others, "the plan is in serious trouble if Brique doesn't show up."

Peruggia had been watching this exchange with grim concentration.

"She's right," he said, his voice calm and even. "If he doesn't return within an hour, she'll have to take his place."

"Are you insane?" Émile blurted out. "We're supposed to be maintenance men, as in *men!*"

"She could go as a charwoman," suggested Madame Charneau.

"That wouldn't work," said Peruggia thoughtfully. "The charwomen never associate with the men. And they're not allowed to handle the paintings."

"There, you see," Émile said.

"This is a colossal waste of time," Julia said, rising from her seat. "Give me one of those caps."

Émile let out an irritated groan as Peruggia picked up one of three workman's caps sitting on the table. Julia took the cap, turned away, and pulled it onto her head, stuffing her hair beneath it. She paused and then turned back to the others.

"Time for you lazy bastards to get off your fat asses," she bellowed, lowering her voice to a husky pitch. "We've got work to do!"

Émile jumped to his feet and threw up his hands in dismay. "This is absurd," he said to the others. But Madame Charneau nodded her head in appreciation, and Peruggia, staring at Julia in cold appraisal, finally announced, "She'll do."

Chapter 23

After walking north to the river and crossing the Pont des Arts, they paid their entrance fee in the Cour Carrée and entered the Louvre. They had waited for Brique until midafternoon, but there had been no sign of him. Left with no other options, Émile reluctantly agreed to let Julia join them on the inside.

Their attire was respectably bourgeois and they easily blended in with the Sunday afternoon crowd thick with tourists. Julia wore a long dress and white blouse topped by a modest yet stylish hat. Peruggia carried a valise that, under more than casual scrutiny, might have seemed unusually large for a typical museum patron.

When Peruggia was out of earshot, Julia whispered a question in Émile's ear. "You did get a chance to test the key, didn't you?"

"You're not even supposed to be in here," he replied dismissively. "It's not your concern."

"But I am in here," she shot back, "and if that key doesn't work, then none of us will be able to get out."

"Just do your job and everything will be fine," Émile said before moving away from her toward Peruggia.

It was at this moment that Peruggia saw the museum director, Monsieur Montand, courting the favor of a haughty-looking older couple at the foot of the main staircase of the Denon wing. They had all been aware of the possibility of coming into contact with

Montand but had decided—taking into account the vast size of the Louvre—that it was a risk worth taking.

Unfortunately, they had no way of knowing that on Sundays the director made a point of hobnobbing with the society types who tended to visit following their morning church services.

Peruggia pulled down the brim of his cap and guided Émile and Julia past the director and up the broad staircase leading to the headless Winged Victory of Samothrace. Reaching the imposing statue, they turned right into a narrow gallery lit by open windows overlooking the Cour du Sphinx, a large interior courtyard. As they continued past an exhibit of Egyptian photographs in the small La Salle Duchâtel, Peruggia nodded his head to draw their attention briefly to a pair of large closet doors set into the wall.

They emerged into the Salon Carré, brilliantly lit by the skylights in the arched, rococo ceiling. The crowd jockeying for position in front of *La Joconde*—secure in her shadow box—was large even for a Sunday. Men tugged at their collars in the warm room while the women cooled themselves with fluted lace fans. A variation of the same sentence, "I didn't realize it was so small," was repeated in a myriad of languages. The three fell in behind the mass of people.

"I could make a fortune in this crowd," Julia whispered to Émile.

He gave her a threatening look.

"This is precisely why they don't allow any copying on Sundays," said Peruggia, peering over the backs of the crowd. "For one thing, there's nowhere for an artist to sit."

"At least it's easy to blend in," commented Julia.

The Italian checked his watch. "Almost closing time," he said and motioned for the others to follow him.

Peruggia led them back in the direction from which they came, but instead of turning into La Salle Duchâtel, he continued past it into the vast Galerie d'Apollon. Here they dallied beneath the ornate arched ceiling adorned with an array of panels paying homage to Louis XIV, the Sun King, until the last patron had exited. When the sound of footsteps died away, Peruggia nodded to the others and they retraced their steps into La Salle Duchâtel.

"Here it is." Peruggia indicated the double closet doors he had pointed out earlier. Below them on the ground floor, chiming bells announced closing time.

Peruggia pulled open one of the supply closet doors. Holding it open, he looked around the gallery as Émile and Julia slipped inside. Satisfied they had not been seen, Peruggia followed them in, pulling the door closed behind him.

The interior of the supply closet was pitch-black.

"Let's hope that device of yours works," Julia said in a half whisper.

"It'll work," Émile said, removing a metal cylinder from his pocket. "At least I hope it will."

Émile slid a switch forward on the cylinder. Instantly, a beam of light shot from his Ever-Ready electric hand torch.

"There, you see? It works."

"But will it *keep* working?" Julia asked.

"Of course it will," Émile replied with some irritation, "it's American. They're very good at this sort of thing."

"I brought candles just in case," Peruggia added.

The museum allowed students and copyists to store their paraphernalia in the closet, which was the size of a small bedchamber. Boxes, easels, paint supplies, and canvases took up most of the space.

"Where are we supposed to sleep?" Julia asked as Peruggia and Émile lowered themselves onto the floor.

"Anywhere you can," Peruggia answered.

"You're the one who wanted to come," Émile reminded her.

"Well, move your feet, you're taking up half the closet," Julia retorted, trying to lower herself into a comfortable position. "I still don't understand why we can't just wait a few hours and take the painting tonight."

"The floors creak," Peruggia said. "The guards who patrol at night would hear us."

Julia gave Émile's foot a kick. "You have to move your legs."

"Be quiet," Peruggia snapped. "Listen."

Everyone held their breath. From the hallway outside came the sound of approaching footsteps.

"The light!" Peruggia hissed.

Émile fumbled for a moment before finding the switch and sliding it off, plunging them once again into what should have been complete darkness. However, a narrow vertical slit of light penetrated the room. One of the closet doors had swung open slightly.

The footsteps stopped and the door creaked slowly open. Silhouetted against the dim light of the corridor was the form of a man wearing a guard's kepi. He stood motionless, peering into the gloom.

It was at this moment that Julia's feet—which she had drawn up close to her body—suddenly slipped forward, making a scraping sound. The guard drew back in alarm. An instant later, a small animal scurried out of the door over the guard's feet. Emitting an oath, the guard drew back and slammed the door shut. The footsteps rapidly receded down the hallway until the only noise in the room was the sound of their own breathing.

"What was that?" Julia said in a tense whisper.

"A rat," Peruggia said.

"You're not afraid of rats, are you?" asked Émile.

"Not with you to protect me."

"He was more afraid of us," said Peruggia.

"There's another one," said Julia suddenly.

Émile jumped as he felt the thing scampering up his arm. With a muffled gasp, he fumbled for the switch on his electric torch. He slid it on and saw Julia's fingers skittering up toward his shoulder.

"Stop being such an idiot," Émile growled. "You'll give us away."

"Sorry, I couldn't resist."

"If you're finished playing games," said Peruggia, "we need to get some sleep. We have much to do tomorrow."

They tried to maneuver themselves into comfortable positions, but it proved next to impossible. Julia settled into a cramped, almost fetal arrangement, grimacing as she inhaled the musty, humid air. It was going to be a long night.

Chapter 24

The match flared in the darkness, releasing a small cloud of sulfurous fumes. Peruggia held it up, and the weak halo of light revealed Émile curled up fast asleep, his head in Julia's lap. Julia groaned slightly and shifted her body but resisted waking. Peruggia transferred the flame to a candle and pulled out his watch. After checking the time, he kicked Émile's foot.

"Wake up."

Émile didn't stir, but Julia's eyes opened, first one and then the other as she adjusted to the candlelight and reoriented herself. She looked down and saw Émile's head in her lap. Smiling, she began to gently stroke his hair.

"Wake up, sleepyhead," she purred with exaggerated familiarity.

Émile shifted in search of a more comfortable position. His eyes flickered open, peered into the folds of Julia's dress, and closed again.

"Comfy?" she asked.

Émile grunted. Then his eyes shot wide open. Suddenly very much awake, he jerked up to a sitting position.

"What . . ." he stammered, "what was I . . . I didn't realize . . ."

"That's all right," said Julia with a grin. "At least you're not a rat."

"You should have pushed me away."

"But you looked so peaceful," she said with a mocking lilt to her voice, "just like a little baby."

"We need to get started," said Peruggia.

Peruggia removed half a baguette and a small flask of wine from his valise, which they quickly shared. Then they started removing their jackets as Peruggia produced three bundles of clothing. Julia immediately began to unbutton her shirt. Still a little dazed, Émile found himself staring at her.

"Maybe you should switch on your flashlight," she said lightly. "You'll have a better view."

Even in the dim light, she could see the mortified look on Émile's face as he quickly turned away. "As if I would even be interested."

"Don't worry," said Peruggia, "these tunics will cover everything."

"It's just as well," Julia said, making a face at Émile as she rebuttoned her shirt.

The two men pulled rough trousers over their own before donning the long white blouses and workmen's caps that comprised the uniform of a museum maintenance man. Julia had to bunch up her skirt when she pulled on her pants. Luckily, the bulge around her waist was covered by the oversized blouse, which went down almost to her knees.

"How do I look?" she asked, gathering her hair up beneath her cap.

"Fine," Peruggia answered.

"Just try to keep your mouth shut," Émile added pointedly. "Even though I know how difficult that is for you."

"Someone got up on the wrong side of the floor," Julia commented.

Peruggia stuffed their jackets along with the hat Julia had been wearing into his valise. "We're ready. Make sure you've left nothing behind."

Satisfied, Peruggia kneeled at the door and listened. He nodded to the others and snuffed out the candle.

Peruggia slowly eased the door open. The closet filled with the pale early morning light that seeped through the windows overlooking the Cour du Sphinx.

"We have five minutes before the museum doors open," he said quietly.

Émile and Julia rose and followed Peruggia into La Salle Duchâtel. While their eyes adjusted to the daylight, they gingerly stretched their limbs in an attempt to work out the cramps left by the long, uncomfortable night. Peruggia checked Émile's outfit, then Julia's. Her blouse was large and her cap a bit too big for her head, but he nodded his satisfaction.

"Émile is right," Peruggia said. "Best to let us do all the talking. Are you both ready?"

Julia and Émile looked at each other, then nodded their heads in assent.

"Good," said Peruggia. "It won't be long now."

Behind one of the museum's smaller arched entrances on the quai du Louvre, François Picquet checked his pocket watch. It was almost time. He smoothed out his newly pressed suit. As head maintenance supervisor, he no longer had to wear a white blouse, and he looked forward to the day when he could afford a new suit. The one he wore was not exactly shabby, but it was dangerously close to becoming so.

At precisely seven o'clock, he threw open the doors of the gate. Immediately, a small army of white-bloused workmen and drably bundled charwomen sorted themselves into a ragged line. The men came in first, each touching his cap or beret as his name was checked off against the list that Picquet held in his hands. The women followed, lifting their long skirts as they shuffled by. It was a particularly large group today as was always the case on the first Monday of the month.

Outside, a guard addressed two very disappointed tourists. "I'm sorry," he said officiously, "but the museum is always closed on Mondays."

Upstairs on the first floor, Peruggia had positioned himself, Émile, and Julia at various places around the large landing presided over by the Winged Victory. He waited until a group of maintenance workers flowed up the wide staircase before nodding to the others. As the workers reached the main landing and began filtering off to the left and to the right, Peruggia and Émile stepped out and blended in with them. When Julia emerged from behind a statue, however, she collided with a large man balancing a length of pipe over his shoulder. The man uttered a muffled oath as she staggered backward.

Julia regained her balance and forced herself to keep her face turned away from him. "Look where you're going, you big oaf!" she said, keeping her voice as husky and low as she possibly could.

The man spat out another epithet and continued on. Émile looked back and, with a terse jerk of his head, signaled her to keep up with them. The three walked back through La Salle Duchâtel, turned into the Salon Carré and up to *La Joconde* as maintenance workers continued to stream in behind them. For a moment, they stood silently before the painting, their gazes fixed on the lady's penetrating yet evasive eyes.

"Now what?" Julia whispered.

"Now," Peruggia said slowly and deliberately, without taking his eyes off the painting, "we take it off the wall."

Julia turned to him.

"That's it?" she said. "That's your plan? Just take it off the wall?"

Peruggia slowly turned his head and gave her a hard look. Then he looked at Émile and spoke in a low, warning tone. "And try not to drop it."

Julia looked around apprehensively as Peruggia put his valise down and he and Émile took positions on either side of the shadow box. Taking hold of the frame, the two men began to lift it from the wall.

Émile grimaced. "I didn't know it would be this heavy."

"I told you," Peruggia said. "The shadow box alone weighs almost forty kilos."

Émile shook his head. "It's not coming off."

"We have to lift together."

"Be careful," Julia added.

Émile gave her a look. "Thanks for the advice."

"Are you ready?" asked Peruggia. "I'll count to three."

"You mean one, two, three, and then heave, or one—"

But Peruggia had already begun his count. "One, two, three!"

Together they lifted the shadow box off its pegs. Émile, however, had not prepared himself properly for the weight and he stumbled and faltered, trying desperately to maintain his grip. Julia stepped quickly forward and reached out to support the box, keeping it from slipping from his hands.

"Put it down," Peruggia said, and the three of them gently lowered it to the floor. Julia looked to Émile, but his eyes caught hers for only an instant.

"You're welcome," she said.

Peruggia looked around. There were four other people in the room, all charwomen, two mopping the floor, and two cleaning the glass on other shadow boxes. None of them seemed particularly interested in the fact that the three of them had just removed the Louvre's most celebrated painting from the wall.

"Ready?" Peruggia asked.

Émile nodded and the two men knelt down, renewed their grip on each end of the shadow box, and lifted it off the floor. Adjusting their grip to balance the weight between them, they shuffled down the gallery like a pair of furniture movers, Peruggia walking backward. Julia picked up Peruggia's valise and followed. It took only a few steps to reach the end of the Salon Carré and the entrance to the Grande Galerie. However, before they could pass through, Picquet, the maintenance supervisor, suddenly stepped around the corner into their path.

"What is this?" Picquet demanded. "Where do you think you're going?"

Knowing he would be recognized, Peruggia could only lower his head and look down at the floor. Émile opened his mouth to speak but nothing came out.

"Well?"

Julia took a step forward. "We're taking it to the photographers' studio," she said in a raspy voice.

The pause that followed seemed to stretch out forever.

Picquet finally spoke. "Again? Don't they have enough photographs already?"

Julia shrugged. "I just do what I'm told."

"Who are you, anyway?" Picquet asked. "One of the new boys?"

"Just started today," Julia answered.

Picquet looked her up and down and then turned to the others. "All right." He stepped aside. "Go ahead." As they shuffled past him, Picquet added, "But tell them down there to let me know in advance the next time."

Once inside the Grande Galerie, the trio turned immediately to their right into a long, narrow gallery known as Salle des Sept-Mètres. Immediately to their right was a double door with ACCÈS INTERDIT stenciled across it. Julia pulled one of the doors open and the two men carried the box onto a small landing above a stairwell leading downward. With a quick look around to make sure no one was watching, Julia followed them in, closing the door behind her.

"That was close," Émile said as he and Peruggia lowered the shadow box to the ground.

"I couldn't speak," said Peruggia. "He might have recognized my voice."

"And what was your excuse?" Julia asked Émile pointedly. "Cat get your tongue?"

"We have work to do," Peruggia said before Émile could respond.

Peruggia knelt and removed some tools from his valise.

"How much time do we have?" asked Julia.

"With good luck, the whole morning," Peruggia replied as he worked a slender crowbar into a join on the shadow box.

"And what if someone decides to pay a visit to the photographers' studio?" asked Émile with a glance at Julia.

"That," Peruggia began, trying to pry the back cover off the box, "would be more along the lines of bad luck."

"It's all I could think of," said Julia. "I remembered what Diego said about his friend."

"You did well," said Peruggia as a nail popped out of the back cover and clinked to the floor. "Put your hand in there and pull," he directed Émile.

Émile placed his fingers in the widening gap between the rear cover and the box frame and tugged. With a creak, the cover came loose, revealing the back of the framed panel. Julia took note of the crucifixlike repair as Peruggia eased it from the box. He produced a small screwdriver and removed four small screws that attached metal straps to short wooden strips glued to the back of the panel, freeing it from its frame. He turned the panel over and stared at it for a moment. Then he looked up at Émile and Julia with an expression of quiet satisfaction.

"Now it looks even smaller," observed Julia.

"Which is good for us," said Peruggia.

Émile stacked the discarded frame and the remains of the shadow box against the wall in a dark corner of the landing. Peruggia stood and slipped the panel beneath his long white blouse. On close examination, a rectangular outline could be discerned, but the painting would be well concealed from the casual observer.

Peruggia nodded to the others and led them down the stairs. After a number of winding turns they came to another door.

"This is the door to the courtyard," said Peruggia.

He grabbed the handle and tried to turn it. As expected, it was locked.

Peruggia turned to Émile. "The key."

Émile removed a shiny new brass key from his pocket and placed it into the lock. For a moment he had trouble getting it in.

"Hurry," said Julia.

He tried again and this time the key slipped in all the way. He turned it. It moved only a fraction before stopping dead. Émile added more force, but no matter how hard he tried, the key would not turn in the lock.

Peruggia and Julia stood frozen, staring at him.

"It's a little stiff," Émile said, straining to turn the key. It still wouldn't budge.

"I thought you said you tried it before," said Julia.

"I never said I tried it." Émile frantically jiggled the key. "I wanted to, but there were always too many people around."

"I don't believe this," Julia groaned.

"It's an exact copy." Émile put all his might behind it this time. "It should work."

Still nothing.

"Maybe you took the wrong key," Émile said to Julia.

"No," said Peruggia, "the large keys the guards carry should work on all outside doors."

An edge of panic crept into Émile's voice. "Then maybe they've changed the lock."

"We need to get that door open now," said Julia.

Peruggia pointed to the valise that Julia was holding. "Hand me that."

He snapped open the valise and removed a large screwdriver. Pushing Émile aside, he knelt down and began to unscrew the door handle plate.

"I'm telling you," said Émile, "there must be something wrong with the lock. The key should have worked."

"Listen," Julia whispered, placing a hand on Peruggia's shoulder. "Do you hear that?"

They all froze. Julia looked from Émile to Peruggia as the cold grip of fear clutched her heart.

A clatter of footsteps floated up from the stairwell. Someone was coming.

Chapter 25

Hurry," Émile whispered frantically.

Peruggia continued to work the screwdriver. "I've almost got it," he said.

The footsteps grew louder.

"What do we do now?" asked Julia, her voice choked with desperation.

"*Santa María!*" Peruggia cursed as the doorknob came loose and clattered to the floor. At the same moment, a man turned the corner, stepped up onto the landing, and stopped dead in his tracks.

He was in his sixties with thinning gray hair and a large white handlebar mustache. Taking in the scene through rheumy, bulging eyes, he resembled nothing so much as a Rembrandt portrait come to life. His stained blouse and large plumber's wrench clutched in one hand revealed his profession.

No one moved or spoke. The plumber looked down at the exposed lock mechanism and sighed.

"You'd think they would have fixed this door by now," he said with a resigned weariness. "Do you have a pair of pliers?"

Exchanging glances with the others, Peruggia took a pair of pliers from his valise and offered it to him. The plumber put down his wrench, took the pliers, and clamped them onto the mechanism.

With his other hand, he produced a key from a pocket of his blouse and inserted it into the lock. He worked both the pliers and the key until he heard a distinct and satisfying click. Then he pushed the door ajar, letting in a sharp beam of outside light.

"Better leave it open," the old plumber said as he handed the pliers back to Peruggia, "in case anyone else needs to go through."

And with a weary shake of his head, he replaced the key in his pocket, picked up his wrench, and continued up the stairs.

The three watched him disappear around a corner before turning to look at each other.

"Well," Julia said, stepping through the door past the two men, "after me."

"That was a bit of luck," said Émile, following her out.

Peruggia only grunted his agreement as he trailed Émile into a small, open courtyard ringed with thick, tall bushes. At one end of the courtyard, a long arched passageway led out to the street. Through this small arcade they could see the quai du Louvre and the Pont du Carrousel spanning the Seine.

"This courtyard is not accessible to the main areas of the museum so it's always unguarded," said Peruggia.

"Is that so," said Julia. "Then who's that?"

Julia nodded in the direction of the passageway. Peruggia and Émile turned in time to see a uniformed guard step out of a small glass-enclosed kiosk set into the wall halfway up the arcade. They retreated behind the bushes as the guard stretched his arms and shoulders before disappearing back inside.

"We'll never get past him," said Émile.

"This is something new," added Peruggia, "and really bad luck for us."

"Then it's time we started making our own luck," said Julia. She removed her cap, pulled her workman's blouse up and over her head, and stepped out of her rough pants. Handing the clothes to Émile, she straightened her skirt and shook out her hair.

"Get my jacket and hat out."

Peruggia removed the articles from the valise and she put them on, adjusting them as best she could.

"Give me five minutes," she said.

"What are you going to do?" asked Émile.

"Keep your eyes on me and you'll find out at the same time that I do."

She edged along the wall to the archway and slowly poked her head around the corner for a view of the guard's kiosk and the street beyond. He stood inside, hunched over a tall desk with his back to her. Turning briefly to look at Peruggia and Émile, she took a deep breath. Then she carefully stepped out from behind the wall, making a point of facing into the courtyard with her back toward the passageway and the street. Looking over her shoulder, her eyes fixed on the kiosk, she began to tiptoe slowly backward.

Émile and Peruggia exchanged puzzled looks. "What does she think she's doing?" Émile whispered.

Peruggia shrugged and shook his head.

With measured steps, Julia moved steadily in reverse, straining her neck to keep the back of the guard's head in sight. If only he would remain like that a little longer. Only a few more steps to go.

The man shifted his position. Julia stopped, holding her breath, but he did not turn. She waited a few seconds before she resumed walking backward. After five or six more steps, she was almost level with the kiosk when her foot landed on a large pebble, causing it to scrape across the cobblestones beneath her feet. A split second before the guard turned, she turned her head to face forward and reversed direction so that now she was walking normally from the street into the courtyard.

"Mademoiselle," the guard said with surprise, "I didn't see you come in. You can't enter through here."

"Oh," said Julia, her eyes wide with innocence. "Isn't this the entrance to the museum?"

"No, it most certainly is not," he replied, stepping out of his kiosk, "and besides, the museum is closed today."

The guard was perhaps forty and sported a trim pencil-thin

mustache. His tight-fitting uniform, shiny with age, had probably fitted him perfectly ten years ago.

"Oh, but I had so hoped to see all the pretty paintings," she cooed.

"I'm sorry, mademoiselle," the guard said, "but you must come back tomorrow and use one of the main entrances."

"Oh, but I'm here now," she said, pouting. "Are you sure you can't bend the rules a little . . . just for me?"

"It's . . . out of the question," the man said, his officious façade cracking a little. "The museum is closed."

"What a pity," she said in resignation. "And, on top of that, I think I'm lost."

"You are at the Louvre Museum, mademoiselle, as you must know."

He tugged at his tunic in a vain attempt to appear more authoritative.

"Of course. But I was supposed to visit a friend afterward on rue de Chartres, and I have no idea where it is."

The guard suddenly brightened. "Ah, now there I can help you. I have a map."

"A map," Julia repeated like an excited child. "What luck that you happened to be here. And with a map no less!"

"Of course," he said, beaming. "Here, I'll show you."

The kiosk was small, barely large enough for two people. The guard went in first. As Julia stepped in to follow him, she glanced back into the courtyard. Peruggia was watching her, his head sticking out slightly from behind a bush. With a small gesture of her hand, she beckoned him on.

"Now let's see, rue de Chartres," said the guard, unfolding a map onto the narrow shelf that served as his desk. "I must admit, I'm not familiar with it."

"Oh, it's very small," Julia said. "Perhaps it's not even on your map."

"No," he said with great confidence, "if it's in Paris, it will be on the map."

As the guard squinted at the unfolded map, Julia stole a look behind her. Peruggia and Émile were slowly and silently tiptoeing up the arcade toward the street. She carefully shifted her position slightly to help block them from the guard's view as they came abreast of the kiosk.

"You are so kind, monsieur," Julia said in a lilting voice.

"*De rien, mademoiselle.* Now, if I could only find your street . . ."

Julia glanced backward again. Peruggia and Émile were almost level with the door of the kiosk but in a matter of seconds would be in a position where it would be almost impossible for the guard not to see them.

Julia looked around the tiny area. She thrust her arm in front of the guard's downturned face and pointed to the back wall. "What's that?"

"Eh?" the guard said, his view of the passageway blocked by Julia's outstretched arm.

"That. On the wall."

The guard turned to look. Julia's finger pointed to a sheet of paper pinned to a vertical wooden support. Scribbled on it was a list of names and times.

"Why, that's our schedule, mademoiselle, with the names of all the guards and their times of duty."

"Which one is you?" Julia asked, as if it were the most fascinating thing in the world.

"That's me there," the guard said, proudly pointing. "Alfred Bellew. Seven in the morning till twelve."

"How exciting," Julia exclaimed, glancing backward in time to see Émile and Peruggia walk through the far entrance into the street.

"Indeed," said the guard, a little unsure how to react. "But the map . . . we still have to find your street."

Julia looked down and randomly picked out a street name near the museum.

"Oh, but I am being too silly," she pronounced. "It is rue Bonaparte, not rue de Chartres."

"But that is right here." The guard indicated a spot on the map. "Just cross the Pont du Carrousel and turn left. The street will be the second one on your right. You can't miss it."

"I don't know how to thank you, monsieur," Julia purred as she stepped from the kiosk and backed away toward the street. "You are so kind, and may I say, very handsome as well."

This had the desired effect of flustering the man even more. "Well, you may say it, of course, but you are the one who is kind, as well as quite enchanting, if I may be so bold."

"I believe you are trying to charm me, monsieur," Julia said with a flirtatious smile and a disapproving wag of her finger. "And, if that is so, then you are succeeding."

By now she had reached the street, the guard following behind her like a smitten puppy dog.

"Perhaps, when I return tomorrow to see the paintings," she added, "I may come and pay you a visit."

"I would be delighted, mademoiselle," he said. "In fact, come to this gate and I'll get you in without having to pay."

She started down the street and glanced back at him. "I wouldn't want to get you into any trouble."

"I'll be expecting you," he called out.

With a final flourish, she threw him a kiss. The man watched her for a moment as she crossed the street onto the Pont du Carrousel. Then he let out a heavy sigh before reluctantly returning to his post.

Walking briskly across the bridge, Julia scanned the throng of people walking along the quai Voltaire, but there was no sign of Émile and Peruggia. No doubt Peruggia was hurrying on ahead to meet Madame Charneau, who was waiting for them in Valfierno's motorcar on rue des Saints-Pères. Émile would stay with him, knowing it was imperative to keep him in sight now that he had the painting.

Reaching the Left Bank, she passed a street artist hawking a number of crudely rendered paintings.

"Special today," the man said, holding out a pathetic copy of *La Joconde*. "Only fifteen francs for the lady!"

"No, thank you, monsieur," Julia said, hurrying past him. "I already have one."

Chapter 26

Madame Charneau had barely opened the door to her house in the cour de Rohan when Peruggia pushed past her into the foyer. He removed the panel from beneath his blouse and bounded up the stairs, hugging it tightly to his chest. The others entered the house in time to hear the door to his room close behind him.

"What's gotten into him?" Émile said quietly. "He hasn't said a word since we left the museum."

"I thought we'd have more time to make the switch," said Madame Charneau.

"Where did you put the copy?" Émile asked Julia.

"In the attic," she replied. "We're going to have to work fast."

Julia led Émile up the stairs. On the first floor, they stopped at Peruggia's room. Émile nodded to Julia, who knocked on the door. After a moment, the door swung open a few inches and Peruggia peered out.

"Yes? What do you want?"

Julia thought she detected an element of suspicion in his tone.

"To come in," Émile said as cheerfully as he could.

"Why?"

"To celebrate, of course," Julia chimed in.

Peruggia hesitated for a moment before pulling the door open to let them in. He immediately went to an open trunk that had been pulled out from beneath his bed. The painting lay on the mattress face-up. Peruggia knelt down, lifted the panel, and placed it into the trunk.

"We should think of a safe place to hide it," Julia suggested.

"Perhaps we should store it in the attic," said Émile, as if the idea had just occurred to him.

Peruggia said nothing. He covered the panel with some folded shirts, closed the lid, and locked it with a key.

"It will be safe here," he said, sliding the trunk back under the bed. He rose and slipped the key into his jacket pocket. "I'm not going to leave this room. I'll take my meals in here."

"That's hardly necessary," said Émile. "I really think the attic—"

But Peruggia stopped him with a stony look. "I told the marquis I would wait, and I will. But not forever. The next time I leave this room, it will be to return *La Gioconda* to its rightful home."

"Of course, but . . ." Émile began before Julia cut him off.

"I'm sure with Signore Peruggia watching over it, it will be perfectly safe," she said with a pointed look to Émile. "After all, without him, it would still be hanging in the museum. We are all grateful indeed." And then, without warning, she turned and threw her arms around Peruggia, catching him by surprise with a tight hug.

"Well, I think we all must be tired," she said, drawing back, collecting Émile, and retreating to the door. "Perhaps we should postpone our celebration for another time. Thank you for all you've done, signore."

As soon as the door closed behind them, Peruggia sat down on the bed. Still wearing his shoes, he swung his legs up and lay on his back, staring up at the ceiling.

Émile pulled Julia away from the door and whispered frantically, "Now what?"

Julia opened the palm of her hand, revealing Peruggia's trunk key. Émile smiled.

"I'll have to return it to him when I bring up his meal," she said, "so be quick. And make sure you do it right this time."

"Don't worry," Émile said with confidence. "This one will be *my* masterpiece."

Part IV

A plague upon it when thieves cannot be true one to another!
—Shakespeare, *Henry IV, Part I*

Chapter 27

For Louis Beroud, Tuesdays never varied. He prided himself on being first in line when the Louvre opened its doors, and he always spent the day seated in front of this masterpiece or that trying to emulate the brushstrokes of the artist. This morning, however, he was delayed by an issue with his landlady. She was going to raise the rent on the first of the following month. This was an announcement with potentially catastrophic implications.

Monsieur Beroud designed his life to be as predictable as a mathematical equation. Ten years ago a distant uncle had died and left him a modest inheritance. It was enough to free him from the normal constraints of steady employment and allow him to indulge himself in his favorite pastime, painting. This did not, however, come without sacrifice on his part. His endowment would last only if he lived under the most spartan conditions. He rented a one-room garret in the Montparnasse district, assembled his wardrobe from only six articles of clothing, and dined solely on soup, bread, cheese, and the cheapest of cheap red wine. These economies bought him time to spend his days wandering about Paris painting whatever took his fancy. Tuesdays were always spent at the Louvre. Though his talents were minimal, his regard for them was prodigious, and this was enough for Monsieur Beroud.

Taking the time to remind his landlady that he had been a loyal tenant for eight years and had no intention of paying more than he already did caused him to arrive at the museum ten minutes after the doors had opened. By the time he reached the supply closet in La Salle Duchâtel, a line had already formed and he was forced to wait for the artists who had arrived earlier to gather their tools before he could collect his. Under the watchful eye of a museum guard, the group of eight or nine men gathered up their easels, paints, and brushes from the closet. When Beroud's turn finally came, he saw one man whose name he had forgotten still rooting about in the supplies.

"Beroud," the man said, "my brushes are not where I left them. Are any of yours missing?"

"No, they're all here," Beroud said as he quickly assembled his paraphernalia and left the man to grumble to himself in the closet.

Trying to make up for lost time, Beroud walked briskly into the Salon Carré and was pleased to note that no one else had chosen to set up there this morning. He stopped at his favorite spot, put down his supplies, and opened a small canvas stool. Setting up his easel, he placed a small wooden panel upon it and arranged his palette, paints, and brushes. Satisfied, he sat down and made the final adjustments. Only then did he look up at the wall.

His face collapsed with disappointment. Between the Correggio on the left and the Titian on the right there was nothing but four iron pegs and a ghostly rectangular outline where the wall was slightly darker. *La Joconde* was gone.

Beroud immediately sought out a guard to complain. The guard informed Monsieur Montand. The museum director checked for himself but was only mildly irritated to see the empty space on the wall. He summoned Monsieur Picquet, the head maintenance man, and asked for an explanation.

"There is no need to worry, monsieur," Picquet told the director with a confident air. "The photographers had *La Joconde* brought down to their studio yesterday."

The director, who in general did not approve of the modern science of photography, was not pleased to hear this. "They had it down there not two months ago. How many more infernal photographs do they need?"

The question did not require an answer, but Picquet was unacquainted with the finer points of rhetoric.

"I'm sure I don't know, Monsieur Director."

His irritation growing by the minute, Montand descended through the ground-floor entresol to the labyrinth of catacombs at the lowest level of the museum, all that remained of the medieval fortress upon which King Philip II had built his original palace. Reaching the end of a dimly lit sandstone passageway, he strode into the photographers' studio and was immediately struck by the strong odor of the chemicals used to process the glass plates. Monsieur Duval, the official museum photographer, was placing one of the new Autochrome plates developed by the Lumière brothers into a large bellows camera. A Rubens rested on an easel set up in front of him. A young apprentice stood to one side ready to make adjustments.

"I've told you previously," Montand began in his most officious voice, "that I need to be informed at least a day in advance before you remove any of the major exhibits."

Duval gave Montand a disdainful look before going back to his work. "I told you about this one last week," he said in a voice that suggested that he did not appreciate pointless interruptions.

"Not *this* one," Montand said, his impatience rising. *"La Joconde."*

"It's not on our list for months yet. We'll let you know in good time."

"I need it returned immediately!"

"That may be so, but I cannot help you."

The man's unconcerned attitude irritated Montand even further.

"You do realize that today is Tuesday! Half the art students in Paris will be here before the morning is out expecting to copy it!"

"That is not my affair, monsieur," Duval said as he adjusted the lens on his camera.

"Ah, but there you are mistaken. It is my affair, and what is my affair is your affair."

Duval shrugged. "Even so, I cannot be of assistance."

"And why not?"

"For the obvious reason that it is not here."

"What do you mean, it's not here?"

"It is a simple statement, monsieur, though I am happy to repeat it for you. It is not here."

Montand started to breathe in short, rapid gasps.

"Then if it's not here," he said, trying in vain to suppress his rising anxiety, "where is it?"

An hour later, Inspector Alphonse Carnot of the Sûreté strode into the Cour Carrée with four smartly dressed gendarmes in tow. Monsieur Montand, flanked by the senior museum guards, waited for him in the center of the room.

"Inspector," Montand began, but Carnot cut him off.

"Monsieur Director," the inspector began harshly, "why do I still see people milling about in the other galleries? You should have closed the museum by now."

"That would have been totally impractical," Montand said, a little flustered. "We have closed the Denon wing of course, but I saw no reason to cause undue alarm."

"The entire museum must be closed at once," Carnot continued. "The commissioner of police himself will join us within the hour. He will be most displeased if it is not."

Montand was not happy with this turn of events. It was still possible that the painting was misplaced somewhere in the museum. Clearing out all the patrons at this point might be an extreme overreaction.

"Well," Carnot said, "what are you waiting for?"

Reluctantly, Montand turned to his head guard. "Do as he says."

"But Monsieur Director . . ." the guard began.

"At once!" Montand ordered.

The guard snapped to attention, turned on his heels, and hurried smartly off.

"Now," Carnot said, smugly satisfied, "shall we proceed?"

As the last disgruntled patrons were being escorted from the museum, the commissioner of the Sûreté himself, Jean Lepine, accompanied by a small entourage of plain-clothed assistants, entered the Denon wing. He wasted no time in locating Inspector Carnot in the Salon Carré. At six feet, with a shaved head and compensatory handlebar mustache, Lepine towered over the inspector in more ways than one.

"Inspector Carnot," he bellowed, skipping any pleasantries, "your report, please!"

"Commissioner," Carnot began, "the head maintenance man, Picquet, reports seeing a group of three men dressed as janitors carrying the painting yesterday morning. The museum is always closed on Mondays for—"

"Yes, yes," the commissioner broke in. "Continue with your report!"

Carnot cleared his throat. "These men informed Picquet that they were delivering it to the photographers' studio downstairs, a routine occurrence. It was never delivered. In my opinion, Commissioner, this was an inside job."

The commissioner gave Montand a disdainful look before turning back to Carnot. "Solving this crime as quickly as possible and recovering *La Joconde* is of the utmost importance. I will not tolerate any mistakes in this investigation."

"Of course not, Commissioner."

With perfect timing, a young gendarme stepped up, snapped to attention, and saluted the commissioner.

"Inspector," he began, turning to Carnot, "some of the copyists report that their equipment has been rearranged in the supply closet."

"The thieves must have used it as a hiding place before the theft," observed Carnot.

"We have also located the empty frame and its shadow box in a stairwell," the gendarme continued. "And furthermore, we have found a fingerprint on the glass."

"Excellent," Carnot exclaimed. "Now we have them."

"A what?" the commissioner asked impatiently.

"A fingerprint, Commissioner," explained Carnot, reveling in the knowledge that he knew something that his superior did not. "It is a new science. The lines on each man's fingertips are unlike any others, and—"

"But how will that help us?" the commissioner demanded.

"Anticipating just such an eventuality, for the last year, I have taken the fingerprints of each and every employee of the museum. If, as I suspect, this is an inside job, we'll have our man within a day, I promise you."

"See that you do," said the commissioner.

Carnot could only smile uncomfortably. Now he would have no choice but to deliver on his hasty promise.

Chapter 28

The Prefecture of Police shared the Île de la Cité with three structures that dated back to the Middle Ages and defined the soul of Paris: the forbidding Conciergerie, the church of Sainte-Chapelle, and that most divine of structures, the Cathedral of Notre-Dame. The island and its sister, the Île Saint-Louis, both sat tethered by numerous bridges in the middle of the River Seine like two stately dowagers. They had always been the heart, the cradle of Paris, the spiritual center of all of France. Here, the Roman legions conquered the Parissi tribe shortly after the time of Christ; here, the original inhabitants of the city took refuge from Barbarian and Viking attacks; here, in the Conciergerie itself, Marie Antoinette spent her final hours before her fatal appointment with Madame Guillotine; and here, Inspector Carnot hoped to impress Police Commissioner Lepine by exposing the man who stole *La Joconde*.

The inspector stood in front of a white wall in a third-floor room of the prefecture. In the middle of the room, a young gendarme named Brousard, who often assisted Carnot, readied two primitive projectors, known as magic lanterns, on a table. Another gendarme stood at the ready by the window, and at a separate table sat Commissioner Lepine himself along with various members of his staff. Unfortunately, a sudden change in the commissioner's schedule had precluded a run-through of the presentation. In spite of this, and a tingle of excited apprehension, Carnot felt confident. He knew the commissioner was skeptical about so-called scientific innovations and that only a concrete demonstration of their usefulness could convince him of their value. Though he wished he had more time to prepare, here was the perfect opportunity for such a demonstration.

The art of fingerprinting had been in use since the 1850s when an English magistrate in India instructed two illiterate merchants to seal the agreement they were entering into by making ink impressions of their palms on a contract. By 1901, fingerprints were being used in England to identify criminals, and on a visit to Scotland Yard in London during the course of an investigation, Inspector Carnot had witnessed the fingerprinting of suspects.

Thinking that he might be able to use this new technique to distinguish himself and further his career, he had tried to introduce the new science at the Sûreté. His ideas had been met with indifference, if not downright skepticism.

His superiors still put their faith in anthropometry, the science of identifying a repeat offender by keeping precise measurements of his physical characteristics, such as his height and the length of his ear. Never mind the occasional innocent doppelgänger sent, at best, to Devil's Island or, at worst, to the guillotine. Justice was never meant to be perfect, only consistent.

Carnot had been undeterred by resistance to the new science of fingerprinting and had taken it upon himself to learn as much as he could about the procedure. He had persevered and, though it was yet to be widely accepted by his colleagues, he had used it himself on occasion, albeit with little success so far.

While investigating a minor theft at the Louvre a year earlier, he had convinced Director Montand to adopt the policy of routinely fingerprinting all employees of the museum. He carefully compiled and filed these fingerprints in the event they would ever be needed. And now that time—and his opportunity—had arrived.

Satisfied that all was ready, Carnot motioned to the gendarme standing by the window. The man pulled down a shade, darkening the room.

"You may begin," Carnot said to Brousard. The young gendarme turned a knob on the lantern, and a large image of a single fingerprint was projected onto the wall.

"This is our man," said Carnot with authority. "His fingerprint was recovered from the glass of the shadow box that held *La Joconde*. By applying a fine talcum powder, and then carefully brushing it off, the fingerprint is revealed. It is then lifted from the surface by the application of transparent cellulose film. This image, of course, is magnified many times over."

The concentric whorls of the fingerprint reminded Carnot of the modern art that had recently come into fashion. Impressionism or something or other, though personally he preferred paintings that actually resembled the objects they were supposed to represent. He nodded to Brousard, who turned a knob on the other projector, and another large fingerprint appeared next to the first.

"This is the fingerprint of one of the almost one hundred employees who have worked at the Louvre in the last year. We simply pressed their fingertips into an inkpad and then onto a thin paper."

Carnot gestured with a wooden ruler. "By comparing the lines, here and here, we can see if the two prints match. As you can see, this one clearly does not. Next, please."

Brousard advanced to the next slide. "Again, as we can clearly see by these patterns, this is also not our man."

The commissioner exchanged impatient glances with his staff. "How long will this take?"

"I shouldn't think much longer, Commissioner." Carnot felt himself beginning to sweat.

A dozen or so prints flickered by with no success. Carnot tried to maintain his confidence as the commissioner grew increasingly fidgety. A few dozen more went by with no matches. At this point, Brousard got to his feet, walked to Carnot, and whispered something in his ear. Carnot's face suddenly drained of all its color.

"Are you sure?" Carnot asked in hushed tones.

"Yes. I'm quite sure."

"Why didn't you mention something before?"

"I only just noticed it, Inspector."

"What's going on?" the commissioner demanded.

Brousard withdrew, and a shaken Carnot gestured to the gendarme by the window to raise the shade. He did so, causing the room's occupants to shield their eyes against the glare.

"Well?" said the commissioner. "Why have you stopped?"

"I am afraid, Commissioner," Carnot began, in a choked voice, "that we may have a small problem."

"What sort of problem?"

"It would seem," he said, drawing a deep breath, "that the print we found was from the thief's left hand."

"And?"

"And, the fingerprints from the workers at the Louvre"—he held his breath for a moment—"were taken from their right hands only."

"And this makes a difference?"

"I'm afraid, Commissioner . . . it does."

The commissioner gave Carnot a long contemptuous look. Carnot could almost hear the door slamming shut on his promotion aspirations. The commissioner would reward exceptional work from his subordinates, but anything regarded as incompetence usually consigned its perpetrator to a windowless basement office, condemned to an endless parade of meaningless bureaucratic tasks.

After what seemed like an eternity, the commissioner rose to his feet, followed by his staff to the sound of much scraping of chair legs across the floor.

"You disappoint me, Carnot. I expected better from you." And with that he turned on his heels and led his staff from the room.

Carnot stood immobilized, the light from the magic lantern silhouetting his face against the screen. Brousard busied himself unplugging and dismantling the projection equipment. The gendarme by the window remained at attention, keeping his gaze fixed on a point on the opposite wall.

Carnot was furious, but not with himself or the commissioner. The rage he felt roiling inside was directed at one source only: the perpetrators of this crime. They had not only taken *La Joconde*, they had stolen the only chance he might ever have to prove to the world that he was more than an insignificant faceless civil servant, that he was indeed a great detective, worthy of the highest honors France could bestow.

In that instant, he made a solemn vow: He would stop at nothing to bring these brazen criminals to their knees before the merciless god of justice.

Chapter 29

NEW YORK TIMES

October 1, 1911

STILL NO CLUES IN THEFT OF MONA LISA FROM LOUVRE!

Leonardo da Vinci Masterpiece Vanished Without a Trace!

AFTER TWO MONTHS FRENCH POLICE STILL IN DARK!

Eduardo de Valfierno placed the copy of the *New York Times* onto the seat next to him. The train rattled around a slight curve and he glanced up at the seventy-seven-by-fifty-three-centimeter package cradled in the overhead luggage rack. The final delivery at last.

He thought back to the previous few weeks. Each delivery had required a separate trip from New York with another panel; it was far too risky to transport more than one at a time.

The deliveries of the first five copies became almost routine. A deferential butler would usher Valfierno into the presence of his client waiting—feverish with anticipation—in a study or a gallery hidden deep within his mansion. Small talk followed, during which the client's eyes kept darting to the wrapped panel, until it came time for the unveiling and the inevitable stunned reaction. Then, there was the exchange of money, which was never counted or hardly even acknowledged by Valfierno, and the giddy banter with the satisfied client almost drunk with greedy delight. Finally, Valfierno would take his leave, waiting until he was seated in his taxi to breathe a sigh of relief as he felt the comforting weight of the small valise or briefcase filled with hundred-dollar bills sitting on his lap.

There had been only one precarious moment. On the fourth delivery, the client's new hunting dog—a jet-black whippet called Maggie—had taken an instant dislike to Valfierno. At first, the client made a joke of it, but the hound's persistent growling prompted him to recall that the previous owner had boasted of the creature's aptitude for judging men's characters. Valfierno was all too aware of the precarious line his clients straddled between self-delusion and suspicion—especially when the whippet started to sniff the painting itself—so it took all his powers of persuasion to gently guide the man to the humorous side of the situation. On taking his leave, Valfierno even ventured a joke, saying that if the man ever grew tired of his hound, he could always find work for her as an appraiser in one of the finer galleries in New York or Paris.

The sudden rush of a train on a parallel track barreling by in the opposite direction wrenched Valfierno back to the present. As the locomotive sped up the Connecticut coast on its way to Newport, his thoughts turned to his current destination: Windcrest, the magnificent house and gardens on the edge of the Atlantic. The home of Mr. and Mrs. Joshua Hart.

From the moment Taggart—instead of Hart's butler, Carter—opened Windcrest's massive oak front doors, Valfierno knew that this transaction would be very different from the others. Hart's bodyguard said nothing, but his steel-gray eyes bored into Valfierno like a predator sizing up his prey.

"Mr. Taggart, isn't it?" Valfierno said, masking his apprehension. "I believe Mr. Hart is expecting me."

Taggart motioned him inside with a jerk of his head.

Valfierno followed the man through the foyer and into the library. He felt a pang of disappointment not to see Mrs. Hart waiting for him as she had been on his last visit. He glanced briefly at the small table by the window where her mother had sat. Of course, he had been to the mansion on a number of occasions in years past without even being aware that Joshua Hart was married; the two women must have been elsewhere in the vast mansion at those times. Perhaps they were in another part of the building now.

Taggart led Valfierno into the study. Hart sat reading the *New York Times* in a large leather chair by the window. Valfierno's eyes briefly glanced at a leather valise sitting on a side table.

"Ah, Valfierno," said Hart, looking up. "It's about time you got here."

Hart's eyes shifted to the wrapped panel beneath Valfierno's arm. He stood up, tossed his newspaper onto the floor, and stepped forward, his eyes fixed on the object.

"I trust that Mrs. Hart and her mother are well," said Valfierno, trying to sound casual.

"What?" Hart responded, momentarily distracted. "Oh, yes." Then he added as an afterthought, "The old woman died." Then, in a tone that suggested Valfierno would completely understand and agree, he added, "Finally."

As Hart turned his attention back to the wrapped panel, Valfierno experienced an unpleasant sinking feeling. He tried to imagine the effect that the death of her mother would have had on Mrs. Hart.

"Your wife must be deeply grieved."

"That's an understatement," Hart said. "I couldn't stand her crying and moping around all day, so I sent her to stay with her relatives in Philadelphia where she can cry all she wants."

"I'm sorry that I missed her," said Valfierno.

"All right, enough about that," said Hart, his attention focused on the panel. "Let's see it."

Valfierno laid it on a mahogany table. With great deliberation, he untied the string and pulled the folds aside, revealing the back of the wooden panel. With a look to Hart, he tilted it up and back, revealing the painting itself. Hart's eyes widened. For a moment, he seemed afraid to approach it.

"It's the most beautiful thing I've ever seen," he finally said before turning to Taggart and adding, "though a bit smaller than I had imagined."

But Taggart was not looking at the painting. He stood as still as a statue, his eyes fixed on Valfierno.

Hart turned back to Valfierno with a look that appeared to seek permission to approach. Valfierno smiled slightly and nodded an almost imperceptible assent. Hart stepped forward and gingerly took the panel in his hands, lifting it and bringing it closer to his face. Valfierno could see the distorted image of the woman in the painting reflected in the man's dilated pupils. Hart turned the panel over briefly and nodded in apparent approval.

Then Hart placed the painting on the table and nodded to Taggart, who stepped forward and handed him a cloth tape measure.

"The most basic test," Hart began. "Twenty and seven-eighths inches by thirty inches. Exact. But don't worry. I know it's real. It's unmistakable. No one but a master could have created such a work."

It was unfailing, thought Valfierno. A man will always see only what he wishes to see; he will always convince himself of that which he is already certain to be true.

Hart nodded to Taggart again. This time, the large man picked up the leather valise.

"Four hundred and fifty thousand dollars," Hart said. "A lot of money." He slowly lifted the painting from the table and added, "But worth every penny."

Valfierno took the valise and bowed slightly to Hart in a show of respectful gratitude.

"Now," Hart said, "let's see how it will look, shall we?"

In the subterranean gallery, Hart placed the bottom edge of the painting on an antique table. The table sat up against the main wall below an empty space, its future place of honor. He leaned the panel against the wall and stepped back.

"I've commissioned a frame from a very discreet source. When it's finished, I'll mount it myself," Hart said, admiring the painting. "I can trust no one else."

Even sitting on a table, the painting was impressive. Valfierno had to admit to himself that Diego had done a remarkable job. He could be looking at the real thing.

"Now, my collection's complete," Hart said, taking it all in.

"Breathtaking," Valfierno said. "It's a pity the world can't share this."

"But that's the whole point," Hart said with relish as he seized the moment to enlighten Valfierno with his guiding philosophy. "All these great works of art now exist for my pleasure alone. They live only for my eyes. That is what makes them so special, unique. Only I can appreciate them now."

"Indeed," Valfierno said, starting to feel a lack of oxygen in the room.

"And when I die," Hart added, walking in a slow circle, taking in the entire collection, "I have arranged with Mr. Taggart to make sure that each and every one of them is destroyed. It will be like taking them with me, like the pharaohs of ancient Egypt."

Hart turned to Valfierno, looking for a reaction, waiting for a response.

Valfierno found himself in the rare position of not being able to think of a single thing to say.

By the time Valfierno's train reached the outskirts of New York City, he had convinced himself it had been fortunate that Mrs. Hart had not been in Newport. If she had been there, he was not sure how he would have reacted, or what he would have said. At the very least, it would have been a complication that was best avoided. Still, he felt genuine sorrow that her mother had died, leaving her alone with her husband. And he gained little satisfaction from the sight of the bulging valise on the seat beside him. Any enjoyment he could have gained from successfully hoodwinking Hart was diminished by the sympathy and concern he felt for his wife.

As the train descended below street level on its final run to Grand Central Station, he forced thoughts of Mrs. Hart from his mind.

"The key to room 137 please," Valfierno said to the clerk standing behind the main desk of the Plaza's lobby.

"Of course, sir." The man turned to the rows of tiny cubbyholes set into the rear wall.

Valfierno allowed himself to feel a sense of relief. He was finished. Tomorrow he would board a boat for France and within a week he would be back in Paris.

"Ah, yes," said the clerk, "you had a visitor, sir." In one hand he held the room key. In the other was a card.

Valfierno felt a stab of apprehension.

"A visitor?" No one on this side of the ocean, not even his clients, knew where he was staying.

"Yes, sir. A lady. She was here all day. In fact, I believe she might still be here. Yes, that's her over there."

A woman was sitting on a divan in the lobby waiting area. Her face was partially obscured by a wide-brimmed hat, but Valfierno recognized her instantly. It was Mrs. Hart.

Chapter 30

I arrived from Philadelphia three days ago. I have a second cousin who lives here. She was kind enough to let me stay with her."

It was late for lunch and early for dinner, so Valfierno and Ellen Hart sat alone in the oak-paneled hotel dining room. It had been closed, but with the help of a large tip Valfierno prevailed upon the management to seat them and serve wine. Her crystal glass remained untouched.

"My husband told me that you would be arriving with the painting this week; indeed, it was the reason he let me travel to Philadelphia. He didn't want my grief over my mother's death to ruin his moment. Where else would you be staying but in New York? And I was sure you would only stay in the best of hotels, so it became a matter of visiting each one. I was lucky. I found you after only three days."

"I'm impressed by your perseverance," said Valfierno, "though, I confess, somewhat mystified as to your motivation."

She flushed slightly at this, turning to look over her shoulder in evident embarrassment.

"I was greatly saddened to learn of your mother's death," Valfierno added.

"Thank you," she said, turning back and composing herself. "Mercifully, she died in her sleep. In a way, it was as if she had never woken up after peacefully drifting off so many years ago, as if for her, indeed for both of us, it had all been one long final dream." She stopped and took a deep breath. "I'm being silly. Forgive me."

"Not at all," Valfierno said with a kindly smile.

"How much longer do you plan to stay in New York?" she asked.

"As a matter of fact, I leave tomorrow for France."

"I see."

He took a sip of his wine. The silence was punctuated by the distant clink of dishes drifting in from the hotel kitchen.

"You once asked me," Ellen finally said, "why I married my husband."

Valfierno raised his eyebrows. "Did I? How impertinent of me."

"Yes, it was impertinent. Yet at the time, part of me wanted to answer the question."

"It was certainly none of my business."

"And it still isn't," she said. "But now I would like to tell you."

Valfierno sat up straighter in his chair, signaling his readiness to listen.

She looked down at the table. "My father left many debts when he died." She let the words hang in the air for a moment before looking up at Valfierno. "I suppose at one time we had been quite wealthy. But in the end, our prosperity turned out to be an illusion."

Valfierno listened intently, occasionally making small comments for clarification but careful not to break the flow of her story. Though the subject was obviously a difficult one, he noticed that as she got deeper into it, the words began pouring out as her shoulders dropped, and her body physically relaxed as if she had been holding her breath for a long, long time.

Ellen Edwina Beach had lived with her father and mother in a large apartment overlooking Central Park in New York City. Her father was an investor. His mood rose and fell with his successes and failures, but for the most part his choices were sound and his disposition cheerful. Railroads had proved particularly lucrative. Indeed, it was through his dealings with railroads that the family became acquainted with Mr. Joshua Hart.

Ellen Beach grew up in a fairy tale. She had a nanny and spent much time playing in the park, rolling hoops in the summer and ice-skating in the winter. She was friendly with the doormen, who turned a blind eye when she roller-skated in the lobby of their apartment building.

As she grew older, it became increasingly difficult to spend as much time with her father as she would have wished; he was always away on business, and when he came back he spent most evenings escorting her mother to a string of social gatherings. That was when business was going well. When it was not going well, he sat alone for hours, unapproachable, brooding in his library. Much as she wanted to, she never disturbed him at these times, though it was difficult to resist the urge to go in and sit on his lap as she had done so many times when she was very young. For the most part, however, she enjoyed a childhood of privilege and contentment.

When Ellen was fifteen, her mother without warning slipped into the unfortunate condition in which she was to spend the rest of her life. At first, her father spent hours on end sitting by her mother's bedside in the sunny bedroom that overlooked the park, but soon he began disappearing for long stretches of time. Ellen saw him only late at night when she peeked from behind her bedroom door as he staggered in, often disheveled and unsteady on his feet, bringing with him the faint smells of cigars, alcohol, and perfume.

Her mother would spend the entire day lying in bed staring up at the ceiling, responding to no one. Eventually, she improved enough to get up, and a live-in nurse would dress her, feed her, and reteach her the basics of taking care of herself. But she passed most of her time sitting by the window staring out at the park. The doctor informed Ellen that her mother's condition most likely would not improve further. There was nothing that could be done.

Ellen was sixteen when she heard that her father had died. He had been on an extended business trip in California, and she hadn't seen him in months. Her reaction to the news had been unexpected: It made her angry. Why had he been so far away from her when he died? Why had he left her all alone?

Ellen's maiden aunt Sylvia—her mother's sister—moved in to run the household. Ellen had never gotten along with the joyless, overbearing women, and her constant presence only served to remind Ellen of the loss—for all practical purposes—of her mother. Then one day Mr. Joshua Hart, a business partner of her father who had visited on a number of occasions since her father's death, sat her down to explain that her father left behind many debts and there was no longer any money to maintain the apartment, the nurse, and the two servants they employed. Aunt Sylvia had no great resources of her own, but Joshua Hart assured Ellen that there was no need to worry. He would personally arrange for things to stay as they were, allowing them to live in the apartment as they always had.

On Ellen's eighteenth birthday, Hart proposed marriage and she accepted. Though he was thirty years her senior, he had been generous, kind even. More to the point, she felt she had no choice. She was certainly grateful for everything Hart had done for her family, yet she had developed no feelings of attachment to him. But feelings had played no part in her decision. She would do whatever was necessary to ensure her mother's welfare, even if it meant marrying a man whom she knew she could never love.

"I was hardly in the position to turn down such a kind offer," she finally said, averting her eyes from Valfierno.

"Hardly," he reassured her.

"He was pleasant enough at first," she continued, "but as time went by, he became more and more distracted by his many business affairs. I began to feel like one of his paintings, part of his collection, the only difference being that instead of hanging on a wall, I was always to be on his arm."

She took her first sip of wine. "I don't suppose I've ever told anyone that story before."

"I am honored," Valfierno said gently.

"And now," she added, "it would seem that my husband has acquired his greatest possession."

"Yes, I suppose he has."

"And you've been paid well?"

"Very well."

"I'm sure you earned it."

"I will admit it was not an easy item to obtain."

"I imagine not." Ellen smiled weakly as she looked down and gently stroked the stem of her wine glass between her forefinger and thumb. The faint sound of voices drifted out from the kitchen.

Finally, she spoke. "I wonder, then, if I might ask you a favor."

Valfierno leaned forward slightly and met her gaze as she looked up.

"Of course. Anything I can possibly do."

"Marquis," Ellen began, "Edward . . . perhaps I can be as forward with you as you once were with me."

"I would hope for nothing less."

"With my dear mother gone, I have no more reason to stay with my husband."

She paused, waiting for a reaction. Valfierno's heart started to beat faster but he wasn't sure if it was from sheer surprise or something else. He knew he should speak, but he was not sure what he was going to say.

"Mrs. Hart—" he began tentatively.

"Please, let me finish. This is not easy for me. I believe you know my husband well, the kind of man he is, I mean. I can assure you that his appreciation for his collection far outweighs his regard for me. Yet he would no sooner let me go than he would relinquish any one of his other acquisitions."

"Perhaps you underestimate his regard for you, or misinterpret the way he demonstrates his affection."

A slightly puzzled look crossed Ellen's face. "The desire to possess is very different from the sentiment of love."

Valfierno allowed this with a slight tilt of his head.

"Therefore," she continued, taking a breath as she gathered

every bit of her resolve, "I would ask you—I would beg you—to take me with you to France."

Valfierno drew back in his chair, unable to hide his surprise.

"Mrs. Hart, I . . ."

"Ellen. My name is Ellen."

"Ellen, I don't know what to say."

"Perhaps, then, I should restate it as a simple question. Will you take me with you?"

He took a deep breath and exhaled slowly.

"I believe, Mrs. Hart . . . Ellen . . . , that I understand your situation, the dilemma you find yourself in, and if I can help in any way, I am happy to be of service. But you must understand that what you're asking is out of the question. No matter what the circumstances, your home is here. Mine is in France. I'm afraid it is impossible. I'm sorry. If I can help financially in some way—"

"I'm not entirely without means. The simple fact of the matter is that I wouldn't know the first thing about . . . escaping, running away, for that's what it would be. And for that I would need your help."

She averted her eyes as she lifted her glass and took another sip of wine.

Valfierno felt a deluge of conflicting emotions. Was this what he wanted to hear above all else? Was the rush of excitement he felt telling him to embrace this turn of events with all his heart? Or was this a warning sign, an emotional alarm cautioning him to not get involved in a situation that could only be fraught with unforeseen complications?

"Ellen," he finally began, surprised that he had difficulty forming his thoughts, "much as I would like to help you in some way, I simply couldn't afford to draw so much undue attention to myself. You must be able to understand that."

She nodded, accepting the obvious logic in his statement. Valfierno could sense how difficult this was for her; bravado did not come easily to this woman. She took another sip of wine as if trying to build up her courage.

"Edward," she began slowly, deliberately, "there is much I know about you, and I am sure that much of what I know would be of great interest to the police, to the authorities." The words came out hesitantly; there was not a hint of threat in her voice.

"This is true," Valfierno responded calmly, "but you'd never be able to say anything without implicating your own husband's role in the crime."

"And you really think that would deter me?"

Valfierno let out a sigh. "You surprise me," he said with an air of gentle indignation. "I have perhaps pictured you as many things, but never as a blackmailer."

She let out a small, ironic chuckle. "Neither have I. Perhaps I picked it up from my exposure to some of my husband's dealings. And even, perhaps, from you."

"Now, you're not going to accuse me of turning you into a cynic, are you?" Valfierno smiled. "As I recall, the little plan to coerce your husband to consummate the deal we had in Buenos Aires was your idea."

"Or at least you allowed me to think it was," she said.

"Well, I don't know about that, but—"

"If I may be frank again," she continued, "even though you and I have met only a few times, I had imagined—perhaps even hoped— that you were not unsympathetic to my situation."

"I can assure you I am very sympathetic, but what you're suggesting—"

"And furthermore," she continued, nervously averting her eyes, "that you might even welcome the opportunity to help me."

Valfierno said nothing. He lifted his glass, gently swirling the dark red liquid. He had learned long ago how to hide the doubt, turmoil, even fear that were unavoidable in his line of work. And though that carefully crafted façade had developed some fine cracks in the past few months, he was still sure of one thing: A man cannot control how he feels about the world, but he can always control the actions he takes in response to them.

"I see," she said. "Your silence is answer enough, which leaves me no choice other than to promise to take more drastic measures to force your assistance in this matter."

Valfierno looked at her. She could be bluffing, of course, but somehow he didn't think so. He had dealt with threats—if this indeed was a threat—many times before. He had always found it best to treat them as nothing more than welcome challenges.

"Ellen," he began, trying to sound like a kindly professor enlightening a naïve student, "you say that you think you know a lot about me, but I wonder if you really do. I have done things in my life that are, at the very least, regrettable. I have been threatened—if I may use so strong a word—before, but I can assure you that those threats have never had their desired effect. I have always done—without hesitation—that which was necessary to counter such attempts at coercion. I will not bore you with the details of these episodes, but I suggest that there are two questions you must ask yourself at this moment. First, in order to protect myself, how do you know that I have never gone to the extreme, even to the point of, shall we say, eliminating all threats against me? And second, and more to the point, if that is the case, how do you know that I would not do the same again?"

His words did not have the effect he had hoped for.

"I believe that there is also something you do not understand," Ellen said coolly. "Even death holds no fear for me. On the contrary, I would much prefer it to returning to life with my husband."

She lifted her glass and drained it. And Valfierno knew that—for the moment at least—she had won.

Chapter 31

Four days later, the telephone rang in the study of Joshua Hart's Newport mansion. Hart picked up the black candlestick base, removed the receiver from its cradle, and put it to his ear. His voice was brusque and impatient.

"Yes?"

"This is Taggart."

"Yes, yes, what have you discovered?"

"I made some inquiries of the staff of the gentleman in question."

Shortly after taking possession of the *Mona Lisa*, Hart was nagged by a vague suspicion that something was not as it should be. At first he had been elated in the knowledge that he now owned the ultimate masterpiece; at last his collection was complete. No other man on earth could match it.

But he kept going back in his mind to the issue of the passport. He had once again compared the forged document to the replacement. Other than the signs of age on the forgery, the two were truly identical in every aspect. This meant one of two things: Either Valfierno's accomplices were capable of making flawless copies—even going so far as to artificially age the documents—or somehow the man had managed to steal his actual passport and pass it off as a forged copy. If it had been the latter, well, business is business; he himself had resorted to underhanded means many times to reach a position of power over his rivals when it came to negotiations.

But if it had been the former, if Valfierno did have resources capable of creating perfect forgeries, why would he stop at passports?

Hart began to examine his collection piece by piece. Most of the works of art had been procured by the persuasive Argentinean gentleman. Valfierno had always been quick to explain that museums had high-quality reproductions they could put up at a moment's notice, but why, out of all the works that Valfierno had obtained, had there never been a single report of a theft until now? Could it be because Hart had insisted that there had to be absolute proof this time that the *Mona Lisa* had indeed been stolen?

Plagued by misgivings, Hart had put Taggart to work. He remembered the name of the potential client Valfierno whispered into his ear on his previous visit—a well-known and powerful business rival. That would be a good place to start, and if anyone could root out information, it would be Taggart.

"I found one of his houseboys willing to part with information for pocket change," Taggart reported. "Shortly before delivering the package to you, Valfierno visited the gentleman in question with a package of similar dimensions. He left not long after with a full carpetbag."

Hart began breathing heavily. "What exactly did he deliver?"

"The houseboy saw it briefly. I showed him the photograph. It was the same one Valfierno delivered to you."

Hart's hands gripped the base and the receiver of the phone so tightly that his arms began to shake. So it was true. Valfierno had tricked him. He had made two copies, even more, for all he knew. How many of the damn things did Valfierno sell?

Taggart broke the silence. "That's not all. You asked me to check up on Mrs. Hart."

Hart was only half listening, his mind consumed with thoughts of Valfierno and how he had let the man make a fool of him.

"I found out," Taggart continued, "that she had traveled to New York by train to stay with a relative."

Hart tried to focus on what Taggart was saying.

"New York?" said Hart. "But she wasn't supposed to leave Philadelphia."

"I made some inquiries," said Taggart, "and discovered that she booked passage on the steamship *Prinz Joachim*. It sailed three days ago for Le Havre."

"What are you talking about?"

Taggart paused before speaking. "When she boarded the ship she was in the company of a certain foreign gentleman."

A crackle of electricity snaked through the line.

"Valfierno . . ." Hart said, the name hissing out of him as if his lungs had been punctured. The silence on the other end of the line was all the confirmation he needed.

"Mr. Taggart," Hart said, his voice tightly controlled.

"Sir?"

"I want you to stay where you are. You will be hearing from me shortly."

"Yes, sir."

Hart replaced the receiver and slowly put the phone down onto the desktop.

Joshua Hart walked quickly through his subterranean gallery, his shoulders stooped, his eyes fixed on the floor to avoid looking at his collection arrayed on the walls. Everything had changed; his suspicions had taken hold and formed a thick mass of dread like a rock in his stomach. He strode past the *Mona Lisa* to the small door at the rear of the gallery. Producing the key, he unlocked the door and walked in, flicking on a light. The room was small, nine feet by twelve, empty except for three things: a stool, an easel, and a round table with a small ornately carved box on it. A framed blank canvas rested on the easel.

Hart stood motionless for a moment before lowering himself onto the stool. He stared at the empty canvas for a full minute. Then he turned his attention to the box, lifting the hinged lid. It contained a row of paint tubes and a collection of brushes of various sizes. A child-size artist's palette fit neatly into the lid. He gingerly took out a fine-tipped brush. He contemplated it for a moment, rolling it in his fingers. Then he removed the kidney-shaped palette, stained and spotted with old, dried splotches of paint. He ran his thumb over the thumbhole, sized for a child and too small for him.

Joshua Hart sat frozen for a moment before carefully replacing the palette and brush in the box and closing the lid. He stared at the blank canvas for a few moments. Then, with a sudden violent sweep of his arm, he knocked over the small table, scattering the contents of the box across the floor. He stood abruptly and left the room, walking directly to his latest acquisition. He reached up and removed it from its pegs. The *Mona Lisa*. Priceless. The most magnificent possession any man could hope to claim as his own, a treasure that had persevered through the centuries while mere mortals hurried to the conclusion of their brief, meaningless lives. And now it was his. No man would ever lay eyes on it again. He and he alone stood at the center of its universe.

And, at that moment, he had absolutely no doubt that it was a fake. The seed of that doubt—so tiny that he had given it only a fleeting thought—had taken root and flowered into a terrible realization: He had been taken in, had been made a complete fool of, by a man who had now spirited away his wife.

He looked at the woman in the painting, at her faintly condescending smile, those slightly hooded eyes, distant and mocking. She looked directly at him, smug and sure of herself. He put the panel on the floor, leaning it at an angle against the wall. Calmly and mechanically, he raised one leg and, with all his might, thrust his foot into the woman's face. A crack snaked at an angle through one eye and across her pursed lips. Struggling to maintain his balance, he drew back his foot and thrust it forward one more time, shattering and splintering the panel where her face had been.

A short while later, Joshua Hart sat exhausted and wet with perspiration in his study, the base of the phone in one hand, the earpiece in the other.

"Yes, Mr. Hart," came Taggart's voice.

"We are going to find them," Hart said slowly and deliberately. "And when we do, after we have recovered my money . . . are you listening, Mr. Taggart?"

"Yes, sir."

"I want you to see to it that, for his sins, this man, Valfierno, will suffer and die. Can you do that for me, Mr. Taggart?"

There was a brief silence before Taggart replied. "Yes, Mr. Hart. I can do that."

Chapter 32

Your head is drooping," Diego said. "Keep it steady. Can't you just look straight ahead?"

He sat on a stool in his basement studio on rue Serpente, one leg slightly raised, his foot resting on a crate on the floor next to him.

Across from him, on the other side of his easel, Julia Conway sat perched on another stool. Except for the long woolen scarf that wrapped around her neck and draped down her back, she was naked.

Julia raised her head, the nagging neck pain reminding her that she had been sitting for almost two hours now. She had never posed for a painting before. She had always imagined it would be easy work. After all, you just sat there doing nothing. But now her back was aching, her bottom was sore, her legs were numb, and she was getting restless, not to mention cold.

At first she had balked at taking her clothes off, but Diego had shown no interest in painting her any other way. He hadn't seemed suggestive or flirtatious about it; indeed, clinical and disinterested would best describe his manner. He had flirted with her before, but as soon as she had agreed to sit for him, his demeanor had changed. He was all business, or perhaps all art would be a better way to put it.

Not that she was particularly attracted to him. He was a bit too

intense for her liking and, though his stocky physique and penetrating eyes lent him a certain animal presence, he really wasn't her
type at all. Still, she felt vaguely insulted that he seemed more interested in his art than in her.

So why, she wondered, had she agreed to pose for him in the
first place? The most obvious answer was boredom. She had been
living for months at Madame Charneau's house and, though she
had spent some time walking around the city and sightseeing, her
strolls had mainly served to tempt her to ply her trade in the ubiq-
uitous crowds of tourists.

She had been particularly amused by the seedy Pigalle Quarter,
which she had visited by way of a series of tram cars after being
warned off by Madame Charneau. Having had a lot of contact with
prostitutes during her stint in Charleston, she instantly recognized
the character of the streets leading into the place Pigalle. Indeed,
within minutes of stepping off the tram, she had not only been so-
licited for sex by a very attractive young woman but also importuned
twice to join the ranks of the poor *grisettes* newly arrived from the
provinces and currently earning their living as *filles de joie*.

She had eventually found her way up through the narrow warren of streets to the foot of the butte Montmartre leading up to the
Basilica of Sacré-Coeur, the Roman Catholic cathedral that resembled nothing so much as a Muslim mosque. She had ridden the funicular railway to the top and prided herself on easily recognizing
the small army of pickpockets preying on the tourists. The high-
light had been when a young man accidentally tripped in front of
her, smearing her dress with syrup from the babas au rhum he
held in his hand. He had barely begun his profuse apologies before she spun around and smacked his accomplice in the face with
the same handbag he had been about to snatch. She had particularly enjoyed berating the two failed thieves for the amusement of
the tourists.

She had been tempted to demonstrate to these amateurs how it
was really done. The problem was that she had promised Valfierno
to resist the urge, and she felt obliged to honor that pledge.

Up to a point, anyway.

Riding the funicular down from the basilica, she found herself sitting behind a large German tourist complaining loudly to his poor wife about something or other and disturbing the entire car. As the passengers filed out at the bottom of the hill, she fell in behind him and relieved him of his wallet. The man deserved it, she reasoned, and she had to stay in practice. Still, in deference to her promise to Valfierno, moments after stepping off the car, she tossed the wallet into the violin case of a young boy sawing gamely away at his instrument for tourist coins.

She had amused herself by observing the different techniques used at the various attractions around the city. Pickpockets who worked the crowds waiting to ascend the Arc du Triomphe, for instance, tended to pose as well-heeled boulevardiers who distracted young couples with charming conversation while an accomplice relieved the gentleman of his wallet; those working the hordes milling about the legs of the Eiffel Tower seemed to be adept at surreptitiously flinging pigeon shit onto fancy frock coats and kindly offering to wipe it off while a cohort lightened the gentleman's load; the busy sidewalks of Saint-Germain featured groups of young boys, two of whom would stage a fight while the others worked the gathering crowd of spectators. All very entertaining, but her inability to participate made Julia lose interest, and before she knew it she had wearied of the many diversions of Paris.

"Aren't you done yet?" she asked Diego petulantly. "When can I see it?"

"Impatience is art's greatest enemy," he replied in an annoyed monotone. "Would you hurry the blossoming of a rose?"

"Well, this rose is starting to wilt."

She had been staring at his zinc tub the whole time. "Do you really bathe in that filthy thing?" she asked with a disdainful grimace.

"On occasion."

The man was hardly paying any attention to her. It seemed impossible to get a rise out of him.

"And why do you have artificial flowers anyway?" she said,

referring to the arrangement in the pot sitting on a stool next to the tub. "Can't you afford real ones?"

"I like the colors better," he answered in a quiet, distracted tone.

"Anyway," she persisted, "my ass is sore."

Diego smiled. He had been, at that very moment, trying to do justice to that particularly pleasing part of her anatomy. But his smile faded. It was not going well at all and he wasn't sure why. It was a perfectly acceptable—if unfinished—work of art, he thought. It did justice to a very attractive subject; there was nothing wrong with it at all. And then he realized what the problem was: There was nothing wrong with the painting. It was like hundreds of others he had done in the past few years. His colleagues—whose regard for his work had changed from initial suspicion and even animosity to an annoyingly passive acceptance—would regard it as just another addition to his growing body of work. This was not the reason he had isolated himself from the world he knew in order to break new ground.

Julia turned at the sound of footsteps on the stairs.

"Please," Diego pleaded, "can't you just keep still?"

"Hello? Diego?" Émile's voice floated down from the top of the stairs.

"Your paramour is here," Diego said to Julia with obvious annoyance.

"Don't be ridiculous," she said, turning her face back to the wall. "It's just Émile."

Émile walked down the steps and stopped cold, his mouth dropping open in surprise.

"What is going on?" he demanded.

"What are you doing here?" Julia asked, making a point of not looking at him.

"Never mind what I'm doing here," he said. "What are *you* doing here?"

"What does it look like? José is painting my portrait."

"José?" Émile stammered in disbelief.

"Take a seat," Diego said. "Learn from the master."

Émile stepped toward Julia, taking note of the pile of clothing heaped on a nearby chair.

"You've taken all your clothes off."

"Your powers of observation are remarkable," she commented drily.

"And you're naked."

"The two often go together. And why shouldn't I be? I'm an artist's model."

"An artist's model?" the young man said with contempt. "And is that what they call it nowadays?"

"What the hell is that supposed to mean?" she demanded, snapping her head around.

"This is useless," Diego said, throwing down his brush in frustration. "You really are spoiling the atmosphere, you know," he added for Émile's sake.

"Spoiling the atmosphere?" Émile said. "I'll show you how to spoil the atmosphere." And with that, he picked up the pile of clothes and threw them into Julia's lap.

"Put these back on."

"What's it to you?" she said, hastily holding up her dress in front of her as she sprang to her feet.

Émile said nothing, momentarily transfixed by the sight of the outer curves of her hips that the dress failed to cover.

"Perhaps you should take your clothes off, too," Diego suggested, "and join her."

"You debased goat!" Émile snarled and took a step toward him.

Diego backed away with an amused smile on his face, which only served to incense Émile further.

"No need to get excited, Romeo," the painter said as Émile took another step toward him.

But before he could make contact, Émile tripped on the crate that Diego had been using as a footstool and stumbled. He grabbed the easel for support, but it collapsed beneath him and he tumbled to the floor on top of the canvas.

"You're ruining my painting!" Julia cried out as she pulled a blanket off Diego's cot and wrapped it around her.

Diego gathered up his worn jacket and cap. "It wasn't any good anyway," he said dismissively.

"What do you mean, it wasn't any good?" Julia shrieked. "Why not?"

Émile tried to get back to his feet but slipped on the gobs of paint on Diego's palette.

"The subject was not inspiring enough," Diego said.

"Not inspiring enough?" Julia said indignantly.

Diego had reached the foot of the steps by the time she hurled a clay pot full of brushes at him. He easily deflected the pot with his arm, sending it shattering into the wall.

"I need a drink!" he called out as he hurried up the steps. "Perhaps some Madeira will provide me with the inspiration I crave!"

Émile struggled to his feet, glaring up in the direction of the staircase. Picking up a rag, he attempted to remove globs of paint from his jacket, in the process only making the stains worse.

Julia turned her attention to the mess on the floor, stooping down and picking up the painting.

Her mouth opened in astonishment. The woman—if you could call it that—looked like something you'd see in a carnival funhouse mirror. For one thing, the proportions were all wrong, the outlines too haphazardly drawn. Her breasts—more like a pair of pastry bags used for decorating a cake—seemed to grow out of her back. The exaggerated curve of her waist flowed down to a pair of oversized buttocks that somehow still managed to convey sensuality.

"My ass isn't that big!" she howled. "And what are those supposed to be?" She pointed to the red-tipped pastry bags in horror.

"What do you mean?" Émile said facetiously. "I think it looks just like you."

Julia let out a growl of frustration.

"You like showing off. You know you do," Émile said as he tried to wipe paint from his face, only to smear it and give himself the aspect of a wild Indian.

Julia picked up a knife that had fallen from the broken vase, and for a moment Émile thought she was going to use it on him. But instead she turned on the canvas, embellishing it with a series of angry slashes.

"You've only got yourself to blame," Émile said with a lofty air.

"What did you say?" Julia hissed as she turned on him, blade at the ready.

"Careful with that knife." Émile drew back.

Julia looked at the weapon in her hand as if seeing it for the first time, and threw it down in disgust. She picked up Diego's paint-smeared palette and smashed it onto what remained of her portrait lying in tatters on the floor. For good measure, she knocked over a small table, spilling an old newspaper, rags, and a full ashtray into the mess.

"You're crazy, do you know that?" said Émile.

"Get out!" she screamed. "Get out!"

Grasping the blanket tightly up to her neck with one hand, she was about to physically push him up the stairs with her other when they were distracted by a voice from above.

"Julia! Émile!" Madame Charneau cried out as she shuffled down the steps, drawing up her skirt to keep from tripping on the hem. "Did you tell her?"

"Tell me what?" asked Julia.

"Signore Peruggia," Émile began, making a gesture that suggested it was her fault he hadn't had the opportunity to tell her earlier. "He's decided to leave."

Safely at the bottom of the steps, Madame Charneau took in the mess around her. "What happened here?"

"Ask her," said Émile, jerking his head toward Julia.

"You should have told me right away," Julia scolded Émile.

"It's all right," Émile said defensively. "He's not leaving for a few days."

"But that's just it," Madame Charneau said frantically, "he's just now informed me that he's leaving this very afternoon. And he's taking the painting with him."

"The copy, you mean," said Émile.

Madame Charneau gave Julia a look.

"You did switch the paintings, didn't you?" he asked them both.

The look Julia exchanged with Madame Charneau gave him his answer.

"I don't believe it!"

"Give me a minute to get dressed," said Julia, exasperated. "I'll explain on the way over."

Chapter 33

He hardly ever left his room," Julia said breathlessly as they hurried to the cour de Rohan. "There was never enough time to get in to replace the original."

"But you've had a copy of the key for months," Émile said.

"Haven't you been listening?" she said. "He's only left his room to go across the hall for a few minutes each day. There's simply been no time and I didn't know he was leaving so soon."

"What time did he say his train was leaving?" Émile asked Madame Charneau.

"He told me that his train for Florence leaves the Gare de Lyon at four o'clock."

"Then we'd better hurry," he said before turning on Julia. "You had one simple thing to do!"

Julia was about to retort when Émile increased his stride and pulled ahead. Instead, she just growled in frustration as she took Madame Charneau's arm to help the older woman keep up the pace.

Fortunately, when they arrived at the boardinghouse a little after one o'clock, they could hear Peruggia moving about up in his room.

"All right, genius," Julia said to Émile in the form of a challenge, "what would you suggest?"

"I don't know," he snapped, trying to keep his voice down. "You're the one who should have taken care of all this by now."

Julia hesitated, thinking. "All right," she finally said. "Madame Charneau, fetch that carafe of brandy from the sitting room and bring it up to my room with two glasses." The older woman nodded and bustled off. "Émile. You go up to the attic. Don't let him hear you. Get the copy and then wait for a signal at the top of the stairs." She removed the key from her pocket and handed it to him. "I only hope you did a better job at copying it than the last one."

"So now you want *me* to do it?" he whispered as she hustled him up the staircase.

On the way up to the second floor, Julia quickly and quietly explained what she wanted Émile to do.

Leaving Émile at the foot of another small staircase leading to the attic, Julia doubled back to the first floor. She reached the door to her room just as Madame Charneau was coming out. Julia whispered instructions to her before disappearing inside. Madame Charneau adjusted her housedress and knocked on Peruggia's door. After a moment, Peruggia appeared. He had eaten very little in the last few months and his rather shabby three-piece traveling suit hung loosely on his frame.

"What is it?" he demanded suspiciously.

"Monsieur Peruggia," Madame Charneau began, "Mademoiselle Julia wishes to say good-bye to you."

He gave her a puzzled look, then poked his head out and peered down the hallway.

"Where is she?"

"She said she wished to say good-bye to you in her room."

Peruggia hesitated for a moment, scrutinizing Madame Charneau's face. She shrugged, gave him a pleasant smile, and began fussing with a vase of flowers sitting on a small side table. Peruggia stood for a moment in the doorway, then stepped out of his room and locked the door. He walked down the hall to Julia's room, smoothed back a lock of hair, and knocked. Almost immediately, the door opened.

Julia looked up at him with a friendly smile. "Signore Peruggia," she said with evident delight.

"Madame Charneau said you wished to say good-bye."

"Yes, please come inside."

He stood motionless.

"Please," she repeated, stepping aside and making a sweeping gesture with her hand.

He hesitated, then walked in. Julia gave a quick conspiratorial look to Madame Charneau and closed the door.

Madame Charneau scurried to the stairs. Émile stood on the upper steps holding the wrapped panel beneath his arm. She gestured with her hand, and he hurried down and followed her to Peruggia's room. Taking out her master key, Madame Charneau unlocked the door.

Julia picked up the carafe from a table, poured two glasses of brandy, and offered one to Peruggia, who stood rather stiffly by the door.

"I'll be sorry to see you go," she said, taking a sip from her glass.

Peruggia took the glass, raised it to his lips, and emptied it.

"I'll miss seeing your handsome face around here," she continued. "Not that we've seen much of it lately."

He remained stone-faced.

Julia managed a pleasant, relaxed smile.

"And where will you be traveling to?" she asked, wondering if the man would ever speak.

Émile unwrapped the copy of *La Joconde* and placed it on the mattress. He reached underneath the bed and pulled out the trunk. Removing the copy of the key from his pocket, he placed it into the lock and twisted it.

The lock didn't respond.

———

"Florence," Peruggia finally answered. "I shall be traveling to Florence."

"Florence," Julia said, refilling his glass. "It sounds so romantic."

"Italy is my home."

"Oh, I'm sure you have a lady friend waiting there for you, eh, Signore Peruggia?"

"My mother lives there," he said, a dour expression on his face. "But I'm not particularly eager to see her."

"Oh, but surely there must be someone."

Peruggia looked suspiciously at Julia. Then he lifted his glass and drained it again.

"There was someone . . . once."

Émile broke into a cold sweat. This couldn't be happening again. When dealing with sophisticated locks, like the ones that would be found on small safes, it could be expected that a copy would not work without some additional filing to make fine adjustments. But with crude locks, such as those found on trunks like this one, even a rough copy should work right away.

He tried to turn the key a number of times with no success. He pulled it out and examined it. He noticed a slight burr on one of the crenellations. Somehow it had escaped his attention when he copied the key. Removing a small file from his jacket pocket, he hurriedly filed it off. Replacing the key in the lock, he took a deep breath and turned it. The lock clicked open.

"I knew it," Julia said, deftly refilling Peruggia's glass. "It would be hard to imagine a catch like you going unnoticed for too long."

Peruggia stared into the dark liquid in his glass as if it were some kind of crystal ball. "She ran off with a butcher."

"A butcher . . ." said Julia, trying desperately to think of an appropriate comment as he drained his glass yet again. Finally, sounding as sympathetic as possible, she said, "For the meat . . . no doubt."

Peruggia nodded his sullen agreement. "She always did have a big appetite."

"There you are, then," Julia said.

There was a moment of awkward silence as the subject trailed off like a dying wisp of smoke. Peruggia suddenly tore himself away from his reverie. "I have to go."

"Oh, so soon?" Julia protested. "But you've plenty of time. Please stay a little while longer."

He fixed his gaze on her. "Why do you want me to stay?"

"Because I enjoy your company, of course." She tried to refill his glass but he covered it with his hand.

"No more," he said, turning to go.

"And besides," she said, stepping between him and the door. "It will be so lonely once you're gone."

Émile opened the trunk and removed a number of folded shirts to reveal *La Joconde*. He gingerly grasped each side of the panel and placed it onto the bed next to the copy.

"Émile," Madame Charneau's voice came through the door.

Wrenched from his intense focus, Émile stepped to the door.

"What is it?" he asked, straining to keep his voice to a whisper.

"You must hurry!" she said through the door.

"Yes, yes," Émile said impatiently before returning to the bed. Kneeling again, he reached for the copy.

He froze.

He looked at the two identical paintings lying next to each other. Which one was the copy? Which one did he put down last?

This is ridiculous, he thought. He had just put them both down. *Ah, yes, of course.* The one on the right was the copy. Or was it the one on the left? No, the one on the right. He remembered distinctly now.

He slid the painting on the right into the trunk. He replaced the shirts on top of it, closed the lid, locked the trunk, and pushed it back beneath the bed.

Julia stood between Peruggia and the door. Her face held a provocative smile.

"And why, all of a sudden, do you like me so much?" he asked, placing his empty glass onto the mantel of the small fireplace. "You've barely spoken to me in months."

"You've kept to yourself so much," she said coyly, "and besides, you know women. We never know our own minds."

Without changing his expression, Peruggia closed his eyes and lowered his face to hers.

He's going to kiss me, Julia frantically thought. *It's the only way to keep him here. I have to.*

But she couldn't. She sidestepped, leaving Peruggia slightly off-balance. He opened his eyes and caught himself by reaching out and propping his hand against the door.

"See what I mean?" she said, smiling lamely.

Peruggia smirked, shrugging slightly. Then he turned the door-knob. As the door opened, Julia stepped once again into his path, took him by the lapels, and turned him around so that his back was to the hallway.

"But I will miss you," she said. Out of the corner of her eye she saw Madame Charneau standing by Peruggia's door signaling her frantically that Émile was still inside.

Julia had no choice. Pulling Peruggia forward and down, she firmly planted her lips on his. They felt wet and rubbery, and she was sure she could taste the Belgian blood sausage she had brought up to him for dinner last night. She cocked open one eye in time to see Émile exit Peruggia's room with the wrapped panel beneath his arms. She kept kissing Peruggia until Émile and Madame Charneau disappeared down the staircase. As soon as they were gone, she let go and stepped back. Julia suddenly became all business as she extended her hand.

"Well," she said, "bon voyage."

Before he could do or say anything else, she gently but firmly pushed him from her room. Closing the door behind him, she leaned back against it, completely drained.

Ten minutes later, Peruggia stood with Madame Charneau at the open front door. He wore his heavy coat and hat, and in one hand he carried his traveling valise. Beneath his other arm, he held the panel, which he had wrapped in cloth.

"Good-bye, madame," he said with a curt nod. "Thank you for your hospitality."

"It has been my pleasure, Signore Peruggia. I hope you have a pleasant journey."

Peruggia started to go, then stopped and turned back. "I think," he began, his voice low and serious, "that the young lady may need a little extra attention for a while."

"Of course, I understand."

With a final awkward bow, Peruggia walked away. Madame Charneau waited until he disappeared from the inner courtyard before pushing the front door shut. Immediately, Émile appeared from the kitchen as Julia hurried down the steps.

"That was close," said Émile.

"You managed to make the switch?" Julia asked breathlessly.

"Of course," Émile answered.

"And the key?"

"It worked perfectly the first time."

"You're my hero!" she chirped, throwing her arms around him.

"Well done, Émile," Madame Charneau said.

When Julia let him go, he stood for a moment a little dazed. Then he quickly patted his pocket to make sure his watch was still in its proper place.

"And you, too," he said to Julia before quickly including Madame Charneau, "the two of you. Well done."

"The marquis will be proud of us all," Madame Charneau said.

"How did you manage to distract him?" Émile asked Julia.

She shared a quick conspiratorial smile with Madame Charneau before answering, "Wouldn't you like to know."

And with that, she darted forward and gave him a quick kiss on the cheek before whirling away and scuttling back up the stairs. Émile watched her in astonishment.

"That's the second time she's done that."

"It's the third time you have to worry about," said Madame Charneau with a twinkle in her eye. Then she turned serious. "Where will you keep the painting now?"

"A very good question. I've actually given it a lot of thought."

"And?"

"And what better place to hide an elephant," Émile began, "than in a herd of other elephants?"

He was halfway down Saint-Germain by the time he realized his pocket watch was missing.

Holding the wrapped panel beneath his arm, Émile knocked on the street-level door to Diego's studio.

"Señor Diego?" he called out. There was no response. "Señor Diego?"

As he had hoped, the artist had not yet returned. Letting himself in with the hidden key Diego always kept in an old rusted gas lamp attached to the wall—the same one Émile had replaced when he, Julia, and Madame Charneau left in such a hurry hours earlier—he let himself in and descended the steps to the basement.

Stepping over the mess on the floor, he went immediately to the small room the artist used as a storage closet. It was a jumble of easels, boxes, canvases, panels, and supplies. The only furniture was a child's wooden school desk jammed into a corner. Copies of La Joconde leaned haphazardly against the walls. Some were incomplete, but one or two looked finished. Some of Diego's copies were smaller than the original, and some were slightly larger. Émile reasoned that they must have been the legitimate reproductions he had been creating for the tourist trade. Diego must have included his correctly proportioned master copy with the frames he had sent to Valfierno. Therefore, Émile thought as he placed the original among them, it would be easy to pick out when the time came because of its unique size and obvious superior quality.

Pleased with his deception, he left the room and walked back up to the street.

Chapter 34

Valfierno stood with Ellen Hart on the stern deck of the *Prinz Joachim* watching the dying sun stain the horizon red.

Ellen had to raise her voice to be heard over the rush of wind and the rumble of the propellers beneath them.

"I hear from the other passengers that we'll dock at Le Havre by midnight, perhaps two o'clock at the latest."

She leaned on the railing next to Valfierno, one hand holding her hat in spite of the wide ribbon tied around her chin.

"And in Paris by morning," Valfierno said.

The voyage from New York had been mostly unpleasant. A nor'-easter brought driving rains and strong winds down from Nova Scotia to lash the ship for much of the journey. Only when they neared the European coast did the storm abate. Valfierno and Ellen spent practically all their time belowdecks in their separate cabins. Their main contact was at the supper table, which they shared with other first-class passengers as well as—on occasion—the captain, so there had been little opportunity for personal conversation.

Ellen suspected that this suited Valfierno fine. He had clearly avoided her, and this made her wonder about his motivation for agreeing to bring her along in the first place. Had she left him with no choice, or had he made his own choice? At any rate, his choice now was to keep their arrangement on a strictly business level, the level that he seemed most comfortable with.

On the day before their arrival at Le Havre, the weather cleared and, following an early supper, she had asked him to join her up on deck for some air.

They both watched as a sliver of orange flame limned the horizon like a mirage before extinguishing itself in the sea.

After a moment, Valfierno turned to her and asked, "What will you do?"

"I have no idea. My family used to have friends in Paris, but that was a long time ago when I was a little girl. I wouldn't even know how to find them now."

"My friend Madame Charneau runs a rooming house near the Latin Quarter," Valfierno said. "I'm sure you would be able to stay there until you're settled."

She nodded. Clearly it wasn't the most pressing issue on her mind.

"Edward," she began hesitantly, "I'm sorry that we haven't had much opportunity to talk."

He nodded but made no response.

She added, "May I ask you something?"

Valfierno stared out at the darkening sea for a moment before answering, "Of course."

"Why do you do it? Is it just for the money?"

"Why else?" he said, shrugging the question off.

"I don't know," she said, answering his rhetorical question. "For the excitement perhaps, the thrill of the con." She embellished the last word with dramatic flair.

"I think you've been reading too many novels," he said lightly.

"There must be something else. Take the present situation. There's no profit in helping me."

"You forced my hand."

"I have a feeling that no one can force you to do anything."

"Besides," he said playfully, "how do you know I won't hold you for ransom?"

"That's not a bad idea," she said with a demure smile. "You could cut off a finger and send it to my husband. Here, I hardly ever use this one."

She held up her small finger. Like everything else about her, Valfierno thought, it was as slender and perfect as that of a porcelain doll.

"Too gruesome," he said dismissively. "Besides, you're the one blackmailing me, remember?"

Ellen dropped her bantering tone and turned serious. "Who would have believed me even if I had gone to the police? And even if they had, my husband would have made sure that everything was hushed up."

"It's true," he said, considering. "He is a powerful man."

"Then why did you help me?"

"Let's just say," he answered, making brief eye contact with her, "that the thought of another long ocean voyage without the company of a beautiful woman was unbearable."

She took a hard look at his profile as he continued to stare out at what remained of the horizon. It wouldn't be easy getting the truth out of this man.

They stood for a moment, both looking out over the wake as it widened and dissipated into the dimpled copper surface of the sea. Finally, he pushed away from the railing.

"We should turn in and get some rest while we can," he said. "Tomorrow will be very busy. I'll bid you good night." He tipped his hat and turned to go.

"Edward."

He stopped to face her. They looked at each other in silence for a moment. Then she stepped forward, placed her hands gently on his arms, slowly lifted her face, and pressed her lips to his. He didn't resist. As the kiss lingered, her fingers tightened around his arms. Did she detect the faintest response, or was he just acting the gentleman? She let go and stepped back.

"Thank you for helping me," she said quietly.

He took a breath as if to say something but stopped himself. Instead, he bowed his head slightly and said, *"De nada."*

She watched him turn and walk away along the deck. After he disappeared down a set of steps, she looked out over the sea. All that remained of the day was a faint wash of ochre lingering on the horizon. As the last traces of light faded and the first stars reclaimed their place in the night sky, she understood she had sailed past the point of no return.

Chapter 35

The yellow-and-burnt-orange buildings lining the Ponte Vecchio stirred to life with a clattering sonata of opening wooden shutters. Walking across the bridge in the direction of the most imposing structure in Florence, the Cathedral of Santa Maria del Fiore—the Duomo—Vincenzo Peruggia stopped to look through a gap in the tightly knit shops. Below him, the Arno flowed gently away from a ring of distant green hills, their crown of cypress trees piercing a cloudless pale blue sky still shrugging off the darkness of the retreating night. He was finally home, and the lingering mist burning off the river could have been the heavy fog lifting from his heart. Catching the first sweet scent of fresh-baked *cornetti* on the warm breeze, he adjusted the wrapped panel beneath his arm and resumed crossing.

With two hours remaining before his appointment at the Uffizi Gallery, Peruggia strolled along the Via por Santa Maria to the Piazza del Duomo. He circled the great domed cathedral again and again, trying to dissipate the intense energy and anticipation that possessed him. The piazza steadily came to life. Beggars staked their claims, assuming their penitent positions near the entrance to the cathedral; market vendors arranged their wares on makeshift tables; artists set up stools and easels to display their caricatures; tourists trickled into the piazza accompanied by the steady click of their heels on the cobblestones.

At ten o'clock, Peruggia appeared at the doors of the Uffizi. He was sure that it would not be long now before his name was acclaimed across his beloved homeland. He would be the man, the hero, who had returned Italy's greatest treasure to its rightful place. He would be famous, not that fame was what mattered, of course. It was justice that he craved, justice for the people of Italy, justice for the nation that was always at the mercy of rapacious tyrants—despots who took what they coveted without mercy or compassion—and justice was what he was about to deliver.

Peruggia sat in an airless anteroom on a wooden bench, the wrapped panel leaning against his knee on the floor beside him. He checked his pocket watch again. It was almost three o'clock. He had been kept waiting for five hours now. Didn't they appreciate the significance of his presence here? No matter. As soon as they realized their mistake, the apologies would flow over him like the River Arno.

The door to an inner office finally opened and out stepped a heavyset, smartly dressed woman, her hair in a tight bun.

"He will see you now," she said, her expression as blank as the walls of the anteroom.

Entering the office, the first thing Peruggia saw was a man—presumably the museum director—writing something at a polished mahogany desk. He was so engrossed in his task that he didn't even look up. How foolish he would soon feel, thought Peruggia, when he realized the significance of the object he possessed.

Only when the heavyset woman closed the door did the man at the desk take notice and raise his head. He was in his sixties, his unnaturally black hair cut in a short style, reminiscent of an ancient Roman emperor. His expression held no welcome, only a vague, surprised curiosity.

"Ah," he began, "Signore . . ."

"Peruggia."

"Yes, yes, of course. Signore Peruggia. I am Signore Bozzetti. *Prego.* Won't you sit down?"

Extending a small, pudgy hand, he indicated a wooden chair on the opposite side of the desk. Peruggia felt a sudden stab of apprehension, as if an inner voice were telling him to leave immediately, to run as far away as possible. But he swallowed his trepidations and sat down, clutching the panel to his chest.

"You had a pleasant journey, I trust."

Signore Bozzetti was not exactly fat, but his soft, round body reminded Peruggia of bread dough. The skin around his neck hung as loose as an ill-fitting suit, though clearly no expense had been spared in custom-fitting his actual suit to his ample body. It was well tailored and shone vibrantly, which made Peruggia all too conscious of his own shabby suit.

"I must admit," Signore Bozzetti continued, "when you telephoned, I was a bit skeptical. You understand that many people claim to have things in their possession that, in fact, exist only in some fantastic recess of their minds."

Was he being insulted? Peruggia wasn't sure, so he remained silent.

"I'm curious," Bozzetti persisted, indicating the panel. "What have I done to deserve such an honor?"

"I understand," began Peruggia slowly, "that you have a certain reputation for discretion."

"That is very true," Bozzetti said, nodding his head with pride, quickly adding, "depending on the situation, of course. You mentioned that your primary motivation was to return the painting to its rightful home."

"My only motivation," Peruggia corrected him.

"Other than the fifty thousand lire you mentioned."

"That is only for my trouble," Peruggia said. Didn't this man understand the nature of fairness, that justice does not come without a price?

"Then you must have gone to much trouble. Assuming, of course, that the painting is genuine."

This is where Peruggia had him. With a satisfied smile, he began to unwrap the panel, taking his time, as if he were removing the petals of a rose.

As the cloth fell away, Peruggia turned the face of the painting slowly toward the museum director, a smug smile on his face.

Bozzetti made a steeple of his forefingers beneath his chin as he appraised it, his eyes narrowing to slits. After a moment, he nodded with cautious approval and looked at Peruggia, his mouth twisting into a condescending smile.

"May I?" he said, opening his hands.

Peruggia hesitated for a moment before holding the panel out from his body. Rising from his chair, Bozzetti leaned over his desk and took it from him. He stepped to the window, turned the panel over and examined the back, his eyes squinting as they explored each quadrant. After a few moments, he turned the panel over. His examination of the painting itself seemed cursory compared to the attention he had paid to the back.

"Very interesting," Bozzetti said, conceding as little as possible in his voice. "Tell me, how did you manage to cross the border with this?"

"I chose a train that I knew would be crowded," Peruggia said. "I thought it was a risk worth taking. As I had hoped, the border guard simply walked through the car and only checked a few passports."

"I see." Bozzetti turned his attention back to the panel. "Do you mind if I ask some colleagues to help me authenticate it?"

Peruggia sprang to his feet.

"We agreed there would be no one else involved."

"It will take only a minute," Bozzetti said as he walked around the desk to the door.

Peruggia felt trapped and the room suddenly grew very hot.

Bozzetti pulled the door open. Two men, both wearing dark suits that appeared a size too small, stepped in without a word. Their hard expressions revealed nothing.

"Signore Peruggia, may I introduce Signore Pavela and Signore Lucci of the carabinieri."

The Italian police! Peruggia's stomach lurched.

Pavela stepped forward and laid a confident grip on Peruggia's arm.

"Signore Peruggia," he said in a flat, officious voice, "I am placing you under arrest for the theft of *La Gioconda*."

Chapter 36

Stuck in his new tiny office in the basement of the Prefecture of Police on the Île de la Cité, Inspector Alphonse Carnot scowled at the file sitting before him on his desk. It detailed the case of one Claude Maria Ziegert, a German national who had lived in Paris for a number of years. Herr Ziegert had recently brought himself to the attention of the police by murdering his landlady, Madame Villon, forty-seven years old at the time of her death. Ziegert was thirty or thirty-one—the record was unclear—and the two were probably having an affair. Perhaps, Carnot considered, he earned a discount on his rent for servicing the woman; or perhaps they had been in love and there had been a lovers' quarrel. Judging by the photograph of Madame Villon's ample body—her throat not very neatly cut—it was probably the former.

The case was now more than three months old and no one had the slightest idea of the whereabouts of Herr Ziegert. The entire affair was as cold as the dead fish sold in the markets of Les Halles and, as far as Carnot was concerned, reeked as badly.

That was why the commissioner had given it to him, of course. Carnot had made the fatal mistake of not only wasting the commissioner's time but also disappointing him, and now he was paying the price.

Disgusted, he closed the file and tossed it into a growing pile of thick folders. Seconds later the door opened and in walked the young gendarme who had been assigned to Carnot when he was in the commissioner's good graces. Although the young man was present at the fingerprint fiasco, Carnot couldn't remember his name.

"Inspector," the young man began brightly, "the Italian police have arrested a man in Florence for trying to sell *La Joconde*."

Carnot's eyes turned to the next file. "And what would that make," he asked dismissively, "the tenth or eleventh time someone has tried to pawn off some amateurish copy?"

"No, Inspector," the young man persisted. "This one is a former employee of the Louvre."

Carnot looked up.

"Come in. Tell me."

The gendarme walked in, delighted that his news had struck a nerve.

"I was there when the telegram came in. It was put into a pile with all the other leads, but I remembered the name. Last year there was a fight in one of the cafés in the Saint-Martin district. The man who started the fight was an Italian named Peruggia, and I remembered that he was employed as a maintenance worker at the Louvre."

"Most observant," said Carnot. "Good work . . . what was your name again?"

"Brousard, Inspector," the young man said, a little deflated.

"Of course, Brousard," Carnot quickly said.

"I was thinking," Brousard continued, "that perhaps you should send someone to interview the man, I mean before the information reaches the commissioner."

"Perhaps you're right," said Carnot. "In fact"—he rose briskly to his feet—"I think I will go myself."

"But Inspector, I thought the commissioner confined you to desk duty."

"Did you?" Carnot said as he grabbed his hat and coat from a stand. "Brousard, you've done a good job. If this lead pays off, it will go very well for me. And, of course, I will make sure it goes very well for you also."

"Thank you, Inspector," Brousard said, drawing himself up straight.

"Oh," Carnot added before leaving, "and if the commissioner inquires of my whereabouts, just tell him I've gone out for a croissant."

Chapter 37

The docking of the *Prinz Joachim* in Le Havre had been delayed by fog, so by the time the train left for Paris it was already full daylight. Valfierno and Ellen Hart spent most of the journey in silence. He buried himself in a pile of newspapers; she stared out the window observing the endless rolling countryside dotted with small farms and villages, each marked by its own distinctive church steeple. The contrast of the trees rushing by just outside the window with the more stately passage of the distant hills and fields had an almost hypnotic effect, allowing her to empty her mind for a while.

She thought of the last night on the boat. She could easily rationalize the kiss as a gesture of gratitude, a way of thanking him for helping her. But if she was being honest with herself, she knew there had been something else, but she wasn't quite sure what it was. Had she wanted him to sweep her into his arms and declare undying love? Had it been a test of some kind? If so, had he failed? He had done nothing in response, or very little, anyway. It was hard to remember now. He hadn't drawn away, but he hadn't given any indication that the kiss had been particularly welcome either.

She tried to push away the thought. It was useless to speculate. She had thanked him, that was all. Another thought brought a wry private smile to her face. Perhaps she had only succeeded in making a complete fool of herself.

"We'll soon be approaching the outskirts of the city," Valfierno said in a matter-of-fact tone.

She looked at him briefly, then turned her face back to the window.

Disembarking at the Gare d'Orsay, Ellen felt a rush of excitement as the frantic energy of the city began to sweep over her. She had been in Paris twice before, once when she was eleven years old with both her parents, and once when she was twelve with just her mother, before she had slipped into her coma. On that occasion, they had visited the *Exposition Universelle* of 1889, but even seeing the newly constructed Eiffel Tower, and the giant halls displaying the endless wonders of the industrial age, did not make her feel as exhilarated as she was now. The sense of adventure and possibility made her heartbeat quicken with anticipation, a feeling she hadn't experienced since she was a little girl. It was pure happiness, even tinged as it was by the specter of an uncertain future.

Exiting the terminus, Valfierno quickly found a motor taxi. What little baggage they had was loaded into the vehicle and he directed the driver to take them directly to Madame Charneau's house. Valfierno traveled with two valises, one of cloth, one of leather. He always kept a particularly watchful eye on the leather valise, and Ellen imagined it contained the fruits of his most recent labors.

The drive through Saint-Germain-des-Prés was far too short for Ellen's taste. She stared with fascination at the endless parade of electric trolleys, horse-drawn carts, motorcars competing with sleek ponies conveying elegant gray-bearded gentlemen in their four-wheeled barouches, men in sandwich boards touting the wonders of the latest *grand magasin,* and tradesmen toting high-backed wicker baskets. Styles had of course changed since her last visit. It was a new century. Women no longer accentuated their bosoms, wasplike waists, and hips into exaggerated hourglass shapes; now the lines were longer and slimmer, fur-trimmed coats taming their bodies into sleek straight lines. Hats were smaller and no longer blossomed into veritable mobile gardens of flowers. One thing hadn't changed: the women being led by small dogs at the end of taut leashes, keeping their balance with tasseled silk parasols, still dressing their pets in tiny outfits to match their own.

If only the journey itself would last forever, she thought as the taxi pulled into the cour de Rohan.

"Of course," Madame Charneau said with a welcoming smile, "any friend of the marquis is welcome to stay here as my guest for as long as she wishes."

Ellen sat across from Madame Charneau in the living room of her boardinghouse. Valfierno stood behind Ellen, while Émile and Julia observed from opposite sides of the room.

"You're very kind, madame," Ellen said. "I'll pay, of course."

"Only here for a few minutes"—Madame Charneau chuckled for the benefit of the others—"and she's already insulting me."

"You are most kind," Ellen said, a slight flush on her face.

"Well," Madame Charneau began, "you've had a long journey. You must be tired. I'll show you to your room."

Ellen rose and glanced at Émile and Julia in turn, smiling her gratitude.

Turning to Valfierno, she said, "Perhaps, Edward, I will see you later."

Valfierno's only response was a slight bow of acknowledgment.

"This way, *chérie*," Madame Charneau said, leading her from the room.

As soon as Madame Charneau and Ellen disappeared up the staircase, Julia started peppering Valfierno with excited questions. "What in the world is going on? How on earth did she end up here? What happened? Tell me everything!"

"Not now, Julia, please," said Valfierno.

"But—"

"Is it all there?" Émile broke in, focusing his attention on the leather valise at Valfierno's feet.

Valfierno was relieved to change the subject. "Minus some necessary expenses and a reasonable incentive to make the customs officials look the other way, and there it will stay for now. We can't afford to draw attention to ourselves by trying to change such a large amount of currency, certainly not before the painting has been safely returned to the museum."

"Then let's take it back now," Émile said. "We'll just leave it on their doorstep or something."

"All in good time," Valfierno said. "It will be done soon, but it must be done right. We have to make certain there will be absolutely no connection, no trail that can lead back to us." After a pause, he asked, "Where is Peruggia?" The question was casual, almost an afterthought.

Valfierno caught the furtive glance the two shared.

"Well?"

"He's gone," Émile said, a little sheepishly.

"Back to Italy," Julia added.

Valfierno looked from one to the other before nodding his head in resignation. "It was inevitable. He was determined. I was hoping that he would at least wait to be paid."

"There was no stopping him," Émile said.

"Not that we didn't try," Julia chorused in.

There was something about the tone of their voices that indicated a shared confidence.

"And you had no difficulty switching the paintings." It was both a statement and a question.

"Of course not," said Julia.

"And the original is in a safe place?"

"Absolutely safe," Émile began. "It's—"

"No." Valfierno stopped him. "I don't need to know where it is. I trust you, Émile. And if I don't know where it is, I won't be tempted to look at it, and if I don't look at it, I won't be tempted to keep it for myself. No one is immune to the lure of great beauty."

Julia noticed that, after saying this, Valfierno glanced over to the staircase in the foyer.

"Well, no matter," he continued, turning to face them. "We'll wait perhaps a few more weeks, see if there is any word of Peruggia. In the meantime we'll devise the best way to return it." He lightened his tone. "So, I was greatly impressed by the various accounts I read of your accomplishment. It was quite a feat."

"It wasn't so bad, really," Émile said with a look to Julia.

"It was amazing," Julia said, excited as a child, "and I had to step in at the last minute to go inside the museum. That idiot, Brique—"

"Yes," Valfierno cut in, "where is he?"

"He disappeared before the theft and we never heard from him again," said Émile. "Lucky for us, he knew nothing of what we were planning."

"I had to step in and take his place," Julia persisted. "You wouldn't believe what I had to—"

Valfierno stopped her with a gentle motion of his hand. "I'll hear all about it soon, but for now I'm very tired from the journey. I slept little last night."

"Of course," Julia said, unable to hide the disappointment in her voice.

"Émile," Valfierno said, "would you be so kind as to take my bag out to the car?"

Émile reached down and grabbed the handle of the leather valise.

"No, just the other bag, please. I'll take this one."

With an awkward smile, Émile replaced the leather valise on the floor and walked to the foyer to gather up Valfierno's travel bag.

Valfierno picked up the valise and he and Julia followed Émile into the foyer.

"And the two of you are getting along all right?" Valfierno asked Julia after Émile had walked out into the courtyard with the bag.

"The two of us?" said Julia lightly. "Oh, like two peas in a pod. In fact, between you and me, I think he's madly in love with me."

Valfierno stopped at the front door.

"Well," he said with a smile, "I'm glad at least that you're getting on together."

"Speaking of which . . ." Julia made a gesture with her head toward the upstairs.

"Señora Hart?" Valfierno responded almost dismissively. "I can assure you that it wasn't my idea to bring her back. She left me with little choice."

"I see. And tell me, what does Mr. Hart think about all this?"

"You know, it's a funny thing," Valfierno said with a sly smile as he walked out into the courtyard, "but I never did get the opportunity to ask him."

Chapter 38

As soon as he arrived in Florence, Inspector Carnot went straight to the Comando Provinciale on Borgo Ognissanti and demanded to see the local commissioner of the carabinieri, Signore Caravagio.

By introducing himself as the official representative of the Sûreté in Paris come to take possession of the stolen masterpiece and custody of its thief, Carnot knew he was taking the biggest gamble of his life. Commissioner Lepine had given him no such authority. If he succeeded, the point would be moot. The newspapers of Paris would splash his name all over their front pages. The commissioner would make sure his own name was also prominently displayed, of course, but he would not be able to take anything away from Carnot, the man who actually recovered *La Joconde* and delivered its thief.

If he failed . . . well, he would not fail; he could not fail. Both the painting and the man were in the hands of the Italian police. It was just a matter of convincing them to release them both into his custody.

Or so he thought.

"I'm afraid, Inspector," began Signore Caravagio, "that the painting in question is a forgery."

"A forgery?" Carnot said. "Are you sure?"

"It has been thoroughly examined by three experts in the field," Caravagio said with an air of impatient authority. "Mind you, it is a very good forgery. Expertly done, they say, but a forgery nonetheless. You may discuss the matter with the director of the museum, Signore Bozzetti, if you like."

Carnot's insides twisted in turmoil. By now, his absence from the Sûreté would have been noted. He really should have thought this through better; perhaps he should have feigned illness to explain his absence. It was too late now, and to return to Paris empty-handed was unthinkable. He would lose his position, probably be demoted to an ordinary *flic* and assigned to the night beat in Pigalle, becoming the laughingstock of the force. But perhaps all was not lost.

"The prisoner," began Carnot with an authority he neither possessed nor felt, "have you told him the painting is a forgery?"

Carnot observed Peruggia through the judas-hole in his cell door. The prisoner sat on the edge of his cot, cradling his head in his hands. A small barred window provided the only natural light. Was this man simply an opportunist who had come into possession of a very good fake, or was he involved in the actual robbery? If the former, then Carnot truly had nothing. But if the latter . . .

Carnot nodded to the uniformed guard, who jerked back the bolt of the lock and tugged on the handle. The door swung open with a grating squeal and the prisoner looked up, squinting against the harsh light from the corridor. Carnot stood silhouetted against the glare for a moment before walking in, motioning for the guard to keep the door open.

"Signore Peruggia. I am Inspector Carnot of the Sûreté in Paris."

The prisoner's only response was to lower his head and stare at his shoes. Carnot walked a few steps to the wall, peering up at the small, barred window near the ceiling. He saw no sky, only the towering prison walls, gray and menacing.

"Not the nicest view in Florence."

Still no response. He nodded to the guard, who brought in a stool and placed it next to the bed. The guard left the cell, standing just outside the door. Carnot lowered his bulk onto the stool.

"Your face," Carnot began, "it is somehow familiar to me. Have we met before?"

Peruggia slowly raised his head and looked at Carnot.

"Yes," Carnot continued, "the Louvre. You used to work there. Am I right?"

Peruggia said nothing, averting his eyes to the floor.

Despite the lack of response, Carnot felt a growing confidence. Peruggia was one of the two men who had dropped the shadow box. A real hothead, he recalled. This had to be played just right.

"Your impulse to return *La Joconde* to its home country was commendable."

Peruggia looked up again and spoke in grave tones. "Injustice is only a word until a man acts to remedy it."

That was more like it, Carnot thought, though he was surprised the man had so much conviction in his voice. He'd have to do something about that.

"Commendable," he said, "but misguided."

"I wouldn't expect a Frenchman to understand."

"Understand what?"

"What a patriot feels when the treasures of his homeland are plundered by an invader."

"An invader," said Carnot, considering. "I assume you are referring to Napoleon Bonaparte."

"Who else would I be referring to?" Peruggia spat out. "My only desire was to save the honor of Italy by returning *La Gioconda*. But this country is run by fools now, fools who cannot recognize the heart of a true patriot."

"A true patriot," said Carnot, mulling over the phrase, "not to mention a very foolish one."

"My mother gave birth to no fools," Peruggia snapped, his eyes narrowing.

"I submit that the record shows otherwise."

Peruggia sat up, bristling. "If you came here to insult me—"

"That was the last thing I came here for," said Carnot. Then his voice took on an almost professorial tone. "Perhaps a little history lesson is in order."

After his interview with Signore Caravagio, Carnot had paid a visit to the Uffizi, where he was reassured by Signore Bozzetti that the painting was indeed an excellent fake. In the course of that meeting he had also learned some interesting facts, facts that were about to come in handy.

"Simply put," Carnot began, "Napoleon did not steal *La Joconde*."

"You don't know what you're talking about!"

"I'm afraid I do. History shows that it was purchased by François the First, king of France, in 1516, from Leonardo da Vinci himself. I believe he paid four thousand gold coins for it." He had made a point of memorizing some important details. "The painting did— for a time—hang in Napoleon's bedroom, but it was finally bequeathed to the Louvre. So, you see, your entire little crusade has, at best, been based on misinformation, and at worst, built on pure fantasy."

"I don't believe you."

"You need only consult any history book, or any expert to confirm the accuracy of what I say."

"I don't care what any of them say," Peruggia said, his defiance starting to show a few cracks.

"But the trouble is," Carnot said, adding a touch of impatience to his voice for dramatic effect, "the rest of the world does."

Peruggia looked back down and grew silent again. Carnot smiled. He was making progress.

"And then, of course," he continued, making an effort to sound sympathetic, "consider the matter of the fifty thousand lire you demanded. A true patriot would hardly expect to profit from his noble gesture."

"No Italian would convict a fellow countryman of returning *La Gioconda* to the land of its birth," Peruggia said.

The conviction was steadily leaking out of the man, thought

Carnot. He slowly got to his feet and stepped to the wall beneath the small window. It was time.

"Perhaps not," he said. "However, they might convict a petty scoundrel for trying to cheat them."

"Cheat them?" Peruggia erupted. "I was not trying to cheat anyone."

"Are you trying to tell me that you were not aware the painting is a forgery? A fake? Surely, you cannot be that naïve."

"Now you're trying to trick *me*."

"Why would I do that? If the painting were genuine, I wouldn't even bother to come and see you. I'd simply return with it to France and leave you here to rot."

"No, it's not possible," Peruggia said.

"It's been appraised by three experts," Carnot said smugly. "The Italians may not know much else but—excluding yourself, apparently—they know their art."

"But I never let it out of my sight." Peruggia said this more to himself than to Carnot. He got to his feet and started pacing, staring down at the cell floor as if it somehow held the truth.

Carnot felt hope stir in his chest. This was the man's first concrete admission of guilt.

"Never?" he asked.

Peruggia stopped cold. Carnot held his breath. He was almost there.

"Those mongrels!" Peruggia finally said, as much to himself as to Carnot. "They swindled me!"

Carnot smiled in satisfaction.

"Tell me about these mongrels, my friend," he said, his voice dripping with empathy.

Peruggia turned to Carnot, his eyes narrowing.

"Why?" the Italian said warily. "Why should I tell you anything? What's in it for me?"

Carnot shrugged in an effort to indicate it was of no great consequence to him.

"Say nothing and you'll not only go to jail for forgery and fraud but also become a pariah in your own country, a traitor who tried to play a hoax on the people of Italy. And you'll expose yourself to the entire world as a classic fool in the bargain. On the other hand, tell me everything and you may very well become the national hero you aspire to be . . . the man who recovered the true *Gioconda*."

Peruggia looked up to the small, high window and the gray brick prison walls beyond. Clenching his fist, he slowly raised his arm toward the fading light. Then, in a sudden, violent move, he slammed the side of his fist into the rough stone wall.

And Carnot knew he had him.

Chapter 39

The people who lived in the city of Dijon and in the small villages along the Plateau de Langres could not remember a worse winter. The short days, made even shorter by the dark, dank clouds that hid sun and sky for weeks on end, had taken their toll on the mood of the populace. And now the rains had come again. All night, the heavy precipitation pounded on the roofs, keeping the inhabitants awake. During the day, the rain cascaded down in sheets, turning people into virtual prisoners in their own dark, fetid houses.

Already, the streams and tributaries that flowed into the Seine had become swollen, rushing torrents. People who made their living loading the *péniches* with wine and goods bound for the Bercy docks and warehouses along the Paris riverfront knew that if this kept up they would be in for hard times indeed. Once the river flooded, it would become too dangerous for navigation.

Everyone agreed. No one could recall a time when there had been so much rain.

Part V

For the rain it raineth every day.
—Shakespeare, *Twelfth Night*

Chapter 40

Since arriving in Paris three weeks ago, Ellen Hart had felt the burden she had carried for almost as long as she could remember ease. She had been surrounded by luxury, attended day and night by a small army of servants, granted every material wish. But all these things had become a millstone around her neck, tethering her to a life she had been forced to choose. Her devotion to her mother had provided her with the only incentive to get through each day; her mother's death had left her with a heart as heavy as lead, her reason for living suddenly gone forever. Only one hope had presented itself, a distant light on the horizon. Eduardo Valfierno. And that hope had now brought her to Paris where, in spite of an uncertain future, she felt as warm and light as the fluid rhythms of the language that surrounded her. Part of her extensive education as a young lady was learning to speak French, the language of diplomats. Indeed, she had spoken French with her mother many times, and using it now brought back fond memories of those interactions. She even found herself conversing with Julia in French. She imagined that Julia felt the same way as she did, that it was more than a language, it was a different way of thinking, of relating to one another, of living.

Her stay at Madame Charneau's house in the cour de Rohan had been comfortable and pleasant. The older woman was like a kindly aunt who had done her best to make her feel at home; Julia could have been a younger cousin chatting endlessly about how naïve Émile was and how Diego was always leering suggestively at her, though whether Julia thought the latter was a bad thing or a good thing was sometimes hard to tell. Ellen found the younger woman friendly and amusing, even though they shared little common ground.

The cloistered courtyards and spiderweb of lanes and arcades within steps of Madame Charneau's front door were an oasis in the midst of the city. The nearby cour du Commerce Saint-André was lined with small shops and businesses, each one more charming and fascinating than the last. Antique shops stood shoulder to shoulder with tiny restaurants, *papeteries,* tea salons, and *chocolatiers.* Ellen's particular favorite was a toy shop with windows festooned with puppets, toy boats, and tin soldiers, all arrayed around a magnificent hot-air balloon, the envelope above the basket so elaborately decorated that it reminded her of a fat Fabergé egg.

Despite the persistent rain that had plagued Paris during the last few weeks, almost every other day she would walk to the river and cross the Petit Pont onto the Île de la Cité. The year-round flower market running along the quai aux Fleurs on the northeast bank of the river never failed to lift her spirits. Ellen had missed the summer with its wild olfactory concert of natural perfumes and fragrances played by a profusion of jasmine, dahlias, and myrtle; and autumn when an endless variety of chrysanthemums held court. But even now, in the dead of winter, Mediterranean greenhouses and the far-off gardens of Chile contributed to an abundance of bouquets, each arrangement trying to eclipse its neighbor.

Indeed, Ellen had brought back so many flowers and potted plants that Madame Charneau sometimes complained with a smile of feeling giddy from the aroma. Thank goodness the American woman didn't become as obsessed with Sunday's Marché aux Oiseaux. The last thing she needed was a house full of canaries, finches, and cockatiels!

Émile visited from time to time, mostly to confer with Madame Charneau. When she was in the house on these visits, Julia seemed genuinely pleased to see him. Émile rarely showed any overt signs of enthusiasm toward Julia, but Ellen suspected that he also enjoyed these encounters. Still, the meetings were often cut short when Émile announced that it was time to be getting back to Valfierno's house.

She had not seen Valfierno since the day they had arrived together in Paris three weeks ago, and though her excursions and observations were a distraction, she still found herself hoping that he would pay her a visit. She would hear a motorcar in the courtyard and her heart would beat a little faster, but when no knock came on the door, the disappointment she felt was palpable.

And so, finally, she had taken matters into her own hands.

Through Émile she had requested a meeting with Valfierno at his house. He had replied that he expected to be visiting the cour de Rohan soon and he could see her then, but Ellen persisted. The rendezvous was finally set for three o'clock in the afternoon of the coming Saturday.

Madame Charneau had offered to take Ellen to Valfierno's house, or at the very least have Émile come and fetch her, but she had insisted on going by herself. She preferred it that way. She had his address and general directions and would be able to find the house. And she wanted to be alone with her thoughts on the way over.

She left the cour de Rohan a little after one o'clock with plenty of time to spare. Thankfully, the morning rain had stopped, though the sky was still overhung with gray, brooding clouds. Crossing the Petit Pont to the Île de la Cité, her attention was drawn momentarily to a group of young people—students from the Sorbonne judging by their fashionably bohemian outfits—looking with interest at the river. She peered over the side briefly to see what they might be looking at. The water had taken on a dark gray pallor, and a few young boys were down on the lower quayside sloshing through ankle-deep water. She watched for a moment before turning and continuing on.

Reaching the island, she glanced up at the great cathedral as she walked toward the Pont Notre-Dame. Reaching the Right Bank, she turned east along the river, then crossed the place de l'Hôtel de Ville. The large square at the foot of the palatial city government building—usually alive with activity—lay empty and forlorn, a sheen of rainwater reflecting the murky cloud cover above. Continuing on, she soon found herself in one of the oldest parts of Paris, the Marais.

Within only a few minutes, she became completely lost in the labyrinth of streets snaking about like an urban maze. This old and unfashionable district of the city had escaped the massive redesign of Paris by Baron Haussmann fifty years earlier by dint of its lack of importance and its general reputation of squalor. Its twisted warren of narrow medieval lanes, laid out without the benefit of rhyme or reason, still confused and tantalized the unwary traveler.

No wide boulevards dominated by walls of uniform five-story edifices and mansards could be found here. Instead, each building seemed to have been erected in a different time, for a different purpose, in a completely different style. Large, gated *hotels particuliers* cloistered by high walls loomed beside tiny cafés; narrow apartment buildings stood shoulder to shoulder, broken only by miniature parks bustling—even in the gloomy weather—with noisy, spirited children; bearded Eastern European Jews plied their trades within a myriad of leather and jewelry workshops; butchers and fishmongers displayed their wares in dozens of small establishments open to the street; bookshops, *magasins d'antiquités*, and galleries, their wooden façades painted in bright red, blue, and green, teetered along the *petit trottoirs*. This was a world apart from the broad, open boulevards of the New Paris.

Not that the Marais was all industry and squalor. Many of the city's bourgeoisie preferred the atmosphere of the old city to that of the renovated, modern city. And the living was much cheaper here, not to mention far more colorful.

At first, Ellen felt completely disoriented by the puzzle of lanes and alleyways, but despite the sporadic outbursts of rain that forced her to seek shelter beneath handy archways or awnings, she found herself enjoying being lost on the streets of Paris. In fact, she had never felt freer in her life. To turn this way and that, to jostle people on the thin ribbon of pavement, to marvel at all the wonders around her, filled her with excitement and anticipation of what she might encounter around the next sharply angled corner.

And the multitude of distractions kept her mind off the apprehension she felt about her upcoming meeting with Valfierno. She had wanted time to consider what she was going to say to him, but the more she thought about it, the harder it became to come up with something. All she knew was that somehow she had to find out once and for all what his true feelings were. She had grown up in a culture where directness was considered the height of rudeness, but she was tired of such games—for games were what they were—and, if she had to, she would simply ask him if he cared for her. So why did she feel that something so simple would be the most difficult thing she had ever done?

She occasionally stopped to politely ask for directions, but the answers were of little help. Everyone seemed to have the attitude that it was inconceivable that she wasn't familiar with the area and therefore shouldn't really need directions in the first place. And so, it was rather disconcerting that when she mentioned rue de Picardie to a butcher arranging his meats in front of his narrow shop on rue de Bretagne, he impatiently pointed to a street corner barely halfway up the block.

"C'est là, madame," he said in a tone that suggested that only a fool would not know she was already there, "c'est là!"

And she was more than a half hour early.

The editorial cartoon depicted a group of Louvre guards standing defiantly in front of the empty space where La Joconde had once hung. The head guard protests, "It couldn't be stolen, we guard her all the time, except on Mondays." Valfierno was considering whether to divert himself by reading an editorial in Le Matin deploring the ineptitude of the museum's security when the clang of his front door knocker drew his attention.

He pulled out his pocket watch. Not yet even 2:30. Knowing of Ellen's anticipated visit, Émile had left earlier for the marketplace at Les Halles, so Valfierno was alone in the house, and he had not expected Ellen to arrive so early. He had made a point of avoiding her since their arrival in Paris. He had thought it would be best for both of them that way. He could have easily left her in New York. Her threats, such as they were, had little weight. But they had provided him with justification for the decision to bring her with him—a very bad idea by all sensible reckoning, but something nonetheless that he was glad to do. Still, he could afford to find room only for his desire to help her; any other feelings would jeopardize everything he and the others had worked so hard for.

He walked to the first-floor window. Looking down, he caught a brief glimpse of a woman standing beneath the small overhang above the front door.

Though he had been trying to prepare himself all day, Valfierno felt his heart race.

Walking down the stairs, he reminded himself that he would do whatever was in his power to help her, but no more.

He paused at the door, allowing himself the brief joy of anticipating seeing her face again. He reached out and turned the knob.

"Eduardo," the woman said as the door swung open, "I thought you were going to keep me standing out here on the pavement all day."

"Chloe," Valfierno exclaimed, stunned.

The last person he would have expected to see at his door was the wife of the art dealer Jean Laroche, the man who had set a gang of street thugs on him so many years ago, possibly at his wife's suggestion.

"Well?" she said coquettishly. "Aren't you going to invite me in?"

"I'm actually expecting someone."

"Are you, now? Well, I wouldn't want to spoil your little tête-à-tête, but surely you won't deny an old friend a few minutes of your time."

Valfierno hesitated, glancing down the narrow empty street.

"Of course not," he finally said. "Please, come in."

Chloe stepped into the foyer, giving him a flirtatious glance as she passed him. She stopped and turned, taking in the surroundings as she removed her black silk gloves.

"So this is where you've been hiding," she said, coyly flashing her pale blue eyes. "It wasn't easy to find you, you know."

"What a delightful surprise that you did," Valfierno said evenly. "And how is Monsieur Laroche?"

"Oh, didn't you hear? He died. You see? I'm in mourning."

She executed a little pirouette to show off her black dress, perfectly fitted from her ample bosom to her wasplike waist. Her hips were delightfully accentuated by the fashionable small hoops beneath the fabric. Somehow, Valfierno thought, she always managed to be both petite and buxom at the same time.

"You have my condolences, madame."

"Thank you," she said with wry sarcasm, "but I already have all the condolences I need."

"How did your husband . . ."

"He killed himself," she said matter-of-factly, "with a pistol. At least he had the decency to do it off in le Bois de Boulogne and not in our house. There's that, at least. And, of course, the small fortune he left behind."

Valfierno was about to inquire further into the matter but thought better of it.

"Well," he began, "as I mentioned, I'm expecting someone."

"Please, Eduardo," she said coyly, "just five minutes of your time and I'll be gone. I promise."

After a brief hesitation, he indicated a small sitting room just off the foyer.

They sat down, Chloe on a small settee, Valfierno on an upholstered chair. She gathered herself together like a flower arranging its petals and looked him straight in the eye. She had the face of one of those bisque portrait dolls they sold at La Samaritaine, round and exquisitely proportioned with large, expressive eyes.

"And so," Valfierno said, "to what do I owe the pleasure of your visit?"

"Ah, yes. Well, it's very simple, really. My husband—being an art dealer—left behind lots of . . . well, you know, paintings and little sculptures and other such things, and now I need help to dispose of it all."

"Then you have come to the right place," said Valfierno brightly. "Within walking distance of this house you will find at least a dozen of the best art dealers in Paris."

"But I was hoping that I could prevail upon you to help me. In fact, I am convinced we would make ideal business partners."

"Alas, madame . . ."

"Chloe."

"Chloe. I have retired from that business, and though I am grateful that you thought of me, I'm afraid I must decline your kind offer. Well, it really has been delightful to see you."

Valfierno began to rise from his chair.

"You're right, of course," she said. "It's such a boring business. I can't wait to get as far away from it as possible, which brings me to the real point of my visit."

Valfierno reluctantly sat back down.

"Don't worry. I won't spoil your little rendezvous. I'll say my piece and then just disappear. Like a little bird." She made a fluttery hand gesture before homing in on him with partially lidded eyes. "You know, Eduardo, I always regretted that we never . . . got to know each other better."

"I'm not sure your husband would have approved of that."

"Indeed. Of course, now that he is out of the picture, that particular concern is no longer relevant."

"You flatter me, madame," Valfierno said, "you really do, but time has a stubborn habit of constantly moving forward. One has as much chance of rewinding a clock as of reversing the course of a river."

"Oh, Eduardo," she said with a disappointed sigh, "you really should have been a poet instead of wasting your life as a cheap charlatan."

"Madame," he said with mock indignation, "a charlatan perhaps, but never cheap."

"Tell me," she continued, indicating herself with a flourish of her hands. "Honestly, how can you possibly turn this down?"

She must be forty at least, Valfierno thought, but she was still one of the most alluring women he had ever laid eyes on.

"It's not easy, I admit," he said as he rose from his chair, "but one must be strong. Well, it has been good to see you again, Chloe."

She stood up, a sly look on her face.

"This guest you're expecting is of course a woman."

"A good friend of mine."

She teasingly placed her hands on his chest. "I was right, wasn't I?" She suddenly turned playfully petulant. "You can tell me. Exactly how good a friend is she?" Her tone was thick with theatrical jealousy.

He gently took her hands in his and lifted them. "Chloe. You've never changed and you never will. The world needs women like you, if for no other reason than to remind men what passion really is, not to mention to show them how beautiful and dangerous someone of your sex can be."

"I'll take that as a compliment."

"You should." He gave her hands back to her. "I only hope that your next husband appreciates the exquisite rose he will be holding."

"Tell me," she said, pulling on her gloves, "is she more beautiful than me? Younger perhaps?"

"Madame," Valfierno replied as he led her from the sitting room, "as for the former, it is not possible to find a woman more beautiful than you in all of Paris; and as for the latter, well, as you are ageless, the point is moot."

"You're very smooth, Valfierno," Chloe allowed, "but I doubt that this woman, whoever she is, is a match for you. If you were smart, you'd realize that if you fell in love with me there would be nothing in the world you couldn't accomplish. Not only would you taste pleasures beyond your wildest imaginings, but between the two of us we could have all of Paris in the palm of our hands in no time at all."

"Chloe," Valfierno said, not unkindly, "the trouble with people like us is that we have forgotten, if we ever knew, how to fall in love. We hold on too tightly to our little worlds, the worlds we have created and know so well. To let go is too painful."

"Oh, I see," said Chloe in a mocking lilt. "We are talking about love now. I didn't realize this was so serious. How generous of you to allow this poor unsuspecting creature into your sordid little world."

"It's been delightful," Valfierno said, ending the conversation as he swung the door open and gently guided her out onto the narrow strip of pavement.

"It's a rare man indeed who would so eagerly show me out to the street."

Valfierno acknowledged this with a knowing smile and a slight tilt of his head.

"Well," she said, resigned, "the least you can do is give me a good-bye kiss."

He took both of her hands and raised them to his lips.

"Good-bye, Chloe," he said, releasing her. "I hope you'll find whatever you're looking for."

She gave a slight shrug, masking her face with a cherubic smile.

"And I am truly sorry that you never will."

She raised herself up on her toes, cupped his chin in her gloved hands, and gave him a lingering, passionate kiss. Then, with a flirtatious backward glance, she sashayed off toward rue de Bretagne.

After Valfierno closed the door behind her, he removed his pocket watch to check the time.

Ellen stared up at the enameled blue plaque on the side of the brick wall: rue de Picardie. Barely more than an alleyway, the cobblestone street was hardly wide enough to accommodate a single cart or motorcar. The buildings on either side, each painted a different pastel color, rose to different heights, which lent the street a pleasant haphazard quality.

Checking her reflection in a shop window, she self-consciously straightened her coat. When she was satisfied, she turned in time to see two people emerge from the third house on the right.

Her heart jumped.

Valfierno stood with his back to her talking with a woman at least a head shorter than he was, dressed in black.

Valfierno took the woman's hands, lifted and kissed them. When he let go, the woman said something before raising herself onto her tiptoes, putting her hands on his face, and giving him a lingering kiss. She couldn't make out Valfierno's reaction. She only saw him gently touch her arm.

The woman stepped past Valfierno and, giving him a backward glance, started to walk toward Ellen. As Valfierno went back inside and closed the door, Ellen quickly spun back to look into the shop window, her heart pounding.

As the woman approached, Ellen could not resist glancing to the side, briefly catching her eye. She turned back to the window and saw the woman's reflection as she walked behind her, catching her eye again in the mirrorlike glass. The woman walked forward for a few steps but, instead of turning into rue de Bretagne, she stopped. After a moment's hesitation, she turned back to face Ellen.

"Excuse me, madame," the woman said, stepping forward.

Ellen turned to her.

"Forgive me," the woman continued, "but have you come to see Monsieur Valfierno?"

Ellen felt suddenly short of breath. She stared at the woman for what seemed like an eternity. It was difficult to tell her age. She was not tall but quite shapely with slender arms and legs. She was dressed entirely in black and her dark hair was bunched beneath a short velvet toque.

"Yes," Ellen finally said, as if in a daze. "Yes, I am."

"I knew it," Chloe said. "I have a special sense for these things. Oh, I'm sorry. I'm being terribly rude. I am Madame Laroche. Chloe Laroche."

Chloe extended a gloved hand. Ellen looked at it for a moment before taking it.

"I'm . . . pleased to meet you," Ellen said.

The woman narrowed her eyes, a slight knowing smile playing on her face.

"You are an American."

"Yes," Ellen said. "I'm afraid my French is not as good as it should be."

"*Mais non.* It is excellent. You must be Eduardo's new friend. He mentioned you."

There was something about this woman's manner that made Ellen uncomfortable. She seemed to be probing for something, as if she had some superior knowledge that she was trying to verify.

"Yes," Ellen answered. "I am Mrs. Hart, Mrs. Ellen Hart."

"*Mrs.* Hart," Chloe repeated with evident surprise. "*Enchanté.* Do you know Eduardo well?"

"Not very well, really. You . . . are his friend?"

"Oh, yes. I should say so," answered Chloe. "We have been . . . friends for quite some time. Since before he left for Buenos Aires. It was unfortunate that he had to leave Paris so suddenly. Between you and me, I do believe there is more to his exporting business sometimes than he cares to reveal."

Ellen felt the sudden urge to get away from this woman.

"Well, it has been a pleasure to meet you." Ellen nodded politely and moved to step away.

"Madame Hart." Chloe put her hand on Ellen's arm to stop her. "I believe I know why you are here."

"You do?"

"Of course. It's very clear. You are in love with him."

Ellen took a sharp breath. "I don't think that is any of your—"

"But my dear, he confides in me totally. As one always does with *une amante. Comprenez?* What's the word I'm looking for? A very special friend, a paramour, you understand?"

Ellen felt suddenly faint.

"He did not tell you?" Chloe asked with mock surprise tinged with sympathy. "Well, that's a man for you. Never wants to hurt a woman, especially a pretty one. And you are quite pretty. You look pale. Are you all right?"

Ellen could think of nothing to say. And the pitiful, sympathetic look the woman was giving her made her want to strike that beautiful face with the back of her hand.

"Excuse me," Ellen finally said, stepping around her.

"There I go again," said Chloe, calling after her. "I just say what I think, whatever pops into my silly head. I'm sure that Eduardo will straighten everything out."

Chloe Laroche let the satisfied smile settle into her face as she spun around and started off down rue de Bretagne, turning the heads of various men as she passed.

Struggling to hold back tears, Ellen approached Valfierno's door, finally stopping on the cobblestones as she raised her hand to muffle the sobs. She stood for only an instant before turning and walking away quickly to the end of rue de Picardie.

Hurrying off down rue de Bretagne back toward the river, tears snaking down her cheeks, she welcomed the rain as it began to fall again, harder than ever.

Even the pelting rain did little to wash the black coal dust from the miners' faces as they trudged through the muddy streets of Lorroy on their way to their midday meal. The livelihoods of everyone in the small community situated fifty miles south of Paris depended on one thing: coal. Most men toiled long hours in mine shafts cut into the hills; others loaded the coal onto barges on the canal to be floated down to the Seine for its journey to Paris and points farther north. But the heavy rains had made it impossible for the barges to return to pick up more loads. The swollen, rushing tributaries feeding into the Seine had stopped all river traffic, the canal docks had overflowed, and the mine carts stood idle, clogged with coal that could not be unloaded. But still the dangerous work of scraping the black gold from the hills of Lorroy continued.

The men were used to hardship, but the relentless rain made their harsh existence almost unbearable. At this time of year, it was dark when they left their homes in the morning and dark when they emerged from the tunnels at the end of the workday. The walk home at one o'clock for their midday meal was their only opportunity to see the sun. But there was no sun this day, as indeed there had been no sun for weeks. Thick, sodden clouds hung over their heads, obscuring the tops of the hills lining the canal. At best, what little light they allowed through made for a constant murky dusk.

Still, as they approached their modest brick homes lined up at the foot of a hill, they could see the lamps burning within and their spirits lifted at the thought of the wine, bread, and cheeses being laid out by their wives and children.

They trudged forward, their heads lowered against the rain. Then, as one, the men stopped in their tracks and exchanged quick, confused looks.

"What is that?" one man asked.

"I don't know," another replied.

They all felt the same thing. The ground beneath their feet was vibrating, rippling the puddles of water all around them.

They stood mesmerized for a moment before one called out, "The hill!"

The men looked up. The hill was moving.

"Avalanche!" one of them screamed in panic.

Trees crisscrossed at crazy angles as the hillside sloughed off and the liquefied mire slid down toward the houses, their houses. In an instant, the wall of mud and timber engulfed the structures, collapsing the roofs, breaking the windows, blowing doors off their hinges, dousing the welcoming lamps.

Lifting their boots from the viscous, clinging mud, the men lurched forward as they called out the names of their wives and children.

Chapter 41

Inspector Carnot had little trouble convincing the Italian authorities to release Peruggia into his custody. His crime, in their eyes, had been relatively minor. He had merely tried to sell a forgery of a recently stolen painting. The copy itself was so accomplished that the price he had asked was actually reasonable. As it turned out, the Uffizi kept the painting and planned to display it as an excellent example of a reproduction. Carnot wondered at first if they were lying to him about the painting being a forgery, but they had little incentive to deceive him, as they would never be able to display the painting as the original. At any rate, he had what he wanted: the man who would lead him to the genuine masterpiece, and more important, to the mastermind of the plot.

The Italian authorities had not yet released information of the arrest to the newspapers, and Carnot convinced them to keep it that way. The less Peruggia's cohorts knew about his situation, the better.

Peruggia said little on the train ride back to Paris. That was fine with Carnot. The man had been cruelly betrayed. Carnot wanted him to have plenty of time to let that sink in. Carnot did not shackle the Italian. He counted on Peruggia's own desire for revenge to keep him from trying to escape, and he needed to gain the man's trust.

Carnot had so far kept his discovery of Peruggia as much under wraps as possible. He had cabled his immediate superior at the Sûreté to inform him that he had traveled to Florence simply to question someone who might have information about the theft. He now had to orchestrate his plan very carefully indeed. He would have some explaining to do to the commissioner, but if he could crack this case, all would be forgiven.

Upon their arrival in Paris, Carnot took Peruggia by motor taxi through the rain-soaked streets to the Île de la Cité and slipped him through a side entrance of the Prefecture of Police. He immediately sought out the young gendarme, Brousard, who had originally brought the intelligence regarding Peruggia, and assigned him the role of the prisoner's keeper.

"Place him in a comfortable cell," Carnot told him. "Make sure he has all he needs."

"What about the commissioner?" Brousard asked. "Shouldn't he be informed?"

"Not just yet. If we do this right, in a few days' time, we will have the whole gang. And that will be a huge feather in both of our caps."

"I understand, Inspector," Brousard said, beaming. Then he quickly added, "There is something else. There are two American gentlemen waiting in your office. They've been here all day."

"American? Who are they?"

"I don't know, monsieur."

"Then why did you let them into my office?"

"They insisted. One of them seems to think he is very important indeed."

"Very well." Carnot wondered what these men wanted. No matter. He would get rid of them and then return to the business at hand.

He dismissed Brousard and went downstairs to his basement office. Upon entering, he saw a tall, solidly built man with a shaved head standing by the window. An older, well-dressed man sat smoking a cigar in the chair behind Carnot's desk.

"Are you Carnot?" the man in the chair asked.

"I am Inspector Carnot," he answered, bristling, "and who might you be?"

"I suppose I might be anybody, but in fact, I am Joshua Hart. Perhaps you have heard of Eastern Atlantic Rail and Coal."

Carnot said nothing. Who had not heard of Eastern Atlantic, one of the largest business empires in the world? And the name, Joshua Hart, yes, he had heard it before. The inspector closed the door behind him. Something about these men made him nervous.

"Yes, I believe I have," he said, trying to sound disinterested as he removed his hat and coat and hung them on a rack.

"This is my associate, Mr. Taggart."

Taggart nodded, a stony expression fixed on his face. Hart rose and stepped to the side of the desk, making a point of relinquishing the chair by gesturing toward it with his hand.

Carnot seated himself. "And what can I do for you gentlemen?" he asked, hoping that he sounded authoritative. "I am a very busy man."

"I believe," Hart began, "that it's more a question of what we can do for you."

"I really don't understand. And, as I mentioned, I am quite busy."

To emphasize the point, Carnot picked up some papers from his desk and began shuffling through them.

"I have information regarding the theft of the *Mona Lisa*," said Hart.

Carnot stopped shuffling and looked from one man to the other. "*La Joconde?*"

"Whatever you want to call it, yes."

Carnot looked back down to his papers, feigning indifference.

"So why come to me?"

"We made some inquiries and heard that perhaps you had a personal interest in the matter."

Carnot looked up at them sharply. "Is that so? Then, in that case, you gentlemen have wasted your time. My interest is purely professional and, besides, I have all the information I need. In fact, it is only a matter of time now before I apprehend the guilty parties."

"I'm impressed," allowed Hart. "Then perhaps we should join forces."

"Monsieur," Carnot said with as much indignation as he could muster, "I am a police inspector. I have no intention of joining forces with anyone."

Hart shared a glance with Taggart. Carnot thought he could see the faint gleam of a smile crack the façade of the larger man's face.

"I see," Hart said, flicking cigar ashes into a small tin ashtray on the desk.

Carnot stood up. This had gone on too long. "I'm afraid I have no more time for this," he said. "I must ask you to leave."

"Let me ask you something, Inspector," Hart said in a casual tone. "I'm curious."

The room was silent for a moment. Then Hart leaned across the desk and fixed Carnot with a hard look. His eyes were so penetrating that Carnot involuntarily drew back.

"Exactly how much money does a police inspector make?"

In spite of himself, Carnot could feel his heart suddenly pumping faster.

"Judging by this office," Hart continued, "I don't imagine it could be very much."

"It is none of your business, monsieur."

"But I would like to make it my business."

"Are you trying to bribe an officer of the law?"

"That would depend . . ." said Hart, stubbing out his cigar in the tin ashtray ". . . on the officer."

Chapter 42

As afternoon faded to evening on the day of Ellen's expected visit, Valfierno's growing impatience gradually changed to a strange mixture of anger and disappointment. Since she had arrived in Paris, he had not led her on in any way. On the contrary, he had done his best to avoid her so as not to give her the wrong idea. Every time he tried to sort out his feelings for her, he came to an impasse. And so he had convinced himself that only when this whole affair reached its conclusion—when *La Joconde* had been returned to the Louvre, when he had learned of Peruggia's fate, when sufficient time had passed—would he be able to resolve his emotional quandary.

He should have been relieved that she hadn't come to her requested meeting, but the initial disappointment he felt was so deep that he became angry at himself for allowing such feelings to run rampant.

When Émile returned that evening and casually inquired about Ellen's visit, Valfierno curtly informed him that she had never shown up.

It only made matters worse when Valfierno, who prided himself on his ability to sleep soundly through even the worst crisis, could find little rest during the night. The constant lashing of the rain on the windows didn't help matters, and he did not fall asleep until a dull gray morning light penetrated through the windows. He awoke in the late morning only to find that the few hours' rest had done little to remove the turmoil of the previous day.

At noon, without a word of explanation to Émile, Valfierno walked to the local garage, climbed into his motorcar, and drove west along the river. He paid scant attention to the gawkers on the Pont-Neuf gathering to witness the growing spectacle of the steadily rising water; the river typically rose at this time of year, and this had been an especially wet winter. Crossing over to the Left Bank, he continued down rue Dauphine.

Within a few moments, he drove into the cour de Rohan. Stopping the car next to a low wall, he hurried through the rain to Madame Charneau's front door, using the cat's-head brass knocker to announce his presence. The door opened almost immediately.

"Marquis!" exclaimed Madame Charneau, astonished. "Come in. Come in. You'll catch your death."

"I've come to see Mrs. Hart," Valfierno said, stepping into the foyer.

"Mrs. Hart?" Madame Charneau said with surprise. "But didn't you know?"

"Know what?"

"Well, I thought she visited you just yesterday to say good-bye."

"Good-bye? Where is she?"

"She's gone. Only a few hours ago. She packed her bags and took a motor taxi to the Gare d'Orsay."

"Where is she going?"

"Vienna, I believe she said. It was all so sudden."

"She didn't tell you why?"

"No. She spoke with Mademoiselle Julia for a while but—"

"Is Julia here?"

"Yes, she wanted to go with Madame Hart to the station but—"

"Where is she?"

"Up in her room."

Valfierno brushed past Madame Charneau and all but ran up the steps to the first floor.

"Julia," he called out at her door. "Julia. Please open the door."

"Go away!" came Julia's voice from inside.

"What did Mrs. Hart say to you?"

"I said go away!"

"Please, Julia."

"How could you? Now, go away."

Frustrated, Valfierno banged his fist on the door before hurrying back downstairs to Madame Charneau.

"She said nothing to me," she began, "only thanked me for—"

"What train is she taking?"

"I don't know. As I said, it happened so quickly. She just announced that she was leaving . . ."

But Valfierno had already left and was hurrying out to his motorcar.

"Marquis!" Madame Charneau called out as Valfierno drove off. "I thought you knew!"

Valfierno realized his mistake too late. He drove along rue Mazarine toward the river only to find it blocked off. A gendarme told him there had been some minor flooding up ahead. He turned around and drove to rue de Lille, his progress slowed by the mass of traffic diverted from the routes along the river. Finally, he pulled to the front of Gare d'Orsay and hurried to the main entrance.

The dim light barely penetrating through the vast skylight gave the expansive station an eerily claustrophobic feel. Valfierno strode to the arrival and departure board. Craning his neck, he scanned the board until he found it. Departure. Vienna. 1:30. He turned to look at the clock above the main entrance. It read 1:16.

He hurried to the railing overlooking the dual train platforms on the lower level. There was only one train, white vapor venting from its locomotive as it built up a head of steam. He pushed through the crowd to the staircase and scurried down.

On the platform, he forced his way through the throng of passengers and well-wishers saying their good-byes, and porters loading baggage into the cars. He reached the end of the platform where only a small handful of people were gathered. There was no sign of Ellen.

"Edward."

He spun around at the sound of the voice.

Ellen Hart stood amid the jostling crowds. She wore a white dress with a brown traveling jacket; her wide-brim hat was pushed back slightly, revealing a guarded look on her face.

Valfierno stepped up to her. They stood for a moment, face-to-face, the swirl of people around them merging into indistinct blurs.

"Ellen, what are you doing?"

"I'm leaving, Edward. I'm sorry I didn't say good-bye, but . . ."

She let the word hang in the air.

"But why are you leaving?"

"I have a cousin in Vienna. His name is Jonathan. He's a third or fourth cousin really. We spent a lot of time together when my father was alive."

"But why leave so suddenly?"

"I don't belong here, Edward. Sometimes I'm not sure I belong anywhere."

Valfierno hesitated.

Ellen continued. "My cousin and I have exchanged letters in the past few weeks. I have reason to believe that he will welcome me, that he can help me. And perhaps more."

All around them, passengers clambered into the carriages, loved ones saying their final good-byes.

"I should get on the train."

Valfierno stepped closer.

"Ellen, your husband may be looking for you. He's bound to follow every lead. You'll be safer if you stay in Paris."

"I'll never be safe from my husband, but the farther away I go the better."

"But I will assure your safety."

"You've already done more than necessary. I'm not sure I've shown you enough gratitude for all you've done."

"Then show it now by listening to me, by staying."

"All aboard!" the stentorian voice of the conductor blared out across the platform.

"I must go." She turned toward the carriage.

Valfierno placed a hand on her arm. "You're making a mistake."

"Am I? And why is that? You've told me you don't think I should go, but you don't tell me why. Oh, I know, for my safety. But that's not enough."

She looked him squarely in the eyes, challenging him to say something.

"Because," he said finally, "because I want you to stay."

She waited for him to say more. Two thin, sharp blasts of the conductor's whistle cut through the babble of voices around them. A man jostled Valfierno from behind as if encouraging him to speak, but he said nothing.

"Edward," Ellen finally said, "you once told me that you take from people only that which they are more than willing to part with. I wonder. Do you also tell them only that which they wish to hear?"

A muffled growl of thunder rattled the canopy of skylights above, a counterpoint to the strident blare of the train horn.

"Good-bye, Edward."

She let a conductor help her up the steps into the carriage. Without looking back, she disappeared into the corridor. Valfierno moved to the side, trying to see her through the compartment windows, but there were only strangers.

With a screech of metal and a hiss of steam, the train lurched into life and started to roll away down the platform. Valfierno could only watch as it receded.

Spectators on the Pont de l'Alma looked down in astonishment at the stone statue of the Zouave standing guard over the bridge.

The soldier, carved in stone and adorning a support pillar, had acted for fifty-six years as an indicator of the river level. Standing proudly and defiantly—his left hand on his hip, his right across his chest—his feet normally stood just above the water level. At times of seasonal high water, the surface of the river rose above his toes; at times of unusually high water, it reached his ankles. The river had now risen above the hand that rested on his hip. How much higher, many in the crowd speculated, could it possibly go?

Ellen stared at her reflection in the window as the train rattled through the tunnel picking up speed. Highlighted against the black tunnel wall, her face appeared old and worn. Or perhaps it was just her mood. Her feelings now were a stark contrast to the exhilaration she felt less than a month ago when she first rode the train into Paris.

The sudden lurching of the carriage pulled her from her reverie. She looked around; the other passengers were turning their heads and murmuring concerns. The train was slowing down. And then it stopped, rocking her slightly forward. A conductor hurried past her toward the front of the train. A passenger asked why they had stopped but the man in uniform only said, "I'm sure we'll only be delayed a moment, monsieur."

Ellen listened to the faint hiss of steam escaping. She was not happy to be leaving Paris, especially under these circumstances, but the physical movement of the train on its way somewhere, anywhere, had given some momentum to her life. But now, as she sat there motionless, she could feel all her doubts and fears closing in on her like the dark walls of the tunnel. She felt the overwhelming urge to get off the train at any cost. The thread of growing panic was suddenly cut by the appearance of the conductor at the front of the car.

"*Messieurs et mesdames,*" he began breathlessly, "I am afraid there is a small problem." A low murmur ran through the passengers. The conductor signaled for quiet. "There has been some minor flooding reported farther along the line. I am afraid that we will have to return to the terminus." A barrage of questions assaulted the conductor as he made his way through the carriage to the next, but he simply waved them off, repeating, *"Je suis désolé, monsieur, je suis désolé . . ."*

The train lurched and started rolling backward. As the rest of the passengers mumbled their complaints, Ellen turned back to the window. Slowly, a faint smile of relief spread across the reflection of her face.

As soon as the train returned to the terminus, the passengers were told that all service had been suspended due to flooding on the track. Reaching the top of the staircase, Ellen noticed people lining the railing and pointing downward. She saw a strange mirrorlike sheen beneath the train where the tracks should have been.

"The river," someone said, and she realized that the tracks were now completely submerged under a layer of water that already covered the bottom rims of the wheels.

"Madame," said the porter who had brought up her luggage, "I will try to find you a motor taxi."

With a last look at the reflection of the terminus lights on the water's oily surface, she turned away and followed him to the entrance.

"I've never seen such weather," Madame Charneau said as she moved Ellen's bags against the wall of the foyer. "Flooding in the train station. What will happen next?"

It had taken Ellen's taxi more than an hour to reach Madame Charneau's house. The streets were jammed with carts and motorized vehicles diverted from the river.

"Did the marquis ever find you, dear?"

"He did," Ellen said. "He came to say good-bye."

"What a fuss he made."

"What do you mean?"

"I don't know what got into him. He burst in here all excited, he didn't seem to know that you were leaving at all. Yet I thought he had seen you only yesterday. Surely you must have told him."

"What did he say?"

"Oh, don't worry about all that now, my dear. Let's get you dry first, and you can stay here as long as you like. The rain will stop soon and all will be well again."

"Ellen!"

They both turned to see Julia standing at the first-floor landing.

"What happened?" she called out as she bustled down the steps.

"The train station was flooded," said Madame Charneau. "Don't bother her with questions now. Help her out of her wet things. I'll make some tea."

As Madame Charneau disappeared into the kitchen, Julia took Ellen's wet coat. "He was here looking for you."

"I know," Ellen said. "He found me at the station right before the train was to leave."

"What did he say to you?"

"I don't know," Ellen began, her voice betraying her weariness. "He said he didn't want me to leave."

"Did he give you a reason?"

"He just said it wouldn't be safe for me to leave Paris."

"That's all he could say?"

"I implied that my distant cousin in Vienna was a young man and that he was interested in me."

"Your cousin?" exclaimed Julia. "You told me that *she* was fifty or something. Oh, you didn't."

"I'm afraid I did," Ellen said with a sheepish smile.

Julia put her hand to her mouth to suppress an involuntary chortle.

Ellen nodded her head as she too began to find this funny. Suddenly they were both trying in vain to suppress their reflexive laughter.

"It's really not funny," Julia said in an unsuccessful effort to control herself.

"No, it isn't," Ellen said, failing to keep a straight face.

It took a moment for their laughter to subside.

"Anyway," Julia finally said, wiping away a mirthful tear, "after what that horrible woman Chloe told you about him, he deserved it."

The last remnants of Ellen's laughter suddenly transformed into real tears, prompting Julia to put her arms around her. "Don't worry. We'll get you into some dry clothes so you can rest. I'll bring up the tea to you."

Before Julia could lead Ellen up the stairs, there was an insistent knocking on the door. The two women drew apart and exchanged puzzled looks.

"Maybe," Julia began, "he heard about the trains being canceled."

Another series of knocks. Ellen hesitated. Julia gave her an encouraging nod and she lifted the latch and pulled the door open.

Standing against the wall of driving rain was a short, heavyset man with a round face.

Inspector Carnot removed his hat, his mouth twisting into a condescending smile. "Madame Hart, I presume."

Chapter 43

Ellen stopped breathing for a moment. Should she deny it, simply say he had the wrong person? But the man, whoever he was, clearly knew that he didn't. And then, the fear that gripped her was suddenly swept away by the realization that, in the depths of her soul, she was no longer Mrs. Hart, and she could simply tell him the truth.

"My name is Beach," she finally said, drawing herself up straight. "Ellen Edwina Beach."

"I am Inspector Carnot of the Sûreté, and, by whatever name you prefer, I have to ask you to accompany me to the prefecture."

"For what reason? I've done nothing."

"Of course not. We'd like to ask a few questions. Merely a formality, I assure you."

"Questions regarding what?"

"It will all be explained at the prefecture, madame."

"You've got no right to take her anywhere," Julia said, stepping up behind Ellen.

"Ah, the other American." The inspector gave Julia an appraising look. "Mademoiselle Conway, I believe."

"What's it to you?"

"A stroke of good fortune. For you see, we would also like to ask you a few questions."

"Do you have a warrant?" Julia demanded.

"And why would I need a warrant, mademoiselle?" Carnot answered, trying to keep his rising impatience in check. "You are not wanted in connection with any crime at the moment. Besides, you are in France now. We do not bother with such things as warrants. Of course, if you prefer that I return with some gendarmes . . ."

"It's all right," Ellen said to Julia. "I can go with him. I have nothing to hide."

"Very wise, madam," Carnot said. "I have a car, so you shouldn't get too wet."

"I'll go with her," said Julia defiantly, before adding in English, "but only to make sure everything is on the up and up."

Smiling amiably, Inspector Carnot moved aside. As Ellen and Julia stepped out the door, Madame Charneau appeared behind them.

"What's the meaning of this?" she asked. "Where are you taking them?"

"It's all right," said Ellen. "We are just going with the inspector to answer some questions."

"What kind of questions?"

"And you are?" inquired Carnot in a challenging tone.

"I am Madame Charneau and this is my house." She drew herself up proudly.

"I see. At some point, we may need to ask you some questions also. In the meantime, madame, do you know the whereabouts of the marquis de Valfierno?"

"I've never even heard of him," she said quickly.

"That's unfortunate," said Carnot, "because he will want to read this." He removed a sealed envelope from his inside pocket and held it out to her.

Madame Charneau's response was to cross her arms and give him a defiant look.

Carnot smiled and tossed the letter onto a small shelf on the hall stand.

"Make sure he gets it."

Inspector Carnot escorted Ellen and Julia out to a car in the courtyard, its motor purring at an idle. He opened the rear door and motioned for the two women to enter. He slipped into the driver's seat, and with an unnerving rattle, the car pulled away. Madame Charneau watched it disappear into a curtain of rain before closing the door and picking up the sealed envelope.

Madame Charneau hurried across the Pont-Neuf, afraid that the driving wind and rain might sweep her off her feet into the rushing river. It was a disturbing sight. Devoid of its usual traffic, the river boiled along with a dark, angry menace. She had never seen it so high, so forceful. A few hardy souls, their coats wrapped tightly around them, their hands pinning their hats to their heads, stood at the bridge's balustrade watching in awe as waves crested up onto the embankments straining to reach up to the street-level quays. Earlier, Madame Charneau had tried placing a telephone call to Valfierno from the Hôtel de Fleurie, but the system was not working.

She reached the Right Bank and hurried along the quai de la Mégisserie in the direction of the Hôtel d'Ville. It was difficult staying out of the puddles and small streams that had formed in the road, and soon her shoes were soaked through.

By the time she reached the entrance to Valfierno's house on rue de Picardie, she was thoroughly drenched. She pounded on the door, the memory of the police inspector driving away with Ellen and Julia replaying in her mind.

Valfierno opened the door and she quickly stepped into the foyer.

"Madame," he said in shock, "what has happened? Is something wrong?"

She took a deep breath and began. "Madame Hart and Mademoiselle Julia have been taken away for questioning by a policeman."

"What are you talking about?" Valfierno said. "Mrs. Hart left Paris hours ago. I saw her get on the train."

"No," Madame Charneau said breathlessly, "her train had to return to the station because of the flooding."

"What's going on?" said Émile, bounding down the stairs.

"Mrs. Hart and Julia have been arrested," said Valfierno.

"Arrested?" Émile blurted out. "I don't understand. You said that Mrs. Hart left—"

"When did this happen?" Valfierno asked Madame Charneau.

"Not half an hour ago. And the inspector told me to give you this."

She handed him the letter, limp and wet despite her efforts to protect it from the rain.

Valfierno picked up an ivory-handled knife from a side table and slit it open. He carefully unfolded a single page. Some of the writing was smudged, but it was still legible. He read it aloud.

"'Monsieur, we have not had the pleasure of meeting but I hope that will be remedied soon. My proposition is simple. You will come immediately to the Saint-Michel Metro station bringing with you the original painting—you know the one I speak of—along with all the money you have collected from your clientele in America. Do not try to deceive me, I warn you. I know more of your scheme than you could possibly realize. This, I assure you, will not be a one-way transaction. As you will know, Madame Hart is in my custody. There will be serious consequences for her should our business not be satisfactorily concluded. Bear in mind that this transaction will be a private one between our two parties. Once concluded, my interest in you will come to an end, a further advantage, as it will provide you with an escape from prosecution. I will expect you at precisely four o'clock.

"'Counting on a timely response, I hope you accept, Monsieur, the assurance of my respect, Inspector Alphonse Carnot.'"

"He's certainly being very polite about it," Madame Charneau commented.

Valfierno handed the letter to Émile and pulled out his pocket watch. The time was 3:05.

"This is outrageous," Émile fumed, quickly perusing the letter. "Who is this Carnot, anyway?"

"I believe he is an esteemed member of the Sûreté," Valfierno answered with a sharp hint of sarcasm.

"A *flic*?" said Émile in surprise. "Why would he play this kind of game with us?"

"I would imagine that the large amount of money we still have in our possession might have something to do with it."

"But how did he find out?"

"I'm not sure. Perhaps our friend, Signore Peruggia, is involved in some way."

"This is what happens when you bring in outside people," said Émile, exasperated.

"But you were the one who brought him to us in the first place," Madame Charneau pointed out.

"Madame Charneau," said Valfierno, "I'm forgetting my manners. Come in by the fire."

He guided her into the sitting room where burning logs crackled in the fireplace.

"I've never seen such a rain." She rubbed her hands together over the fire. "The river will be flowing over the bridges if this keeps up."

"The metro station mentioned in the letter," Valfierno said to Émile. "You know it?"

"Yes, it's just across the river near the Pont Saint-Michel. It's one of the new stations still under construction."

"And completely abandoned on a Sunday," added Valfierno. "The perfect place to avoid prying eyes."

Valfierno stared intently into the fire, deep in thought.

"Émile," he said after a few tense seconds, "retrieve the painting. We can't use the motorcar; by now the police will have blocked off all streets leading to the river. I want you to bring it to the metro station as soon as you can, but it is imperative that you don't reveal yourself until I call for you. Do you understand?"

"It will be too dangerous for you," protested Émile. "Let me go. I'll bring both the painting and the money to him."

"I'm afraid that's not all he wants," said Valfierno thoughtfully.

"But it says right here that you'll be free from prosecution if you follow his instructions," said Émile.

"Free from prosecution, perhaps, but I fear there is more to this than is outlined in this letter."

"I don't understand," said Émile.

"Carnot could have learned about the painting from Peruggia, that's clear. However, Peruggia knew nothing about Mrs. Hart, which makes me think that our policeman, or someone else, wants more than the painting and the money."

"What?"

Valfierno reached behind the mantelpiece clock and pulled out a long, white glove. He contemplated it for a moment, feeling the soft, silky fabric between his fingers.

"Me."

Chapter 44

Émile left the house immediately to retrieve the painting from Diego's studio on the other side of the river. The closer he got to the Seine, the more dramatic became the flooding in the narrow, twisting streets of the Marais. Dirty water bubbled up around manhole covers, making them gyrate and dance like the lids of boiling pots; miniature rivers filled the gutters on either side of the street. Cold rain mixed with flecks of snow fell from sullen clouds. Silvery white frost clung to bare tree limbs and empty park benches, contrasting incongruously with the mud and oily sludge covering the streets.

A block from the river, a horse-drawn cart laden with sandbags clattered past, forcing Émile to jump out of the way. A harried-looking soldier urged the reluctant horse forward and, as it drew even with Émile, a sandbag slipped from the back into a deep puddle, splashing him with cold, filthy water.

Soaked to the skin, he stopped at the Pont au Change leading to the Île de la Cité. The water had risen far above the embankments below street level. The archways through which boats normally traversed had all but disappeared. Barely a yard of space existed between the rushing water and the tops of the arches. Bits of furniture, wooden casks, and all sorts of debris and rubbish built up against the upstream deck of the bridge.

Suppressing a tug of fear in his stomach, Émile took a deep breath and hurried across.

In the basement studio of rue Serpente, water had begun to seep across the floor. Diego rapidly gathered together the artworks he planned to take with him. The last few weeks had been a mad blur of industry; he had not created so many new works in such a short space of time in more than two years.

In a pile next to his zinc tub, he came across the master copy of *La Joconde*, the one he had used as a reference point for making all the others. He briefly thought of taking it with him but discarded the notion; he had reached a new pinnacle of artistic creativity and he was no longer interested in the fruits of his creative sabbatical.

The copy of *La Joconde* reminded him of the pile of incomplete forgeries and other canvases in his storage closet. Taking the master with him, he hurried into the small room, leaned it against the wall, and rummaged through the reproductions in search of anything of interest he had overlooked. Finding nothing, he went back into his studio, leaving the master copy behind.

Émile walked rapidly past the Prefecture of Police to the Pont Saint-Michel, which joined the island to the Left Bank. The rushing water seemed even more ferocious here, but he swallowed his fear and started across, passing a group of onlookers peering down at the turbulent water.

The river had turned a sickly yellow color and held little resemblance to the usually placid and stately Seine. The channel was clogged with debris. A logjam of barrels and lengths of wood fought to break through the rapidly diminishing arches of the bridge. Furniture smashed and broke apart against the abutments. He even caught sight of something that looked like the carcass of a pig spinning like a bizarre merry-go-round in the swirling water.

On the far bank, a bearded officer was exhorting a group of a dozen or more soldiers to unload the same wagon that had passed him before.

"Hurry up there!" the officer bellowed. "Leave no gaps between the bags!"

The officer turned his attention to the people on the bridge. "You!" the man shouted. "All of you! Off the bridge now! Can't you see the danger?"

The various citizens of Paris turned their heads toward the officer with more curiosity than alarm. Trading a few laughing remarks with each other, they chose to ignore him and turned their attention back to the raging spectacle below. One man—with the help of another holding on to his belt—was even attempting to reach down and retrieve a wine cask.

"*Imbéciles!*" the officer cried before turning back to scream once again at his men. "Work faster! We have to buttress this entire section! Pry up the paving stones and use them if you have to!"

Émile crossed the street to the Place Saint-Michel, where he took note of the ornate cast-iron arch supporting a sign in scripted lettering: MÉTROPOLITAIN. Beneath it, a temporary shack covered the mouth of the street-level entrance of the future Saint-Michel metro station, the meeting place designated by Inspector Carnot.

He crossed the *place* and hurried down rue Danton. The water bubbling up from the manhole covers filled the street to a depth of three or four inches, slowing Émile's progress, but he finally reached rue Serpente. Outside Diego's basement studio stood a large hand cart. A tarp covered it, but he could see the edges of a number of panels outlined beneath it. Émile lifted the tarp to reveal a stack of canvases. Flipping through them, he found no sign of *La Joconde*. In fact, he didn't recognize these paintings at all. He stepped out of the sunken road onto the pavement, which was still dry and acted as a sort of dam, protecting the steps leading down into the basement.

Émile went through the open door and descended to the studio. The floor was slick from seeping ground moisture. Diego stood before a table stacked with painted canvases stretched over wooden frames. He was wrapping them, one by one, in cloth.

"What are you doing?" Émile asked.

"The rats have already vacated. I'm following their wise example."

Émile picked up a canvas from the pile. It was the most bizarre image he had ever seen. A woman, or rather, parts of a woman, were piled on the seat of an armchair. Half of her head had been sliced neatly off at a forty-five-degree angle; rivulets of multicolored hair cascaded down from the featureless, partial face; something—a hand, perhaps, or a claw—held part of a newspaper, an actual newspaper, *Le Journal*, which had been pasted onto the canvas, as had real wallpaper on the wall behind the chair. The woman's breasts floated freely—my god, they were Julia's breasts, the ones from her so-called portrait, the ones that looked like pastry bags. They appeared to have been cut out and pasted into the center. Her derriere was partially covered by a piece of cloth painted to look like some sort of frilly undergarment. He felt as if he was looking through some sort of nightmarish kaleidoscope at the disjointed pieces of a human puzzle that could have been imagined only by a blind madman.

"You like it?" Diego asked.

"I don't even know what it is," Émile said.

Diego picked up what was left of the original portrait of Julia. Large pieces were missing. The slashed canvas, smudged and smeared by the palette Julia had thrown onto it, echoed the same disjointed quality as the one that Émile held.

"Inspiration!" Diego said.

"But this is not your name." Émile pointed to the signature in the lower corner of the canvas he held in his hands.

"Ah, but it is. It's the name I reserve for my true art. My name is Pablo Diego José Francisco de Paula Juan Nepomuceno María de los Remedios Cipriano de la Santísima Trinidad Ruiz y Picasso." Diego took a breath and shrugged. "For short, just Picasso."

Putting down the damaged painting, Picasso took his original from Émile and added it to his bundle. "The inspiration came to me like a flash of lightning, thanks to your beautiful and spirited Julia."

Émile looked into Picasso's eyes. The man was clearly mad as a March hare.

"*Au revoir*, Monsieur Émile. And you can keep my cut of the money. I have rediscovered something that no amount of money can buy. My soul. Kiss the lovely Julia good-bye for me. I think she would like that."

Picasso pulled a paint-stained beret onto his head and disappeared up the steps with the last of his canvases. Émile watched him go for only a moment before stepping into the storage room.

The room was a shambles, canvases and supplies strewn about the wet floor. Fending off a surge of panic, Émile knelt and began shifting through the mess. He collected all the panels with images of *La Joconde*, discarding the obviously incomplete reproductions until he was down to four.

He cleared the small desk in the corner, placing the four panels on it. Two were of identical proportions; the other two were slightly larger but also identical in size.

The panic returned. There should be no others the same size as the original. He searched again among the remaining panels on the floor. All were obviously unfinished, so he got to his feet, his mind racing. He had seen all the paintings that Diego had taken, and it wasn't among them. It must be here. He must have missed the identical-sized copy when he had first hidden the original.

Then he remembered: the master copy. That was the same size as the original. That must be the other painting.

This was not a problem. He could pick out the real one. He wished he remembered the exact dimensions—not that it would have mattered as he didn't have a measuring tape. He examined the two smaller panels. They were both excellent but definitely too small. It had to be one of the larger paintings, but which one? He turned them over. They both had the crucifixlike repair at the top. Just to be sure, he checked the backs of the smaller panels. They had similar repairs, though on opposite sides. That made no sense. It didn't matter, they were too small.

He balanced the two larger panels side by side on the desktop. He looked from one to the other then back again. They were identical.

Time was running out. He placed one on top of the other and hurried back into the studio. He wrapped them both in a piece of cloth and bounded up the stairs two at a time.

Chapter 45

Valfierno convinced Madame Charneau that she had done all she could and to stay in his house. He left not long after Émile but almost didn't make it across the Pont au Change in time. Gendarmes and soldiers were clearing the roadway of gawkers and attempting to deny access to the Île de la Cité. One gendarme was more interested in tacking a poster to a tree announcing that citizens had twenty-four hours to turn in anything removed from the river. Clutching the handle of his leather valise, Valfierno took advantage of the confusion and slipped across before the last group of onlookers was expelled from the bridge. He passed behind a military officer arguing with a gendarme. The officer was advocating using dynamite to clear the logjam of debris to release pressure on the bridge. The gendarme was trying to explain that the sandbag walls might not be able to withstand the sudden surge of water.

As he reached the far end of the Pont au Change, Valfierno paused to look down at the river. Frothy and muddy, it had taken on a lead gray pallor. Water pounded into the bridge abutments with such force that Valfierno wondered if it was strong enough to hold. Then, in the midst of the debris rushing by on the river, he saw the body of a woman floating facedown. She was dressed in rough peasant clothing, her arms and legs spread-eagled as she slowly spun in the raging current. He watched transfixed as she hit a bridge abutment and held there for a moment before being sucked through a narrow opening at the top of one of the debris-choked arches. Valfierno turned away, hurried across the Île de la Cité to the Pont Saint-Michel, and crossed to the Left Bank.

It wasn't long before he reached the same ornate MÉTROPOLI-TAIN sign that Émile had passed earlier. Valfierno tried the door to the rough wooden shack erected above the metro entrance and found it unlocked. He slipped inside.

Water trickled down the steps as Valfierno descended into the darkness. After two turnings, he stepped onto a station platform dimly lit by a line of incandescent lightbulbs running along the top of the arched ceiling. Attached halfway up the curved wall was a large enamel plaque with SAINT-MICHEL in white letters against a blue background.

To Valfierno, the space looked like a vast crypt. The first metro line had opened in 1900, shortly before he left for Buenos Aires. The few times he used the metro he had not been impressed. He resented how it drew business away from the street-level *autobuses* and the once popular *bateaux-mouches*. He had found the metro to be unnatural, not to mention unpleasant; it inhabited a dark nether-world filled with the roar and clatter of steel wheels echoing from tiled walls. He preferred invigorating walks aboveground, or the opinionated observations of taxi drivers. He saw little difference between metro trains and the mechanical trolleys that had been installed in selected sewers to cater to the curious tourists drawn to Paris's most unlikely subterranean attraction.

A dark red wooden metro car sat on sunken tracks. The trench through which the tracks ran was already filled with water to the depth of about a foot and a half. Extending perhaps sixty feet in length, the platform terminated in an arched rear exit with steps leading upward. A section of flat tiled wall separated this rear exit from the archway of the track tunnel. Not all of the lights were illuminated, and the sound of dripping water echoing off the walls contributed to the dank, forbidding atmosphere.

"Marquis de Valfierno?"

Valfierno turned. A figure stood partially hidden by darkness in the mouth of a small, unlit connecting pedestrian passageway.

"Inspector Carnot?"

Carnot stepped out into the dim light.

"Officially, yes," the inspector said, "but for these purposes, 'Monsieur Carnot' will suffice. I believe you know Signore Peruggia."

The lanky Italian stepped out of the passageway behind Carnot. Valfierno tried to conceal his surprise.

"Yes, we're well acquainted," he said, nodding his head slightly. "Good to see you again, signore."

"You tricked me," Peruggia muttered. "You switched the painting with a copy."

"And I do apologize, but you see, my friend, the Italian authorities would have returned the painting to France anyway. And you were, after all, to be well paid."

Peruggia squinted at Valfierno. Then an awkward smile grew on his face.

"And now I'll be even better paid."

"Yes," Valfierno said.

He turned his attention to Carnot. "Shall we get down to the business at hand before we're all swept away?" For effect, he lifted a foot from the platform and shook off some water.

"Soon enough," said Carnot, "but I'm not finished with the surprises."

Carnot looked back into the passageway and stepped aside. Valfierno followed his gaze, expecting to see Ellen and Julia.

Out of the darkness stepped Joshua Hart, followed by Taggart. Valfierno could not hide his shock at seeing these two men.

"Marquis," said Hart with a gruff amiability, "what a pleasure to see you again."

Valfierno did his best to regain his composure. "As always, señor, the pleasure is all mine."

Hart stepped forward. "I believe that we have some unfinished business to attend to. Foremost, I would like to take delivery of the painting for which I have already paid you in full. In addition, I would like not only my own money back, all four hundred and fifty thousand dollars of it, but I think I shall have everyone else's money also. If my calculations are correct, I believe that should come to almost three million dollars."

"I'm afraid," Valfierno began, unable to suppress a smile, "that your calculations are somewhat optimistic. In truth, the other buyers all paid considerably less than you did."

Hart's jaw clenched as he tried to control his anger.

"Though indeed," Valfierno added, "it still represents a great deal of money."

"And that's not all," Hart said, regaining his composure with a smirk. "I would also like an apology. A sincere apology."

Valfierno managed to muster a small laugh. "The first two items you mention will be no problem at all, but the third . . . whatever would I need to apologize for?"

"For a start, you could apologize for running off with my wife."

"Perhaps it is you who owes her an apology."

"Now why on earth would I owe her an apology?"

"Oh, I don't know," Valfierno said mildly, "perhaps for being an unscrupulous, malevolent pirate who profits from the misery of others, who seeks to snatch up all that's beautiful in the world only to lock it away for his own perverted pleasure, and in truth couldn't tell a Pissarro from a piss pot."

The smirk on Hart's face evaporated. Taggart stepped toward Valfierno, but Hart put his hand up to stop him.

"Not yet," Hart said. Then he nodded toward the valise that Valfierno carried. "The money. It's all there?"

"Most of it. New York, as you know, tends to be somewhat expensive."

Hart motioned to Taggart, who took the valise from Valfierno. He unfastened the clasp and rummaged through the wads of bills, then turned and nodded to Hart before fastening it again.

"Good," said Hart. "That's mainly to punish you. What I really want is the painting. And make sure it's the real one this time."

"Where are they?" asked Valfierno.

"I assume you're referring to my wife and your lovely . . . niece?"

"I have to see that they're safe first."

"You're in no position to bargain," Hart snapped.

"Perhaps not, but I still have to see them."

"They are close by. Where is the painting?"

"Also close by."

Hart and Valfierno stared at each other.

"Taggart," prompted Hart.

Still holding the valise, Taggart crossed the platform to the door of the metro car. He turned its handle and pulled it open. Valfierno took a step closer. Ellen and Julia sat inside on a bench, their hands bound behind them and their mouths gagged. Julia was struggling against her bonds. Ellen sat still, looking at Valfierno, her composure belying her predicament.

"Release them first," said Valfierno.

Hart exploded in anger. "Enough of this! Where's the goddamn painting?"

Taggart slammed the carriage door shut.

Valfierno turned on Hart. "Do you think I'm fool enough just to hand it over to you? The *Mona Lisa* is so well hidden that if you don't release them right now, you will never hope to possess it. Unless you do exactly as I say, I can assure you that neither you nor anyone else will ever lay eyes on the painting again."

Valfierno's statement seemed to have had the desired effect on Hart, who could not find the words to respond immediately. At least it might have had the desired effect if the moment hadn't been shattered by a panicked scream. Everyone turned toward the main entrance as Émile slid on his back down the steps onto the platform, the wrapped panels slipping from his hands, breaking loose from their wrapping, and skidding across the floor to come to rest at Peruggia's feet.

Valfierno looked with astonishment into the young man's shocked, embarrassed face.

"Sorry," Émile said, grimacing with pain and motioning with his head to the steps. "Slippery."

As Émile struggled to his feet, Carnot took his arm and pushed him toward Valfierno.

"You definitely need to work on your timing," Valfierno said with a wry smile.

Peruggia picked up the panels, staring at them both in astonishment.

"What is this?" Hart snarled, motioning toward the paintings.

"I wasn't sure which one it was," Émile said, "so I brought both of them."

Hart stared at the panels for a moment before fumbling in his pocket and pulling out a tailor's tape measure. With Peruggia still holding the paintings, he hastily began measuring the sides.

"Where are they?" Émile quietly asked Valfierno.

Valfierno nodded toward the carriage.

Before Émile could say anything more, Hart bellowed out at the top of his voice, "They're both too damn big!"

Ripping the panels from Peruggia's hands, Hart threw them across the platform and stepped menacingly toward Émile.

"I was sure it was one of those," Émile stuttered, "but I could have been mistaken. There were two others."

Hart turned to Valfierno, his face reddening. "After all this you're still trying to swindle me?"

"No," Émile protested, turning to Valfierno. "I tried to pick the right one. Everything was such a mess."

"Diego's studio?" Valfierno asked.

"Yes," replied Émile, then added, "only he's calling himself something else now."

"He's telling the truth," Valfierno said to Hart. "It's only a few streets away. Go back with him."

"If it's not there," said Hart, barely controlling his anger, "you'll regret it, I promise you. You'll all regret it!"

"Your wife had nothing to do with the painting," Valfierno said. "Don't punish her."

Hart stepped up to him, his jaws clenching. "You think I would still have her for my wife after what she's done to me? After what you've done? You are all in this together, and you will all suffer together if I don't get that goddamn painting!" He wheeled on Taggart. "Watch him. You know what to do."

Taggart smiled as he withdrew a silver Colt .45 automatic pistol from a shoulder holster hidden beneath his jacket. Placing the valise onto a small bench built into the wall next to him, he racked back the slide to strip a cartridge from the magazine and feed it into the chamber.

Carnot's eyes widened. "You said there would be no violence."

"And if everyone cooperates," Hart said ominously, "there won't be."

After getting a nod from Valfierno, Émile led Hart up the stairs and out of the station. Valfierno, Carnot, and Peruggia stood on the wet platform looking at Taggart. The sound of dripping water echoed from the tunnel.

Finally Peruggia spoke, his sullen voice thick with resentment. "Nobody said anything about a gun."

Chapter 46

Hart followed Émile down rue Danton away from the river. Cold, dirty water seeped into his patent-leather shoes and undulating sheets of rain soaked his overcoat. The older man was having trouble keeping up the pace, and this gave Émile a certain satisfaction. Hart deserved all the discomfort he was being subjected to.

"Does it always rain like this here?" Hart grunted as he vainly tried to keep his trouser cuffs from trailing in the water.

"Only every hundred years or so," Émile answered with a quick glance back over his shoulder.

Hart's foot became momentarily entangled in a sodden newspaper, which he angrily tried to kick off.

"We have to hurry," said Émile, waving him forward.

Giving up on the newspaper, Hart sloshed off after him.

In the metro station, Carnot paced nervously across the platform. Taggart stood implacably, tapping the barrel of his gun into the palm of his left hand. Peruggia moved closer to Valfierno and whispered, "This was not my idea."

"I think," said Valfierno, lowering his voice and turning away from Taggart, "that Señor Hart and his friend have enough ideas for all of us."

"They'd better hurry," said Carnot to no one in particular, his eyes fixed on the water seeping steadily down the steps. "I'm not staying down here forever."

As Émile and Joshua Hart turned into rue Serpente, they were hailed by a gendarme hurrying along the opposite side of the street.

"You must get away from the river," the gendarme shouted. "They are going to dynamite the obstructions in the arches of the upstream bridges. The sandbags may not be able to hold the surge! The soldiers will be firing warning shots first! Get as far away as you can."

Hart looked worried, but Émile took his arm and led him to the door of the studio. He pulled it open and indicated that Hart should go down the steps.

"I'm not going down there," Hart protested.

"Suit yourself," said Émile as he scurried downward, "but this is where the paintings are."

Hart hesitated a moment before warily following him.

The water on the floor now reached above Émile's ankles.

"Where are they?" Hart said, looking around.

"In here." Émile led him into the storage closet.

Hart took in the disarray of scattered canvases, panels, and equipment as Émile moved to the wooden desk that held the two smaller panels.

"It has to be one of these," Émile said.

Hart removed the cloth tape from his pocket and measured the sides of each panel.

"Yes," he said, anticipation starting to override his apprehension. "These are the correct size."

His eyes darted back and forth between the two paintings. They were indistinguishable from each other.

The distant crack of rifle fire penetrated the street-level window.

"We have to leave now," said Émile, grasping Hart's arm. "That's the warning."

Hart angrily shook him off, his eyes never leaving the paintings. The sound of another rifle shot reached their ears.

"Take them both," Émile said. "We have to go. Now!"

"But if there are two, there may be more," Hart said, looking around the room.

Émile felt an almost overwhelming urge to grab this man by the throat and strangle him there and then. Instead, he looked at him with contempt and said, "Then drown for all I care."

With that, Émile raced from the room and bounded up the steps two at a time.

Hart sweated profusely, his eyes darting from one painting to the other. There was no mistaking it. The one on the right. The depth. The muted colors. The electric feeling of genius it imparted. That was the one! He was positive.

Then he looked again at the one on the left and quickly back to the other. His confidence drained away. He could not tell them apart.

Panic and doubt rose in his chest. What if it wasn't either of these paintings? What if it was somewhere else in the room?

Hart heard a muffled crump like the report of a distant cannon firing. It was followed by a low rumbling vibration in the floor. It was time to leave. Placing one panel on top of the other, he lifted them and hurried from the room.

As soon as Émile emerged from the studio, he heard a distant explosion from the direction of the river. The rain had diminished to a steady drizzle and there was an ominous silence for a moment, followed by a low, menacing rumble, as if hundreds of horses with muffled hoofs were stampeding. Bits of debris were rushing by his feet. A small army of rats frantically clawed at the water as the current swept them along. He looked back down the steps. There was no sign of Hart. He had seen and heard enough. He had to get back to the metro station as soon as possible, but he couldn't go back the way he had come. Turning away from the sound, he ran as fast as he could through the filthy ankle-deep water.

By the time Hart put his foot on the steps, the low rumbling noise had become much louder. Clutching the two *Mona Lisa* panels close to his body, he struggled upward, his heart pounding as if trying to escape his chest.

Reaching the street, he stopped and leaned over, desperately gasping for air. The noise of his own heaving breath began to be replaced by a new sound, the roar of rushing water. He straightened up and turned toward rue Danton as a wall of water, more than three feet high, surged around the sharp corner. With a crescendo, the water crashed into the buildings on the opposite side and ricocheted back into rue Serpente, toward him. Despite the funneling effect of the narrow street, the oncoming wave appeared at first to have lost some of its force, and for a moment he thought he might be able to stand his ground. But the growing pressure around his legs quickly changed his mind and he turned to run. He managed only one faltering step before the wall of water hit him with the force of a tidal wave, knocking him down and ripping one of the panels from his hands.

Chapter 47

At the precise moment the wall of water swept into rue Serpente, Émile reached rue Hautefeuille, a narrow side street about fifty yards to the east. Glancing toward the river, he saw another wave, compressed in the narrow space, rushing toward him and threatening to cut off his escape. Hurrying across, he reached the opposite side seconds before the deluge passed behind him. The surge created a moving dam that cut across rue Serpente, diverting the main wall of water. Momentarily sheltered from the flow, Émile continued to struggle along rue Serpente, lifting his feet high out of the water with each step.

Behind him, Joshua Hart still managed to cling desperately to one panel as the moving dam of water dragged him helplessly farther away from the river up rue Hautefeuille.

Émile reached the intersection with Saint-Michel, a wide boulevard leading directly to the river where it merged with rue Danton into Place Saint-Michel. Rows of chestnut trees rose from the water on either side, lending an almost swamplike aura to the scene. Unlike the narrow streets behind him, the broad boulevard allowed the flow of water to spread out, taming its ferocity somewhat. The water here, though still moving swiftly, reached barely to his knees, making movement easier.

The Saint-Michele metro station was to his left, directly toward the angry gray water that surged over the now indistinct bank of the river. To reach the station he would have to fight against the oncoming flow. An instinct for survival screamed at him to get as far away from the river as possible. If the station had already flooded, it would be too late to save them anyway and pointless to throw away his own life. He made his decision.

Observing the pattern made by the debris in the swirling stream, Émile judged that the current was stronger in the middle of the boulevard and weaker along the sides. Keeping close to the façades of the buildings, he began to make his way toward the river. It was hard going. The water was cold and he had lost much of the feeling in his feet; it was up to his knees, and his thighs ached from the effort it took to move forward.

About two-thirds of the way to the metro station, Émile lost his footing and he fell face-forward into the water. The current immediately grabbed him and, gasping for air, he flailed about trying to find something to hold on to. Even though the water was barely three feet deep, a cold helpless panic rose in his chest. He tried to get back to his feet but the current was too strong. As he swallowed a mouthful of filthy water, his left hand raked violently along a line of metal gateposts. In spite of the searing pain, he managed to grab hold of one of the posts to stop his momentum. With all his might, he pulled himself closer to the gate, got a grip with his other hand, and stood up.

Clinging tightly to the gateposts, he tried to catch his breath as he gauged the remaining distance to the metro station. The rising water and growing force of the current tugging at his legs made it seem impossibly far away.

Still gasping for air, a heavy cloak of utter exhaustion fell over him. His legs felt like blocks of stone, and he was struck by the urge to let go and surrender to the rushing water. He thought of Valfierno. What would he say? You've done all you can, perhaps, or, It would be foolish to risk your life further. He knew what Julia would be thinking: She wouldn't be expecting him to make it back. After all, he couldn't even copy a key correctly. Thinking of this made him angry. She thought she knew everything, but in reality she knew nothing at all about him. She had no idea what he was capable of. He felt the rage slowly rising in his chest, breaking through the dull fatigue.

He lifted his foot and took a step forward.

Chapter 48

Inspector Carnot stared nervously at the increasing flow of water cascading down the steps from the street.

"It's getting worse," he said, his voice tight with apprehension.

"It doesn't look good," agreed Peruggia.

Valfierno's and Taggart's eyes remained locked together as the water swirled around their feet seeking the lower level of the sunken tracks.

"He's right," said Valfierno, trying to sound reasonable. "We all need to get out of here now."

Taggart lifted the barrel of his gun slightly. "We stay."

"Then we need to at least get them out." Valfierno indicated the carriage.

Taggart slowly shook his head. "We do nothing until Mr. Hart returns."

"And if he doesn't?" Carnot asked, a shrill panic seeping into his voice.

Taggart's eyes never left Valfierno. "We stay here."

The sound of a muffled shot filtered down from the street.

"What is that?" asked Peruggia.

"Rifle fire," said Carnot. "It's a warning signal of some kind."

"Mr. Taggart," said Valfierno, his voice gaining urgency, "this is clearly not the place to be if the flood gets worse."

"This has gone too far," said Carnot, stepping toward Taggart. "In my capacity as an officer of the Prefecture of Police, I insist that we—"

In one swift movement, Taggart swung his gun toward Carnot and fired. In the enclosed space, the explosion was deafening. By the time the inspector fell backward onto the wet platform, he was dead. In spite of the dampening effect of the water, the report echoed off the station walls.

"*Madonna*," muttered Peruggia, staring down at Carnot's lifeless body.

"We stay here," said Taggart, swinging the gun back toward Valfierno. His tone remained calm and even.

Another muffled rifle shot penetrated down from outside. Valfierno made up his mind.

"I'm getting them out now." He turned toward the carriage.

"I wouldn't do that," Taggart warned.

"Are you going to shoot everyone?" Valfierno asked without looking back.

Taggart extended the gun toward Valfierno's back, his finger tightening on the trigger.

Valfierno reached the carriage door and gripped its handle.

The gun fired.

Valfierno cringed but felt no impact. He turned and saw Peruggia and Taggart thrashing about on the platform, wildly struggling for possession of the gun.

Valfierno heard yet another distant explosion. He turned back to the carriage, pulled open the door, and stepped inside.

Ellen's eyes looked hopefully at him as he slipped her gag off.

"I knew you'd come," she gasped.

"I would never disappoint you," Valfierno said before untying her hands.

Her hands free, Ellen started to untie her feet. Valfierno turned to Julia and removed her gag.

"It's about time!"

"Sorry, mademoiselle," Valfierno said, struggling with the bonds around her wrists, "but I was delayed by the weather."

Valfierno looked back toward the platform. Taggart and Peruggia were both on their feet in a frozen tableau. Taggart had retrieved his gun and held it not two feet from Peruggia's face.

Valfierno stepped over to the carriage door. As he did, the carriage began to vibrate. A low rumbling tremor, like a small earthquake, rolled through the station.

Taggart smiled.

"Don't shoot!" Valfierno shouted.

Taggart's gaze shifted to Valfierno. He was smirking. He was back in control.

The vibrations increased in intensity as if something ominous was approaching from deep within the black tunnel.

"I warned you," said Taggart, his voice a cool monotone.

Oblivious to everything else, Taggart turned to Peruggia and pulled the trigger. Only the sound of a sharp click penetrated the low rumble. A look of surprise replaced the steely smile on Taggart's face. He pulled back the slide on the barrel. Peruggia leaped at Taggart, struggling for the gun a split second before the rumble became a rushing roar. A torrent of water exploded down the steps at the same time that a violent surge sluiced out from the tunnel to the rear of the carriage. The car's occupants braced themselves as the deluge rocked them from side to side. The churning wall of water knocked Peruggia and Taggart down like a pair of ninepins, sweeping them, along with Carnot's body, onto the tracks and into the dark mouth of the tunnel in front of the carriage.

Then, as suddenly as it had appeared, the flood of water began to subside.

"What happened to them?" Ellen asked.

"Peruggia, Taggart, and the policeman are gone," Valfierno said. "The river must have broken through the sandbag wall. It's let up now. In a few minutes, we should be able to make it back up to the street."

Julia looked with astonishment out at the flooded platform. "What about Émile?" she asked frantically. "Is he all right?"

Valfierno looked at her. "I don't know."

Émile moved across the fronts of the buildings until he was parallel to the metro entrance across the wide boulevard Saint-Michel. The small breach in the sandbag wall had caused the initial rush of water, but it looked like most of the barrier was still in place holding back the river. At least for now. Water seeped between the remaining bags and Émile knew that it was only a matter of time before the entire barrier collapsed.

Beneath the MÉTROPOLITAIN sign still held up by its arched iron support, the entrance to the station was a gaping hole, its temporary wooden work shack having been swept away. A steady stream of water flowed into the yawning mouth as if it were a giant drain. The thought of going down those steps filled Émile with an ice-cold dread and he froze in place. To die up here in the open air was one thing, but he couldn't bear the thought of being trapped in the suffocating, flooded tunnels.

His attention was suddenly drawn to a bundle of ragged clothing sweeping through the break in the sandbags. It careened across the street and became entangled on a jumble of chairs and tables that had piled up against the front of a corner café. A strip of cloth that was caught on one of the chairs began to steadily unravel as the current tore at the bundle. Then it broke free and swirled toward him.

He saw that it was not a bundle of clothing after all. It was a body, the small body of a child. Émile watched with horror as it approached him on a direct collision course.

And then, when it was only a few yards away, one of the legs snagged on something beneath the surface. The body spun around, turning slightly onto its side and revealing a face.

Émile felt as if all the breath in his lungs had been violently sucked out.

The sound of the rushing water faded as he realized that the body in the water was his sister Madeleine. An unnatural silence descended around him and Émile became nine years old again. His heart filled with a curious mixture of joy and immense sadness: joy that he had at last found her, and heartbreaking sadness that he was too late to save her. The irrational feelings coursed through him in a terrible conflicting surge of emotion.

Then the reality of the moment and the sounds of the flooding city rushed back as the body broke free and swept past him, revealing the corpse of an old woman. The desiccated body, small and frail as a child, must have been pulled from its grave somewhere upriver. Transfixed, Émile watched it drift away down the middle of the boulevard into the heart of Paris.

Another explosion, closer this time, pulled his attention back to the river. Water was spilling over the barricades. What remained of the sandbag wall was starting to collapse.

Standing at the carriage door, Valfierno looked out over the platform, trying to gauge the strength of the current as the water continued to subside.

"Is it safe?" asked Ellen.

"Hardly," replied Valfierno. "But I think it's safer than it was. Are you ready?"

"Do we have a choice?" asked Julia, trying to bolster her courage.

Valfierno gave them both a reassuring look. "We'll have to use the main entrance." He indicated the staircase to the right. "The other exit could be blocked."

Julia followed Valfierno's gaze to the valise still sitting on the bench against the side wall.

"Is that what I think it is?" she asked.

"Yes, and I suppose it would be a good idea to take it with us," he replied with a sardonic smile. "We'll hold each other's hands. I'll go first and pick up the valise on the way."

He held his hand out to Ellen. She took it and in turn held hers out to Julia. Valfierno stepped onto the platform. The water was above his ankles but the current did not seem too strong. Holding on to each other like links in a chain, they all moved across the platform at an angle toward the curved wall. As Valfierno reached out with his left hand and gripped the handle of the valise, he heard the distant thump of the second explosion and felt a shuddering tremor beneath his feet.

Above them, the wall of sandbags began bulging inward. It was only a matter of seconds before the remaining section of wall gave way. Émile raced across to the station entrance. Pumping his legs wildly to raise them above the flow, he quickly covered the remaining distance. At the same instant that he grabbed a leg of the iron arch supporting the MÉTROPOLITAIN sign, what was left of the sandbag barrier collapsed, releasing a deluge of water into the street.

He looked down the steps, gripped a side rail, and started descending into the black hole. When he was halfway down, the wall of water plunged into the entrance above and a second later hit him with the impact of a giant fist. The irresistible force tore his grip loose from the rail and swept him into a narrow side passageway. Tumbling helplessly in the roiling water, he held his breath and flailed about for something to hold on to. His bursting lungs were about to reflexively fill themselves with water when he opened his eyes and saw her again.

Just ahead—her small figure shimmering and indistinct in the water—his sister Madeleine held out her hand to him. His consciousness rapidly fading, Émile reached out and grasped it, but instead of the soft hand of a child, he felt the cold, hard steel of a metal handrail.

Chapter 49

Their hands locked tightly together, Valfierno, Ellen, and Julia were within a few yards of the steps leading up to the main entrance when they were struck by a sudden blast of air rushing down from above.

"What's that?" cried Ellen.

Valfierno hesitated for only a second. "We have to turn around," he shouted. "The other entrance, quickly!"

Ellen and Valfierno let go of each other's hands and turned in unison. Julia felt Ellen's hand slip from hers as she saw a wall of water surging down the steps. She began running toward the rear exit. It was easier to run with the flow than against it, but it became trickier to maintain her balance.

Valfierno reached his empty hand to Ellen. Before she could take it, her feet shot out from beneath her and she tumbled onto the platform, the rising water cushioning her fall. Valfierno was about to pull her up when the wall of frigid water slammed into them.

Running ahead of Valfierno and Ellen, Julia had almost reached the rear exit when the column of water hit her. She was thrown violently up against the steps where they met the side wall that separated the rear exit from the track tunnel. Reeling from the pain, she desperately tried to resist the current pulling her toward the tracks. She reached out toward the corner of the rear exit for something to hold on to, but all she found was the slippery surface of the steps.

Then, seconds before the raging water peeled her away, someone grabbed her wrist and yanked her out of the flow and up onto the steps.

Breathless, she looked up into the face of her rescuer.

"Émile!" she gasped, her eyes wide with amazement.

"Are you all right?" he asked, kneeling down.

For a moment, she just stared into his eyes, her own wide with delight. Then her face tightened.

"Where have you been?" She scowled, letting the tension of the last few hours drain from her in a flash of anger.

"Trying not to drown," he said before urgently adding, "Where are the others?"

"I don't know. They were right behind me."

Émile looked out across the cauldron of water raging down the steps of the main entrance and diagonally across the platform, striking the side of the carriage before it swept onto the tracks. There was no one in sight.

Then he heard someone call out Julia's name.

The force of the terrible wave knocked Valfierno off his feet. Dragged helplessly by the flow, he managed to lift his head in time to see Ellen careening off the platform onto the tracks before disappearing into the tunnel. He caught a brief glimpse of someone pulling Julia up onto the rear exit steps before the wave pinned him to the connecting wall. Winded, he looked toward the rear exit directly to his left.

"Julia?" he called out.

Émile poked his head around the corner. A big surprised smile formed on the young man's face as he reached out and shouted, "Take my hand!"

"Catch this!" Valfierno swung up the valise and tossed it toward the steps. Émile reached out to grab it but the sodden bag was heavier than Valfierno had judged and it fell short. Valfierno didn't hesitate. Sacrificing his balance, he reached out with both hands and grasped the handle as the valise swept back past him. An instant later, the rush of water carried him off the platform and into the dark maw of the tunnel.

Chapter 50

Julia grabbed Émile by his arm as he instinctively took a step onto the platform.

"What do you think you're doing?" she demanded.

"Going after him."

"Can you even swim?"

Émile hesitated. "No."

"Then you're not going to help him by drowning yourself!"

Émile grunted in frustration and, overcome with exhaustion, sat back dejectedly onto the steps, burying his face in his hands. Julia put her arms around his shoulders.

"Émile," she said. "You did everything you could. You saved my life."

He didn't respond. She put her hand under his chin and lifted his face toward her. In her other hand she held out his pocket watch. "Here, maybe this will cheer you up," she said, grinning tentatively.

He stared at it with a dazed expression before looking up at her. A tired smile formed on his face as he gently took it.

"And you might as well have this too," she added, then leaned forward and kissed him on the lips.

He returned the kiss for a moment, then drew back.

"That was the third time you've done that," he said, a little bewildered.

"I had no idea you were counting."

"Don't ever do that again," he said.

She looked at him, hurt and confused. "What? Kiss you?"

"No," he said as if explaining something to a child. "Steal my watch."

Her smile returned as she threw her arms around his neck and kissed him. Then he took her by the wrists, removed her arms, and gently pushed her away.

A new determination burned in his eyes. "Let's go. We're not finished yet."

Valfierno broke the surface of the water. Behind him, the arched tunnel entrance shrank into the distance as the underground river swept him away and darkness eclipsed the dim light of the platform. The current was irresistible, but the water was less than six feet deep so he was able to kick his feet off the tunnel floor to gasp for air. The bitter cold water stung the exposed flesh of his face and hands. Despite the strong urge to let go of the valise to free up his arm, he forced himself to maintain a tight grip on the handle.

Every fifteen feet or so, a dim ceiling lamp faintly illuminated the tunnel like a haunted-house ride at a carnival. Rushing along, he could see little ahead of him other than the long curving line of bulbs. Then something white appeared on the wall to his right. Rapidly approaching, he saw to his amazement that it was Ellen, hanging on to a vertical pipe that climbed the wall to the ceiling. About six feet closer, a metal ladder clung to the wall running parallel to the pipe. With only seconds to react, he switched the valise to his left hand, reached out with his right, and grabbed the side rail of the ladder.

Valfierno jerked to a sudden stop, almost dislocating his shoulder in the process. But he kept his grip and managed to gain a foothold on one of the rungs, wrapping his elbow tightly around the side rail of the ladder. He looked around to get his bearings. The pipe and the ladder were attached to a perpendicular section of wall set into the otherwise curved tunnel. It was too dark to see the top of the ladder clearly, but he assumed it must lead to some kind of access door.

Ellen clung to the pipe perhaps four feet away. She held on with both arms, but the swift current tugged at her legs, lifting her body almost horizontally. Valfierno could see the exhaustion and fear in her eyes.

"Edward," she called out over the noise of the rushing water, "I can't hold on."

"You have to," he said.

Switching the valise between hands, he hooked his elbow around the downstream side rail before returning the valise to his left hand. This enabled him to hang on to both the ladder and the valise with the same arm. He reached out as far as he could, his back up against the side of the tunnel. She was still almost an arm's length away.

"Can you get closer?" he called out.

With great effort, she pulled herself closer to the pipe and stretched out her hand as far as she could toward Valfierno, but the force of the water held her back and their fingertips barely touched.

"I can't . . ." she gasped, her voice growing weaker.

"A little more," he said, but she had reached her limit. Valfierno knew that it would be only a matter of seconds before she lost her grip entirely and surrendered herself to the current.

He had to do something quickly. He looked at the valise. It held no small fortune. He turned back to Ellen and he knew in an instant the terrible truth: He couldn't possibly hope to save them both . . .

The loud, insistent knocking tore Roger Hargreaves from Valfierno's story like an alarm rips a sleeper from a vivid dream.

Chapter 51

PARIS—1925

The sudden pounding on the door stopped Valfierno in mid-sentence. He exhaled, a long forlorn sigh, and his head sank deeper into his pillow.

Hargreaves turned to the door, his face tight with agitation. "What is it?" he demanded.

In spite of the insistent knocking that preceded it, Madame Charneau's voice sounded muffled and tentative through the door. "I was just checking to make sure everything is all right, monsieur."

"Yes, yes," Hargreaves snapped. "Everything is fine." He turned back to Valfierno. "What happened? Did you save her? What happened to the money? To the painting?"

Valfierno's words seeped out like the dying hiss of a punctured tire. "I hesitated . . . a moment too long . . ."

He was barely audible now. Hargreaves leaned forward, straining to hear, but Valfierno was drifting away.

". . . and in the end," his voice trailed off, "I lost everything."

Valfierno tensed, choking on a sharp, desperate intake of air.

His eyes locked frantically with Hargreaves's, and his hand shot up and clutched the man's lapel. Lifting his head slightly, Valfierno pulled Hargreaves down until their faces were only inches apart.

"I almost held the greatest treasure a man could ever possess . . . but I let her slip through my fingers . . ."

"What do you mean?" Hargreaves spluttered. "The painting? The money? Mrs. Hart? What treasure?"

Valfierno's expression tightened in fear, his eyes focusing on some unnamed terror approaching from the distance. The correspondent tried to draw back, but Valfierno would not release his grip. Hargreaves felt a horrified fascination as the older man's eyes lost focus as if they were sinking backward into bottomless, black wells. Dilated pupils drifted up beneath his sagging eyelids before they fluttered closed, sealing those wells shut forever.

A final rattling breath escaped from Valfierno's throat as the strength drained from his arm muscles and he lowered himself back down to the bed, his mouth locked open in a hollow silent cry.

There was a dreadful frozen silence before Hargreaves realized Valfierno's hand still clutched tightly to his lapel. Sickened, he needed considerable strength to release the cold death grip before he could stand up and back away from the bed.

"Madame," he managed to call out. "Madame. Come quickly!"

Madame Charneau hurried into the room and bustled to the bedside, where she lifted Valfierno's hand, feeling for a pulse. Then she lowered her head and put her ear next to his gaping mouth.

"He's gone, monsieur," she said solemnly. "May God rest his soul."

She took a box of matches from her apron pocket and lit a lamp on the side table. Evening had crept into the room without Hargreaves even noticing. As Madame Charneau rose to the window and used the lamp to signal the men waiting in the courtyard below, an object on the table caught Hargreaves's eye. He picked it up.

It was a glove, a single long, white silk lady's glove.

———

Roger Hargreaves and Madame Charneau stood next to each other in the courtyard, watching the monks slide the heavy coffin into the back of the hearse. The undertaker and the three hooded men had not spoken a word when they brought the casket up to Valfierno's room, placed him in it, and carried him back down.

The monks clambered into the back of the hearse, and the undertaker closed the door behind them. The tall man climbed back up onto the front bench and solemnly doffed his stovepipe hat to Madame Charneau. Taking up the reins, he signaled the horses with a slight flick of his wrists. The animals stirred to life, and the hearse clattered from the courtyard.

"Well, monsieur," Madame Charneau said with an air of finality, "I hope you got what you came for. *Bonne nuit.*"

Madame Charneau disappeared back into the house. Surveying the empty courtyard, Hargreaves realized that he had been so enthralled with Valfierno's tale that he had neglected to take notes. And he had lost interest in the evening's entertainment at the Moulin Rouge. He felt drained and exhausted, and wanted only to return to the hotel for a few hours sleep before catching the train to Calais for the ferry back to England.

As he walked out of the cour de Rohan toward Saint-Germain, he thought back through all Valfierno had told him. It seemed to have the quality of a dream, some parts indelibly etched in his mind, some already beginning to fade.

The details were not important, he thought. The essential part was that he now knew almost the entire story of the most intriguing crime of the new century. The mystery could now be brought to its bittersweet conclusion and any credit would be his.

The marquis de Valfierno, of course, still remained a cipher, but that was probably for the best. Though the public liked to see loose ends tied up neatly, they also liked their facts seasoned with a dose of mystery. He'd probably have to come up with a background story for the man, perhaps make him a nobleman whose family had fallen on hard times—there were certainly enough of them in Paris—and was forced by circumstances to take up a life of deceit and crime. Yes, that sounded about right.

But he could think about all that tomorrow. Now he felt drained and tired. He would sleep on the train, and then again on the ferry. Yes, when he arrived in Dover, rested, he would remember everything with more clarity.

The three monks, seated on a wooden bench next to the coffin, swayed gently to the rhythm of the moving hearse. Beneath them, a wheel sank into a hole in the cobblestones and the carriage lurched, forcing them to involuntarily reach out to each other for support. It also caused the unhinged and unsecured coffin lid to slide partway off. The monks made no attempt to push it back in place but instead watched silently as a hand slowly emerged from inside, its fingers wrapping around the edge of the lid. With a forceful jerk, the hand pushed the lid off, and Valfierno slowly rose to a sitting position.

"Will they never fix this road?" he said with a devilish smile.

One of the monks raised his arms, pulled back his hood, and Émile's head emerged from beneath the rough cloth.

"I can hardly breathe in this," he said.

"It wasn't my idea to wear these things," said Julia as she pulled back the hood of her robe.

Ellen tossed back her hood and said, "So much for our vows of silence."

They all turned to the sound of knocking. Vincenzo Peruggia, sitting up on the driver's seat, looked down at them, smiling, as he rapped his knuckles on the glass partition.

"So," Ellen said, extending a helping hand to Valfierno, "did you tell Mr. Hargreaves our little story?"

"Indeed," Valfierno replied, taking her hand for support as he clambered out of the coffin. "Although I might have left out one or two minor details . . ."

Chapter 52

PARIS—1913

. . . Valfierno released his grip on the money valise. The current immediately snatched it, carrying it off into the darkness. He unhooked his elbow from the ladder rail, let his arm slip for an instant, and caught the rail with his left hand. His reach now extended, he stretched out his other arm and gripped Ellen's wrist.

"Take my wrist!" he shouted.

She did as instructed, strengthening their connection.

"Let go of the pipe!"

He responded to the fearful look in Ellen's eyes by gently nodding his encouragement.

"I won't let go of you."

She took a deep breath and released her grip on the pipe. The underground river fought for her, not wanting to relinquish its prey. Valfierno pulled with every ounce of strength he could muster, gradually drawing her closer to the ladder. Growing weaker by the second, Ellen made a final effort and gripped the rail with her free hand. In a few seconds, they were both securely perched on the steps of the ladder.

Slowly regaining her strength, Ellen peered down the length of the tunnel for a moment before turning back to Valfierno.

"The money . . ."

He smiled and shrugged. "It was only paper."

"And the painting?"

"Only paint and wood. I couldn't even begin to tell you where it is right now."

She gave him a tired smile and, pushing against the current, leaned her face toward him. He met her halfway and they kissed as passionately as they could under the circumstances.

She slowly drew back and said, "I love you, Edward."

He smiled. A warm, genuine smile.

After a moment, she said, "Well?"

He hesitated a moment more before speaking.

"And I—"

A loud grating noise from above snared their attention. They looked up, squinting against a light shower of water dripping onto their faces. A sliver of light grew in size like a crescent moon waxing to full as a manhole cover slid loudly away. Julia's face, backlit by the harsh light of an incandescent bulb, appeared over the rim.

"They're down there!" she shouted.

Émile's face appeared next to hers.

"Are you all right?" he called down.

"Émile," Valfierno said with relief, "your timing has definitely improved."

The collapse of the sandbags that flooded the streets relieved the pressure from the rising river, allowing the water to begin to subside. Farther downstream, near the Gare d'Orsay, a group of exhausted soldiers rested on a pile of sandbags.

"Look," cried a grizzled sergeant, pointing to a body careening toward the bank. "He just washed out of that pipe." He indicated a wide iron drainage pipe extending from the river wall. The soldiers scrambled down the stone steps in time to take hold of the man's clothing and pull him up out of the water.

"Is he dead?" a young private asked.

As if in response, the man's body convulsed and he coughed up water. The sergeant firmly slapped the man's face, and Vincenzo Peruggia's eyes popped open.

The descending evening cloaked the city of Paris in a murky darkness it had not known in almost a century. Public works crews could no longer reach the gas lamps to light them; the city's electricity-generating plants upstream in Bercy had ceased to operate. Emergency generators kept some lights on in public buildings, and naphtha-flare lamps wielded by soldiers and gendarmes pierced the night like fireflies on a summer's evening.

The streets of the Latin Quarter were still awash. A waning full moon, lurking behind a thin veil of clouds, washed the scene in an otherworldly light. *Passerelles*, hastily constructed wooden walkways and footbridges, had already started to appear between buildings. Makeshift rafts of barrels and planks shared the urban lakes with Berthon boats, each operated by two sailors propelling the collapsible waterproof canvas crafts with long poles. It was from the bow of one of these boats that a gendarme caught sight of something at the edge of the circle of light cast by his outstretched lamp. A man's inert body was draped against a low wrought-iron railing, his jacket caught on the sharp points of the balusters. He held something in his arms. His eyes were closed, but his head was moving slightly and he seemed to be trying to speak.

"He's still alive," the gendarme said as the boat closed in.

The gendarme and one of the sailors hoisted the victim over the side and into the boat. The man was middle aged, heavyset, and well dressed. He clutched a small wooden panel.

"Don't worry, monsieur," the gendarme said, "you are safe now."

After directing the two sailors to pole the boat toward a temporary infirmary in a nearby church, the gendarme put down his lamp and tried to unwrap the man's arms from around the rectangular panel. Despite being only semiconscious, the victim refused to relinquish it, holding on with a deathlike grip.

Joshua Hart protested with incomprehensible grunts as the panel was finally pried loose from his grasp. The gendarme turned it over, lifted his lamp, and stared into the faintly mocking smile of *La Joconde.*

A few miles downstream from the city, where the Seine ran through one of its many serpentine curves on its way north, the body of a large bald man drifted facedown with the current. He was accompanied on his journey by a flotilla of hundred-dollar bills. They floated around him like green lilies, many with the profile of Benjamin Franklin staring up in wonder at the slowly clearing night sky.

Nearby, on the bank of the river, a farmer named Girard searched through the shallows by the feeble light of the veiled moon for a calf he thought might have drowned in the high water. Something caught his eye and he waded over to a rectangular wooden panel caught in some overhanging branches. He picked it up. It was a painting of a woman, her hands crossed in her lap, a slight smile on her face. It was not bad. And there was something vaguely familiar about the eyes.

As luck would have it, it was his wife's birthday soon. The panel was wet but appeared undamaged. Perhaps Claire would like it as a present.

Chapter 53

Monsieur Duval, official photographer for the Louvre, stood in the midst of the crowd gathered in the Salon Carré for the official rehanging of *La Joconde*. Politicians, dignitaries, military officers, and their wives filled the salon, barely leaving room for a harpist and string quartet stuck in a corner. Scarcely two weeks had passed since the recovery of the painting by a gendarme from the flood-soaked streets of the Latin Quarter. Remarkably, the painting and the panel were virtually undamaged. The many layers of lacquer that had been applied over hundreds of years to both the front and rear of the panel had protected it during the apparently short time it had been subjected to the elements. Under the supervision of Monsieur Montand, the museum director, various curators had quickly authenticated the painting, and this ceremony had been hastily arranged.

Duval himself had been allowed only a perfunctory examination of the painting. His job had been to compare it with recent photographs, which had not helped much. It had always been difficult to capture the image with consistent lighting, and this made precise comparison problematic. His inclusion in the process had been only a matter of form, anyway. Within minutes, the panel had been taken from him and he had been thanked for his services. Montand had obviously been in a hurry to get the painting back up onto the wall and put the whole unfortunate incident behind him. Following the theft, thought Duval, Montand must have had to pull in every favor he had ever accumulated to keep his position.

As various politicians and patrons looked on, the painting—already ensconced in a new shadow box—was hoisted onto its pegs on the wall between the Correggio and the Titian. It was at this moment that Duval realized what had been bothering him since his token examination. The painting itself seemed genuine enough; it was hard to imagine any artist so perfectly re-creating the master's technique. No, it was something else. Something about the panel itself, and not the front of the panel, but the back. Still, it was impossible to be sure.

Then he remembered: Of all the photographs taken of the masterpiece, only one had been made of the rear panel to document a repair from the last century.

Of course.

He pushed backward against the tide of spectators pressing forward for a better view. He had to get back to his office to see the photograph.

Standing before the eager crowd, Monsieur Montand thought briefly of Inspector Carnot as he acknowledged Police Commissioner Lepine standing in the front row. Carnot had completely disappeared two weeks ago. It was suggested that he perished in the flood, perhaps even taken the opportunity to drown himself rather than endure the shame brought on by his miserable failure to apprehend the thieves. It was of no consequence. Montand never did care much for the man's manner, not to mention his cheap, ill-fitting suits.

And now, the speeches had been given by the various dignitaries, praise had been apportioned to both the police and the museum curators—including, of course, Monsieur Montand himself—for making this day possible. Montand could be confident that his position as director—which he had come perilously close to losing—was now assured, at least for the foreseeable future.

After the recovery, the other curators had been in complete agreement: The quicker *La Joconde* took its rightful place on the wall of the Salon Carré, the better. No need to wait for the arrival of the self-proclaimed Italian experts who had offered their services to authenticate the painting; the French could handle it very nicely alone, thank you. Duval had insisted on being part of the process so Montand had been forced to allow him to examine the panel, albeit for as little time as possible.

And now it was done. The world had demanded that the masterpiece be returned to the people of France, and it had been accomplished.

Of course, there had been that one small detail Montand had to take care of to make sure everything would go smoothly. Though he was an expert in many things related to the thousands of artworks under his care, he found himself strangely unmoved by them. He was more interested in the technical aspects of art and spent no small amount of time studying the technique of well-known forgers. It was with this eye that he appraised *La Joconde*. The painting recovered from the flood—the same one that now hung on the wall in the shadow box—was exquisite. The man must be a master in his own right, and Montand himself would have been fooled. If it hadn't been for one thing.

No matter how magnificent their skill, the nature of their work relegated forgers to complete obscurity. To counteract this, many had affected a mark—a sort of signature—that only they would recognize. This man had been devilishly clever. While most forgers changed some minuscule aspect of the image—an extra strand of hair or blade of grass—he had made his mark on the rear of the panel. Not one man in a hundred would have noticed that the cross-like strip of wood, applied in the last century to repair damage caused by the removal of the original frame, should have been right of center, not left of center as this one was. He considered the possibility that this could have been an error on the forger's part, but the painting itself was too perfect, too flawless; the incorrect positioning of the cross had to be the forger's mark. It had made Montand smile. Such a simple change. Such a bold statement. Such perverse genius.

And then he had remembered Duval.

The man had always irritated him. Montand had never seen the value in the contributions of the photographers' studio; it was expensive to operate, especially when one considered Duval's salary. Indeed, he had unsuccessfully tried to close down that particular department on a number of occasions. For this reason, he always kept a close eye on everything Duval did, and he remembered something he had seen on a surprise visit shortly before the theft. He had demanded to see all the photographs taken of *La Joconde* during the department's existence. There were many images and Montand had hoped to use this fact as evidence of unnecessary expenditure. Why did so many expensive photographs have to be taken, anyway? Weren't there already enough? But his complaint to the Board of Trustees had fallen on deaf ears; they were too captivated by this relatively new science.

But shortly after authenticating the painting, he had remembered one particular photograph he had seen, one unlike any of the others. It seemed especially worthless at the time. What possible use could there have been for a photograph of the back of the painting? How ironic that this one photograph could have ruined everything, including the reputation he had just worked so hard to restore. But there was no longer any reason to worry. He had taken care of it personally.

Monsieur Duval pulled open the large sliding drawers containing his photographic collection. He was a meticulous man and immediately located the series of photographs of *La Joconde*. They were numbered sequentially and he remembered that the image of the rear of the panel would be somewhere in the middle.

Methodically, he shuffled through the prints. The one he had taken of the rear of the panel was missing. Indeed, the numbers abruptly jumped from 26 to 28. Someone had removed number 27.

He went to a large cabinet where the original Autochrome glass negative plates were stored. Each sat in its own cardboard slot to keep from touching the plates on either side. As he had feared, plate number 27 was also missing.

There was no doubt. Someone had removed both the negative glass plate and the only print he had of *La Joconde*'s rear panel. He had been unable to put his finger on what it was exactly that bothered him, and, without the photograph, he would have no proof that the painting being mounted at this very moment was not the original. Indeed, without the photograph, he would never even be sure himself.

Part VI

And thus the whirligig of time brings in his revenges.
—Shakespeare, *Twelfth Night*

Chapter 54

NEWPORT, RHODE ISLAND—1925

Three weeks after its publication in the *London Daily Express*, Hargreaves's story was reprinted in the *New York Times* as a curiosity piece, all but buried in the arts reviews. Appearing as it did almost fifteen years after the sensational robbery, the article did not create much of a stir, though it was noticed by the financial secretary of Mr. Joshua Hart, who read it to his employer.

Hart sat in the wicker seat of his wheelchair positioned in front of the easel in his cramped studio at the rear of his subterranean gallery. At seventy-five, he might easily be mistaken for a man ten years his senior. Paralyzed from the waist down as a result of injuries sustained in the great Paris flood, he had ordered an elevator to be constructed, really no more than a glorified dumbwaiter, to transport him to and from his studio. In the years since the flood, his mind had steadily deteriorated, and now he depended on the help of a small army of nurses and servants who attended him around the clock.

He remained convinced of two things: He had held in his hands—if only for a tragically short time—the greatest masterpiece of the ages; and, even though he would never lay eyes on it again, it still belonged rightfully to him and him alone. And now he had the satisfaction of knowing, once and for all, that the marquis de Valfierno—the man who had dared to cheat him—was dead. He had always hoped that he had drowned, but there was never any proof. Now the newspaper story confirmed that, although Valfierno survived the flood, he ended his days destitute, withering away, and ravaged by a life of sin and deceit.

The story made no mention of Hart's part in the affair. Solicitors from the *London Daily Express* had contacted Hart's financial secretary and an agreement guaranteeing complete discretion was quickly put into place. The story did include a report that Valfierno's companion—referred to in the article as Ellen Stokes—had drowned in the flood. Hart felt a tinge of unexpected regret. The feeling quickly faded, replaced by relief. He had always felt afraid that she might be tempted to use her knowledge of his various unscrupulous business dealings—not to mention his art dealings—against him. Besides, she had gotten only what she deserved. Over the years he had spent a great deal of money on private detectives in an attempt to hunt down both Valfierno and Ellen. There would be no need for their services anymore.

These days, Hart came in contact with his collection only while being pushed in his wheelchair on his way to and from the tiny studio in the rear of the gallery. It was in this room that he spent most of his time.

He lifted his brush and added more detail to the tree in the painting. He had been working on it for months now, or was it years? The trees he had painted were so lifelike that their branches seemed to sway in the gentle breeze blowing across the imagined landscape. Light from a blazing sun coruscated off the fluttering leaves, reflecting back into a blue sky feathered with wispy clouds. A family— mother, father, and child—stood hand in hand on a gently sloping hillside.

The door behind Hart opened, and Joseph—a large man whose coal-black skin contrasted with his spotless white uniform—approached the wheelchair. He was the only one of Hart's attendants allowed into the gallery.

"Are you all right, sir?" Joseph asked, noting the sweat beading on his employer's face. "Mighty hot down here. Maybe it's time I took you upstairs."

Joshua Hart spoke in a thin, raspy voice. "Joseph, what do you think of it?"

Joseph looked at the canvas on the easel. He saw a hopeless mixture of colors and meaningless shapes haphazardly strewn across the canvas as if by a small child. Rivulets of paint had dripped over the lip of the easel, forming dried splotches on the floor. Indeed, a child could have done better than create this mess, a mess that seemed to grow worse each day.

"It's real nice, Mr. Hart. Real pretty."

"Do you see the trees, the sky, the sun, Joseph?"

"Well, sure I do."

"Do you see the family?"

"Real nice family, Mr. Hart. It's the prettiest picture I ever seen, and that's a fact."

Hart grunted, already tiring from the effort it took to talk.

"It's time to go up now, sir."

Joseph gently removed the brush from Hart's hand and placed it into a jar filled with dirty water. He released the brake on the wheelchair and spun it around, maneuvering it out of the room.

"Maybe we should turn on some more lights down here, sir," Joseph said as he pushed the wheelchair through the dimly lit gallery. "You know, so you can see all your nice pictures."

Hart didn't respond. He kept his eyes on the floor, never looking up once.

Chapter 55

Five months following the publication of the *London Daily Express* article concerning the theft of the *Mona Lisa*, seventeen men, uncomfortably warm in their starched collars and suits, sat in three rows of elegantly carved chairs in the top-floor salon of the Hôtel Athénée. They had grown impatient waiting in the oppressive summer heat, so when the door finally opened and a well-dressed gentleman in his fifties walked into the room, they greeted him with a murmur of excited anticipation. Followed by an entourage consisting of two men and two women, the older man—his steel-gray hair flowing back like the bow wave of a ship—strode over to a set of heavy drapes drawn across a large window and held up his hands to signal for silence.

"I am Victor Lustig," he began, "and I apologize for keeping you waiting. My associates and I welcome you most heartily, and I can assure you that the patience of at least one of you will be well rewarded."

His associates sat down on chairs arranged in a row behind him.

"You have been carefully selected," Lustig continued, "as the lucky group who will have the privilege to bid on this once-in-a-lifetime opportunity. You have distinguished yourselves as among the most successful, the most sagacious entrepreneurs ever to grace your singular and noble profession."

The men visibly puffed with pride.

"As junk dealers extraordinaire, you have taken your place among the elite of the true leaders of the Third Republic. But nothing has prepared you for the monumental commission the boldest of you must now undertake."

He nodded to one of his female associates. She rose, stepped to the drapes, and took ahold of a thick hanging cord.

"The effort required will be monumental," he continued, "but the profits to be gained have hitherto only been dreamed of, for whoever bids the highest in the next few moments will have the distinguished honor of dismantling for scrap metal the greatest architectural eyesore ever created by man . . ."

Some of the men in the audience leaned forward, their eyes wide with anticipation.

". . . that odious column of bolted metal . . ."

A whispered buzz, like the hum of nectar-starved bees, rose from the assemblage.

". . . that monstrous erection . . ."

A girlish snigger escaped from the young female associate still seated, only to be cut short by the sharp elbow belonging to the young man next to her.

". . . that giant and disgraceful skeleton . . . that hideous iron asparagus . . ."

His buildup reaching its crescendo, Valfierno turned to Ellen and nodded. With a yank, she pulled aside two heavy curtains, bathing the room in light and revealing a perfect view across the Seine. Valfierno's voice rose in climax:

"*La Tour Eiffel!*"

A gasp rose from the audience. Émile, Julia, and Peruggia stood up and began clapping. On cue, the men erupted into applause, jumping to their feet like puppets yanked up by hidden strings in the ceiling.

Ellen and Valfierno exchanged triumphant grins as the men, all caution stripped away by Valfierno's performance, shouted out their frenzied bids.

Epilogue

GIVERNY—1937

If a man is capable of dying from loneliness, then certainly such a fate befell the farmer called Girard. His wife, Claire, had died suddenly a year earlier; one minute she was tending her garden behind the house and the next she was gone forever. With her, she had taken Girard's heart and soul, and left behind a man as hollow and fragile as a rotted tree trunk.

The things she left behind in the farmhouse provided a certain amount of comfort at first, but they quickly became painful reminders, and he had methodically removed them from sight. He hid the small figurines she had cherished so much in boxes in the backs of dark closets; all her clothes were bundled together and taken to the local church for distribution to the poor; even the decorative bowl that held her fresh tomatoes and pears was consigned to a dark corner of the kitchen pantry.

And then there was the painting, the one he had presented on her birthday so many years ago. She had treasured it above everything else she owned. For twenty-four years it had graced the mantel above the fireplace. Each night as she sat knitting before the fire, she would look up every now and then and smile. Girard had even seen a likeness between his wife and the woman on the wall. Of course, the woman never aged, never suffered the ravages of time, while his wife's face showed all too clearly the hardships of a life as a simple farmer's wife. Only Claire's eyes never seemed to age. Like those of the woman in the painting, they remained clear and focused and kind until the end.

So, when the day came that he could no longer bear looking into those eyes, he took the painting down, carried it out to one of the barns, and placed it on a shelf in the hayloft.

Each night after that, before he lay his head on his pillow, he muttered only one prayer, that he would never wake again but instead join his beloved Claire in the Kingdom of the Father. And one night, a few days ago, his prayers had finally been answered.

Monsieur Pilon, the local magistrate, pulled the door to the farmhouse closed, inserted a padlock into the newly installed hasp, and locked it shut. Girard, the farmer who owned the house, had no children and, as far as Monsieur Pilon could discover, no living relatives. The farmhouse would have to remain locked until the estate could be settled. To make matters worse, it was a bad time for such things. Rumors of a coming war had been brewing for months now, and what the future would bring was anyone's guess. All Pilon knew was that he had already done his bit in the last war. Let the young men sort this one out.

Pilon walked back to his car, tugging at his collar as the heat of the day lingered even as the sun descended into the west. As he reached for the door handle, the harsh cawing of a crow made him turn back toward the barn. Silhouetted against the late afternoon sun, a line of the large black birds adorned the roof ridge as if patiently waiting to take possession of the farm. Wiping the sweat from his forehead with the sleeve of his jacket, Pilon climbed into the car, pushed the self-starter button, and drove off.

As soon as the whine of the car's engine faded away, the crows lifted from the barn roof and wheeled away into the fields to feast on the neglected harvest. But a solitary bird broke rank, alighting on the sill of the open hayloft. Small clouds of dust mixed with slivers of dried hay rose from the floor of the hayloft as the crow hopped down in search of an insect or a dead mouse. The sound of something scuffling in the darkness stopped the bird as still as a statue. The creature's head darted this way and that, alert for danger. A movement on the wall drew its attention. A thin shaft of sunlight had found its way through a crack in the siding and was slowly snaking down the wooden planks.

Reflecting like white pinpoints in the crow's black eyes, the light moved across a patch of skin, revealing another pair of eyes staring straight back at the bird like a predator waiting in the darkness. Another scuffle from the corner spurred the crow to action. Cawing madly, the bird flapped its wings and, in a cloud of billowing dust, escaped through the hayloft door out into the gathering evening.

On the wall, the blade of light moved slowly below the eyes, down across a long aquiline nose to lips pursed in a patient, eternally amused smile.

In less than a minute, the light had moved on, once again veiling the face with darkness.

Author's Note

Leonardo da Vinci's *Portrait of Mona Lisa*—known in France as *La Joconde* and in Italy as *La Gioconda*—was stolen from the Louvre Museum in 1911 in a manner similar to the one depicted in this novel. Two years later, an Italian named Vincenzo Peruggia attempted to return it to Italy. He was arrested for his troubles. In 1925, a story appeared in the *Saturday Evening Post* purporting to be an interview with one Eduardo de Valfierno, a self-professed con artist who claimed to have masterminded the theft as part of an elaborate forgery scheme. The world-renowned artist with whom I have taken inexcusable liberties was actually questioned by the police in connection with the theft. Jean Lépine was Prefect of Police at the time of this story. All the other characters are entirely products of my imagination.

In the early part of the twentieth century, the River Seine did overflow its famous banks, inundating streets, flooding metro stations, and making thousands of Parisians homeless. *L'inondation de Paris* actually took place in 1910, a year before the *Mona Lisa* was stolen. I trust the reader will forgive me for moving that event forward for dramatic purposes.

Acknowledgments

A novel, like a child, takes a village. In chronological order of their contributions to this book, I'd like to thank: Paul Samuel Dolman for reading the earliest incarnation as a screenplay, and on whom I could always depend for encouragement; Julie Barr McClure for listening to my story before a word had been written. Cody Morton, Toni Henderson, Beverly Morton, Jim Herbert, and Peter Dergee for being intrepid early readers and providing invaluable feedback and suggestions; Jill Spence for lending her ears to a final reading; Marie Bozzetti-Engstrom for eagerly volunteering to be my first editor and for all those breakfasts at Bongo Java; Gretchen Stelter for her insightful editorial suggestions; my agent at the Victoria Sanders Agency, Bernadette Baker-Baughman, for her confidence and tenaciousness; the entire team at St. Martin's Press for their professional skills; and my editor at Minotaur Books, Nichole Argyres, for her brilliant editorial guidance and unflagging support.

Anyone interested in reading further about the places and events depicted in this book should consider the following books, which were extremely helpful to me in my research: *Paris Then and*

Now by Peter and Oriel Caine, *Becoming Mona Lisa: The Making of a Global Icon* by Donald Sassoon; *Paris: Memories of Times Past* (with 75 Paintings by Mortimer Menpes), by Solange Hando, Colin Inman, Florence Besson, and Roberta Jaulhaber-Razafy; and *Paris Under Water: How the City of Light Survived the Great Flood of 1910* by Jeffrey H. Jackson.